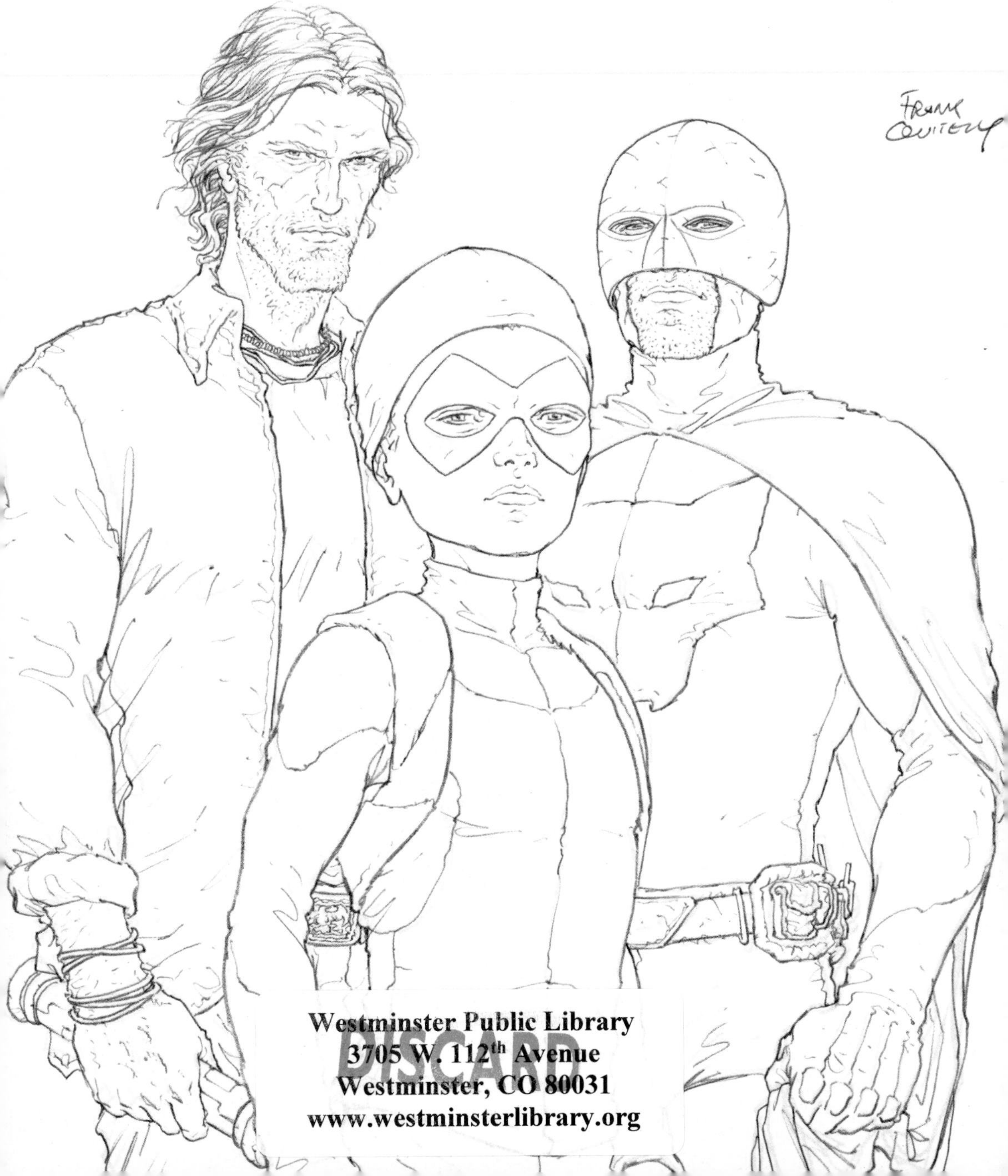
FRANK QUITELY

JUPITER'S LEGACY

VOLUME 4

MARK MILLAR
WRITER & CO-CREATOR

FRANK QUITELY
ARTIST & CO-CREATOR

SUNNY GHO
Colors

PETER DOHERTY
Letters, Design & Production

ROB MILLER
Digital Art Assistant

RACHAEL FULTON
Editor

MELINA MIKULIC
2020 Collection Cover Design

LUCY MILLAR
CEO

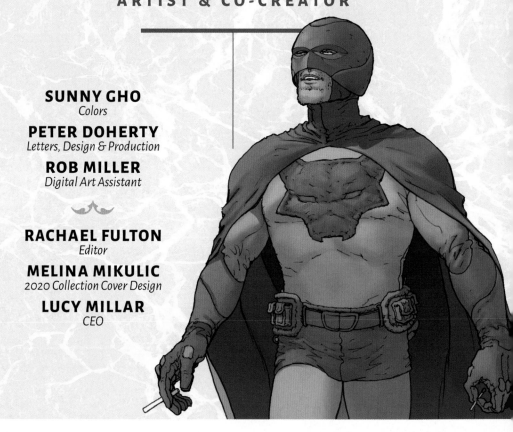

IMAGE COMICS, INC. · Todd McFarlane: President · Jim Valentino: Vice President · Marc Silvestri: Chief Executive Officer · Erik Larsen: Chief Financial Officer · Robert Kirkman: Chief Operating Officer · Eric Stephenson: Publisher / Chief Creative Officer · Nicole Lapalme: Controller · Leanna Caunter: Accounting Analyst · Sue Korpela: Accounting & HR Manager · Marla Eizik: Talent Liaison · Jeff Boison: Director of Sales & Publishing Planning · Dirk Wood: Director of International Sales & Licensing · Alex Cox: Director of Direct Market Sales · Chloe Ramos: Book Market & Library Sales Manager · Emilio Bautista: Digital Sales Coordinator · Jon Schlaffman: Specialty Sales Coordinator · Kat Salazar: Director of PR & Marketing · Drew Fitzgerald: Marketing Content Associate · Heather Doornink: Production Director · Drew Gill: Art Director · Hilary DiLoreto: Print Manager · Tricia Ramos: Traffic Manager · Melissa Gifford: Content Manager · Erika Schnatz: Senior Production Artist · Ryan Brewer: Production Artist · Deanna Phelps: Production Artist · IMAGECOMICS.COM

CHAPTER 1

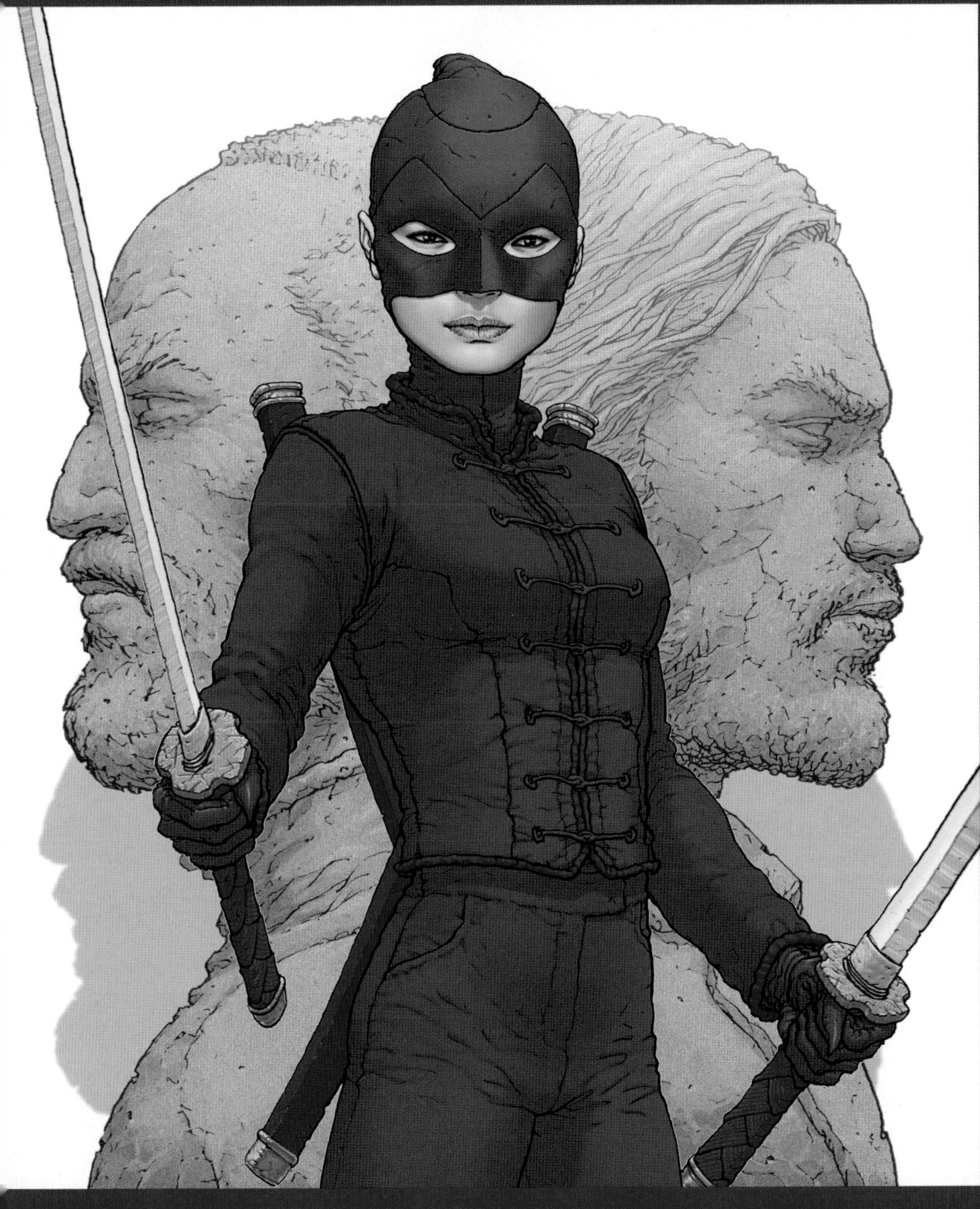

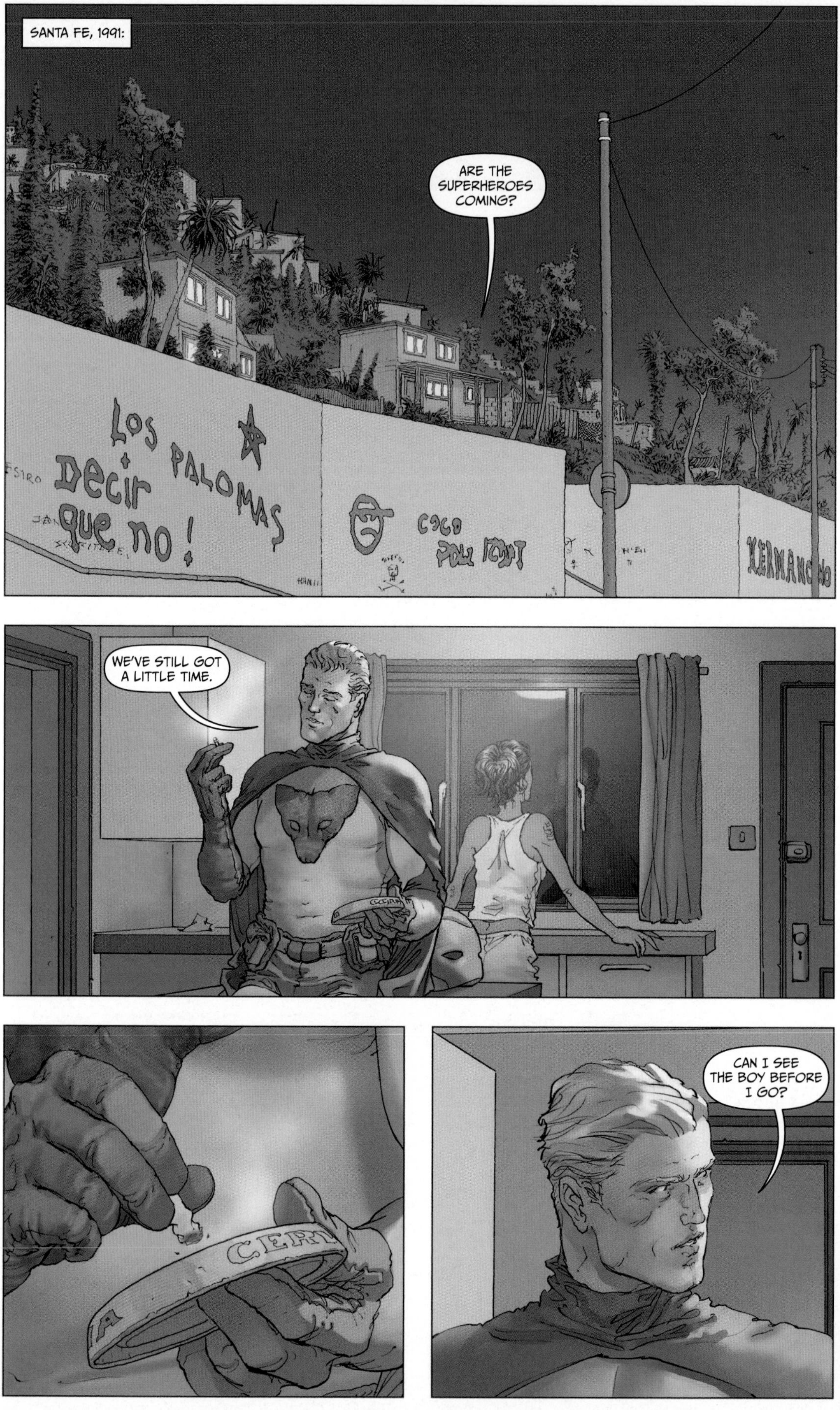

SANTA FE, 1991:
ARE THE SUPERHEROES COMING?
LOS PALOMAS
Decir que no!
WE'VE STILL GOT A LITTLE TIME.
CAN I SEE THE BOY BEFORE I GO?

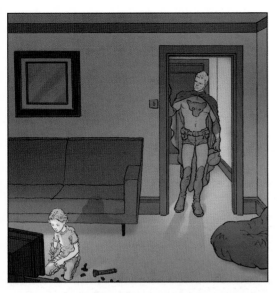

WHAT ARE YOU WATCHING?

THE REAL GHOSTBUSTERS.

WHY'S IT CALLED REAL IF IT'S ONLY A *CARTOON?*

I DON'T KNOW.

ARE YOU MY *DAD?*

YEAH.

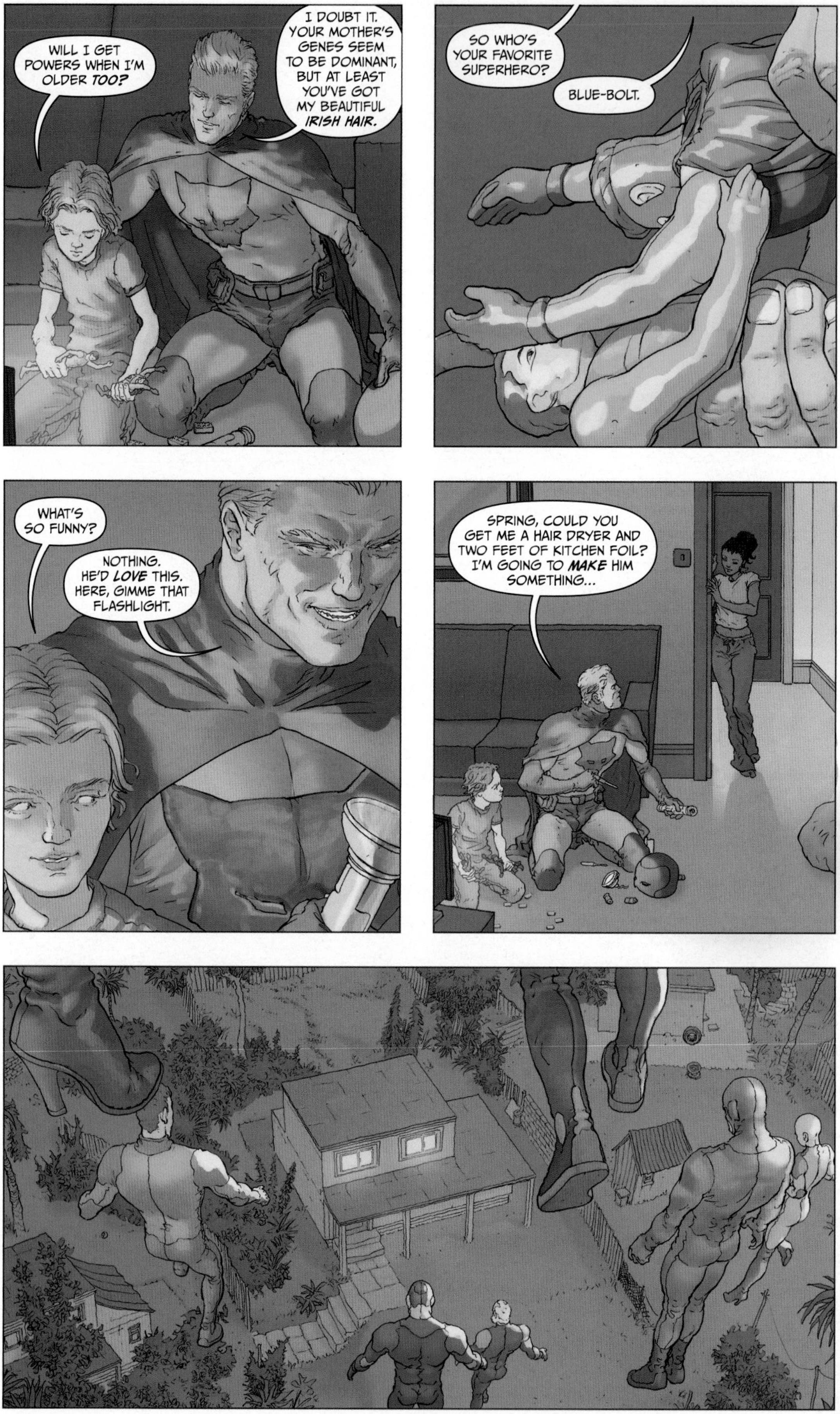
WILL I GET POWERS WHEN I'M OLDER TOO?
I DOUBT IT. YOUR MOTHER'S GENES SEEM TO BE DOMINANT, BUT AT LEAST YOU'VE GOT MY BEAUTIFUL IRISH HAIR.
SO WHO'S YOUR FAVORITE SUPERHERO?
BLUE-BOLT.
WHAT'S SO FUNNY?
NOTHING. HE'D LOVE THIS. HERE, GIMME THAT FLASHLIGHT.
SPRING, COULD YOU GET ME A HAIR DRYER AND TWO FEET OF KITCHEN FOIL? I'M GOING TO MAKE HIM SOMETHING...

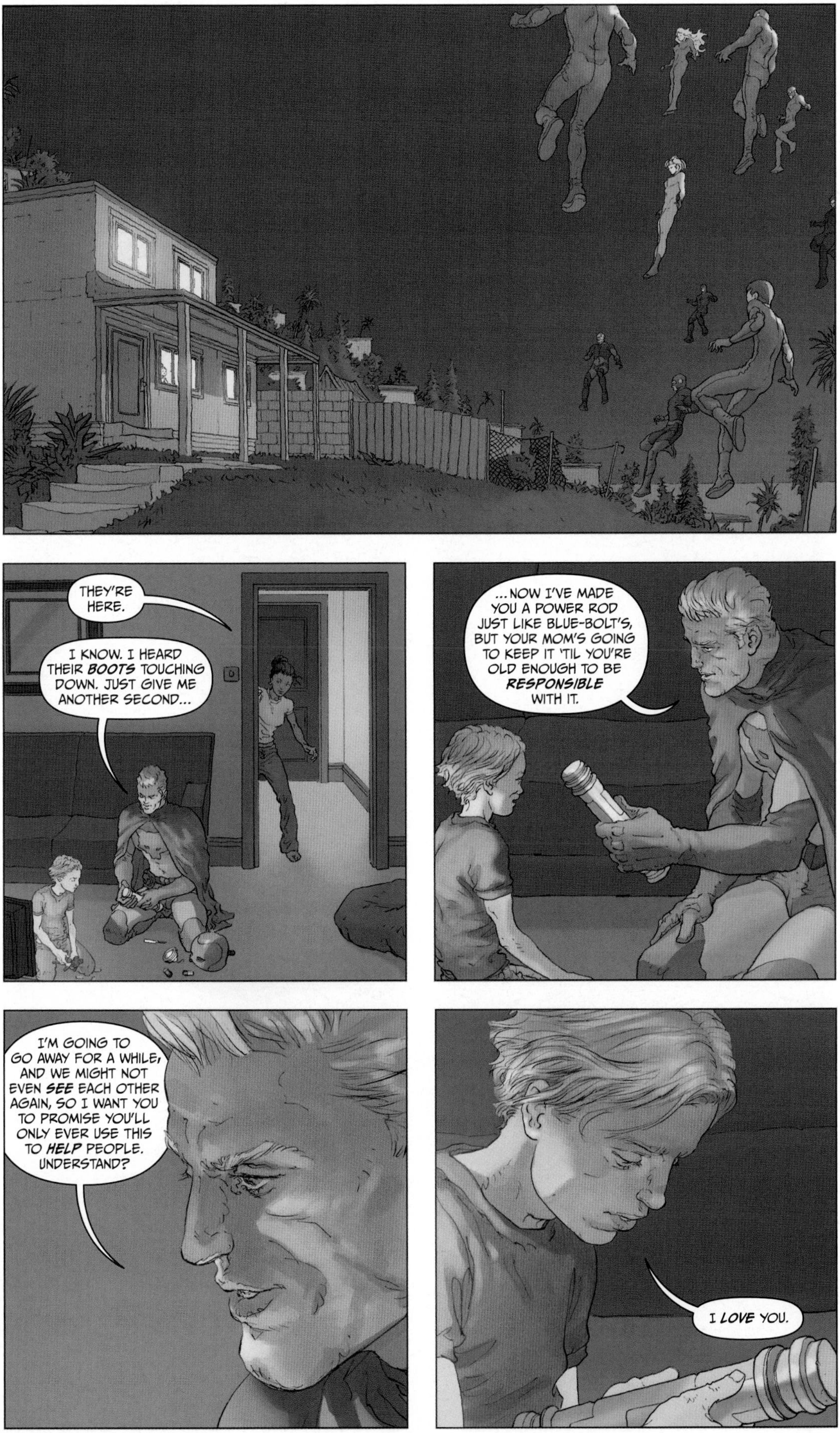
THEY'RE HERE.
I KNOW. I HEARD THEIR *BOOTS* TOUCHING DOWN. JUST GIVE ME ANOTHER SECOND...
...NOW I'VE MADE YOU A POWER ROD JUST LIKE BLUE-BOLT'S, BUT YOUR MOM'S GOING TO KEEP IT 'TIL YOU'RE OLD ENOUGH TO BE *RESPONSIBLE* WITH IT.
I'M GOING TO GO AWAY FOR A WHILE, AND WE MIGHT NOT EVEN *SEE* EACH OTHER AGAIN, SO I WANT YOU TO PROMISE YOU'LL ONLY EVER USE THIS TO *HELP* PEOPLE. UNDERSTAND?
I *LOVE* YOU.

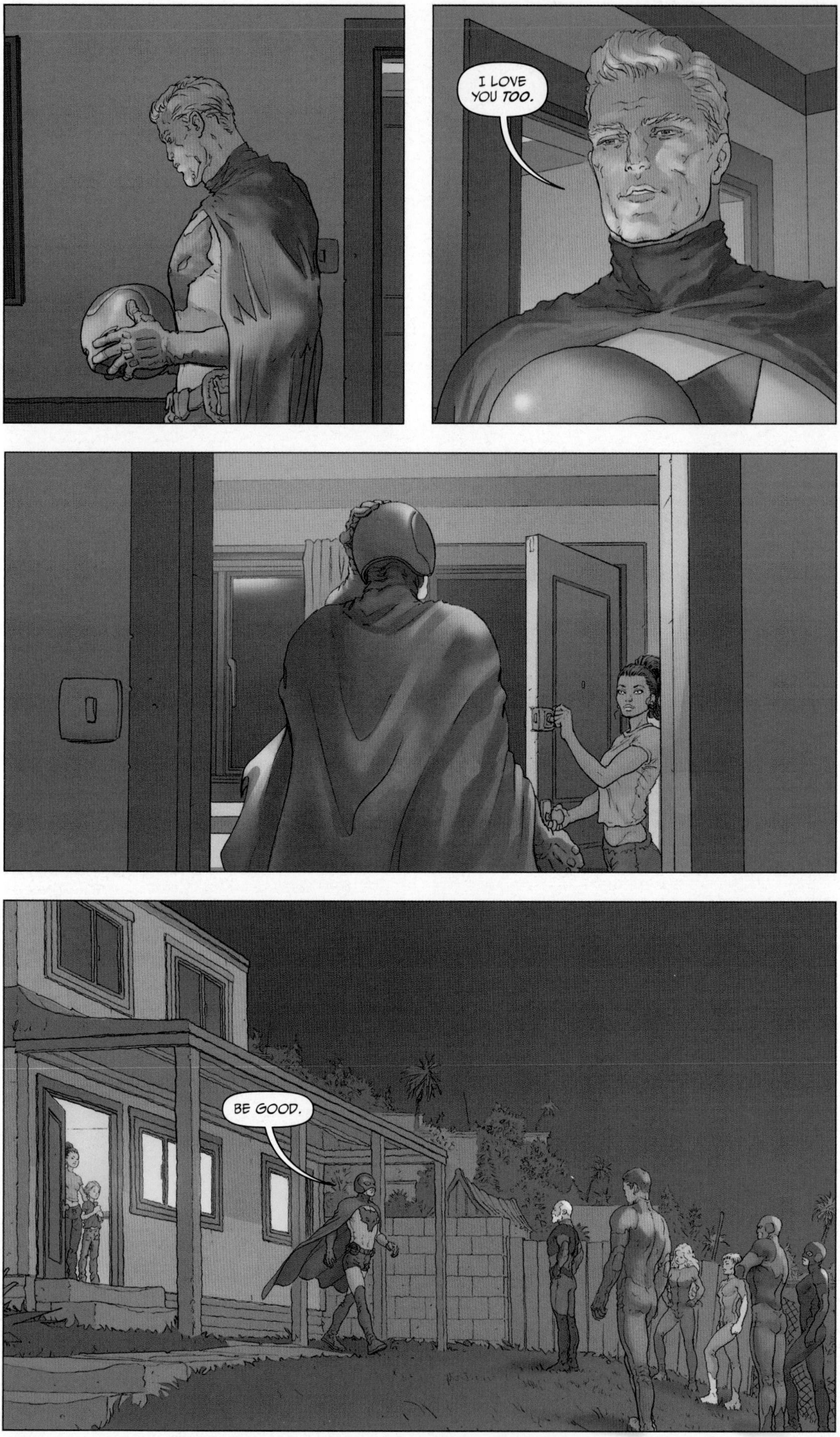
I LOVE YOU TOO.
BE GOOD.

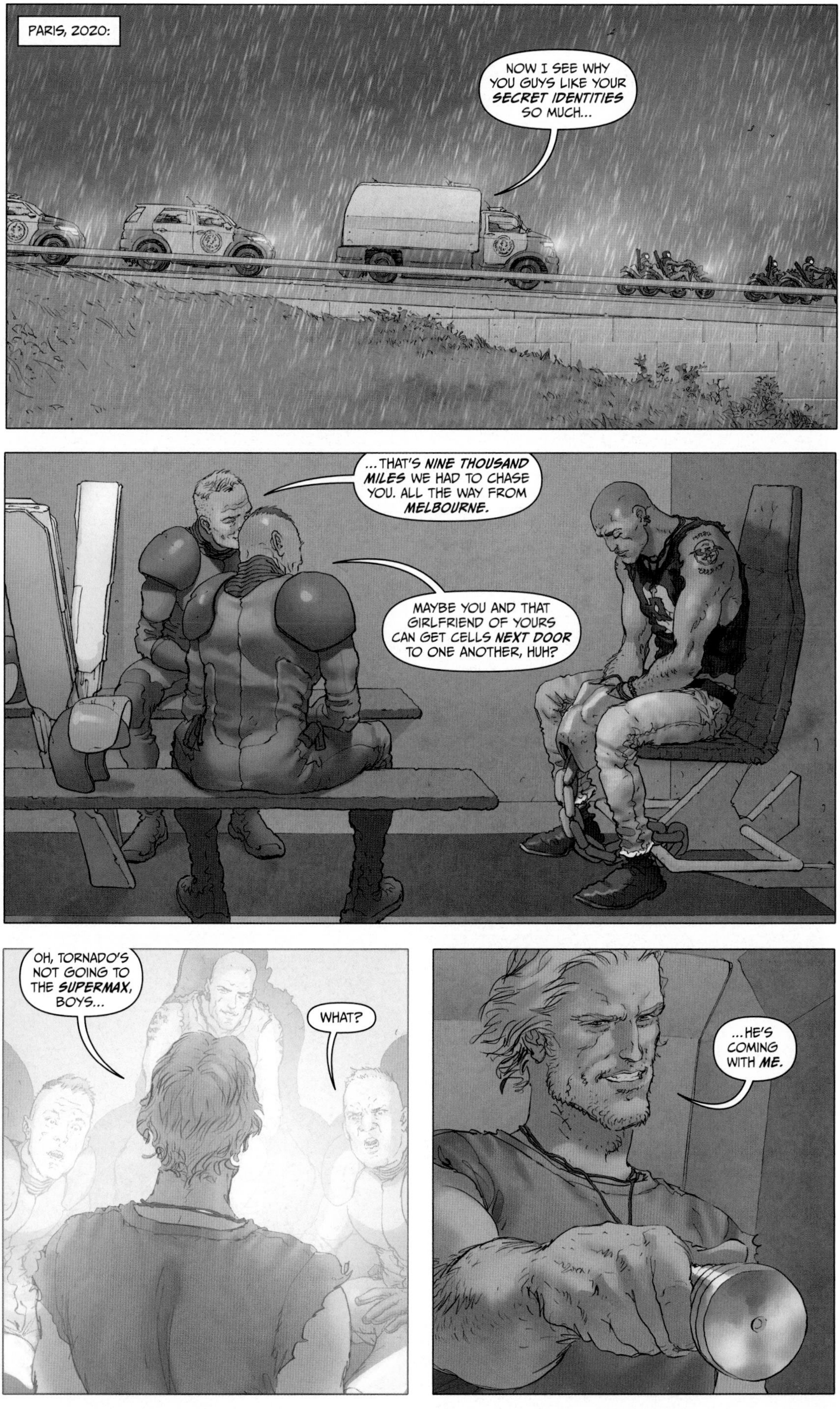
PARIS, 2020:
NOW I SEE WHY YOU GUYS LIKE YOUR SECRET IDENTITIES SO MUCH...
...THAT'S NINE THOUSAND MILES WE HAD TO CHASE YOU. ALL THE WAY FROM MELBOURNE.
MAYBE YOU AND THAT GIRLFRIEND OF YOURS CAN GET CELLS NEXT DOOR TO ONE ANOTHER, HUH?
OH, TORNADO'S NOT GOING TO THE SUPERMAX, BOYS...
WHAT?
...HE'S COMING WITH ME.

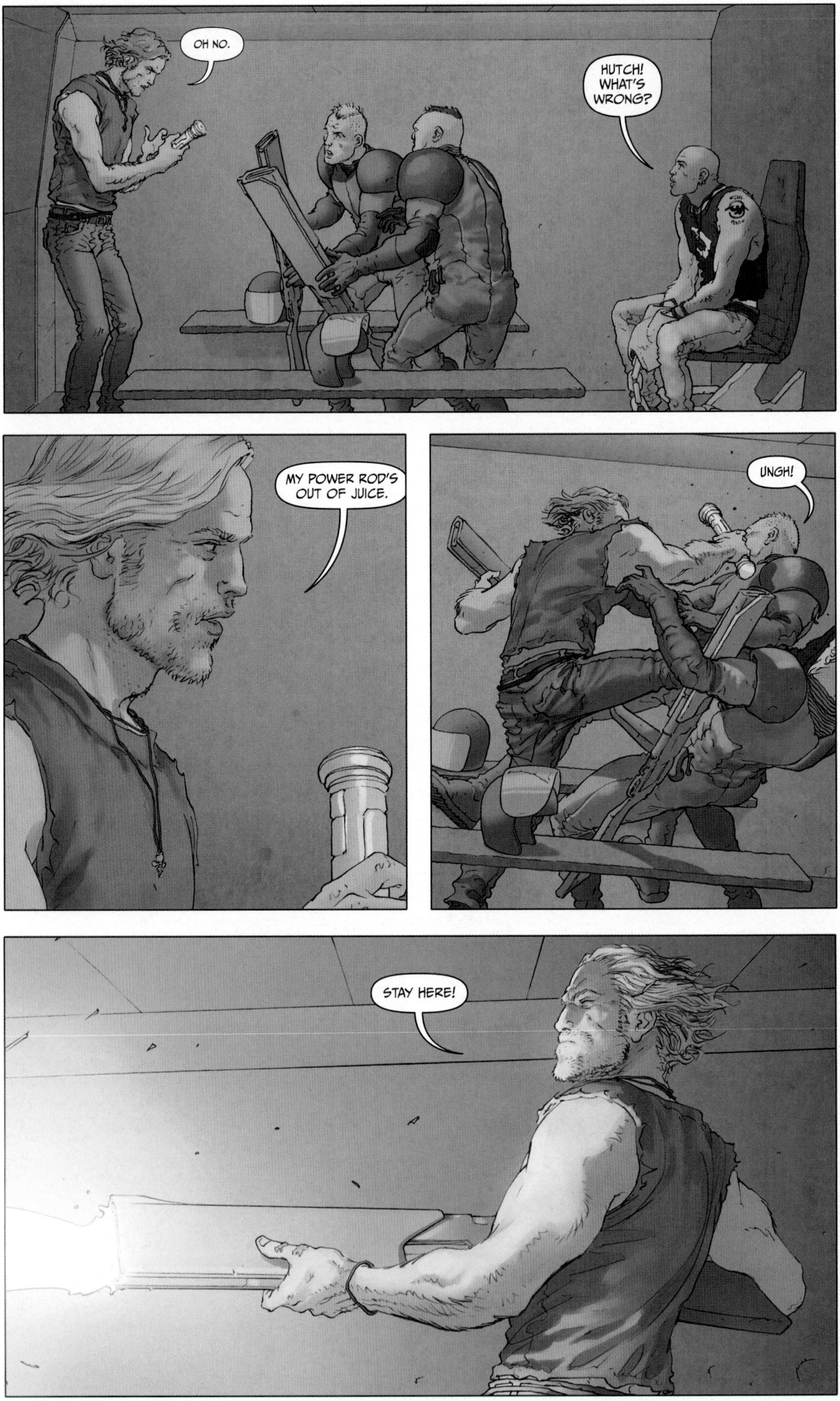
OH NO.
HUTCH! WHAT'S WRONG?
MY POWER ROD'S OUT OF JUICE.
UNGH!
STAY HERE!

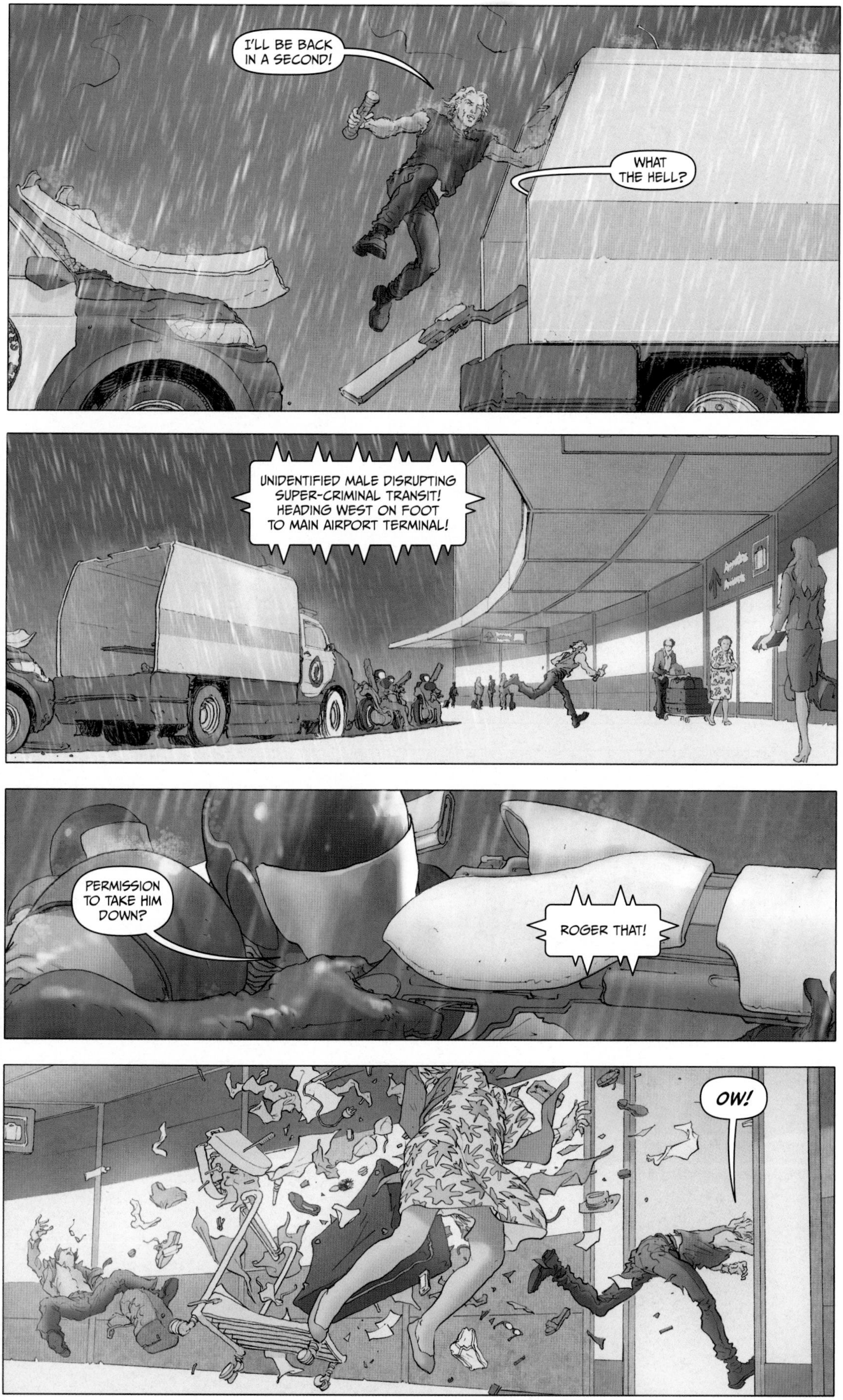
I'LL BE BACK IN A SECOND!
WHAT THE HELL?
UNIDENTIFIED MALE DISRUPTING SUPER-CRIMINAL TRANSIT! HEADING WEST ON FOOT TO MAIN AIRPORT TERMINAL!
PERMISSION TO TAKE HIM DOWN?
ROGER THAT!
OW!

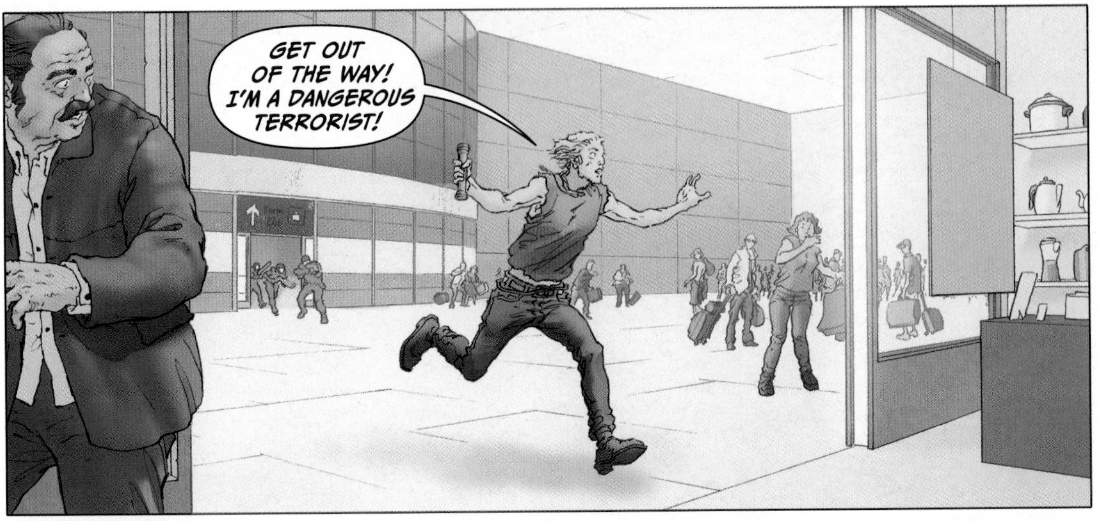
GET OUT OF THE WAY! I'M A DANGEROUS TERRORIST!

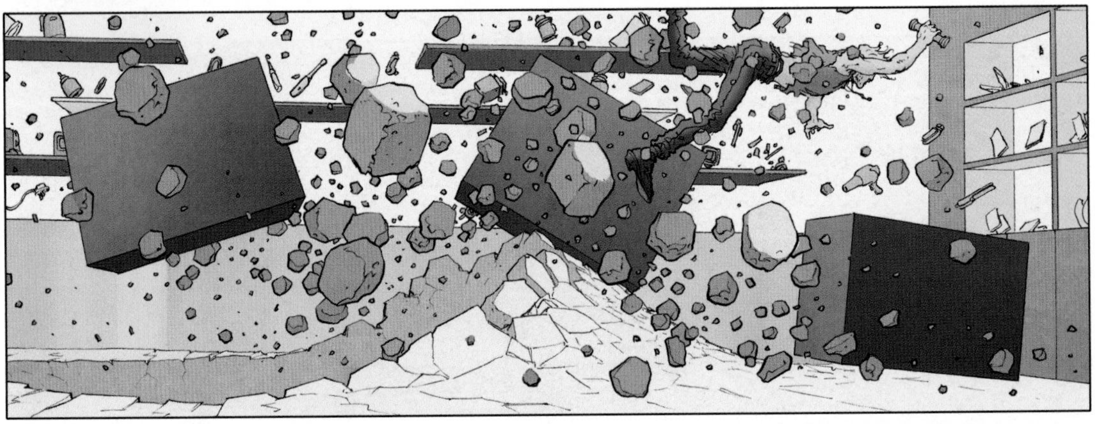

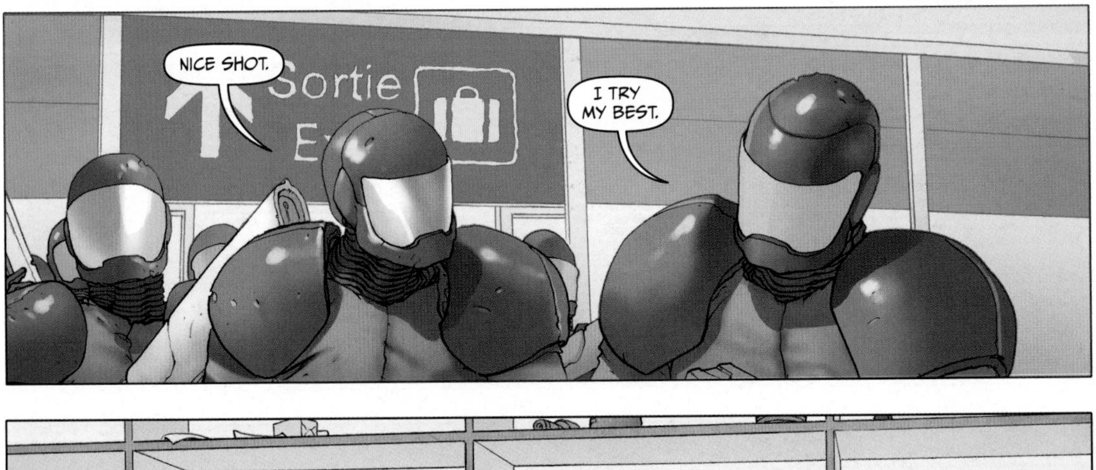
NICE SHOT.
Sortie
I TRY MY BEST.

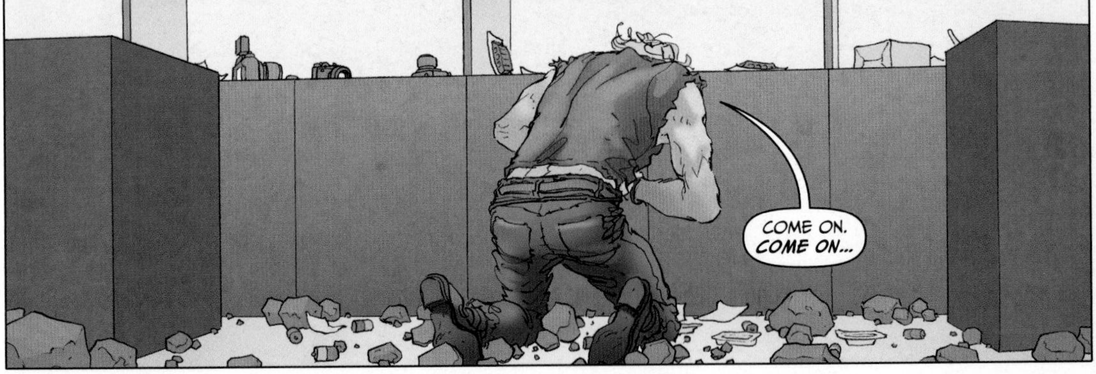
COME ON. COME ON...

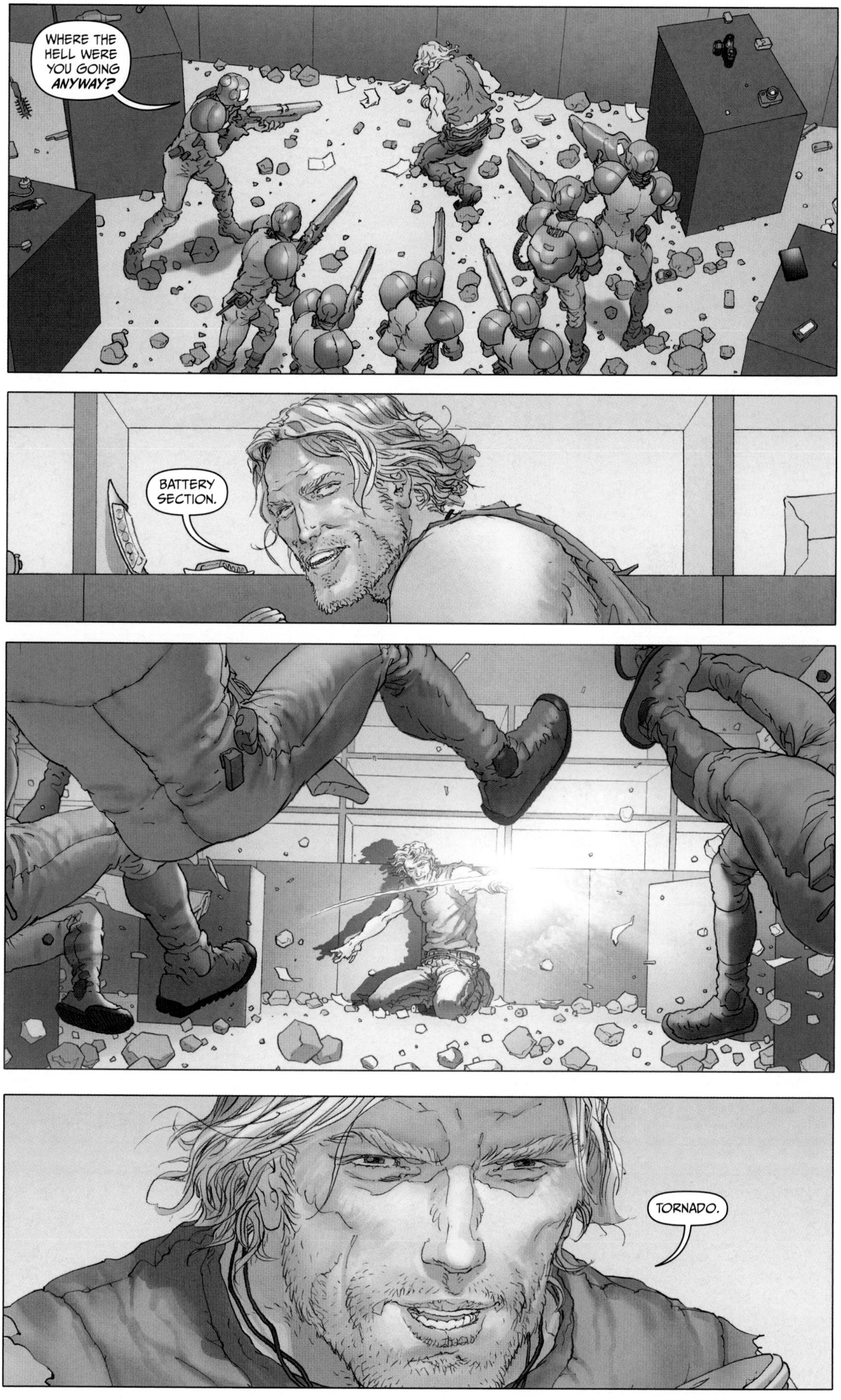
WHERE THE HELL WERE YOU GOING *ANYWAY?*
BATTERY SECTION.
TORNADO.

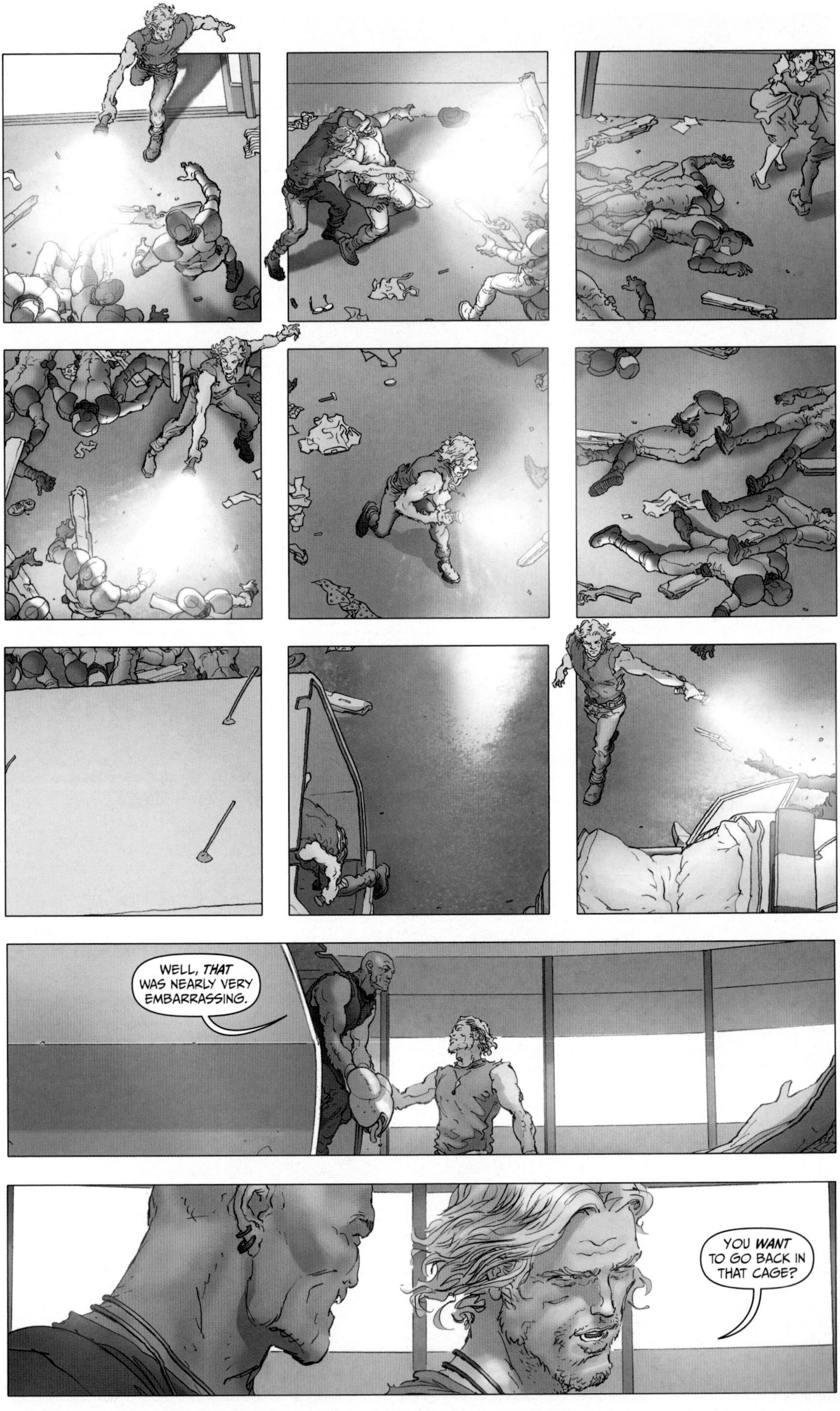
WELL, *THAT* WAS NEARLY VERY EMBARRASSING.
YOU *WANT* TO GO BACK IN THAT CAGE?

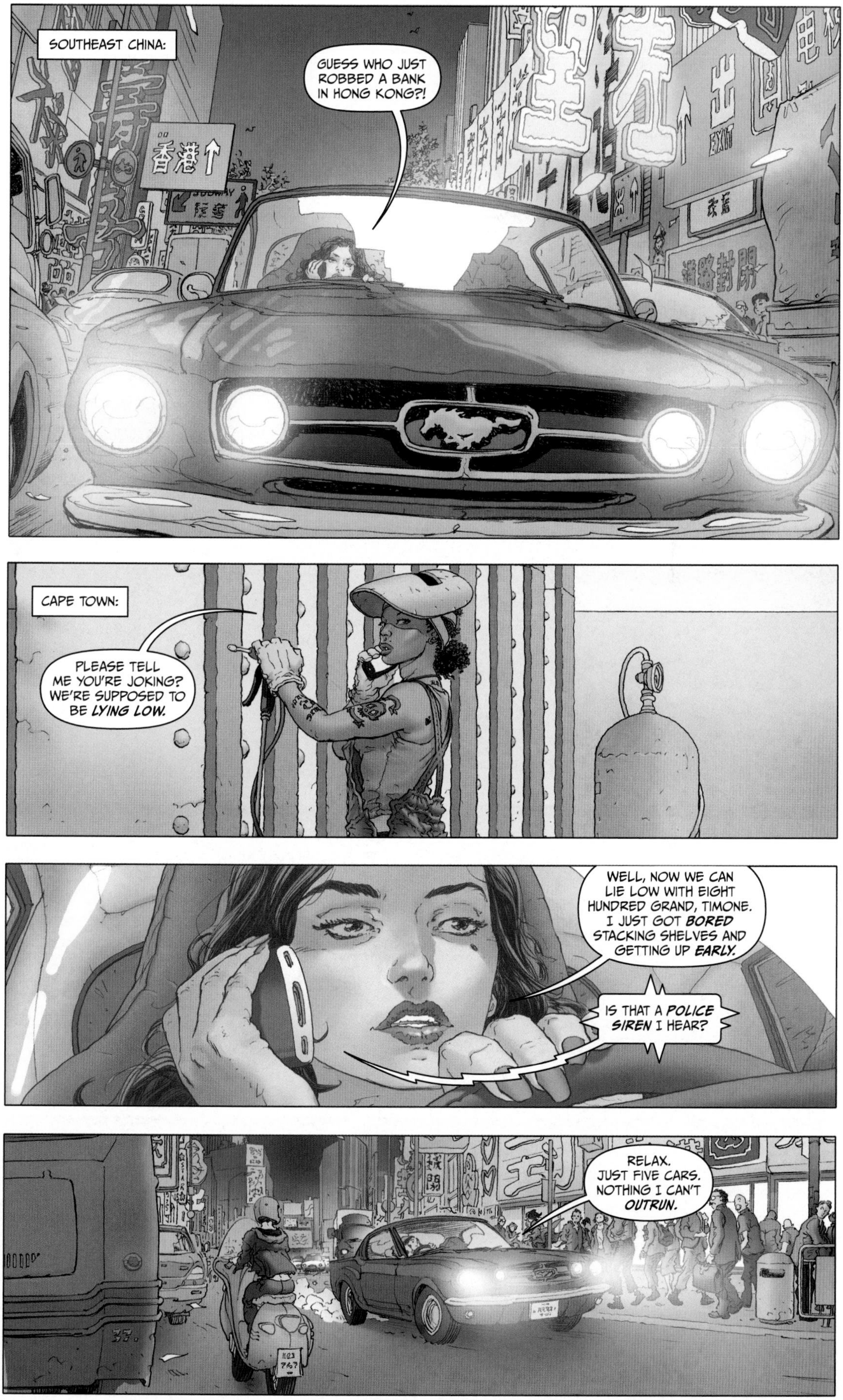
SOUTHEAST CHINA:
GUESS WHO JUST ROBBED A BANK IN HONG KONG?!
CAPE TOWN:
PLEASE TELL ME YOU'RE JOKING? WE'RE SUPPOSED TO BE *LYING LOW.*
WELL, NOW WE CAN LIE LOW WITH EIGHT HUNDRED GRAND, TIMONE. I JUST GOT *BORED* STACKING SHELVES AND GETTING UP *EARLY.*
IS THAT A *POLICE SIREN* I HEAR?
RELAX. JUST FIVE CARS. NOTHING I CAN'T *OUTRUN.*

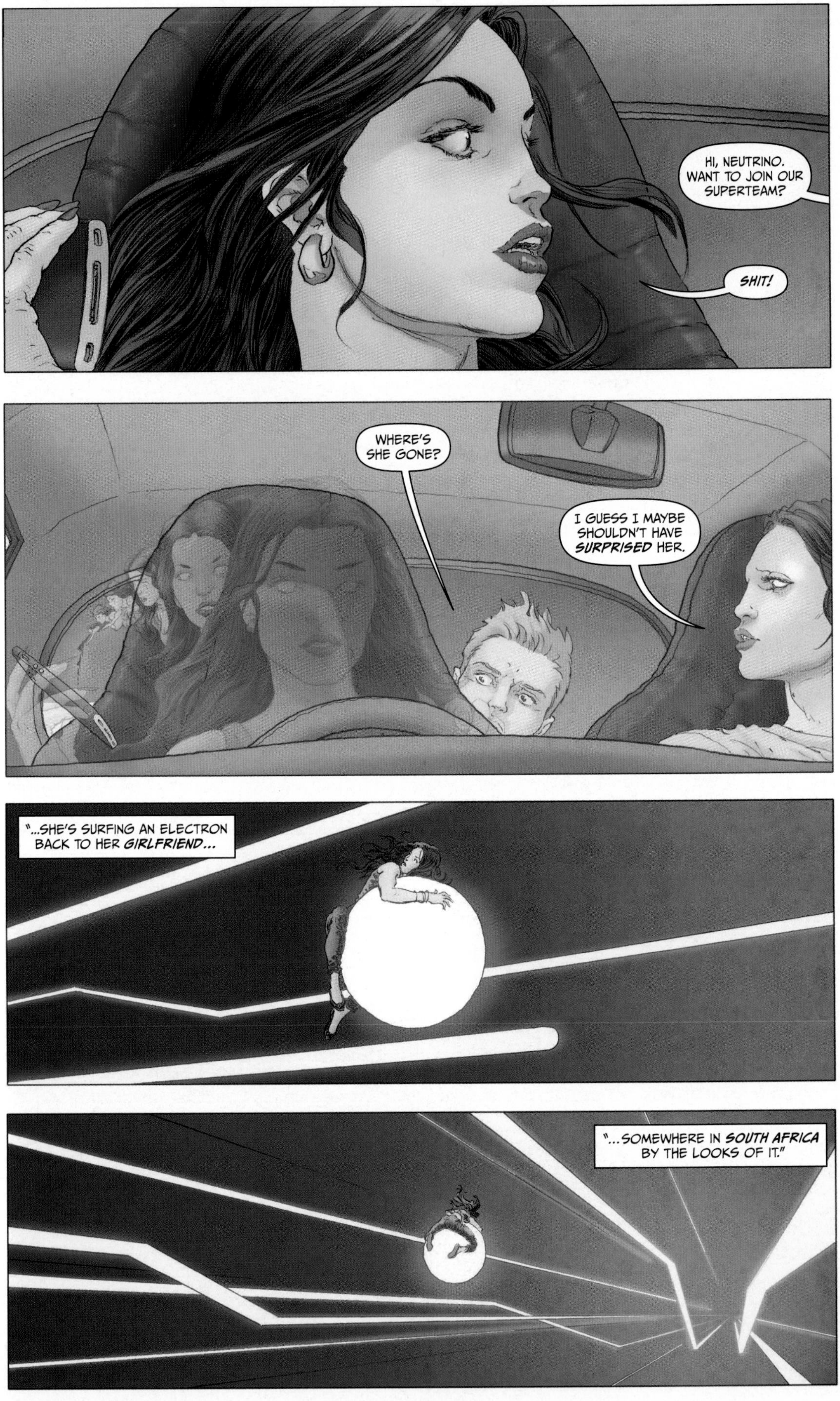
HI, NEUTRINO. WANT TO JOIN OUR SUPERTEAM?
SHIT!
WHERE'S SHE GONE?
I GUESS I MAYBE SHOULDN'T HAVE SURPRISED HER.
"...SHE'S SURFING AN ELECTRON BACK TO HER GIRLFRIEND...
"...SOMEWHERE IN SOUTH AFRICA BY THE LOOKS OF IT."

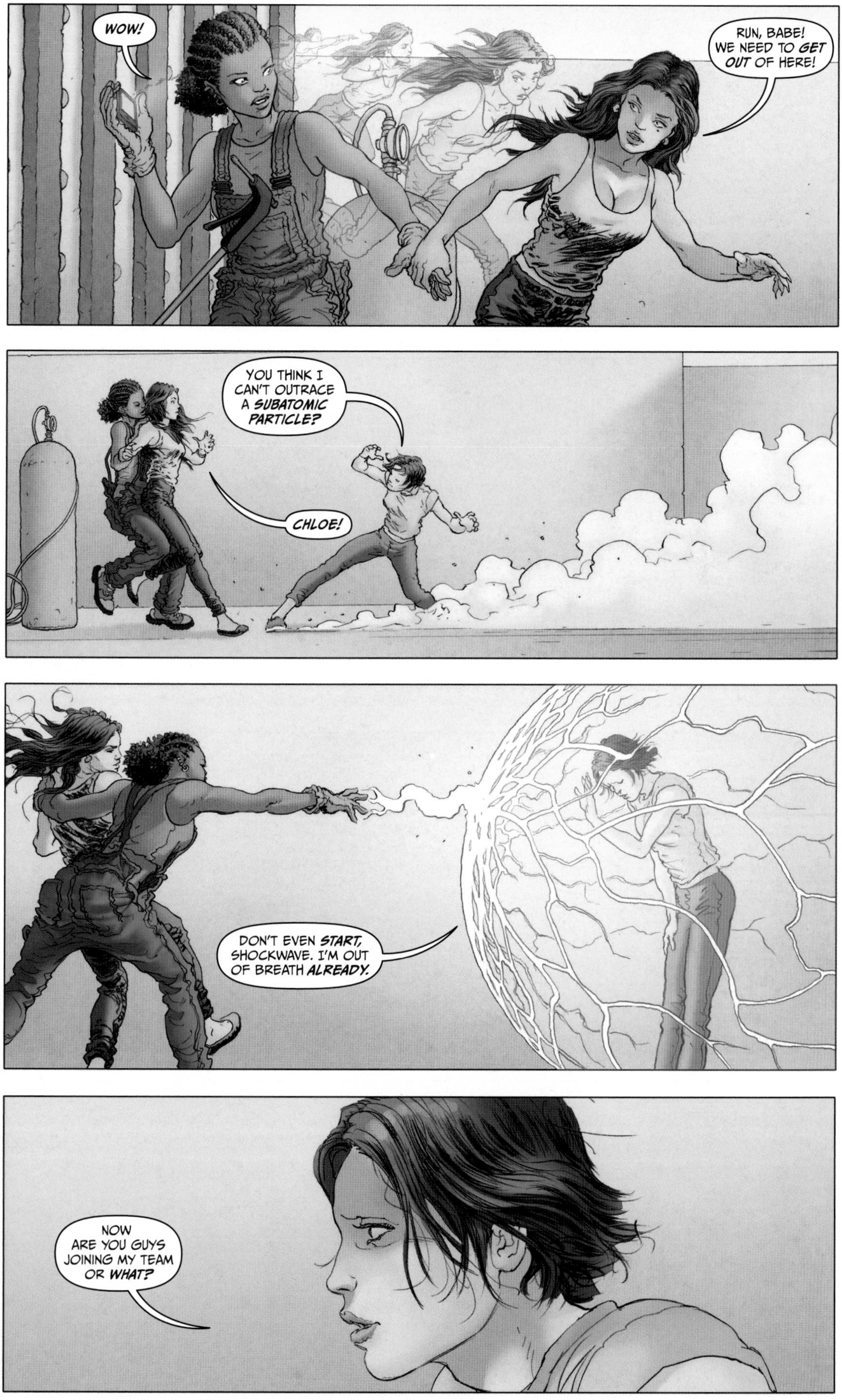
WOW!
RUN, BABE! WE NEED TO GET OUT OF HERE!
YOU THINK I CAN'T OUTRACE A SUBATOMIC PARTICLE?
CHLOE!
DON'T EVEN START, SHOCKWAVE. I'M OUT OF BREATH ALREADY.
NOW ARE YOU GUYS JOINING MY TEAM OR WHAT?

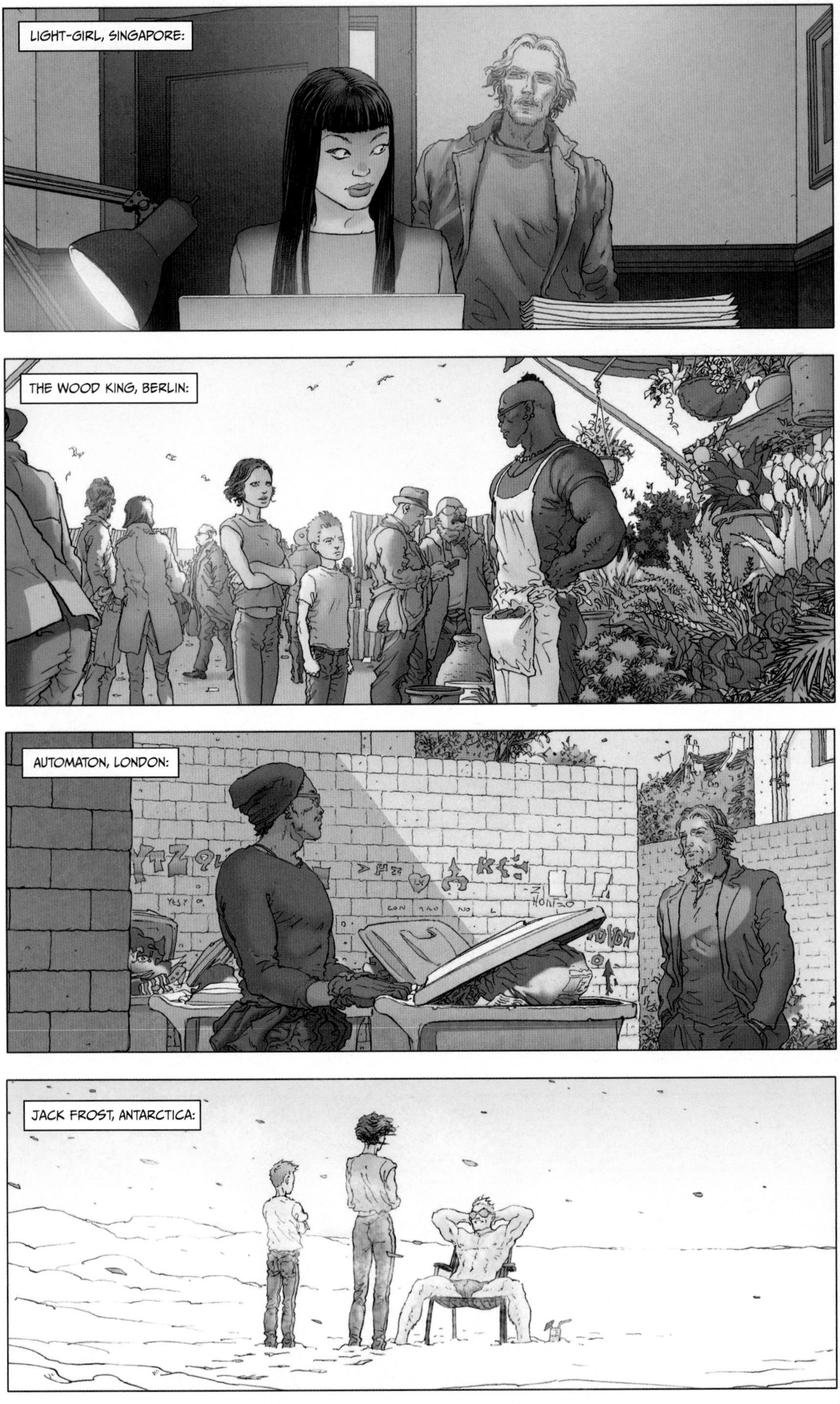
LIGHT-GIRL, SINGAPORE:
THE WOOD KING, BERLIN:
AUTOMATON, LONDON:
JACK FROST, ANTARCTICA:

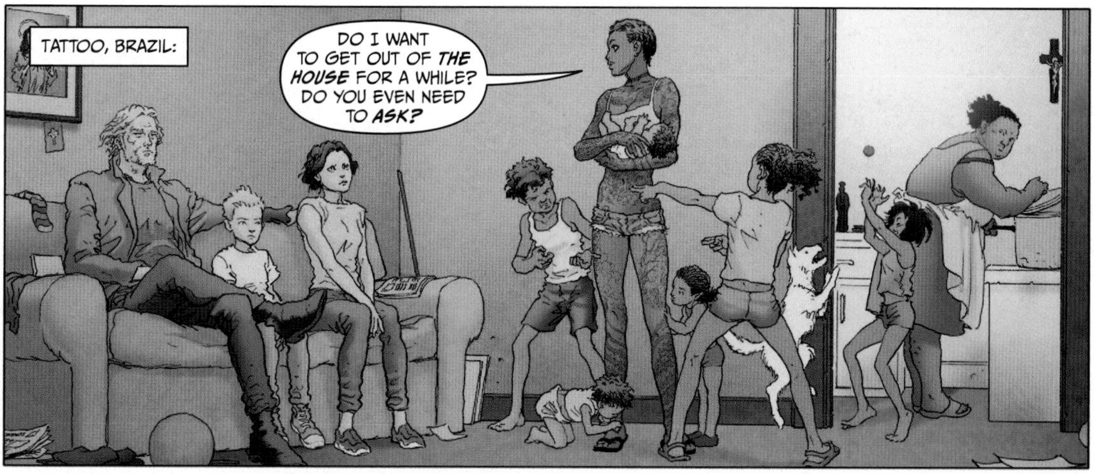
TATTOO, BRAZIL:
DO I WANT TO GET OUT OF THE HOUSE FOR A WHILE? DO YOU EVEN NEED TO ASK?

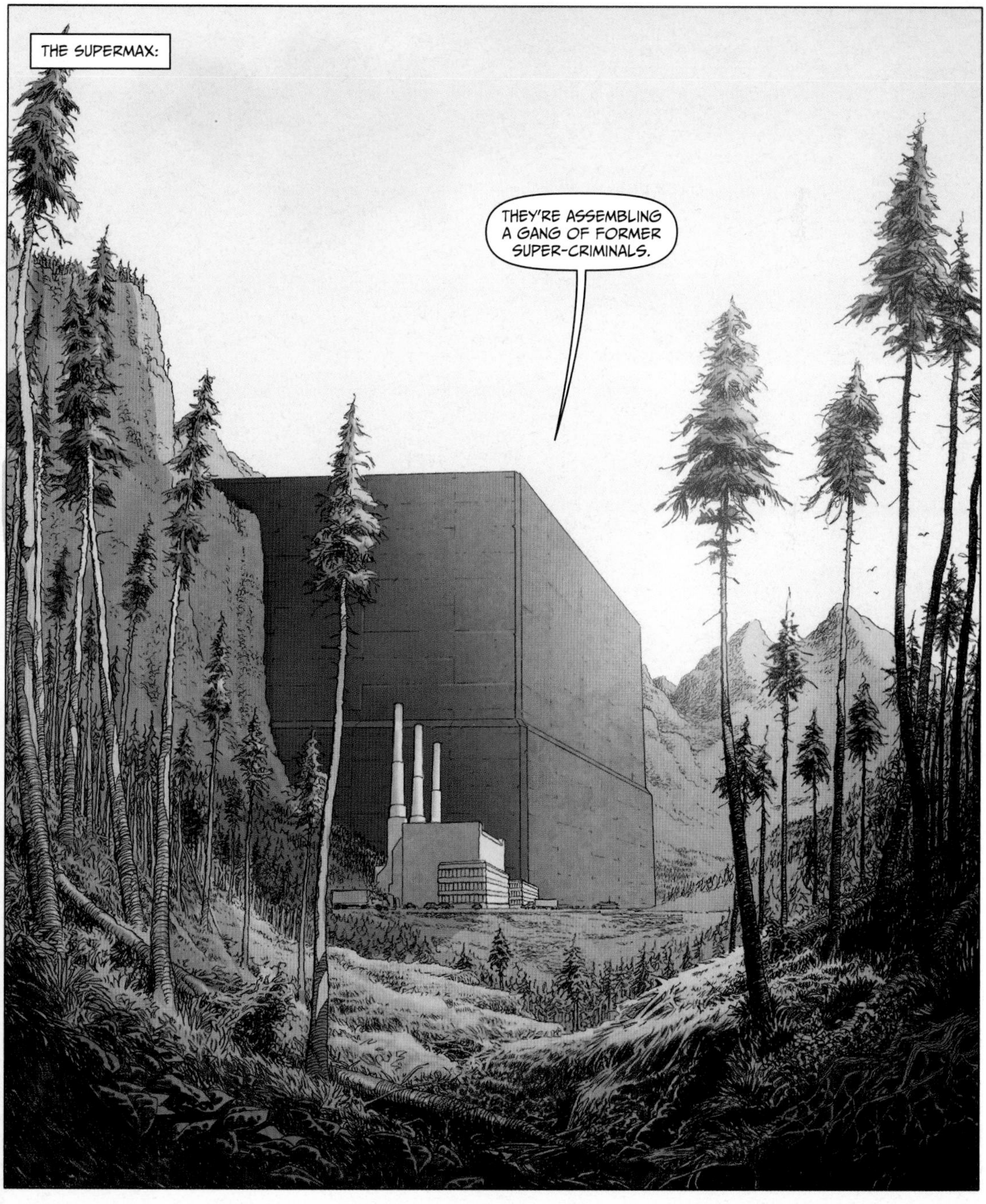
THE SUPERMAX:
THEY'RE ASSEMBLING A GANG OF FORMER SUPER-CRIMINALS.

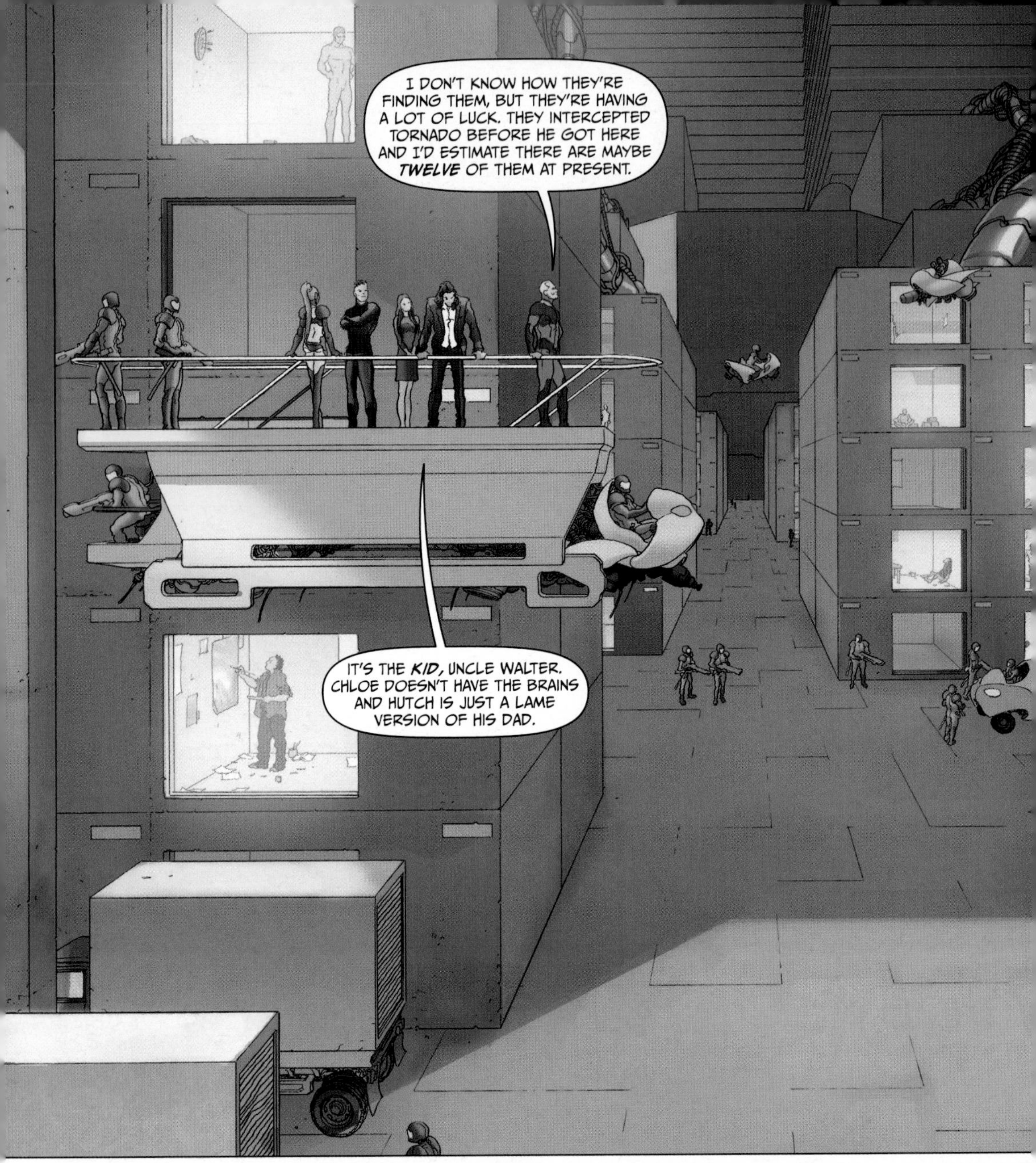
I DON'T KNOW HOW THEY'RE FINDING THEM, BUT THEY'RE HAVING A LOT OF LUCK. THEY INTERCEPTED TORNADO BEFORE HE GOT HERE AND I'D ESTIMATE THERE ARE MAYBE *TWELVE* OF THEM AT PRESENT.
IT'S THE *KID,* UNCLE WALTER. CHLOE DOESN'T HAVE THE BRAINS AND HUTCH IS JUST A LAME VERSION OF HIS DAD.

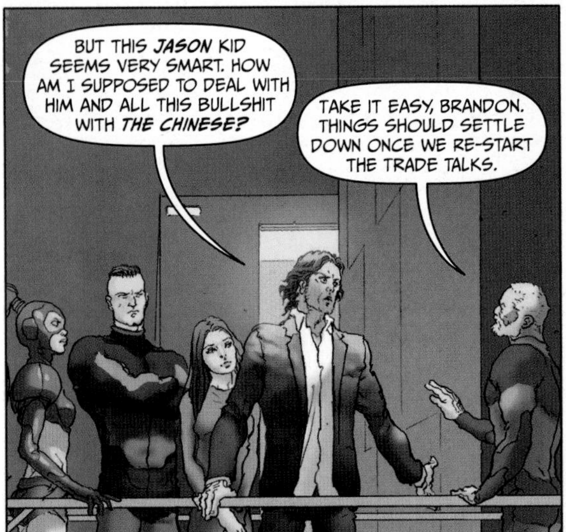
BUT THIS *JASON* KID SEEMS VERY SMART. HOW AM I SUPPOSED TO DEAL WITH HIM AND ALL THIS BULLSHIT WITH *THE CHINESE?*
TAKE IT EASY, BRANDON. THINGS SHOULD SETTLE DOWN ONCE WE RE-START THE TRADE TALKS.

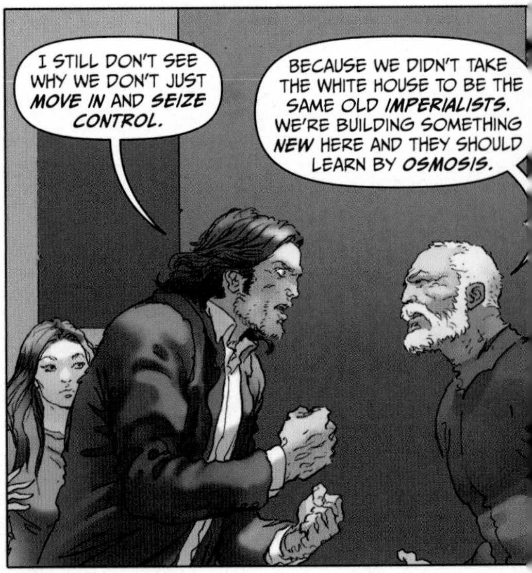
I STILL DON'T SEE WHY WE DON'T JUST *MOVE IN* AND *SEIZE CONTROL.*
BECAUSE WE DIDN'T TAKE THE WHITE HOUSE TO BE THE SAME OLD *IMPERIALISTS.* WE'RE BUILDING SOMETHING *NEW* HERE AND THEY SHOULD LEARN BY *OSMOSIS.*

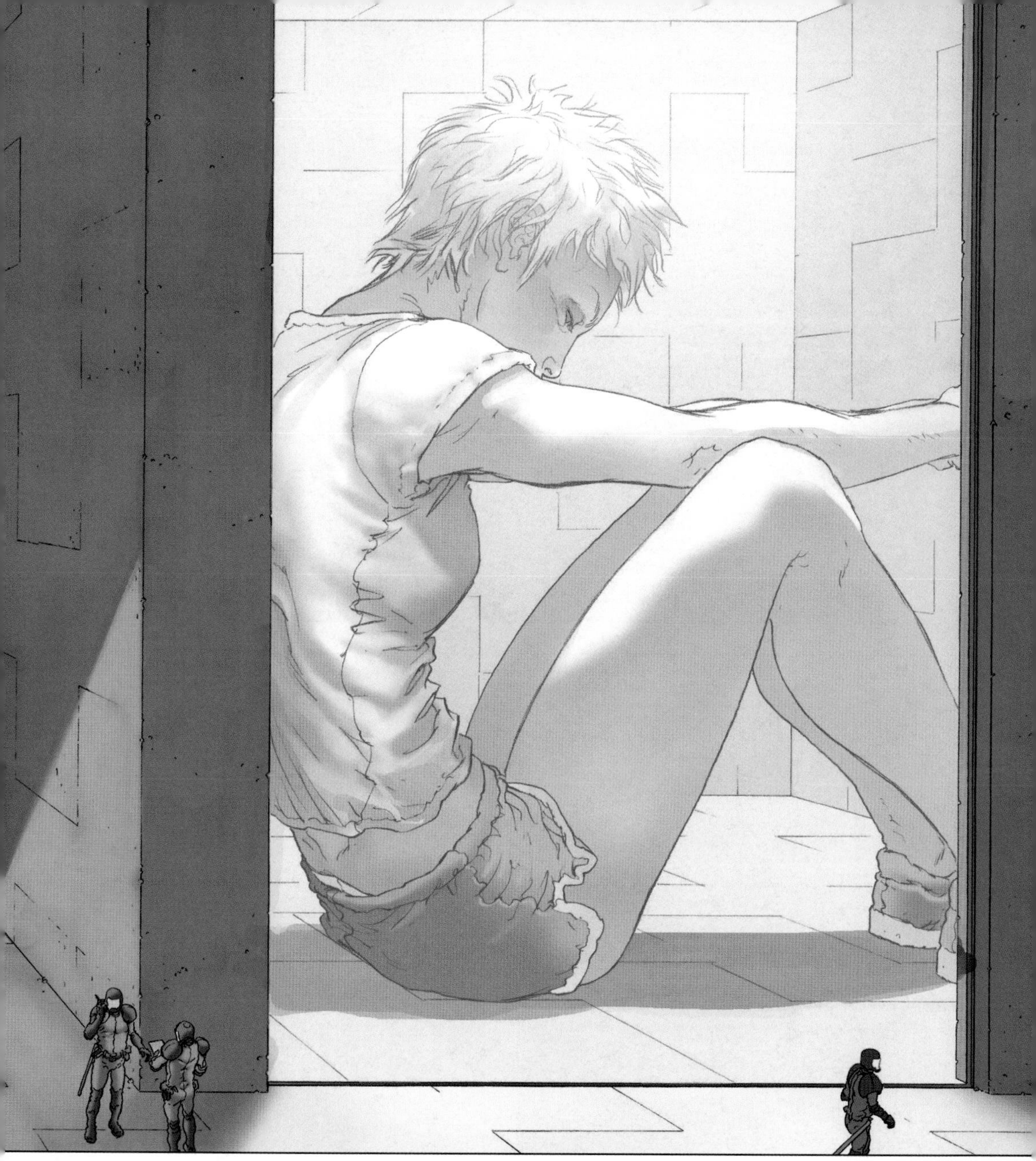

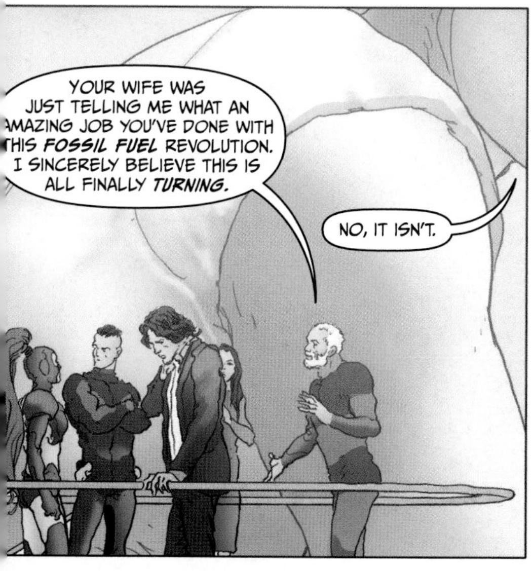
YOUR WIFE WAS JUST TELLING ME WHAT AN AMAZING JOB YOU'VE DONE WITH THIS FOSSIL FUEL REVOLUTION. I SINCERELY BELIEVE THIS IS ALL FINALLY TURNING.
NO, IT ISN'T.

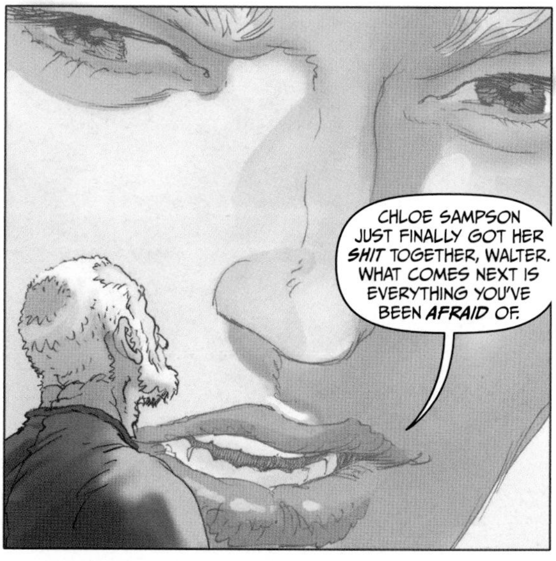
CHLOE SAMPSON JUST FINALLY GOT HER SHIT TOGETHER, WALTER. WHAT COMES NEXT IS EVERYTHING YOU'VE BEEN AFRAID OF.

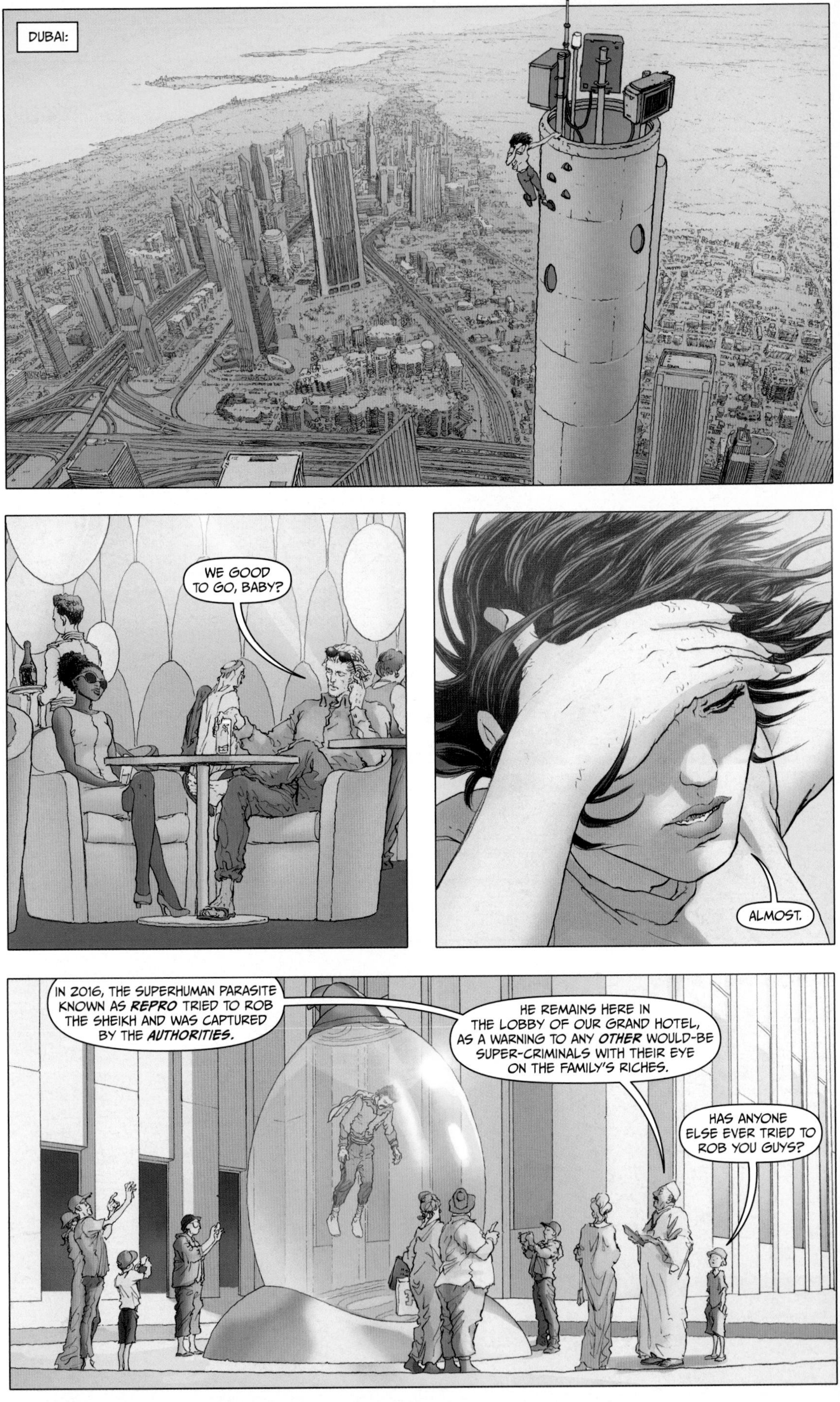
DUBAI:
WE GOOD TO GO, BABY?
ALMOST.
IN 2016, THE SUPERHUMAN PARASITE KNOWN AS REPRO TRIED TO ROB THE SHEIKH AND WAS CAPTURED BY THE AUTHORITIES.
HE REMAINS HERE IN THE LOBBY OF OUR GRAND HOTEL, AS A WARNING TO ANY OTHER WOULD-BE SUPER-CRIMINALS WITH THEIR EYE ON THE FAMILY'S RICHES.
HAS ANYONE ELSE EVER TRIED TO ROB YOU GUYS?

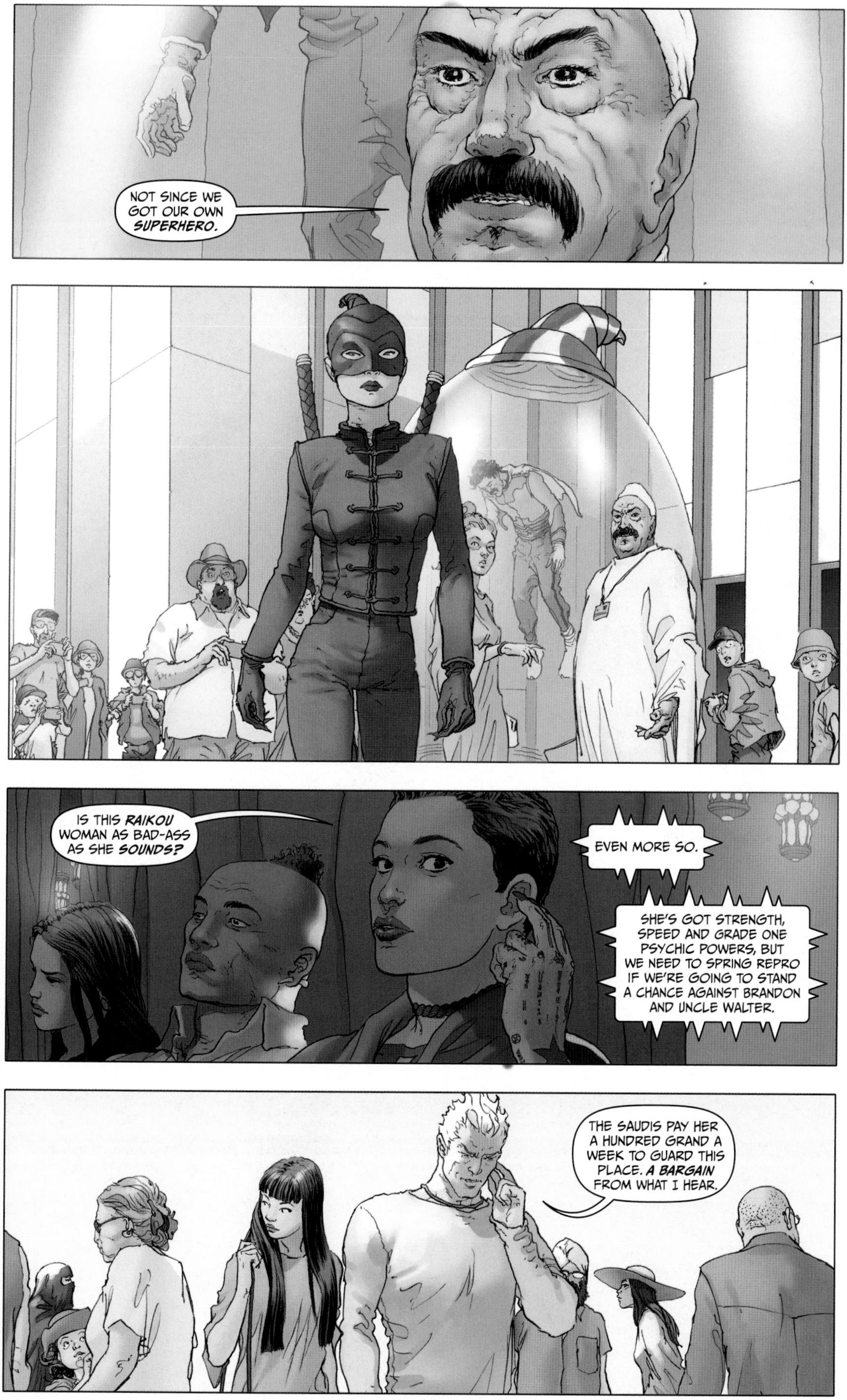
NOT SINCE WE GOT OUR OWN SUPERHERO.
IS THIS RAIKOU WOMAN AS BAD-ASS AS SHE SOUNDS?
EVEN MORE SO.
SHE'S GOT STRENGTH, SPEED AND GRADE ONE PSYCHIC POWERS, BUT WE NEED TO SPRING REPRO IF WE'RE GOING TO STAND A CHANCE AGAINST BRANDON AND UNCLE WALTER.
THE SAUDIS PAY HER A HUNDRED GRAND A WEEK TO GUARD THIS PLACE. A BARGAIN FROM WHAT I HEAR.

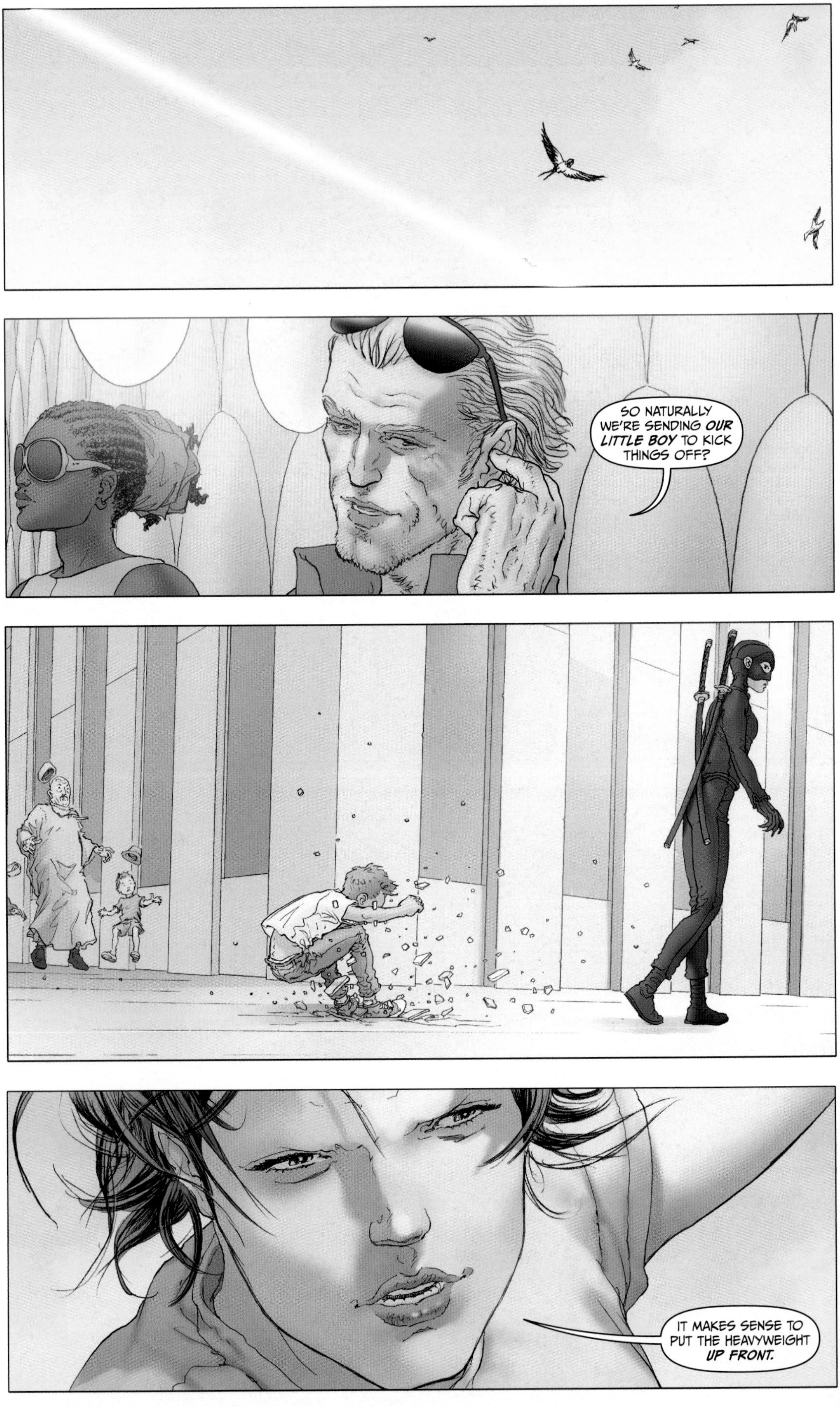
SO NATURALLY WE'RE SENDING *OUR LITTLE BOY* TO KICK THINGS OFF?
IT MAKES SENSE TO PUT THE HEAVYWEIGHT *UP FRONT.*

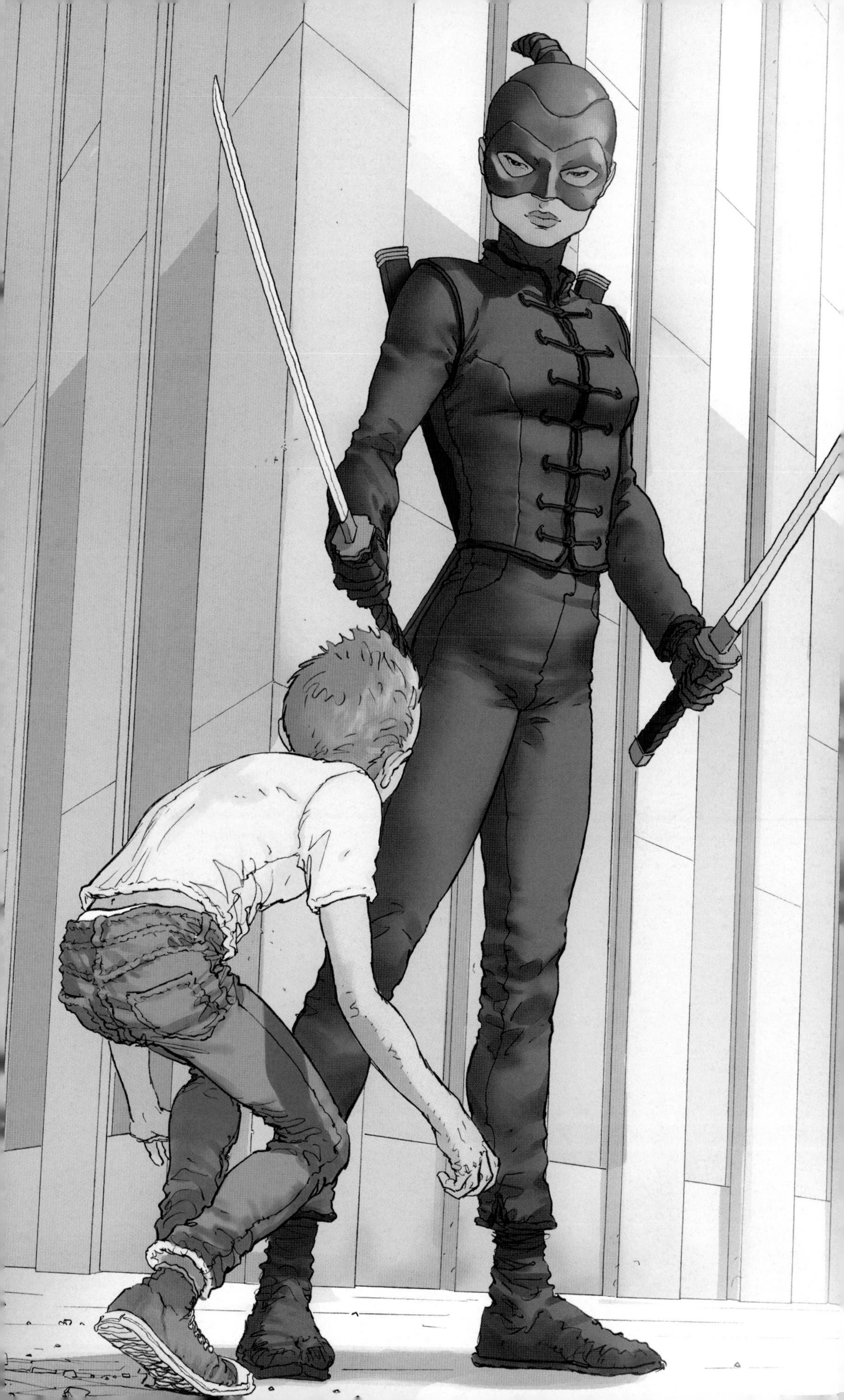

CHAPTER 2

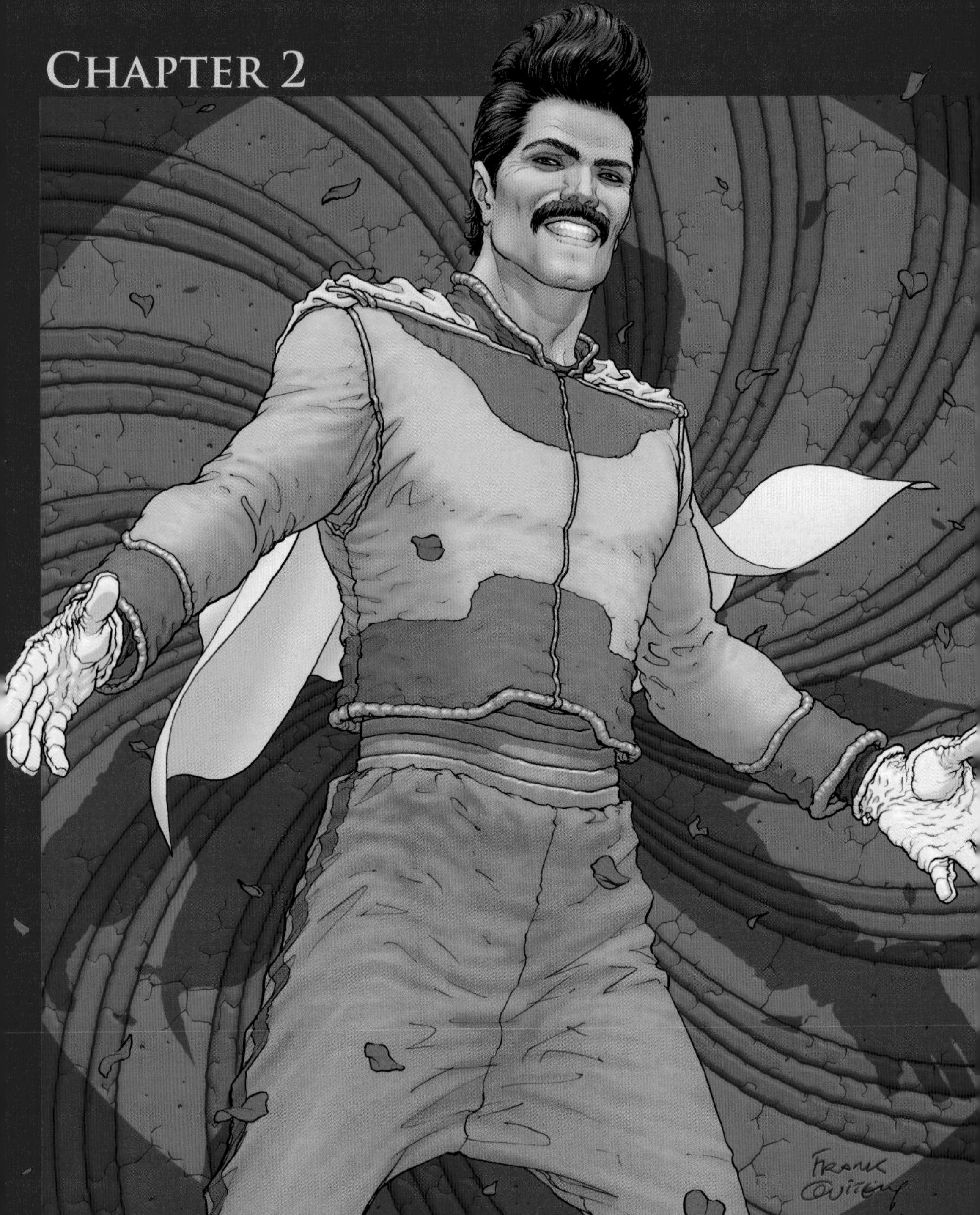
FRANK
QUITELY

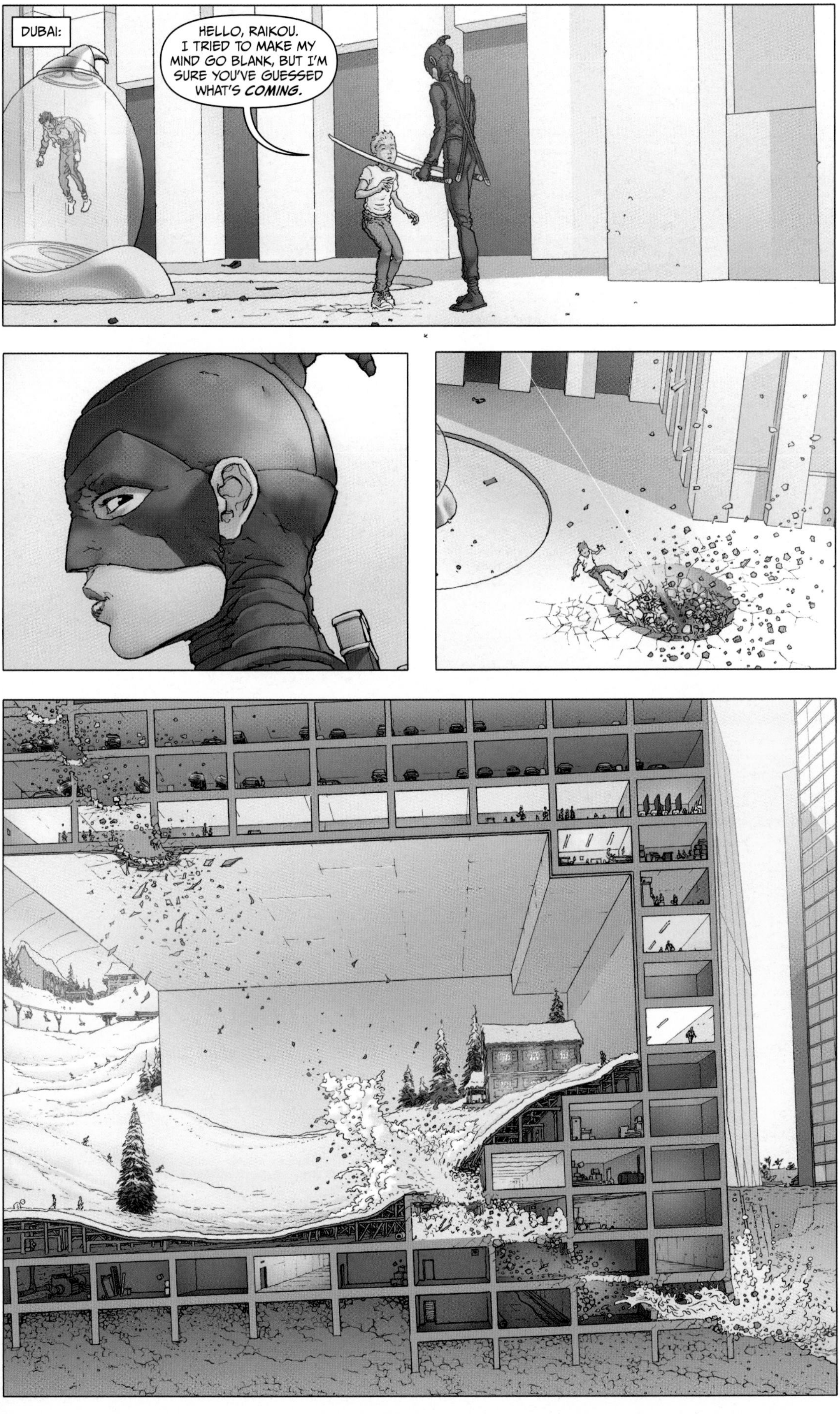
DUBAI:
HELLO, RAIKOU. I TRIED TO MAKE MY MIND GO BLANK, BUT I'M SURE YOU'VE GUESSED WHAT'S *COMING.*

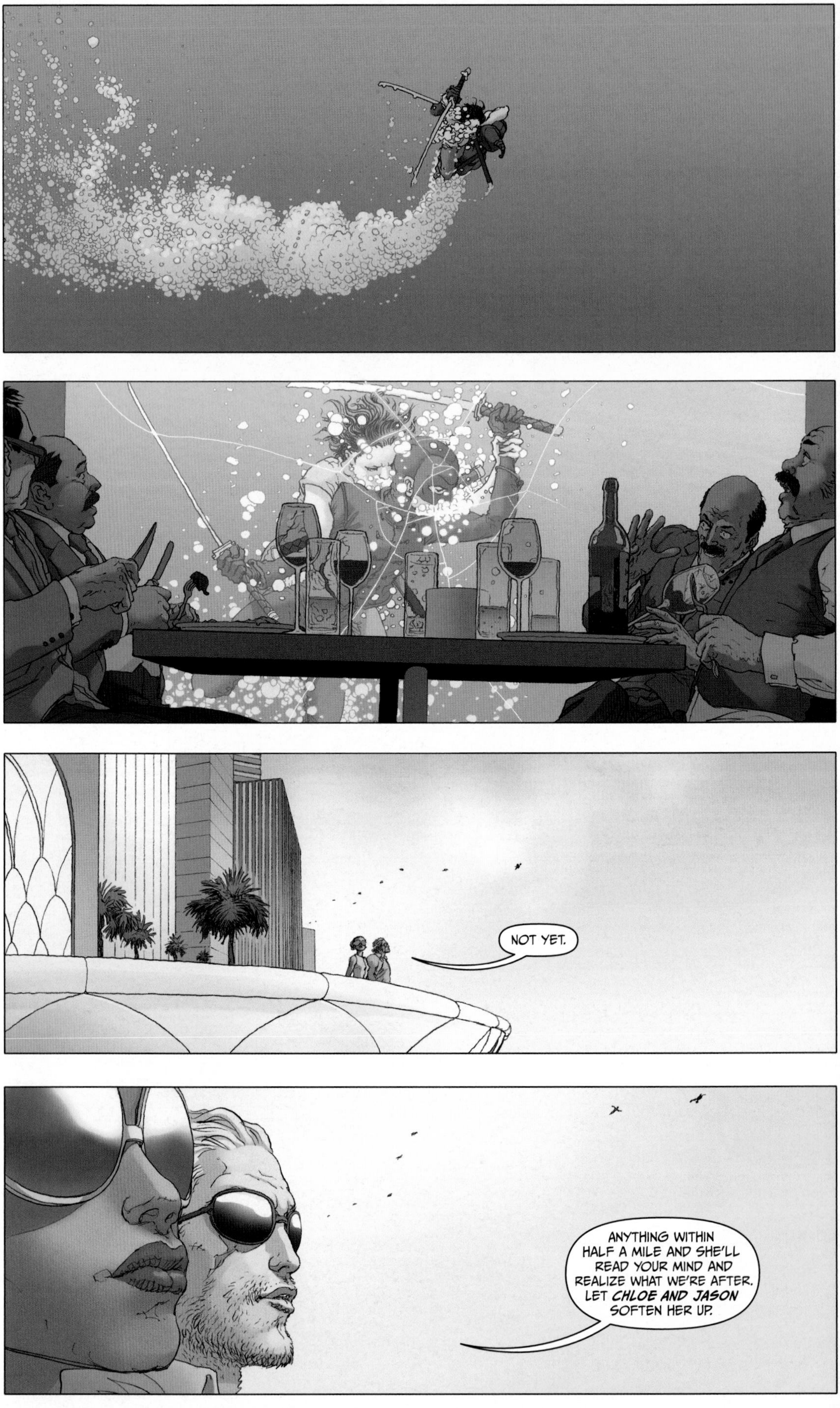
NOT YET.
ANYTHING WITHIN HALF A MILE AND SHE'LL READ YOUR MIND AND REALIZE WHAT WE'RE AFTER. LET CHLOE AND JASON SOFTEN HER UP.

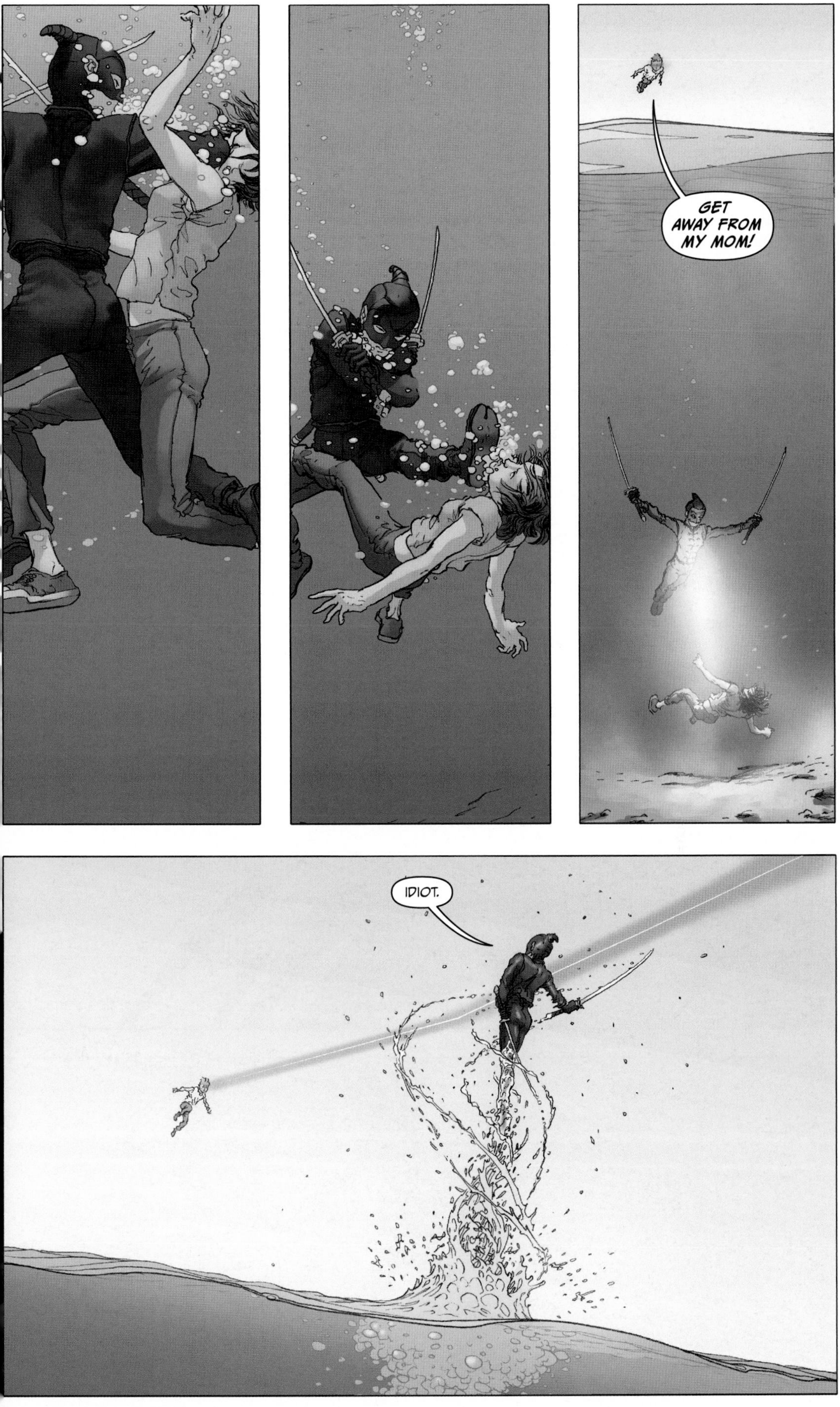
GET AWAY FROM MY MOM!
IDIOT.

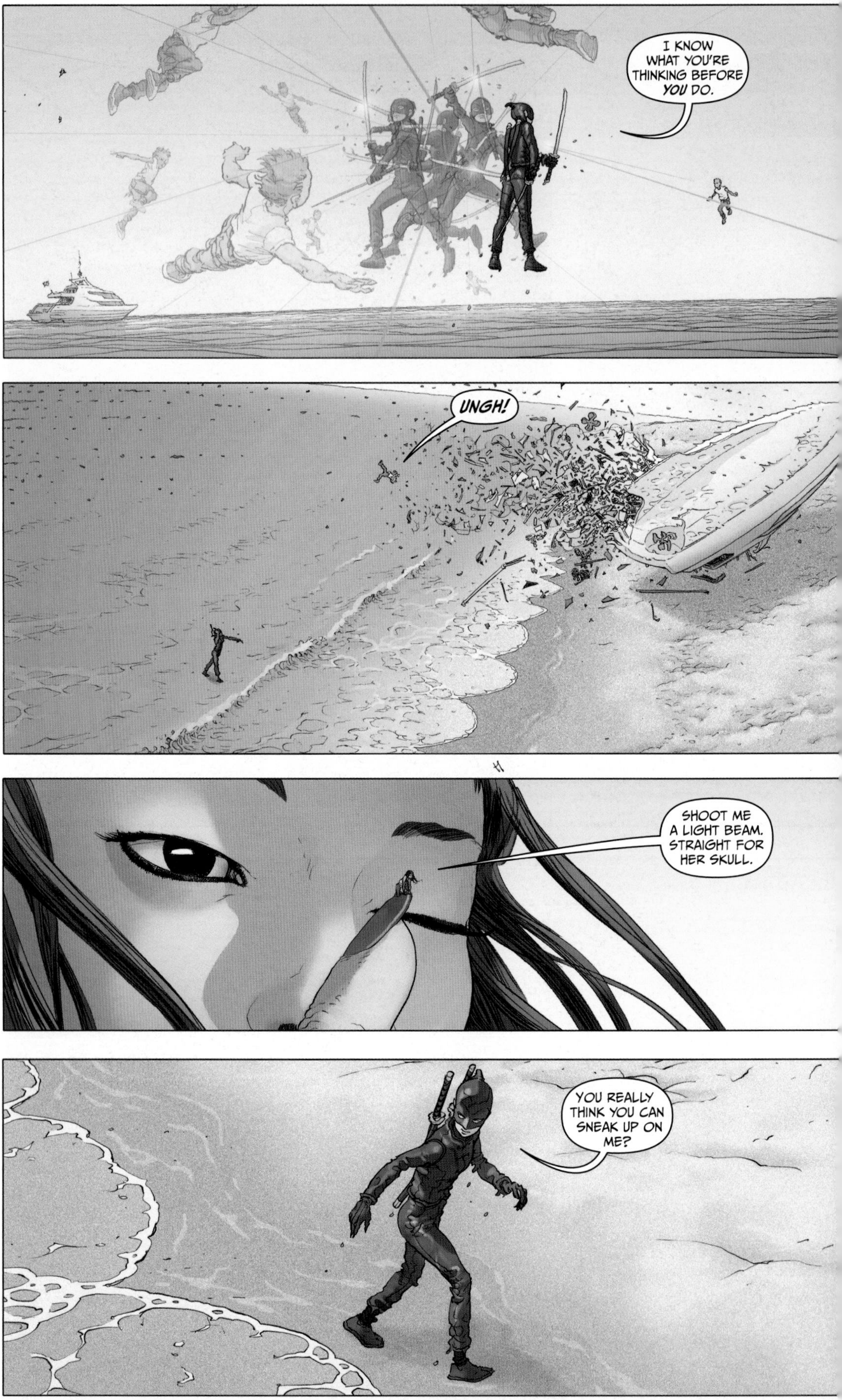
I KNOW WHAT YOU'RE THINKING BEFORE *YOU* DO.
UNGH!
SHOOT ME A LIGHT BEAM. STRAIGHT FOR HER SKULL.
YOU REALLY THINK YOU CAN SNEAK UP ON ME?

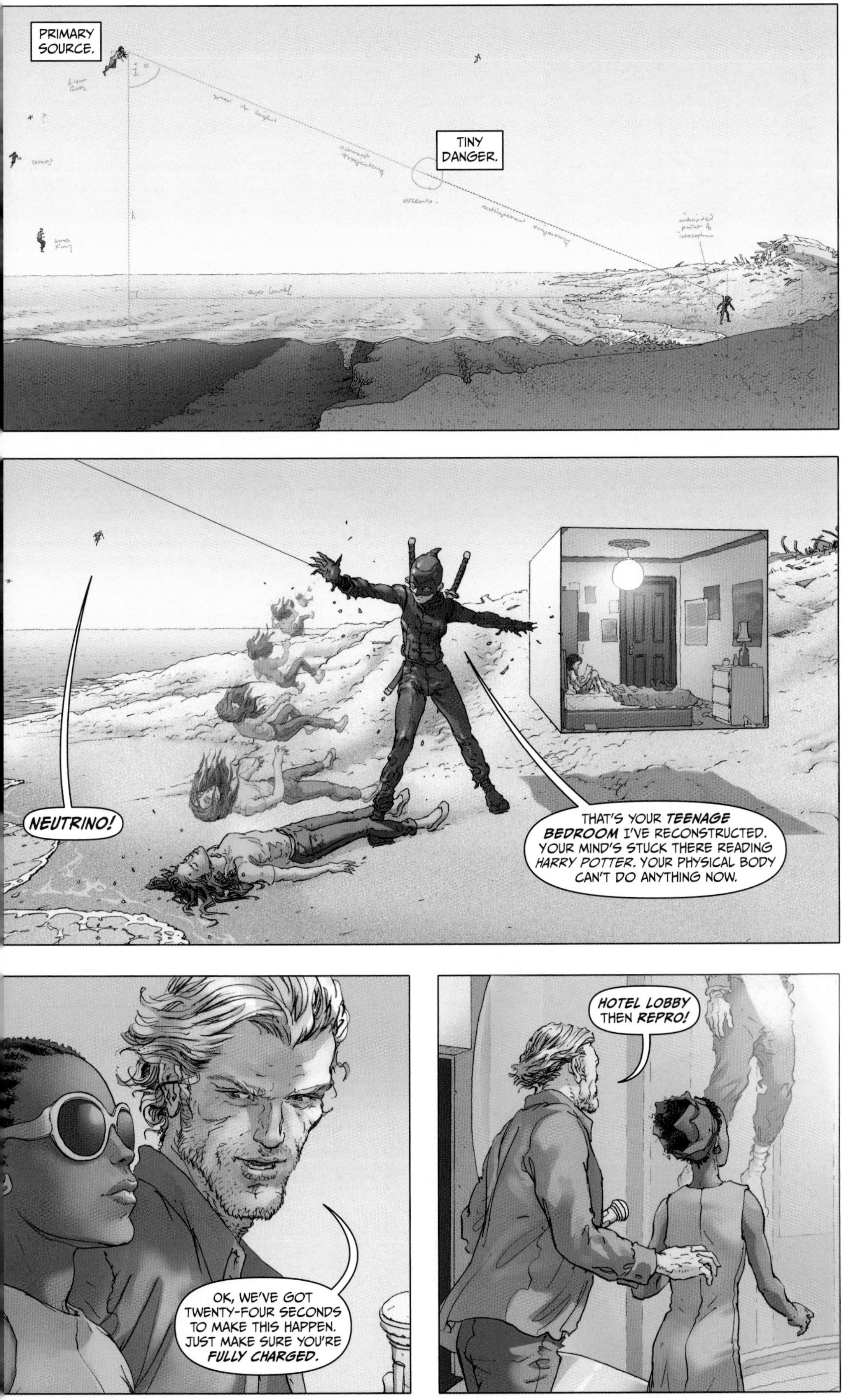
PRIMARY SOURCE.
TINY DANGER.
NEUTRINO!
THAT'S YOUR TEENAGE BEDROOM I'VE RECONSTRUCTED. YOUR MIND'S STUCK THERE READING HARRY POTTER. YOUR PHYSICAL BODY CAN'T DO ANYTHING NOW.
OK, WE'VE GOT TWENTY-FOUR SECONDS TO MAKE THIS HAPPEN. JUST MAKE SURE YOU'RE FULLY CHARGED.
HOTEL LOBBY THEN REPRO!

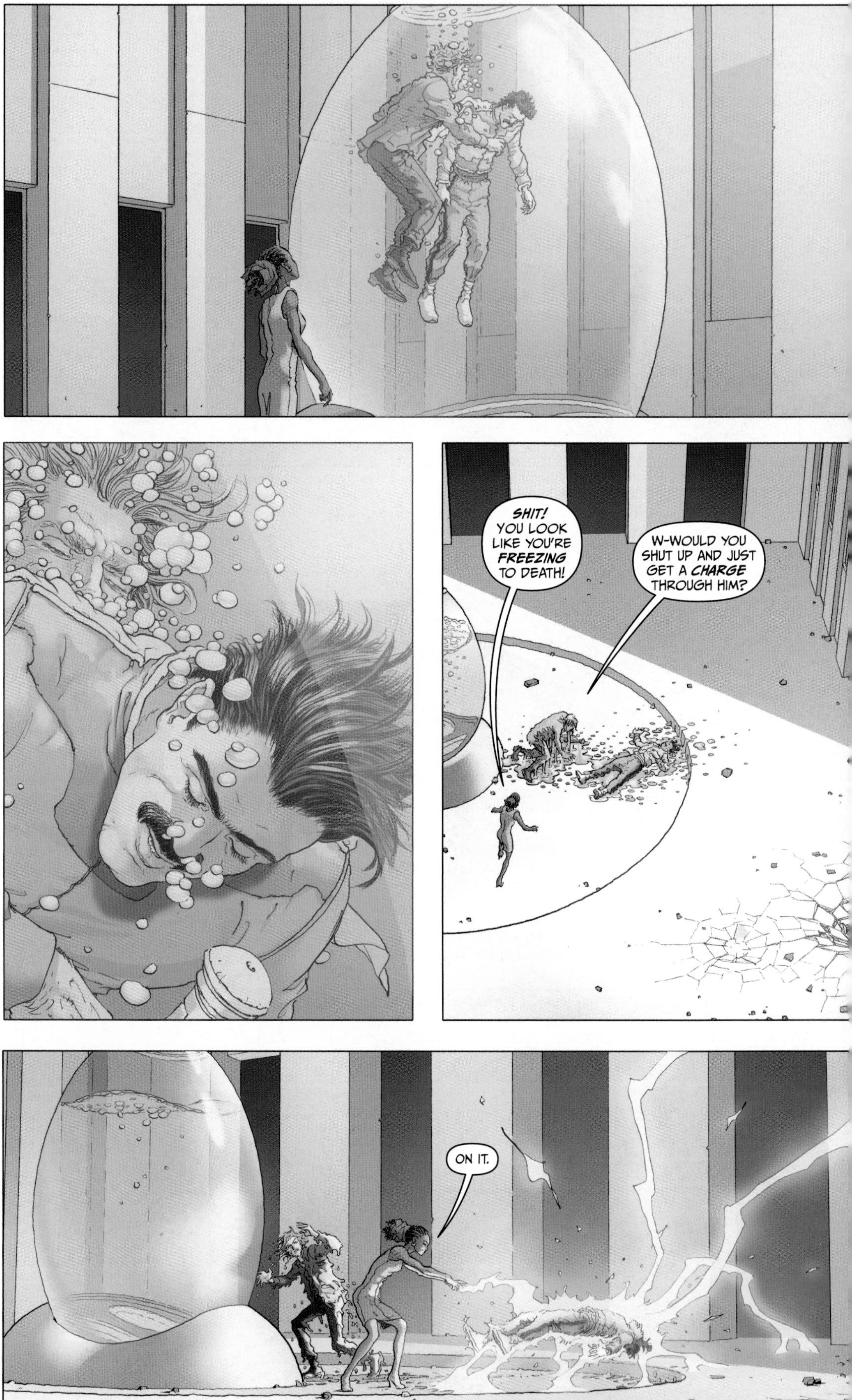
SHIT! YOU LOOK LIKE YOU'RE FREEZING TO DEATH!
W-WOULD YOU SHUT UP AND JUST GET A CHARGE THROUGH HIM?
ON IT.

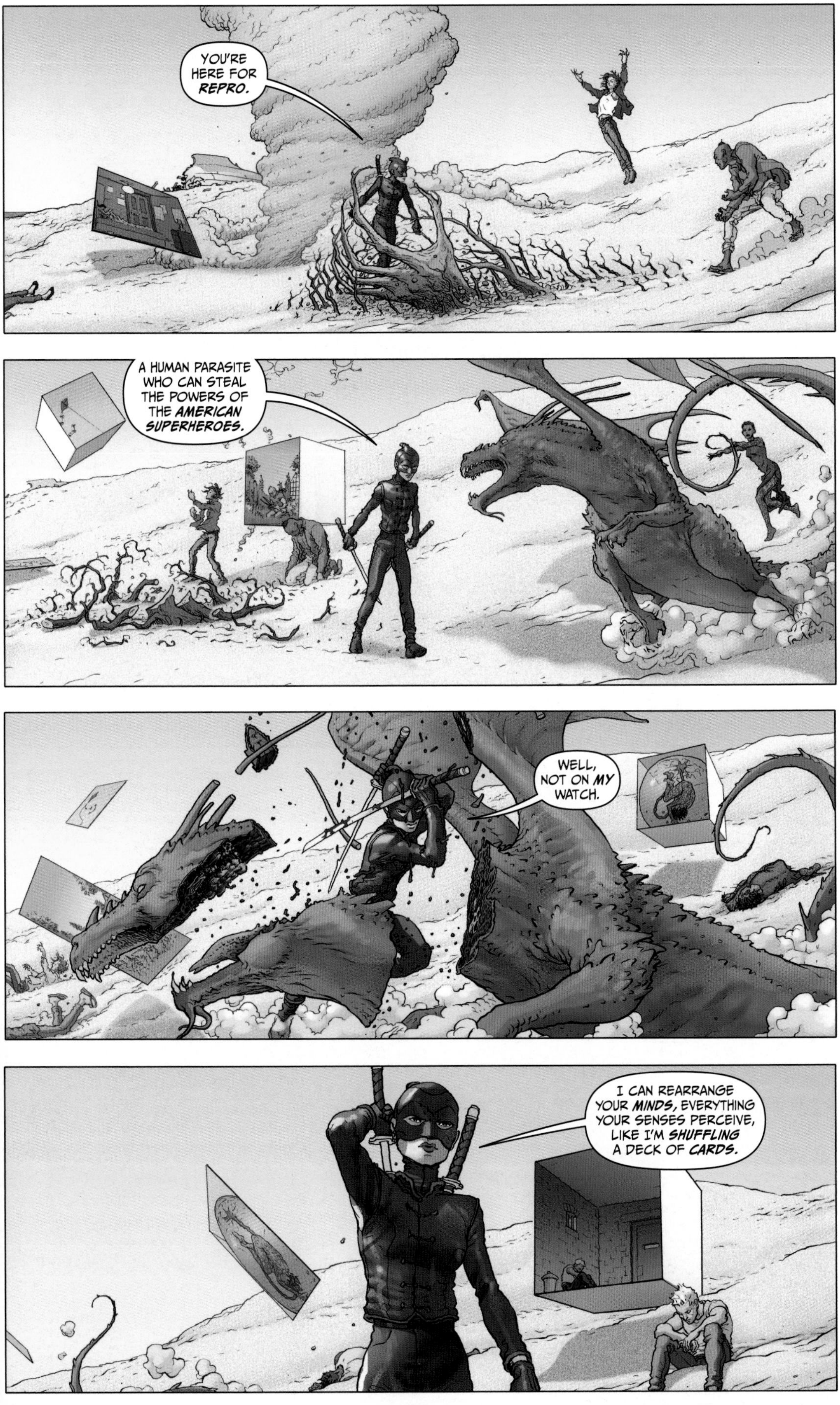
YOU'RE HERE FOR REPRO.
A HUMAN PARASITE WHO CAN STEAL THE POWERS OF THE AMERICAN SUPERHEROES.
WELL, NOT ON MY WATCH.
I CAN REARRANGE YOUR MINDS, EVERYTHING YOUR SENSES PERCEIVE, LIKE I'M SHUFFLING A DECK OF CARDS.

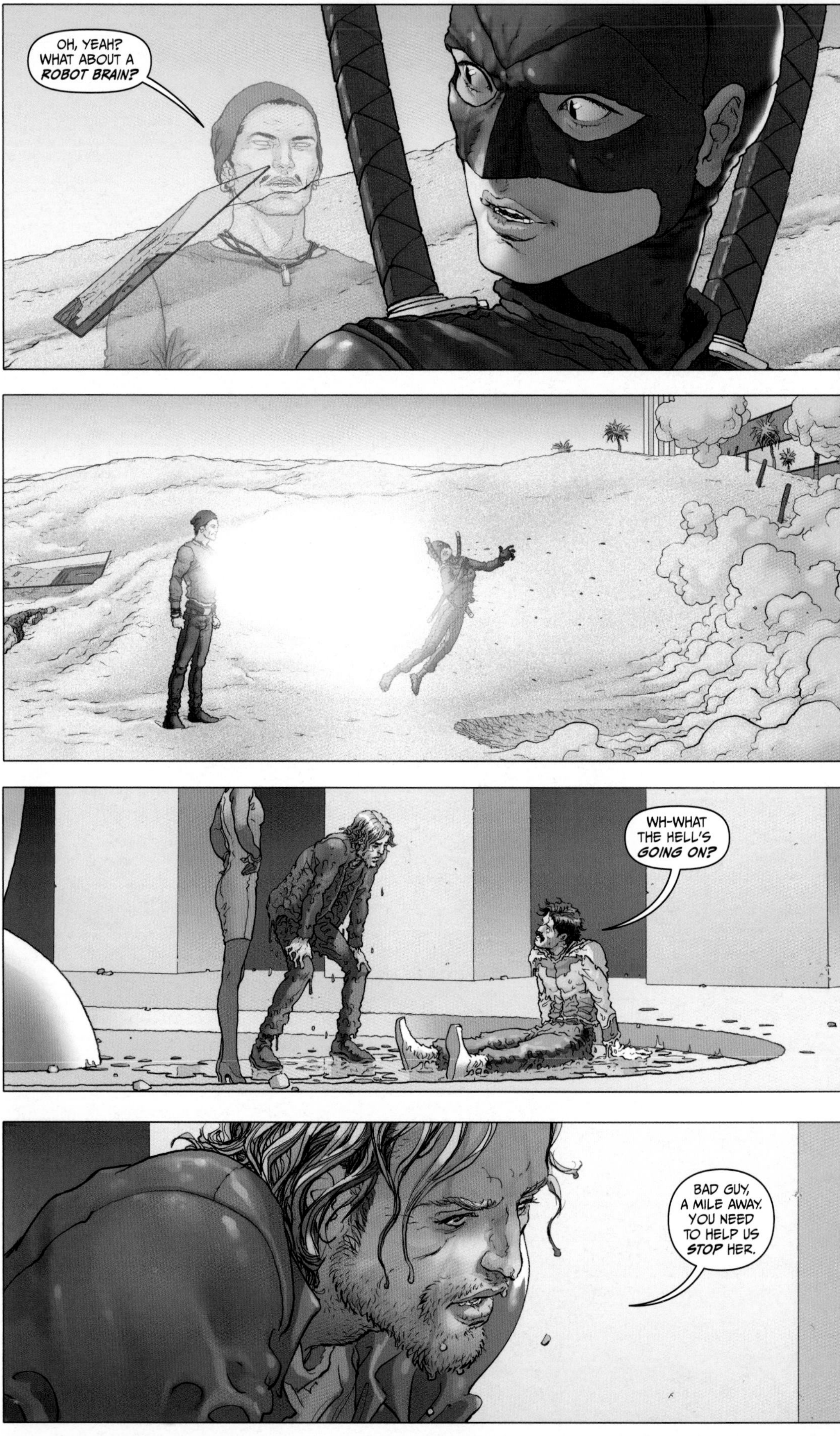
OH, YEAH? WHAT ABOUT A ROBOT BRAIN?
WH-WHAT THE HELL'S GOING ON?
BAD GUY, A MILE AWAY. YOU NEED TO HELP US STOP HER.

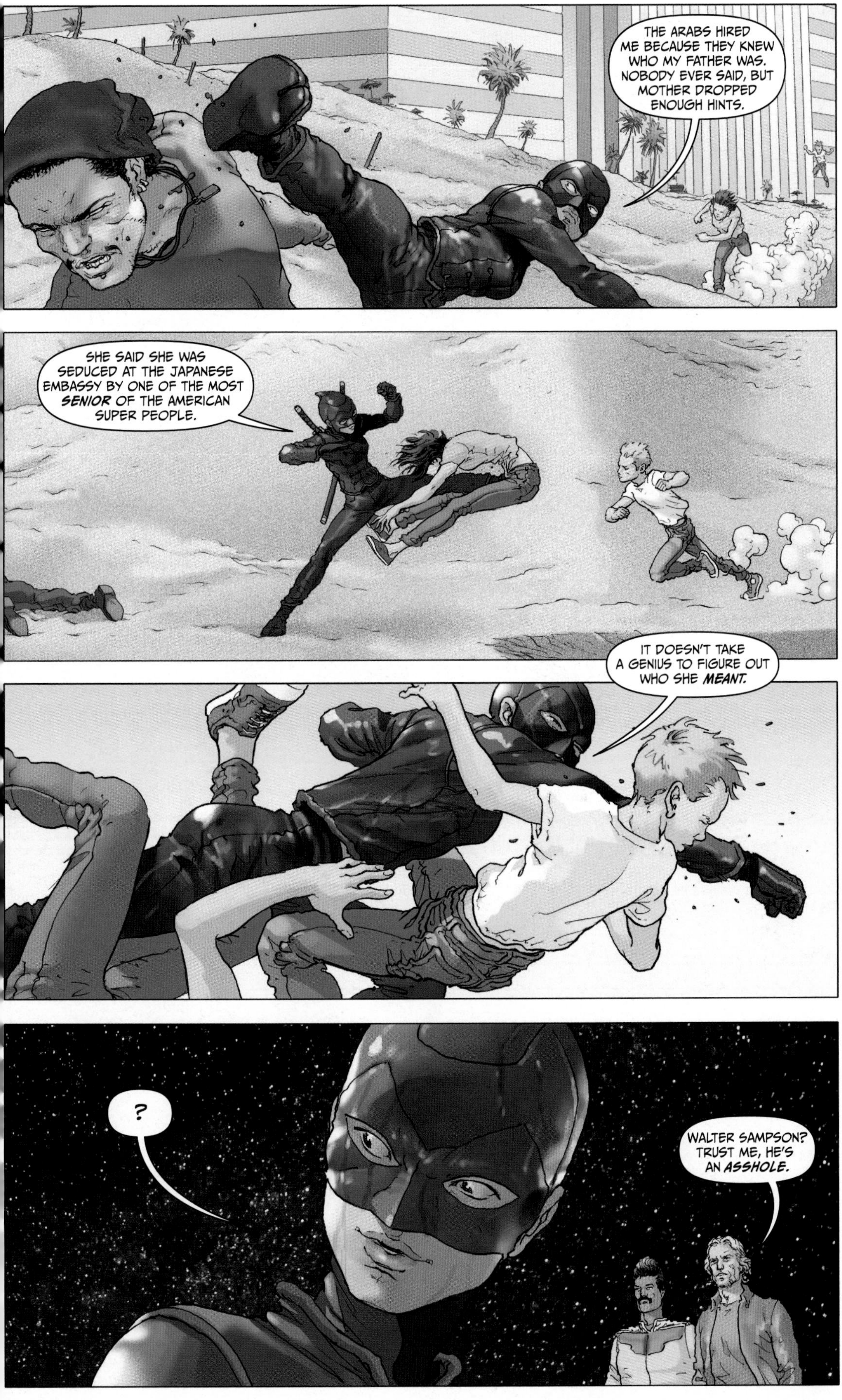
THE ARABS HIRED ME BECAUSE THEY KNEW WHO MY FATHER WAS. NOBODY EVER SAID, BUT MOTHER DROPPED ENOUGH HINTS.
SHE SAID SHE WAS SEDUCED AT THE JAPANESE EMBASSY BY ONE OF THE MOST SENIOR OF THE AMERICAN SUPER PEOPLE.
IT DOESN'T TAKE A GENIUS TO FIGURE OUT WHO SHE MEANT.
?
WALTER SAMPSON? TRUST ME, HE'S AN ASSHOLE.

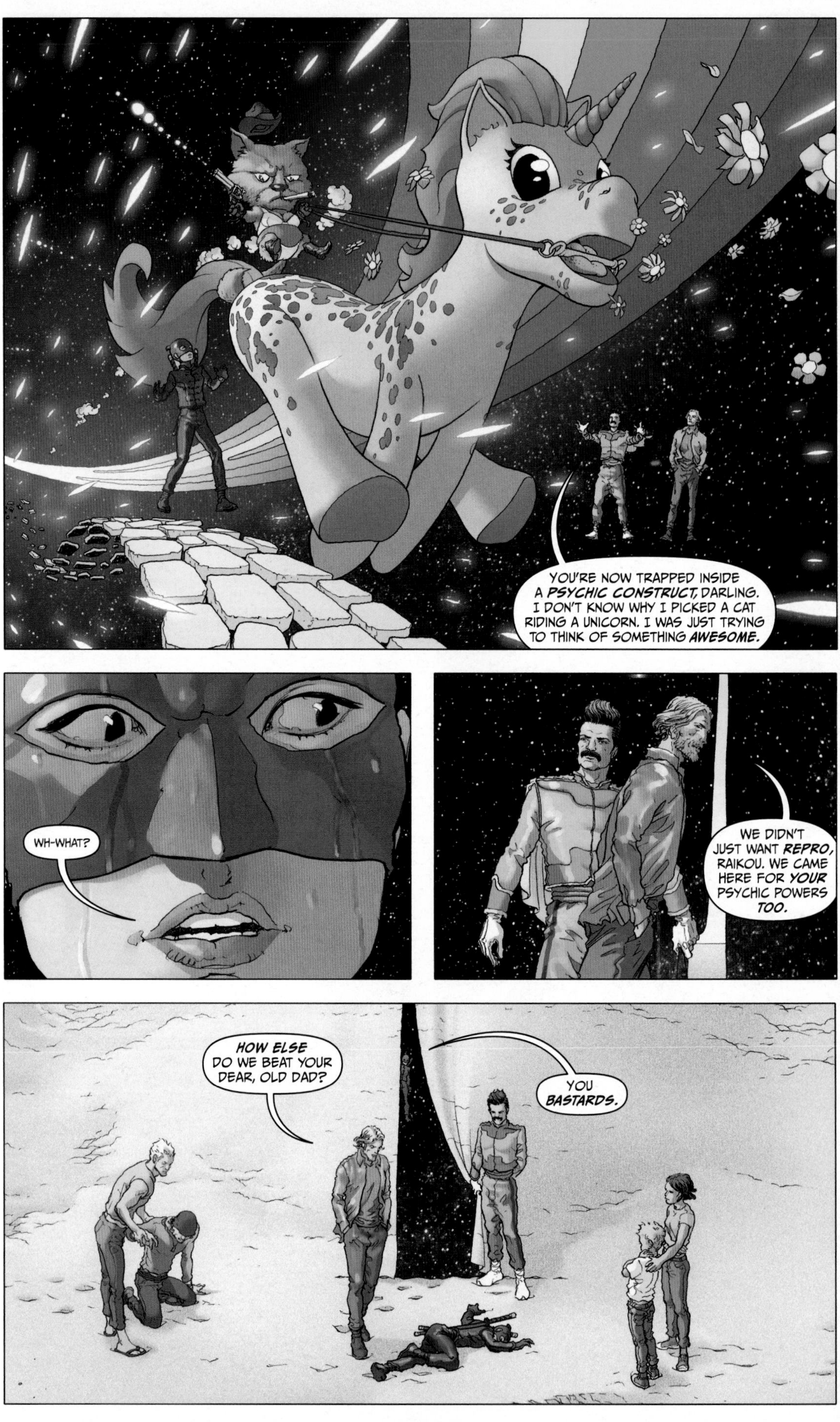
YOU'RE NOW TRAPPED INSIDE A PSYCHIC CONSTRUCT, DARLING. I DON'T KNOW WHY I PICKED A CAT RIDING A UNICORN. I WAS JUST TRYING TO THINK OF SOMETHING AWESOME.
WH-WHAT?
WE DIDN'T JUST WANT REPRO, RAIKOU. WE CAME HERE FOR YOUR PSYCHIC POWERS TOO.
HOW ELSE DO WE BEAT YOUR DEAR, OLD DAD?
YOU BASTARDS.

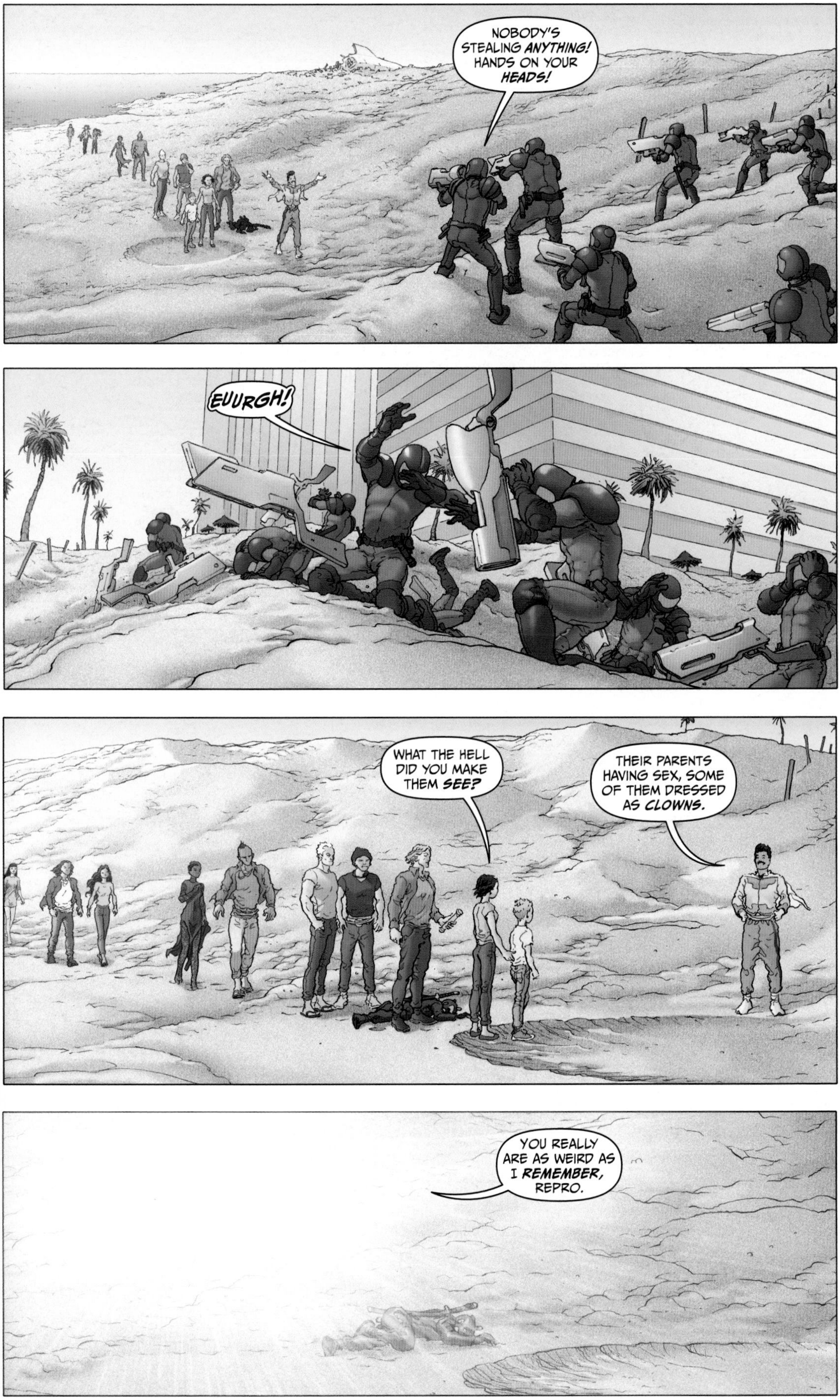
NOBODY'S STEALING ANYTHING! HANDS ON YOUR HEADS!
EUURGH!
WHAT THE HELL DID YOU MAKE THEM SEE?
THEIR PARENTS HAVING SEX, SOME OF THEM DRESSED AS CLOWNS.
YOU REALLY ARE AS WEIRD AS I REMEMBER, REPRO.

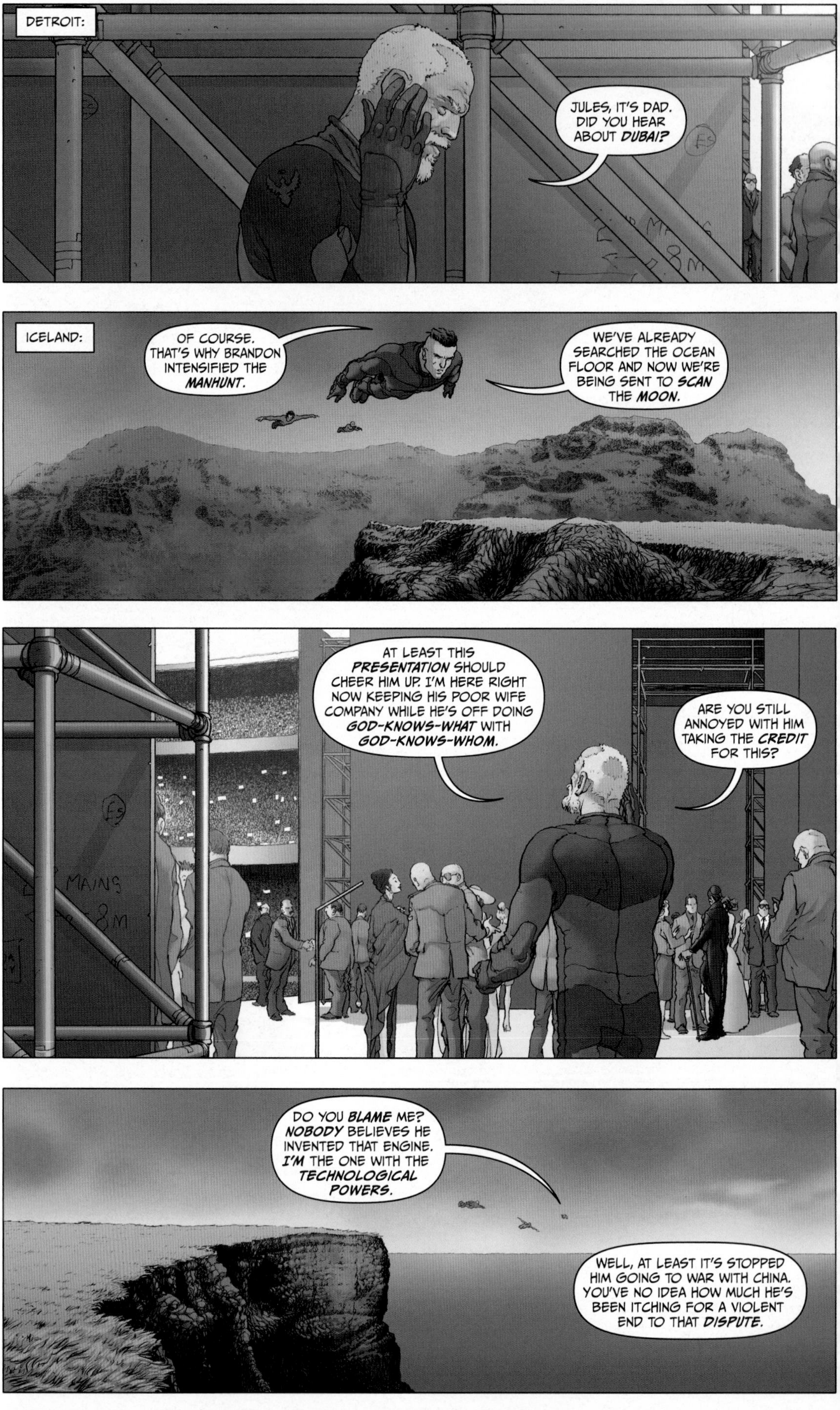

DETROIT:
JULES, IT'S DAD. DID YOU HEAR ABOUT DUBAI?
ICELAND:
OF COURSE. THAT'S WHY BRANDON INTENSIFIED THE MANHUNT.
WE'VE ALREADY SEARCHED THE OCEAN FLOOR AND NOW WE'RE BEING SENT TO SCAN THE MOON.
AT LEAST THIS PRESENTATION SHOULD CHEER HIM UP. I'M HERE RIGHT NOW KEEPING HIS POOR WIFE COMPANY WHILE HE'S OFF DOING GOD-KNOWS-WHAT WITH GOD-KNOWS-WHOM.
ARE YOU STILL ANNOYED WITH HIM TAKING THE CREDIT FOR THIS?
DO YOU BLAME ME? NOBODY BELIEVES HE INVENTED THAT ENGINE. I'M THE ONE WITH THE TECHNOLOGICAL POWERS.
WELL, AT LEAST IT'S STOPPED HIM GOING TO WAR WITH CHINA. YOU'VE NO IDEA HOW MUCH HE'S BEEN ITCHING FOR A VIOLENT END TO THAT DISPUTE.

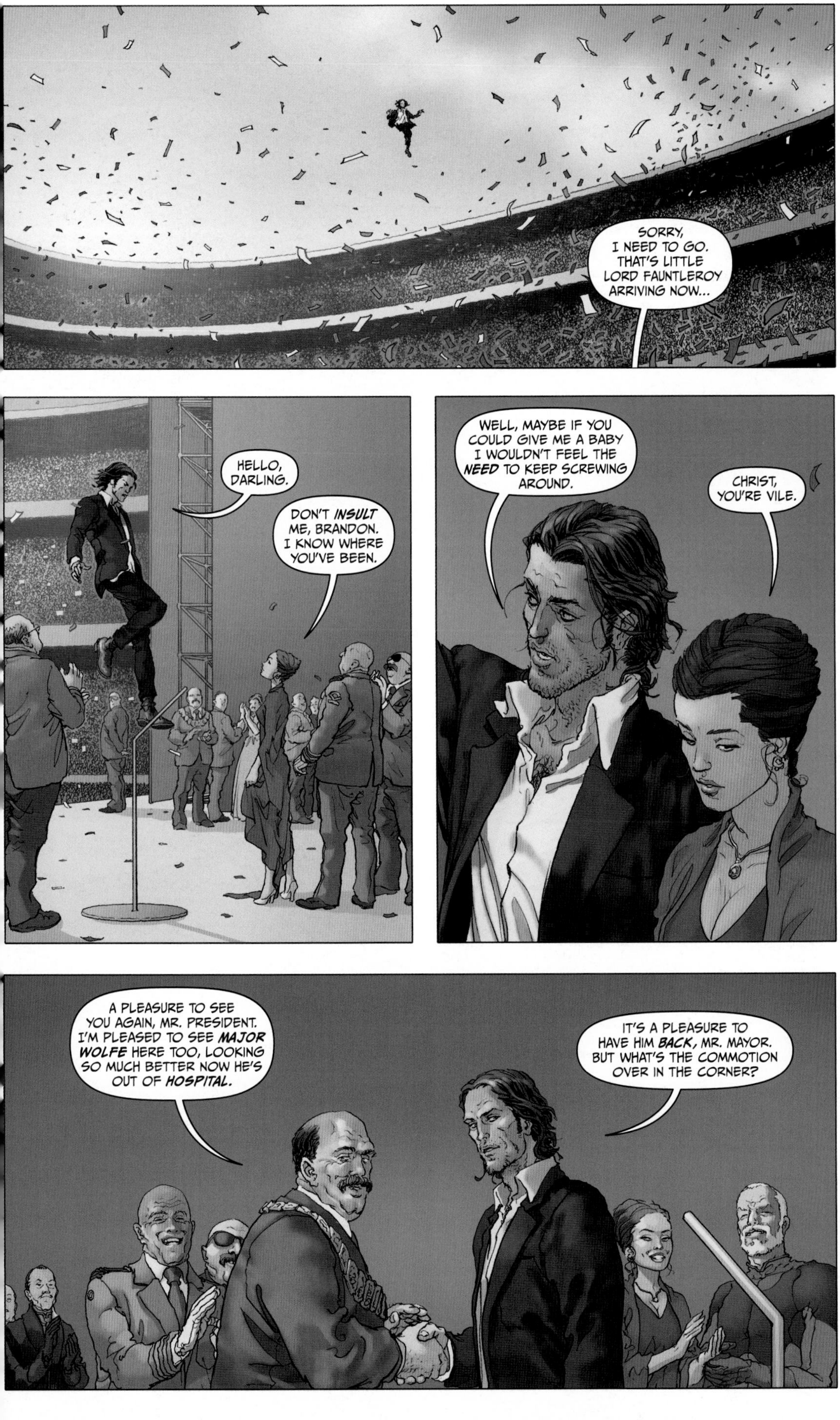
SORRY, I NEED TO GO. THAT'S LITTLE LORD FAUNTLEROY ARRIVING NOW...
HELLO, DARLING.
DON'T INSULT ME, BRANDON. I KNOW WHERE YOU'VE BEEN.
WELL, MAYBE IF YOU COULD GIVE ME A BABY I WOULDN'T FEEL THE NEED TO KEEP SCREWING AROUND.
CHRIST, YOU'RE VILE.
A PLEASURE TO SEE YOU AGAIN, MR. PRESIDENT. I'M PLEASED TO SEE MAJOR WOLFE HERE TOO, LOOKING SO MUCH BETTER NOW HE'S OUT OF HOSPITAL.
IT'S A PLEASURE TO HAVE HIM BACK, MR. MAYOR. BUT WHAT'S THE COMMOTION OVER IN THE CORNER?

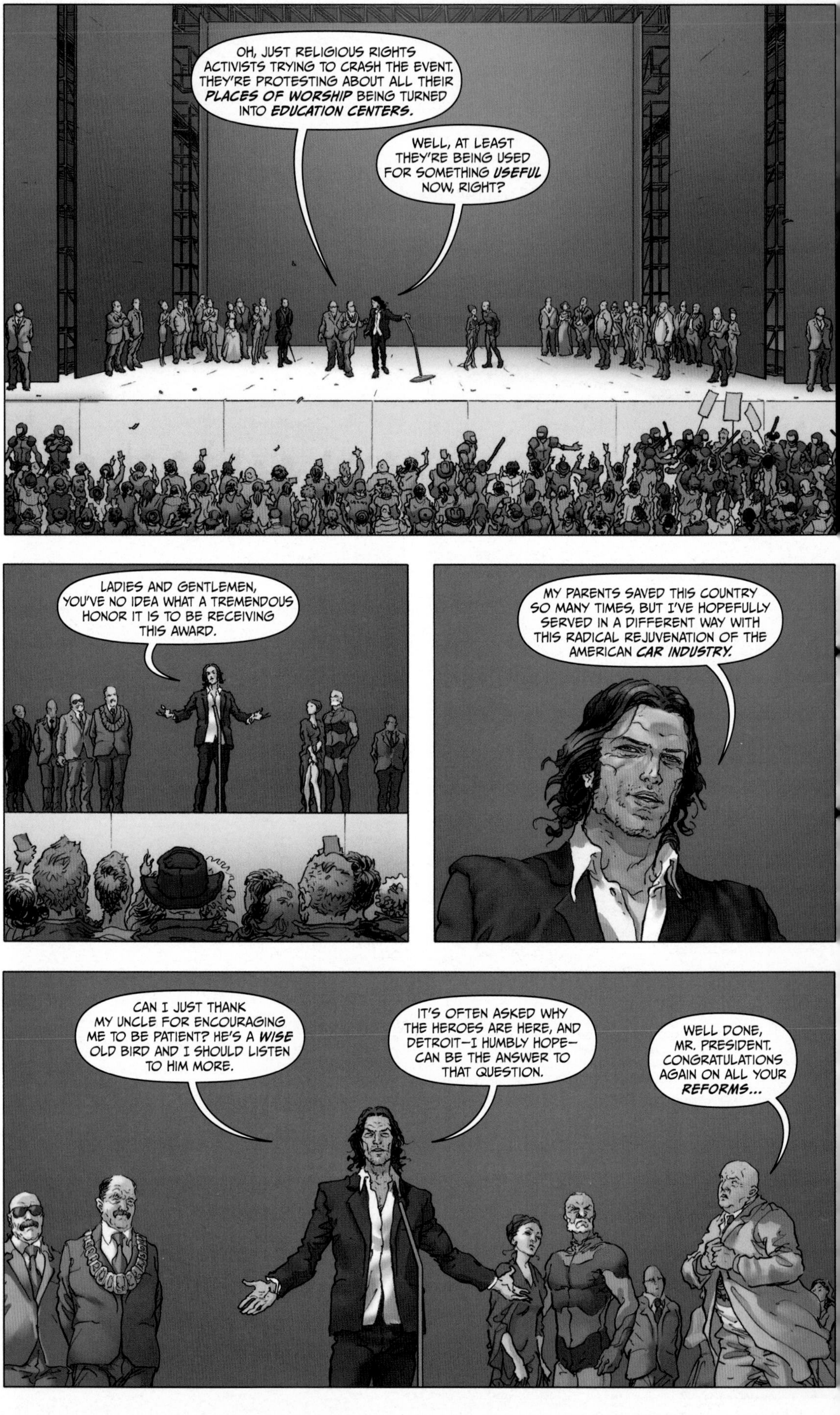
OH, JUST RELIGIOUS RIGHTS ACTIVISTS TRYING TO CRASH THE EVENT. THEY'RE PROTESTING ABOUT ALL THEIR *PLACES OF WORSHIP* BEING TURNED INTO *EDUCATION CENTERS.*
WELL, AT LEAST THEY'RE BEING USED FOR SOMETHING *USEFUL* NOW, RIGHT?
LADIES AND GENTLEMEN, YOU'VE NO IDEA WHAT A TREMENDOUS HONOR IT IS TO BE RECEIVING THIS AWARD.
MY PARENTS SAVED THIS COUNTRY SO MANY TIMES, BUT I'VE HOPEFULLY SERVED IN A DIFFERENT WAY WITH THIS RADICAL REJUVENATION OF THE AMERICAN *CAR INDUSTRY.*
CAN I JUST THANK MY UNCLE FOR ENCOURAGING ME TO BE PATIENT? HE'S A *WISE* OLD BIRD AND I SHOULD LISTEN TO HIM MORE.
IT'S OFTEN ASKED WHY THE HEROES ARE HERE, AND DETROIT—I HUMBLY HOPE—CAN BE THE ANSWER TO THAT QUESTION.
WELL DONE, MR. PRESIDENT. CONGRATULATIONS AGAIN ON ALL YOUR *REFORMS...*

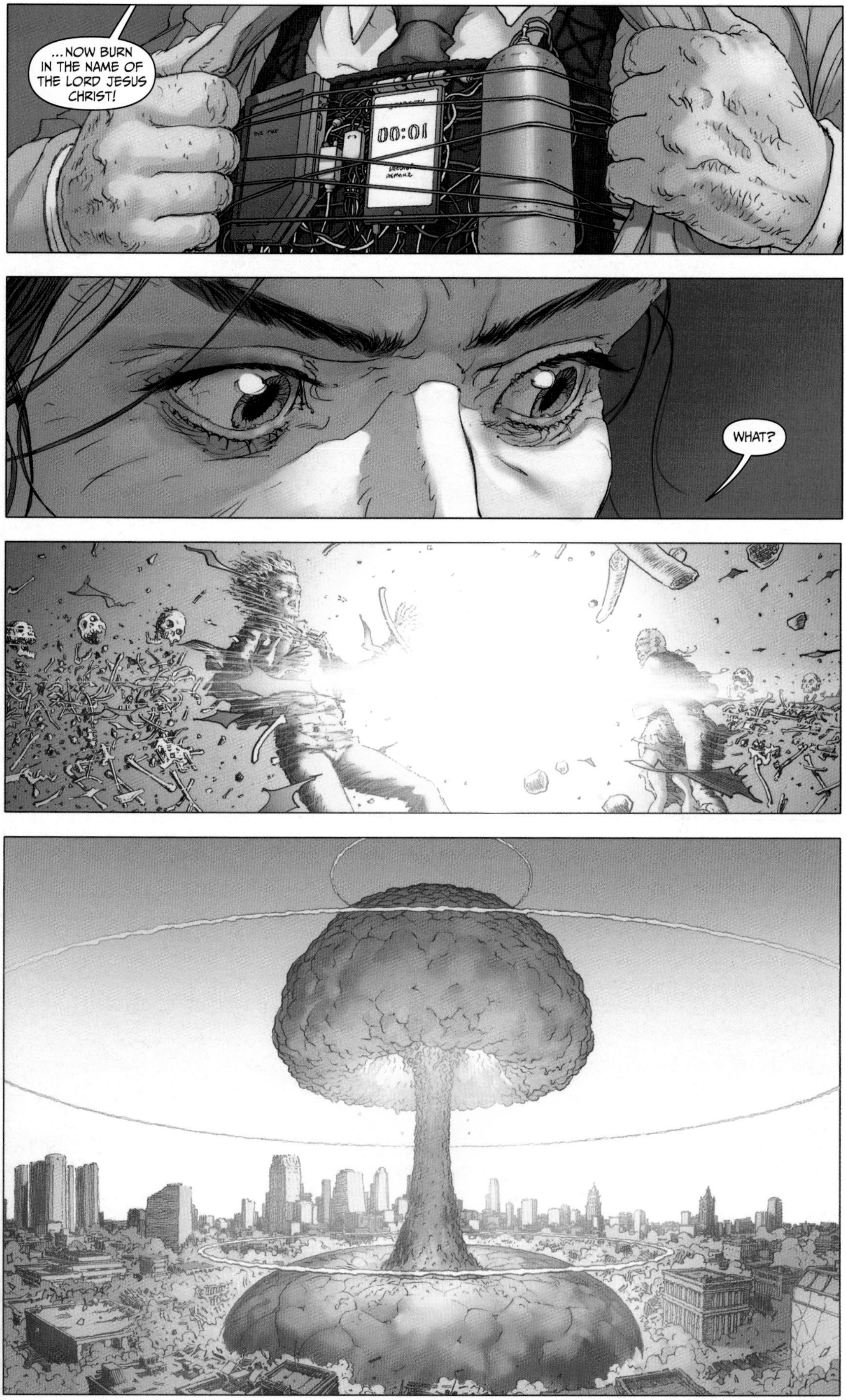
...NOW BURN IN THE NAME OF THE LORD JESUS CHRIST!
00:01
WHAT?

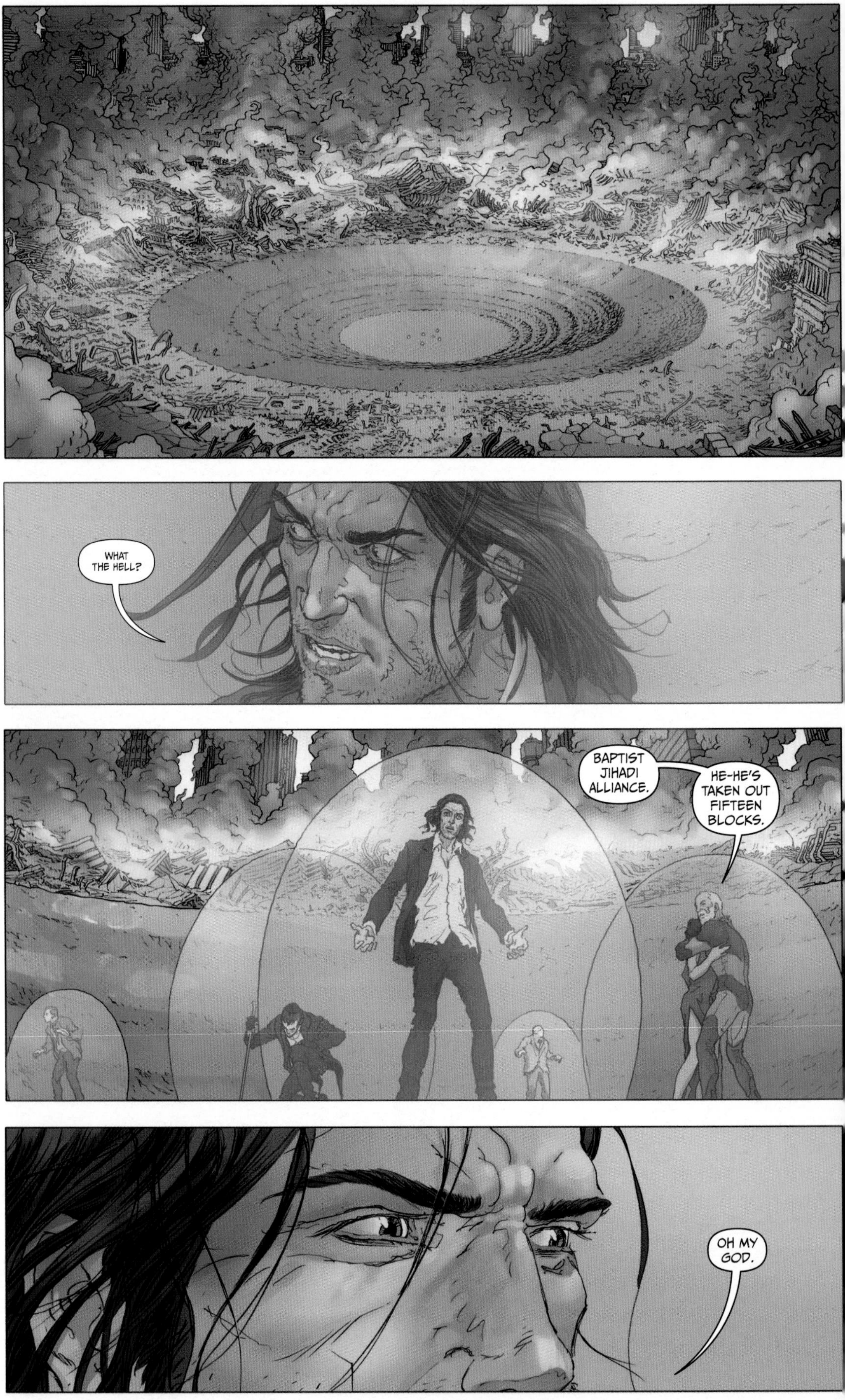
WHAT THE HELL?
BAPTIST JIHADI ALLIANCE.
HE-HE'S TAKEN OUT FIFTEEN BLOCKS.
OH MY GOD.

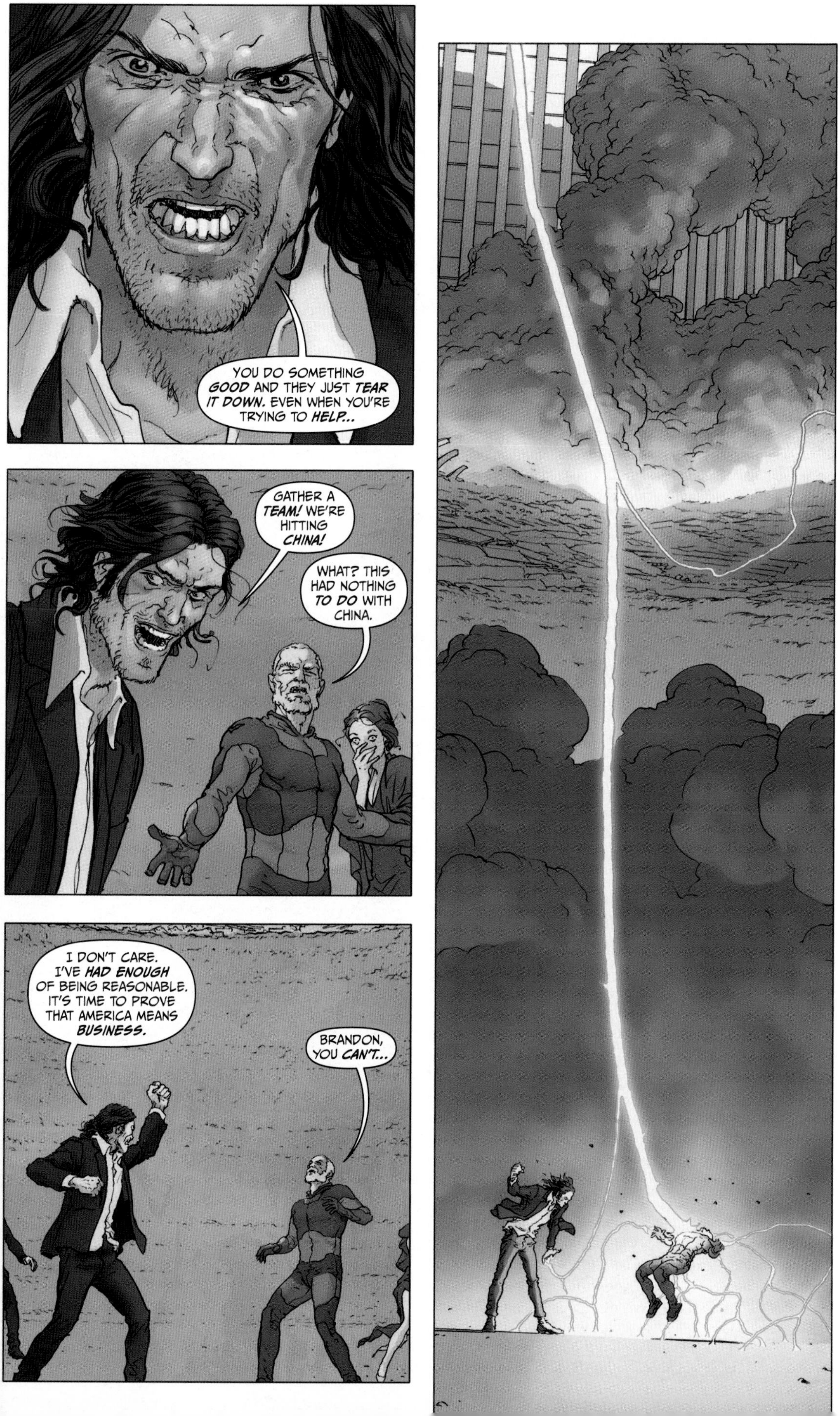
YOU DO SOMETHING GOOD AND THEY JUST TEAR IT DOWN. EVEN WHEN YOU'RE TRYING TO HELP...
GATHER A TEAM! WE'RE HITTING CHINA!
WHAT? THIS HAD NOTHING TO DO WITH CHINA.
I DON'T CARE. I'VE HAD ENOUGH OF BEING REASONABLE. IT'S TIME TO PROVE THAT AMERICA MEANS BUSINESS.
BRANDON, YOU CAN'T...

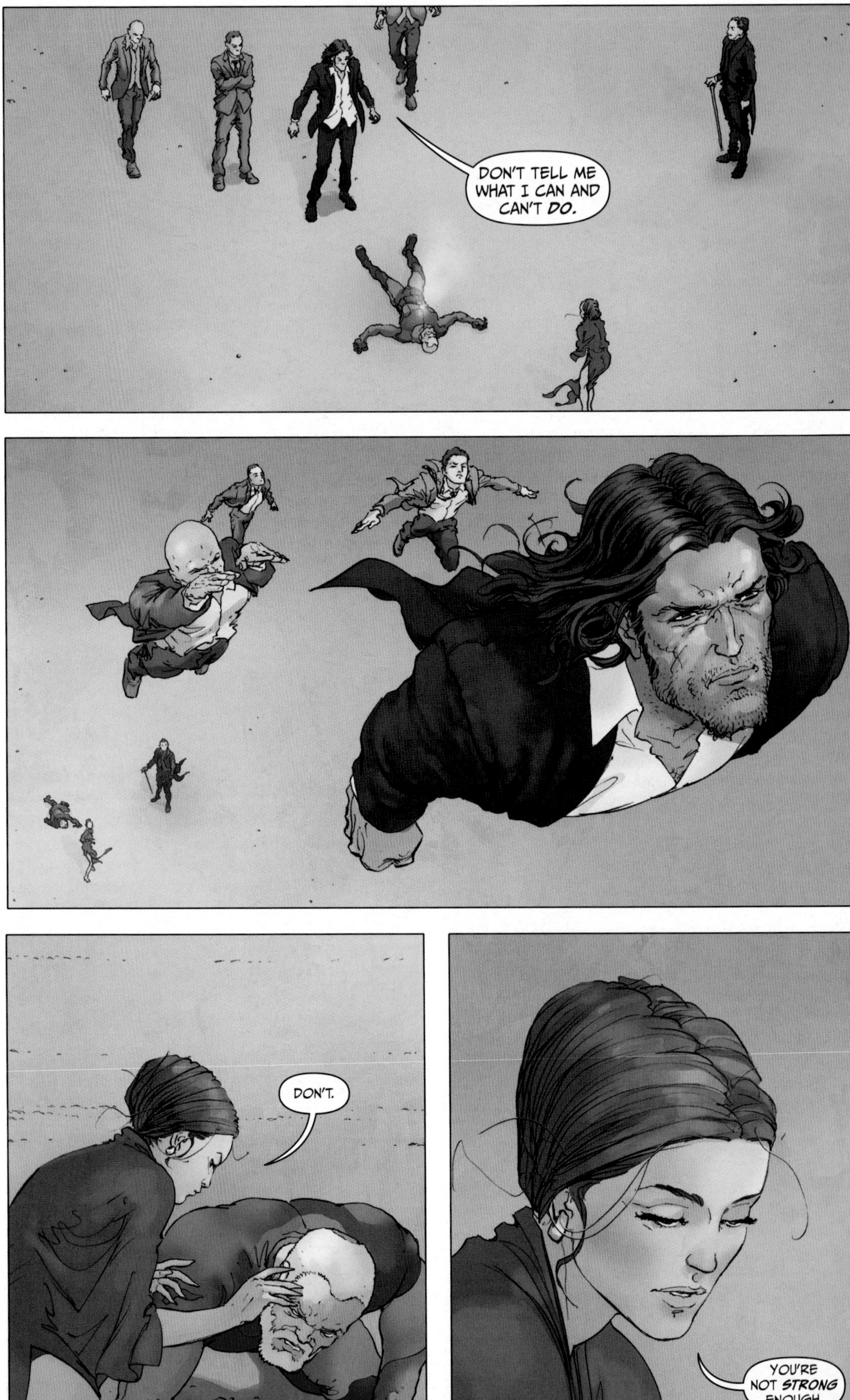
DON'T TELL ME WHAT I CAN AND CAN'T DO.
DON'T.
YOU'RE NOT STRONG ENOUGH.

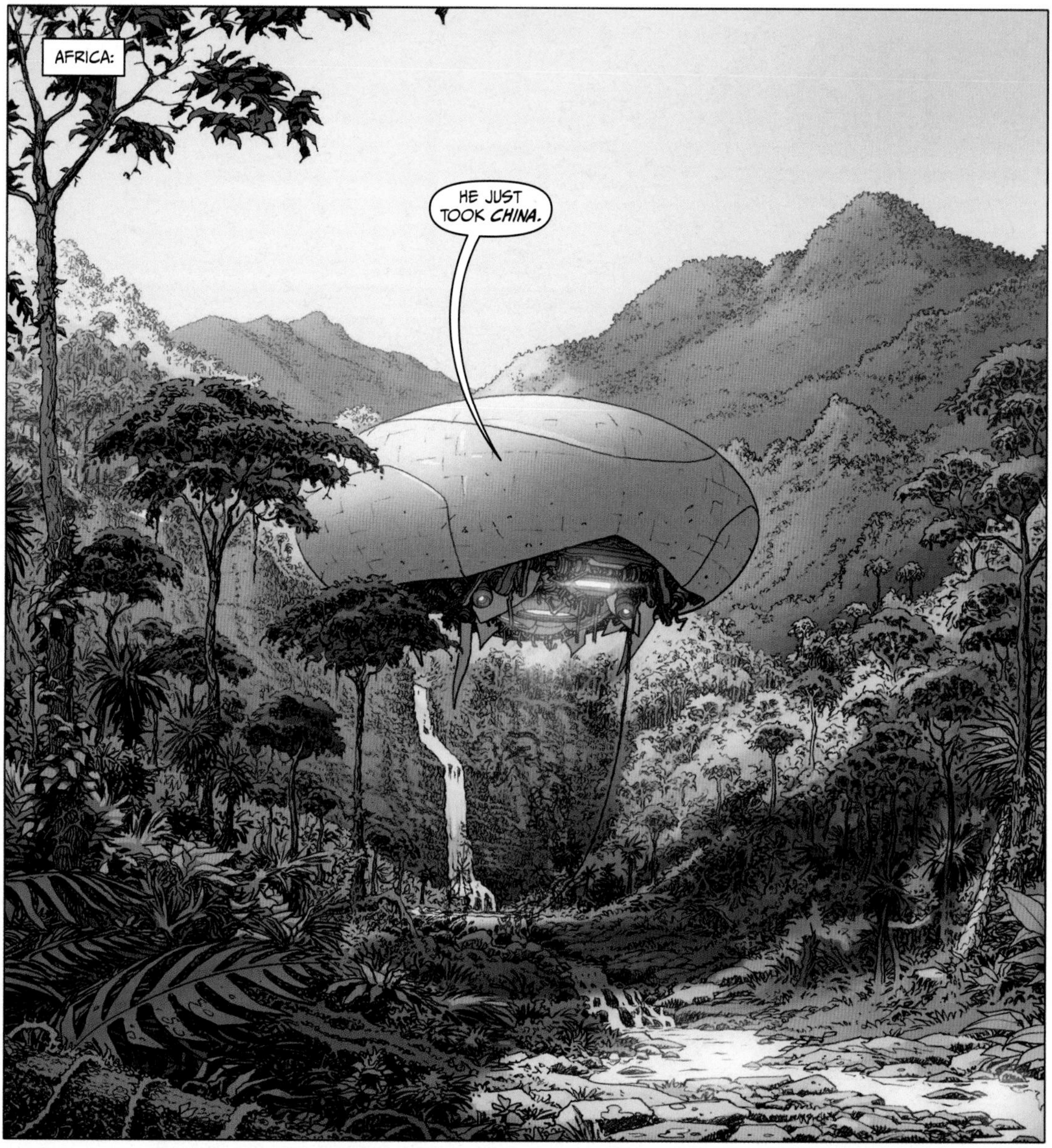
AFRICA:
HE JUST TOOK *CHINA.*

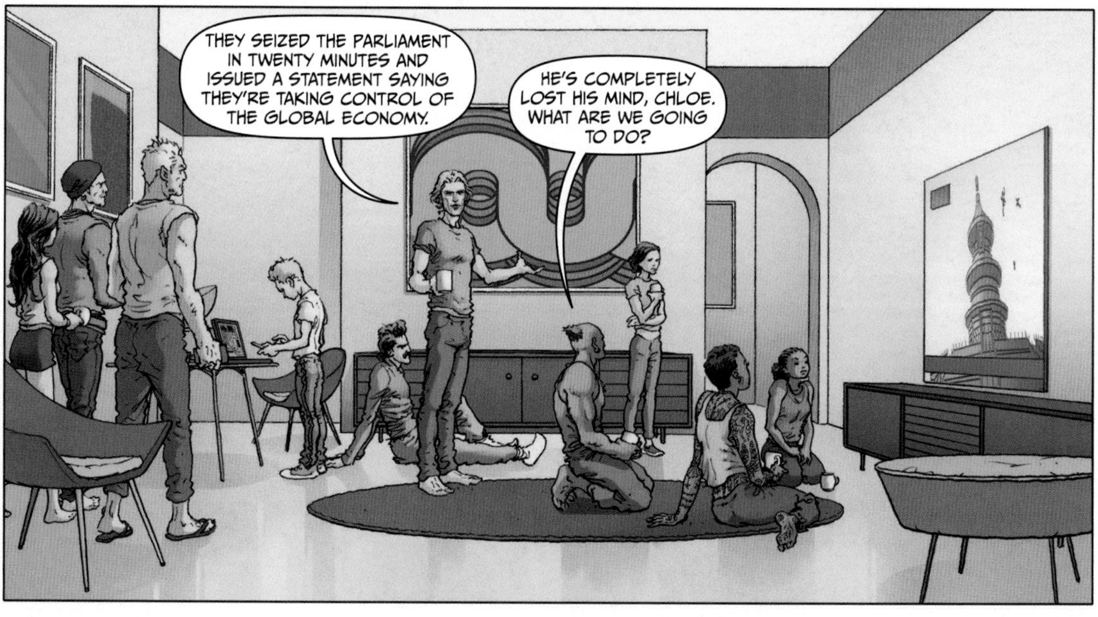
THEY SEIZED THE PARLIAMENT IN TWENTY MINUTES AND ISSUED A STATEMENT SAYING THEY'RE TAKING CONTROL OF THE GLOBAL ECONOMY.
HE'S COMPLETELY LOST HIS MIND, CHLOE. WHAT ARE WE GOING TO DO?

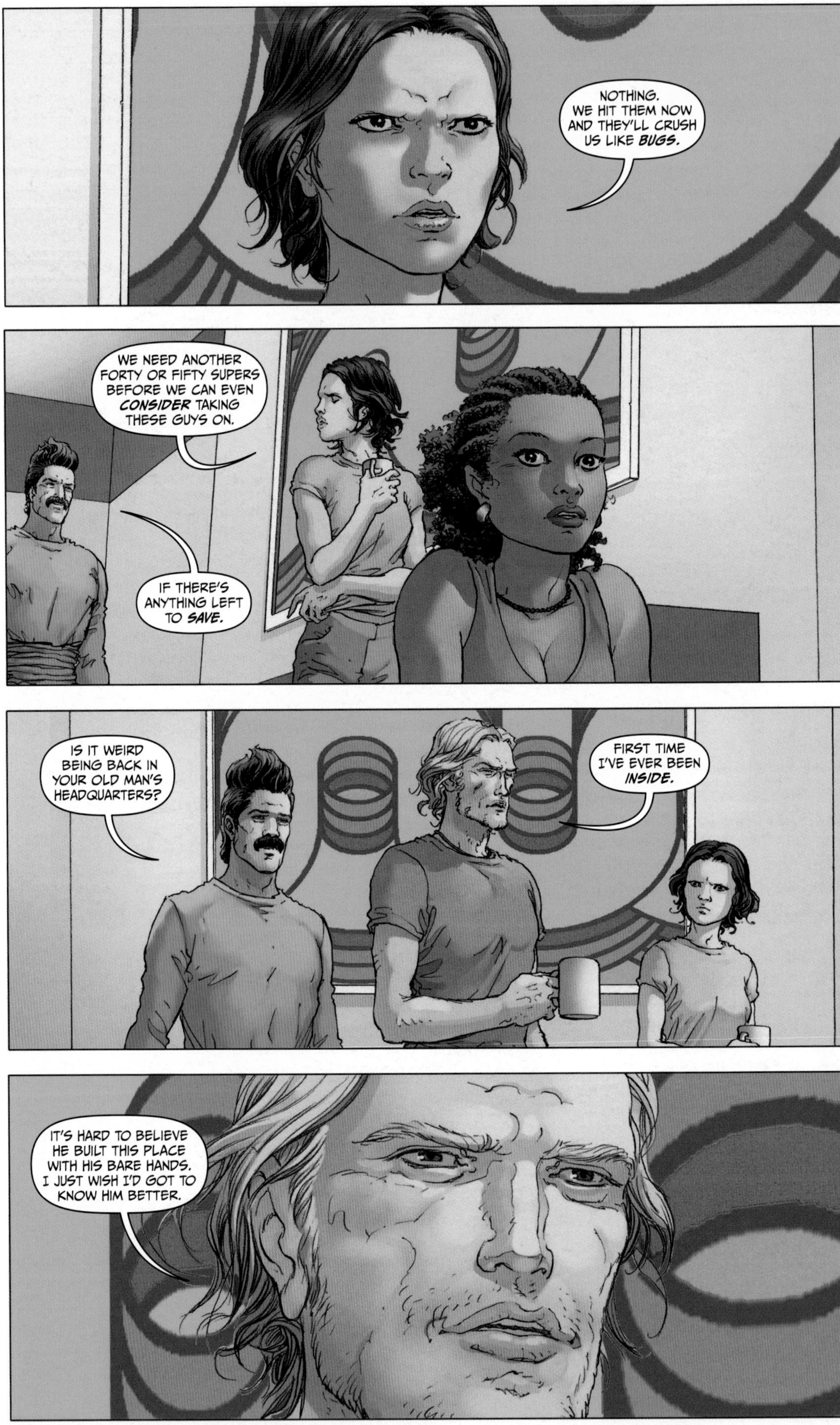

NOTHING. WE HIT THEM NOW AND THEY'LL CRUSH US LIKE *BUGS.*
WE NEED ANOTHER FORTY OR FIFTY SUPERS BEFORE WE CAN EVEN *CONSIDER* TAKING THESE GUYS ON.
IF THERE'S ANYTHING LEFT TO *SAVE.*
IS IT WEIRD BEING BACK IN YOUR OLD MAN'S HEADQUARTERS?
FIRST TIME I'VE EVER BEEN *INSIDE.*
IT'S HARD TO BELIEVE HE BUILT THIS PLACE WITH HIS BARE HANDS. I JUST WISH I'D GOT TO KNOW HIM BETTER.

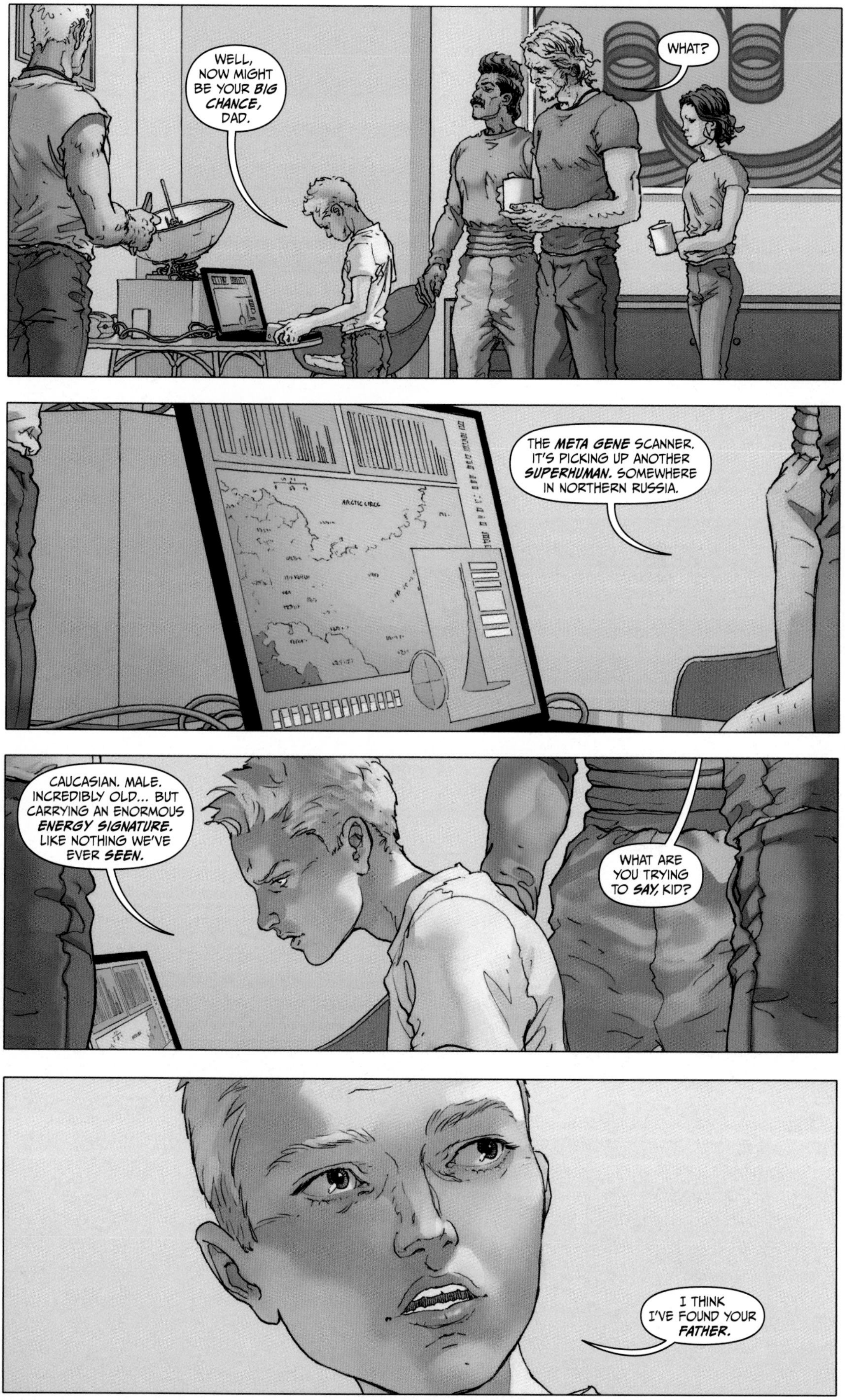
WELL, NOW MIGHT BE YOUR BIG CHANCE, DAD.
WHAT?
THE META GENE SCANNER. IT'S PICKING UP ANOTHER SUPERHUMAN. SOMEWHERE IN NORTHERN RUSSIA.
ARCTIC CIRCLE
CAUCASIAN. MALE. INCREDIBLY OLD... BUT CARRYING AN ENORMOUS ENERGY SIGNATURE. LIKE NOTHING WE'VE EVER SEEN.
WHAT ARE YOU TRYING TO SAY, KID?
I THINK I'VE FOUND YOUR FATHER.

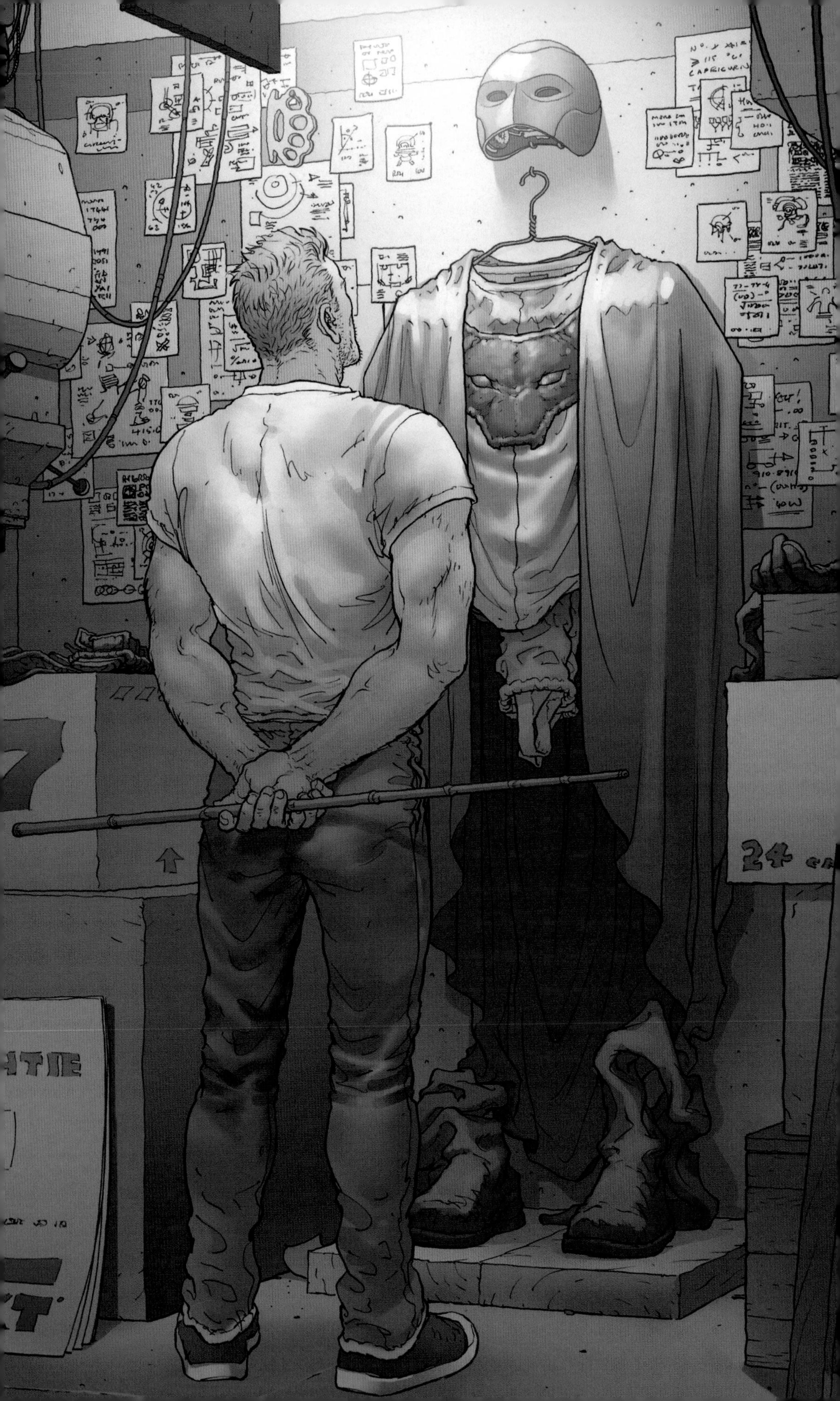

CHAPTER 3

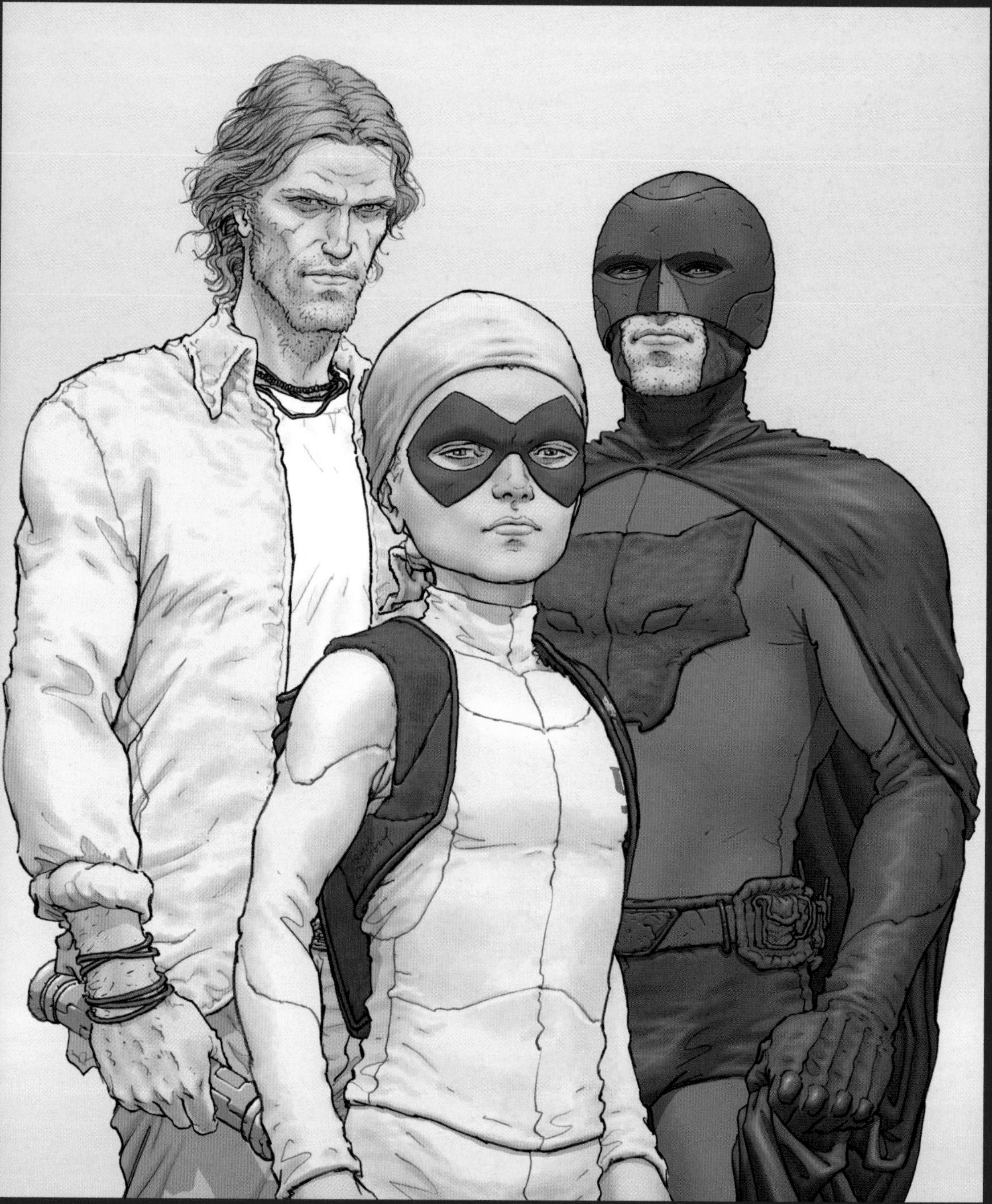

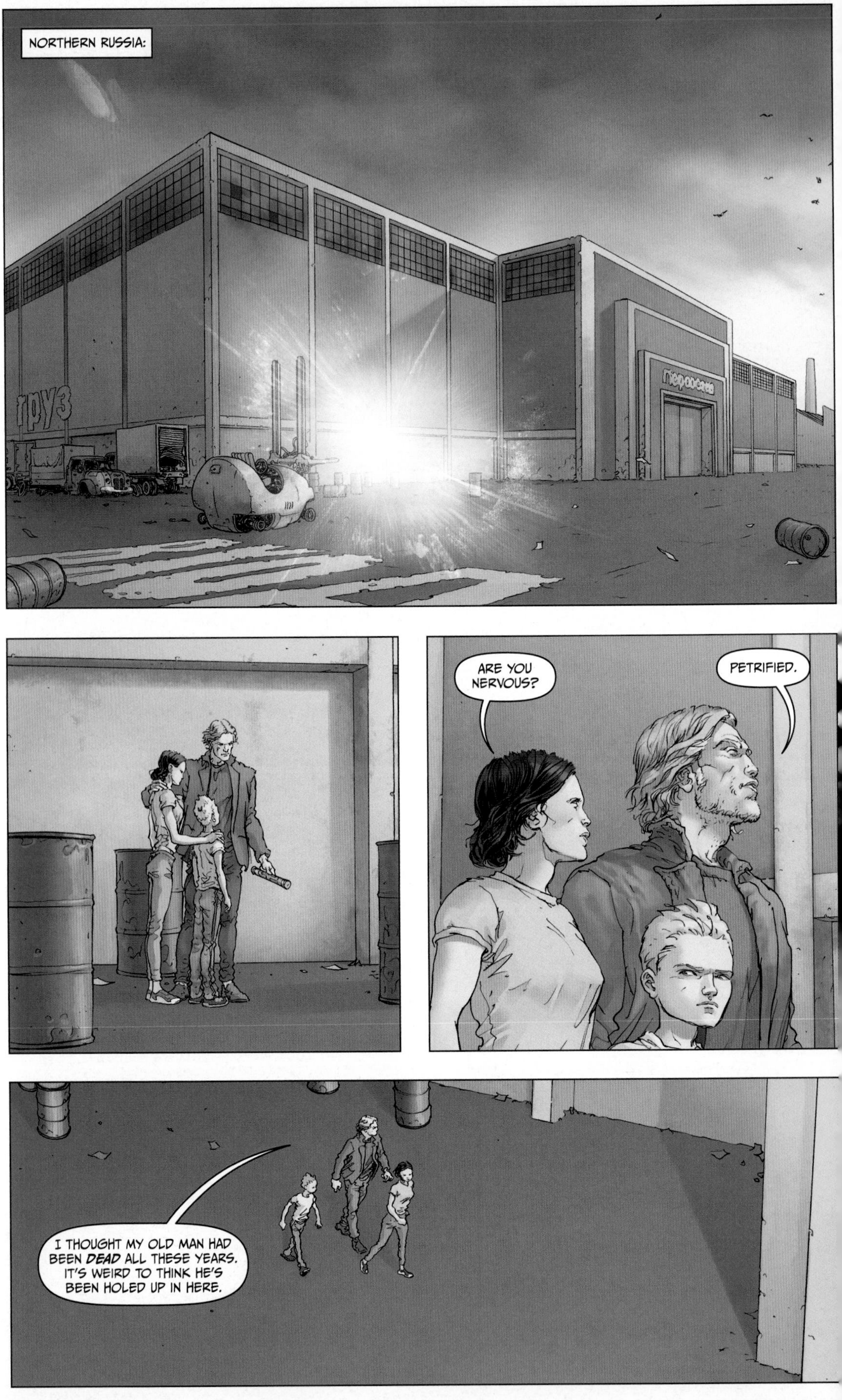
NORTHERN RUSSIA:
ARE YOU NERVOUS?
PETRIFIED.
I THOUGHT MY OLD MAN HAD BEEN *DEAD* ALL THESE YEARS. IT'S WEIRD TO THINK HE'S BEEN HOLED UP IN HERE.

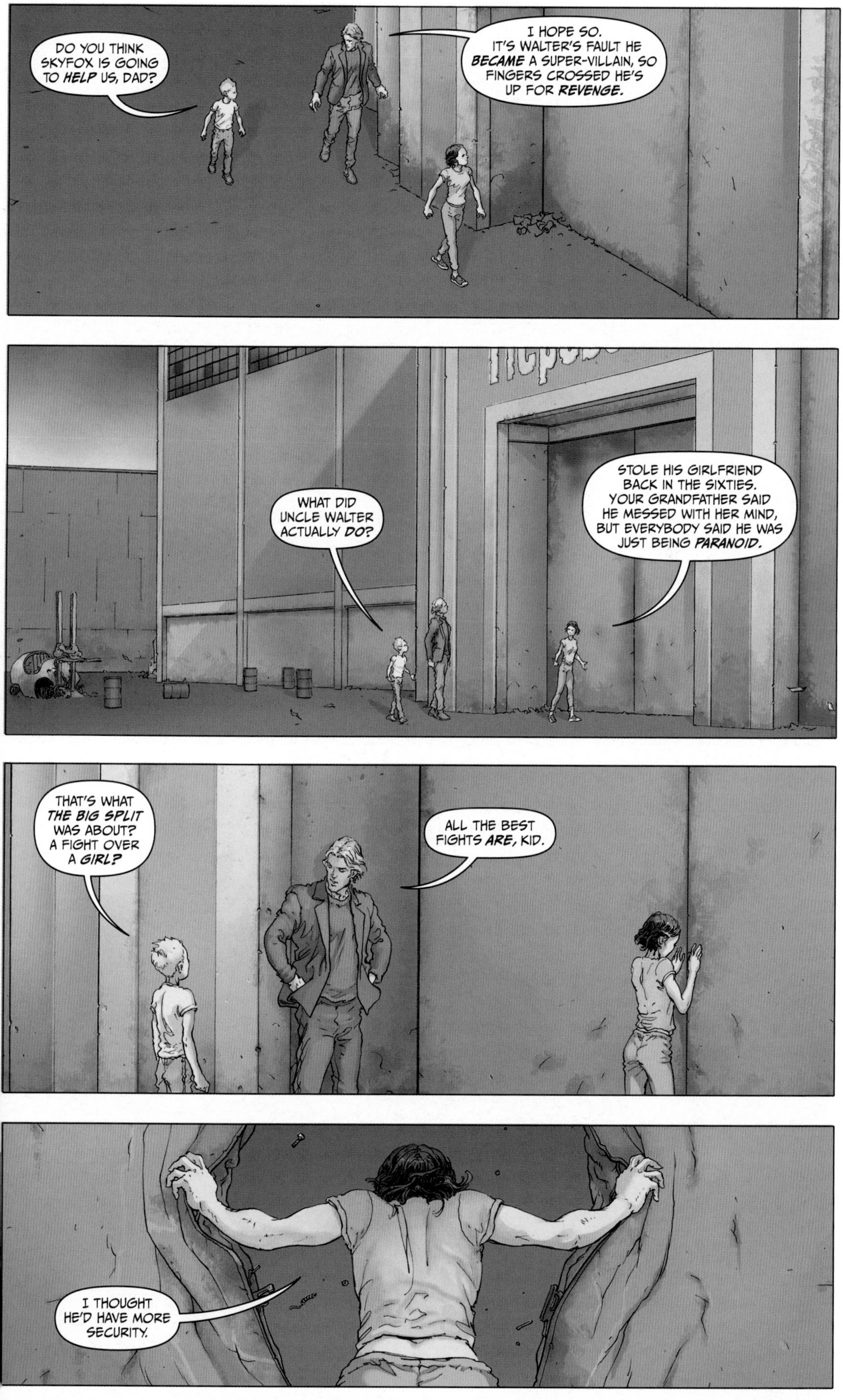
DO YOU THINK SKYFOX IS GOING TO HELP US, DAD?
I HOPE SO. IT'S WALTER'S FAULT HE BECAME A SUPER-VILLAIN, SO FINGERS CROSSED HE'S UP FOR REVENGE.
WHAT DID UNCLE WALTER ACTUALLY DO?
STOLE HIS GIRLFRIEND BACK IN THE SIXTIES. YOUR GRANDFATHER SAID HE MESSED WITH HER MIND, BUT EVERYBODY SAID HE WAS JUST BEING PARANOID.
THAT'S WHAT THE BIG SPLIT WAS ABOUT? A FIGHT OVER A GIRL?
ALL THE BEST FIGHTS ARE, KID.
I THOUGHT HE'D HAVE MORE SECURITY.

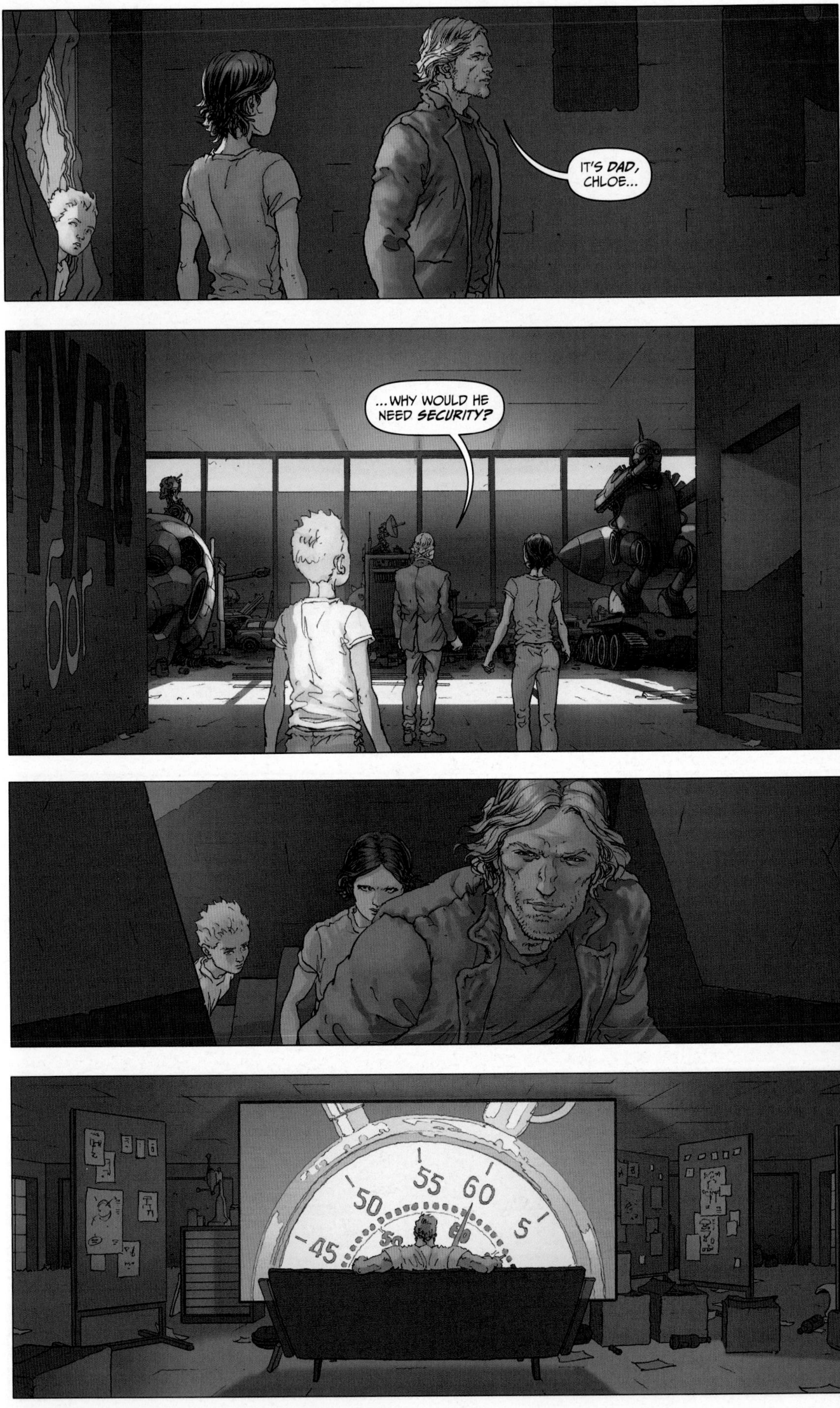
IT'S DAD, CHLOE...
...WHY WOULD HE NEED SECURITY?
55 60
50
5
45

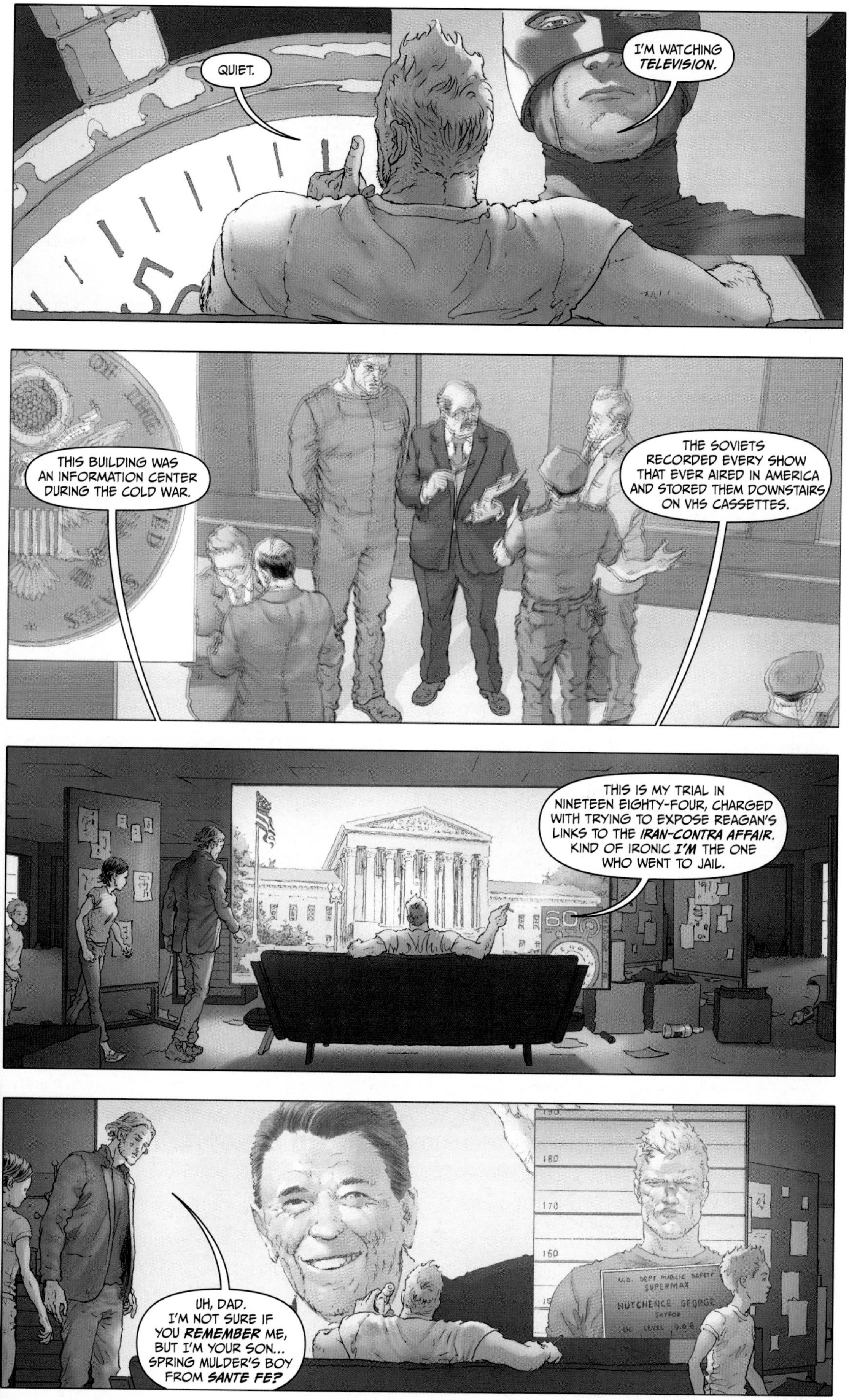
QUIET.
I'M WATCHING *TELEVISION.*
THIS BUILDING WAS AN INFORMATION CENTER DURING THE COLD WAR.
THE SOVIETS RECORDED EVERY SHOW THAT EVER AIRED IN AMERICA AND STORED THEM DOWNSTAIRS ON VHS CASSETTES.
THIS IS MY TRIAL IN NINETEEN EIGHTY-FOUR, CHARGED WITH TRYING TO EXPOSE REAGAN'S LINKS TO THE *IRAN-CONTRA AFFAIR.* KIND OF IRONIC *I'M* THE ONE WHO WENT TO JAIL.
UH, DAD. I'M NOT SURE IF YOU *REMEMBER* ME, BUT I'M YOUR SON... SPRING MULDER'S BOY FROM *SANTE FE?*

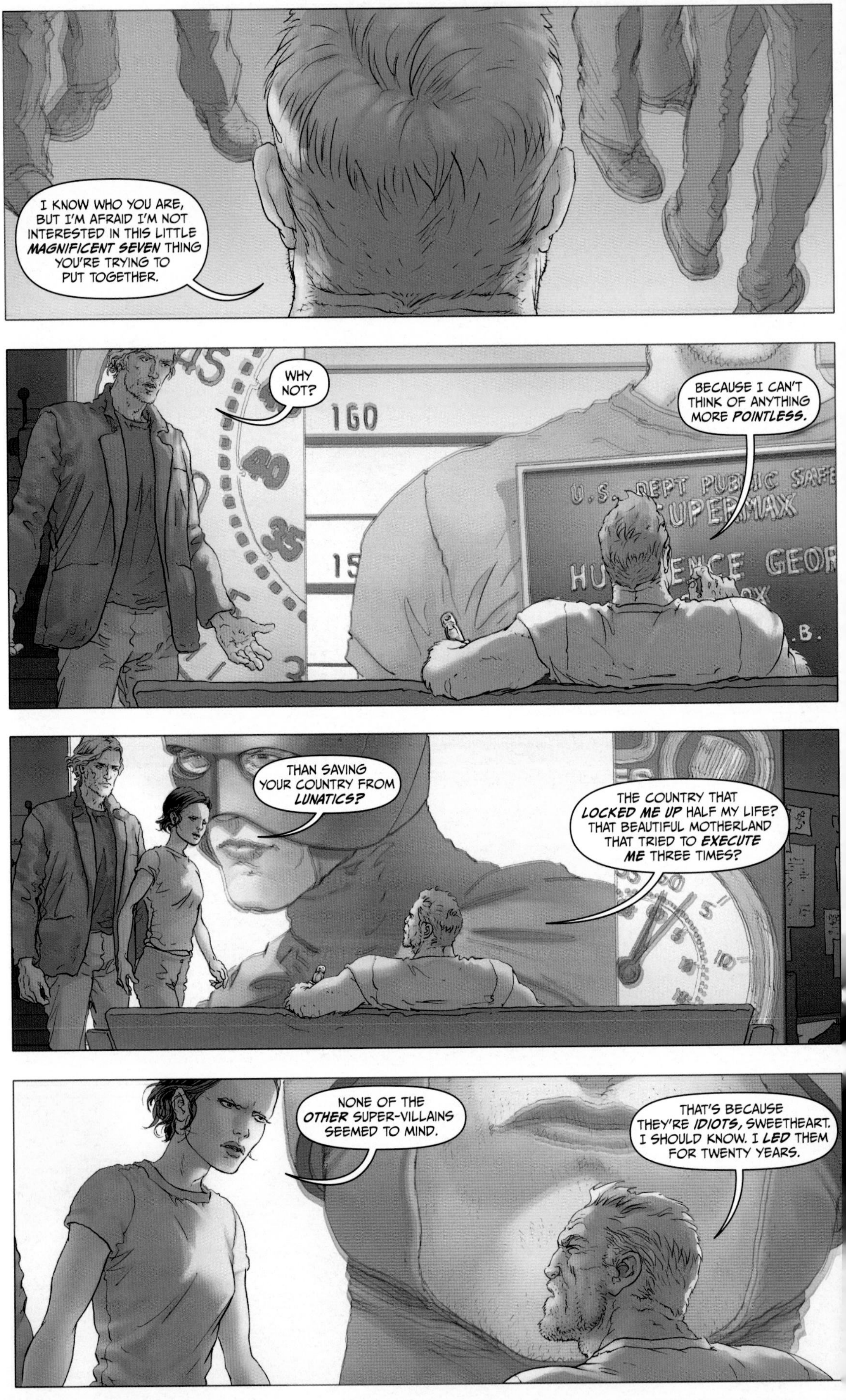
I KNOW WHO YOU ARE, BUT I'M AFRAID I'M NOT INTERESTED IN THIS LITTLE MAGNIFICENT SEVEN THING YOU'RE TRYING TO PUT TOGETHER.
WHY NOT?
BECAUSE I CAN'T THINK OF ANYTHING MORE POINTLESS.
U.S. DEPT PUBLIC SAFE
SUPERMAX
THAN SAVING YOUR COUNTRY FROM LUNATICS?
THE COUNTRY THAT LOCKED ME UP HALF MY LIFE? THAT BEAUTIFUL MOTHERLAND THAT TRIED TO EXECUTE ME THREE TIMES?
NONE OF THE OTHER SUPER-VILLAINS SEEMED TO MIND.
THAT'S BECAUSE THEY'RE IDIOTS, SWEETHEART. I SHOULD KNOW. I LED THEM FOR TWENTY YEARS.

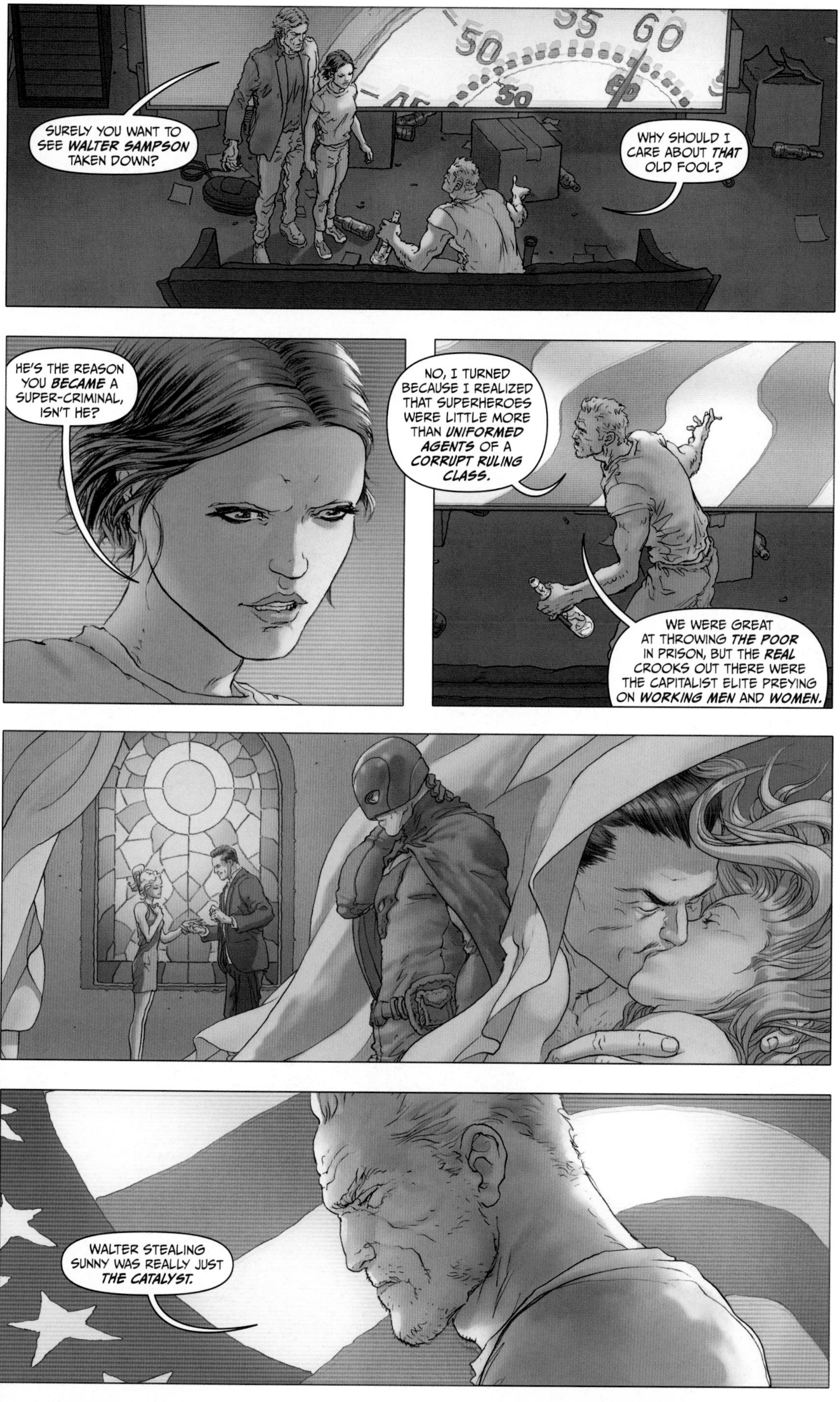
SURELY YOU WANT TO SEE WALTER SAMPSON TAKEN DOWN?
WHY SHOULD I CARE ABOUT THAT OLD FOOL?
HE'S THE REASON YOU BECAME A SUPER-CRIMINAL, ISN'T HE?
NO, I TURNED BECAUSE I REALIZED THAT SUPERHEROES WERE LITTLE MORE THAN UNIFORMED AGENTS OF A CORRUPT RULING CLASS.
WE WERE GREAT AT THROWING THE POOR IN PRISON, BUT THE REAL CROOKS OUT THERE WERE THE CAPITALIST ELITE PREYING ON WORKING MEN AND WOMEN.
WALTER STEALING SUNNY WAS REALLY JUST THE CATALYST.

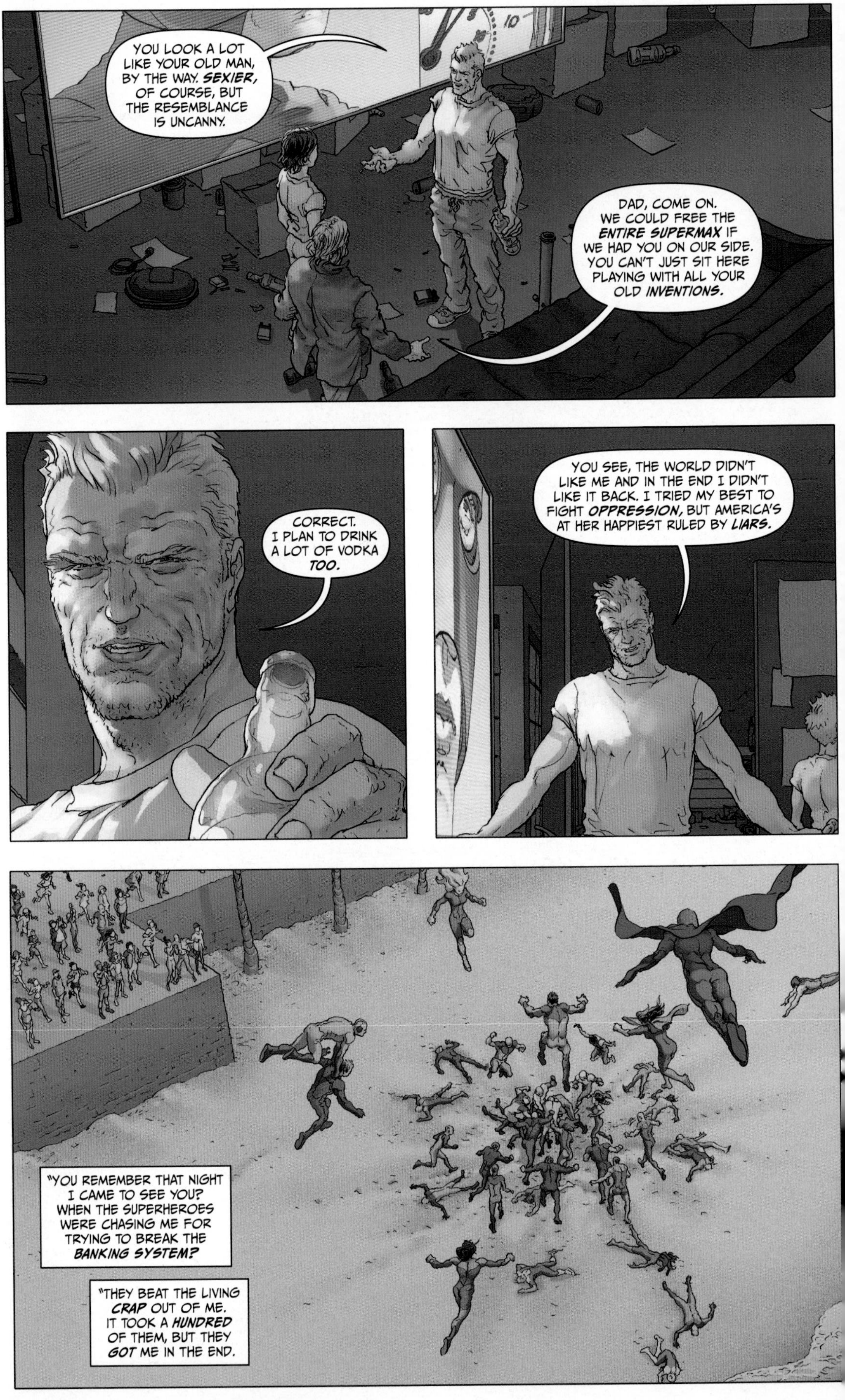

YOU LOOK A LOT LIKE YOUR OLD MAN, BY THE WAY. SEXIER, OF COURSE, BUT THE RESEMBLANCE IS UNCANNY.
DAD, COME ON. WE COULD FREE THE ENTIRE SUPERMAX IF WE HAD YOU ON OUR SIDE. YOU CAN'T JUST SIT HERE PLAYING WITH ALL YOUR OLD INVENTIONS.
CORRECT. I PLAN TO DRINK A LOT OF VODKA TOO.
YOU SEE, THE WORLD DIDN'T LIKE ME AND IN THE END I DIDN'T LIKE IT BACK. I TRIED MY BEST TO FIGHT OPPRESSION, BUT AMERICA'S AT HER HAPPIEST RULED BY LIARS.
"YOU REMEMBER THAT NIGHT I CAME TO SEE YOU? WHEN THE SUPERHEROES WERE CHASING ME FOR TRYING TO BREAK THE BANKING SYSTEM?
"THEY BEAT THE LIVING CRAP OUT OF ME. IT TOOK A HUNDRED OF THEM, BUT THEY GOT ME IN THE END.

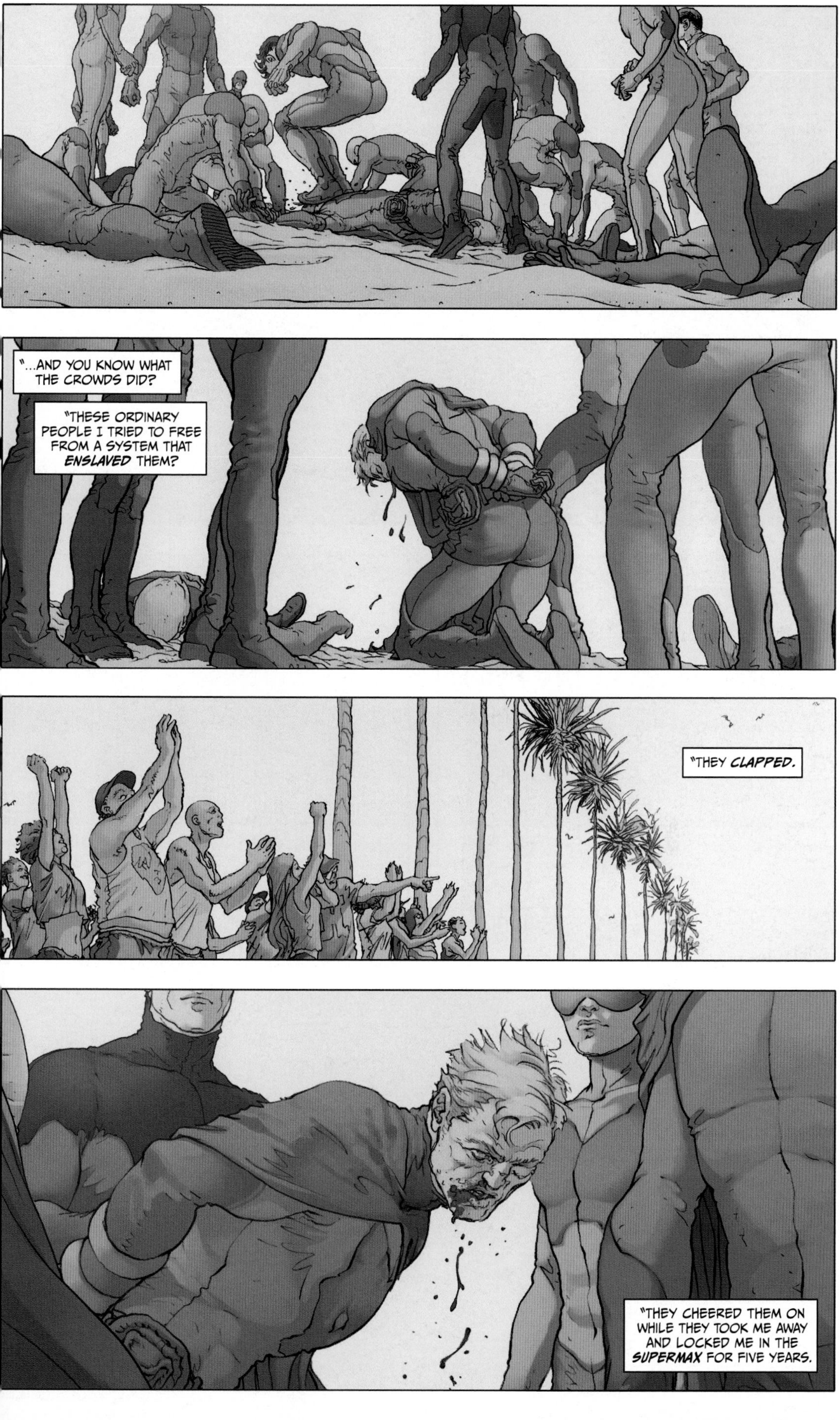
"...AND YOU KNOW WHAT THE CROWDS DID?
"THESE ORDINARY PEOPLE I TRIED TO FREE FROM A SYSTEM THAT ENSLAVED THEM?
"THEY CLAPPED.
"THEY CHEERED THEM ON WHILE THEY TOOK ME AWAY AND LOCKED ME IN THE SUPERMAX FOR FIVE YEARS.

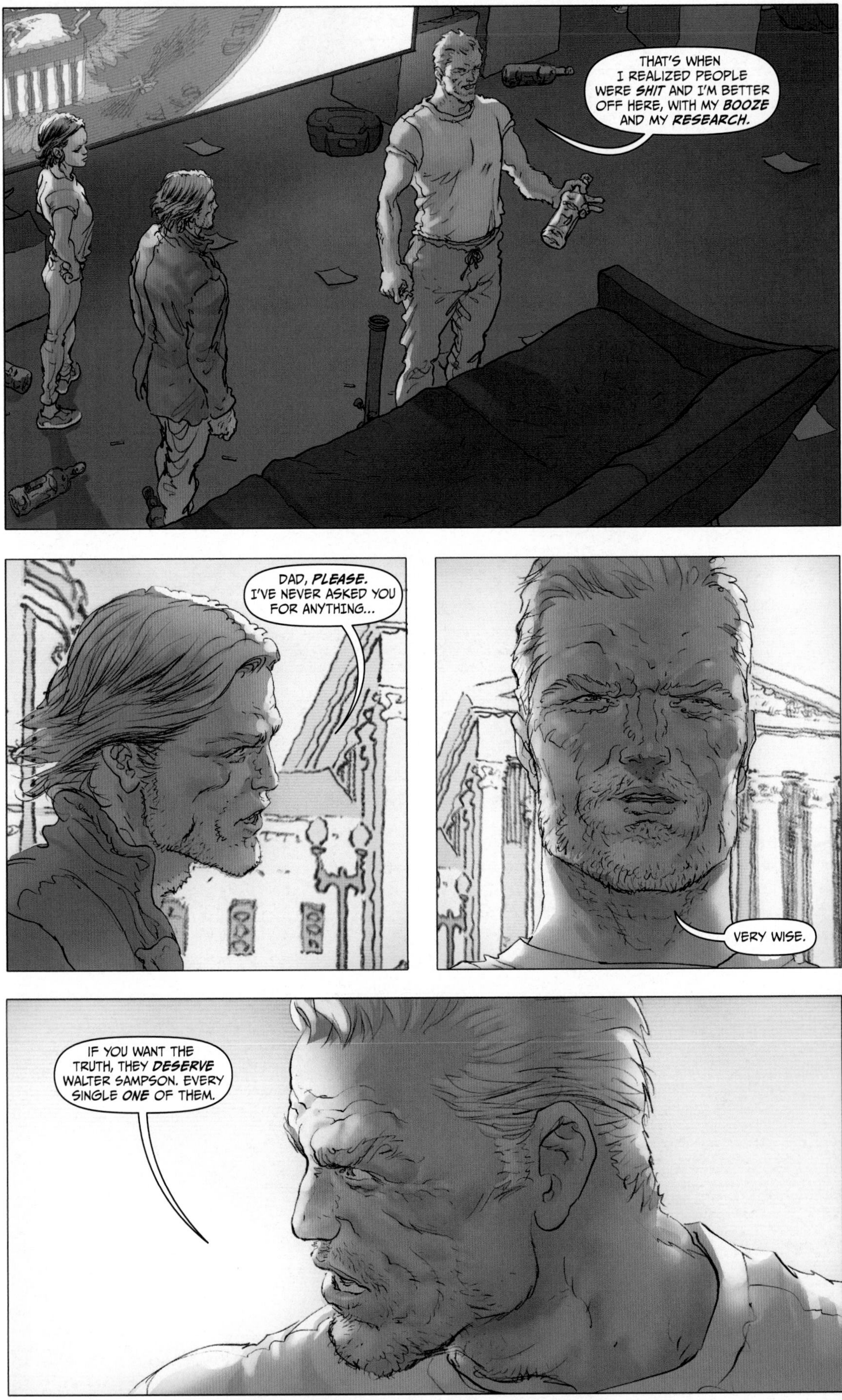

THAT'S WHEN I REALIZED PEOPLE WERE SHIT AND I'M BETTER OFF HERE, WITH MY BOOZE AND MY RESEARCH.
DAD, PLEASE. I'VE NEVER ASKED YOU FOR ANYTHING...
VERY WISE.
IF YOU WANT THE TRUTH, THEY DESERVE WALTER SAMPSON. EVERY SINGLE ONE OF THEM.

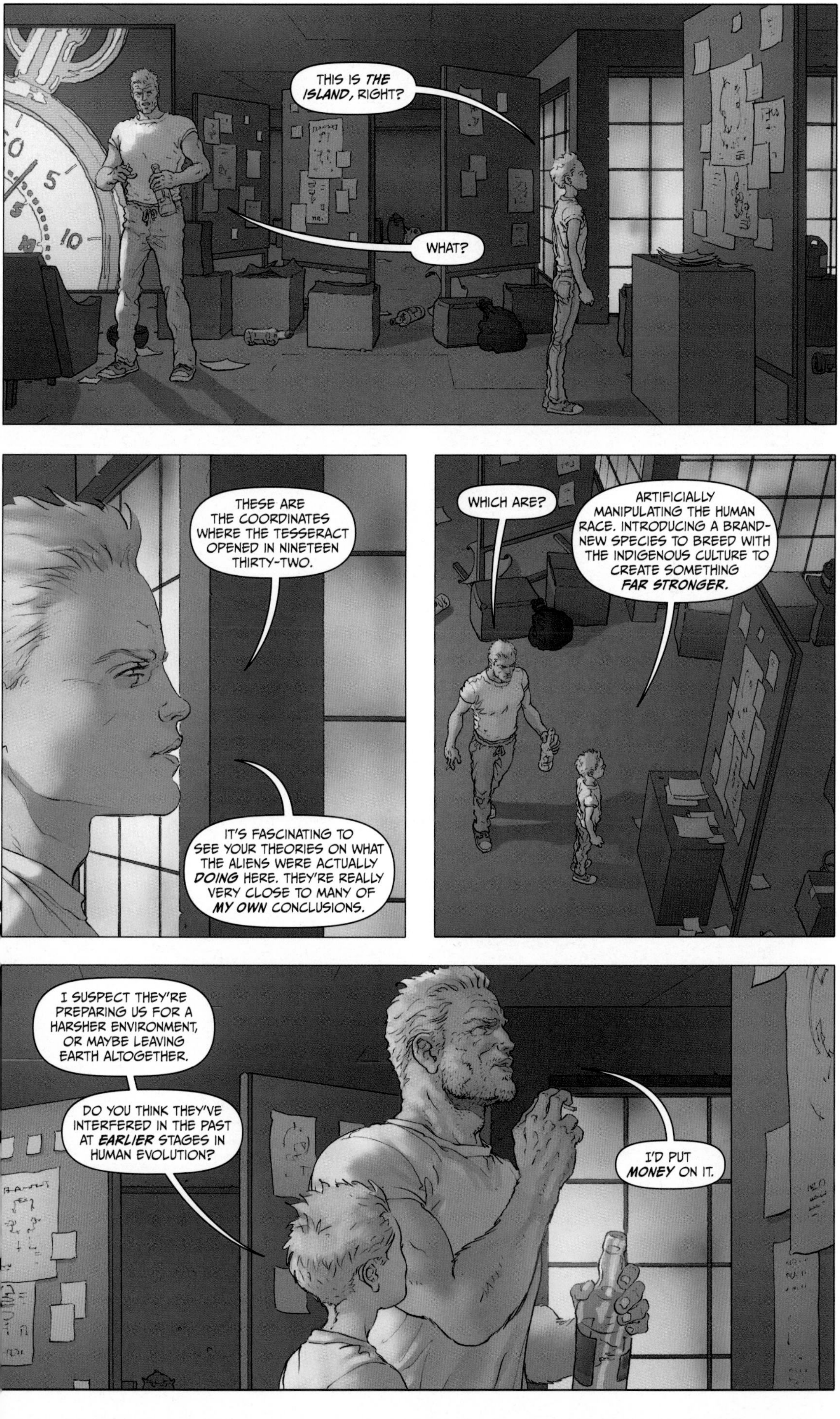

THIS IS *THE ISLAND*, RIGHT?
WHAT?
THESE ARE THE COORDINATES WHERE THE TESSERACT OPENED IN NINETEEN THIRTY-TWO.
IT'S FASCINATING TO SEE YOUR THEORIES ON WHAT THE ALIENS WERE ACTUALLY *DOING* HERE. THEY'RE REALLY VERY CLOSE TO MANY OF *MY OWN* CONCLUSIONS.
WHICH ARE?
ARTIFICIALLY MANIPULATING THE HUMAN RACE. INTRODUCING A BRAND-NEW SPECIES TO BREED WITH THE INDIGENOUS CULTURE TO CREATE SOMETHING *FAR STRONGER.*
I SUSPECT THEY'RE PREPARING US FOR A HARSHER ENVIRONMENT, OR MAYBE LEAVING EARTH ALTOGETHER.
DO YOU THINK THEY'VE INTERFERED IN THE PAST AT *EARLIER* STAGES IN HUMAN EVOLUTION?
I'D PUT *MONEY* ON IT.

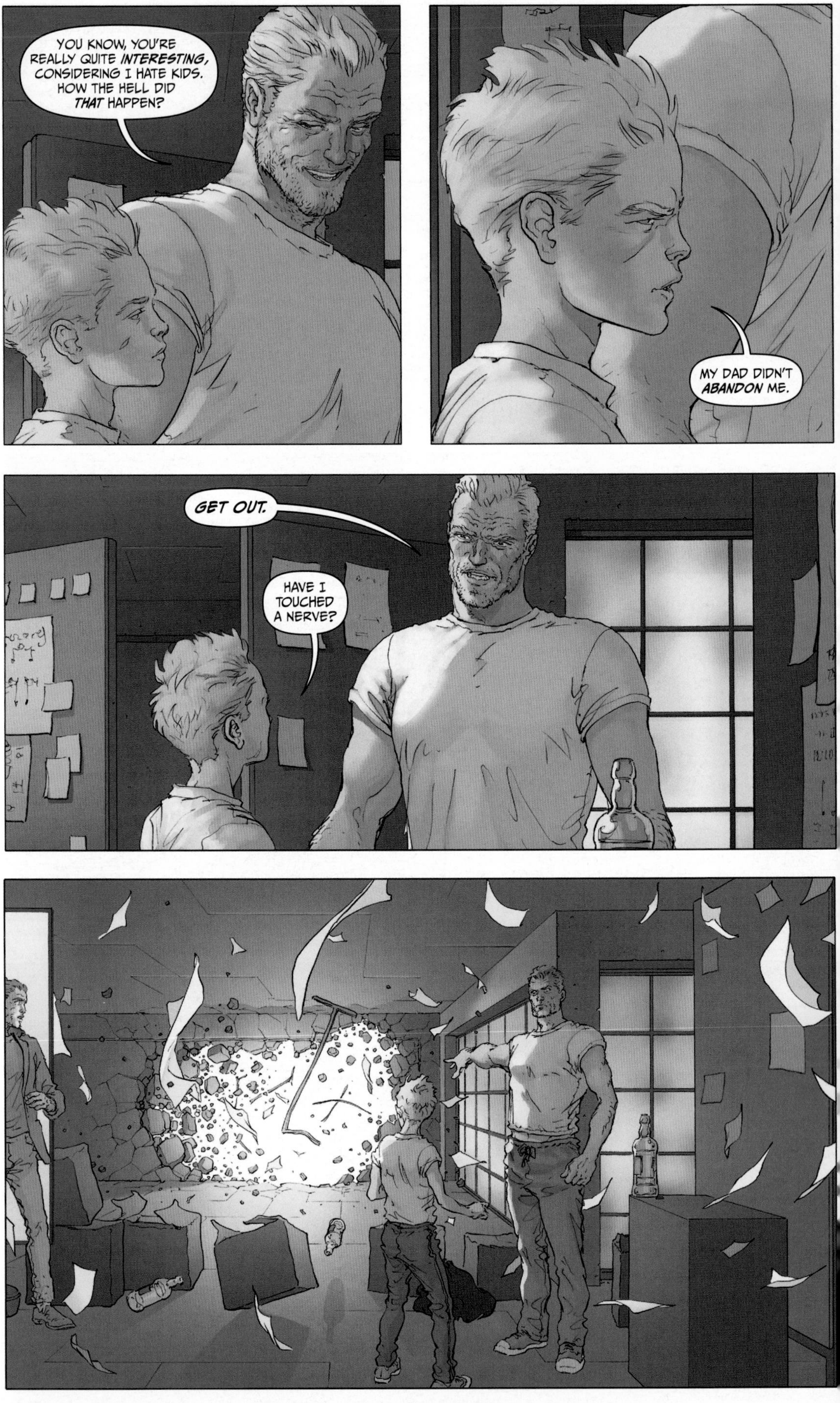
YOU KNOW, YOU'RE REALLY QUITE *INTERESTING*, CONSIDERING I HATE KIDS. HOW THE HELL DID *THAT* HAPPEN?
MY DAD DIDN'T *ABANDON* ME.
HAVE I TOUCHED A NERVE?
GET OUT.

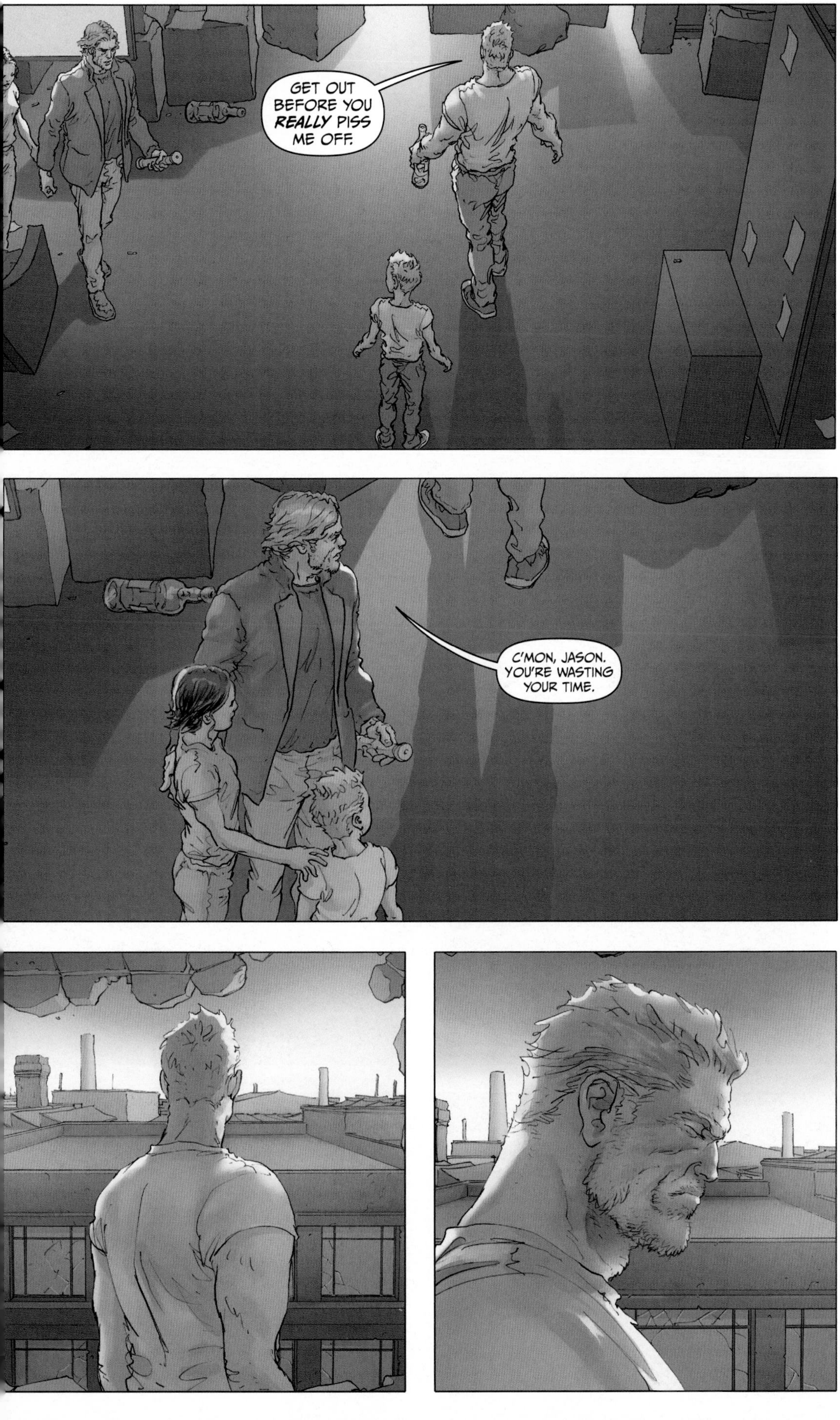
GET OUT BEFORE YOU *REALLY* PISS ME OFF.
C'MON, JASON. YOU'RE WASTING YOUR TIME.

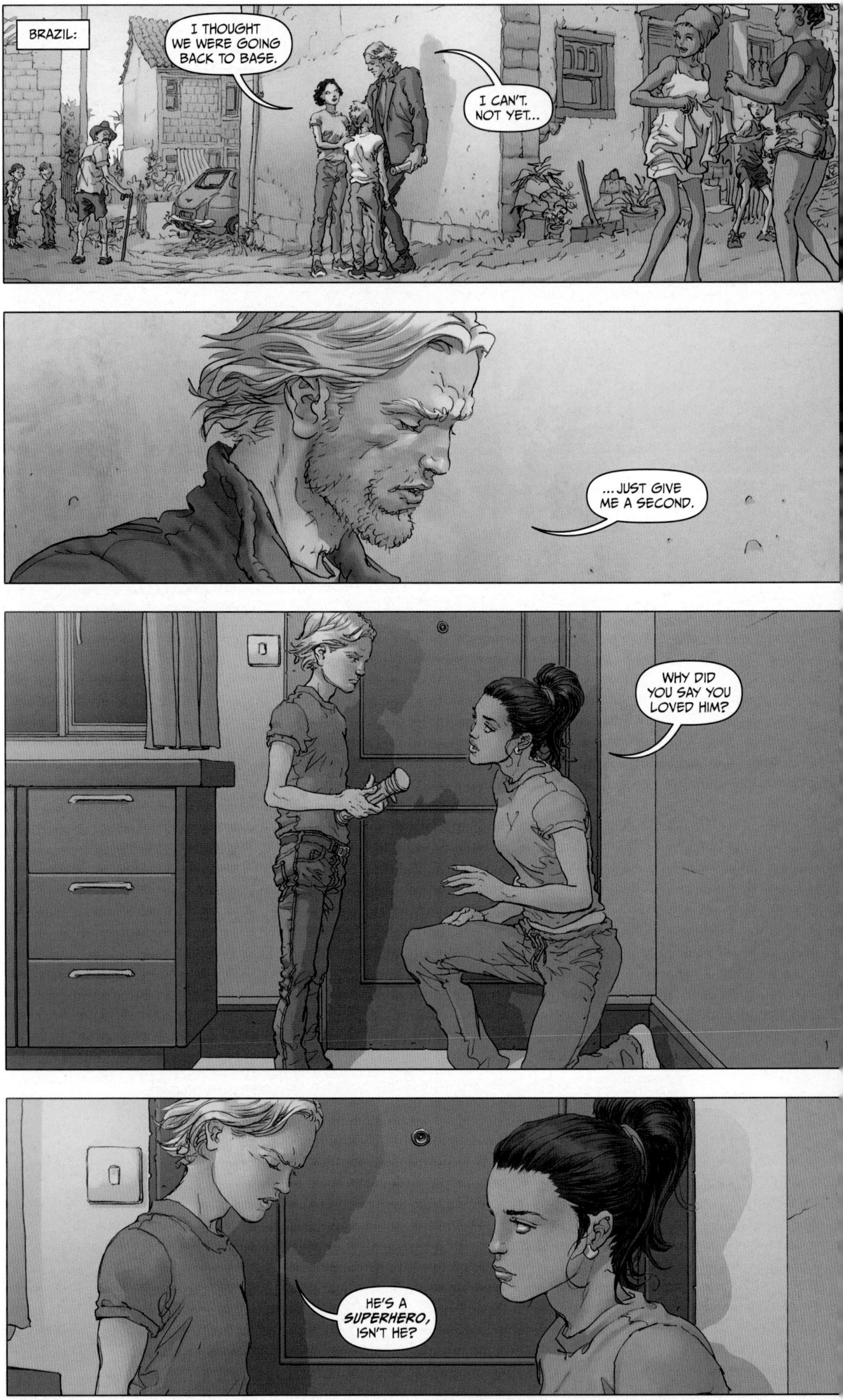

BRAZIL:
I THOUGHT WE WERE GOING BACK TO BASE.
I CAN'T. NOT YET...
...JUST GIVE ME A SECOND.
WHY DID YOU SAY YOU LOVED HIM?
HE'S A *SUPERHERO*, ISN'T HE?

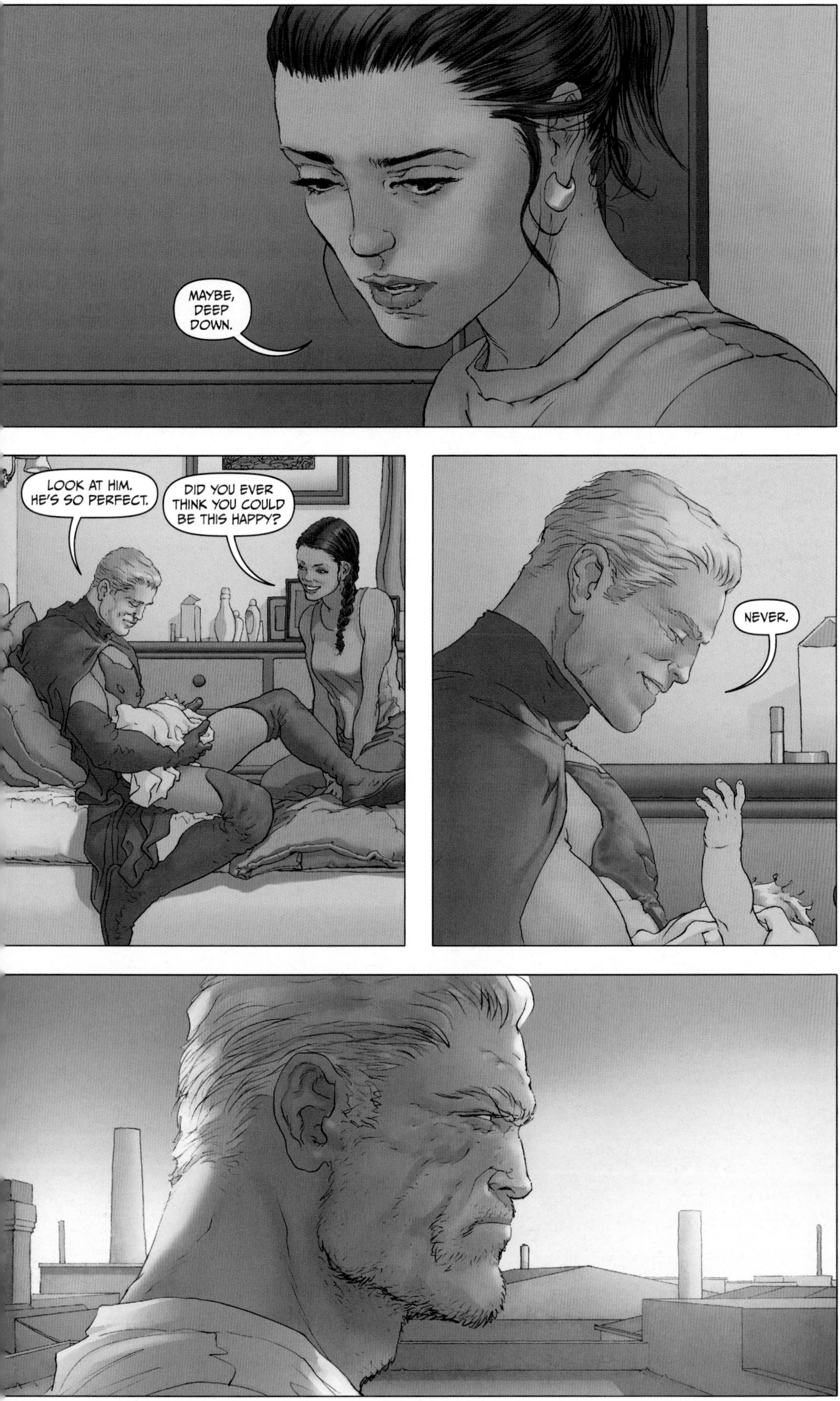
MAYBE, DEEP DOWN.
LOOK AT HIM. HE'S SO PERFECT.
DID YOU EVER THINK YOU COULD BE THIS HAPPY?
NEVER.

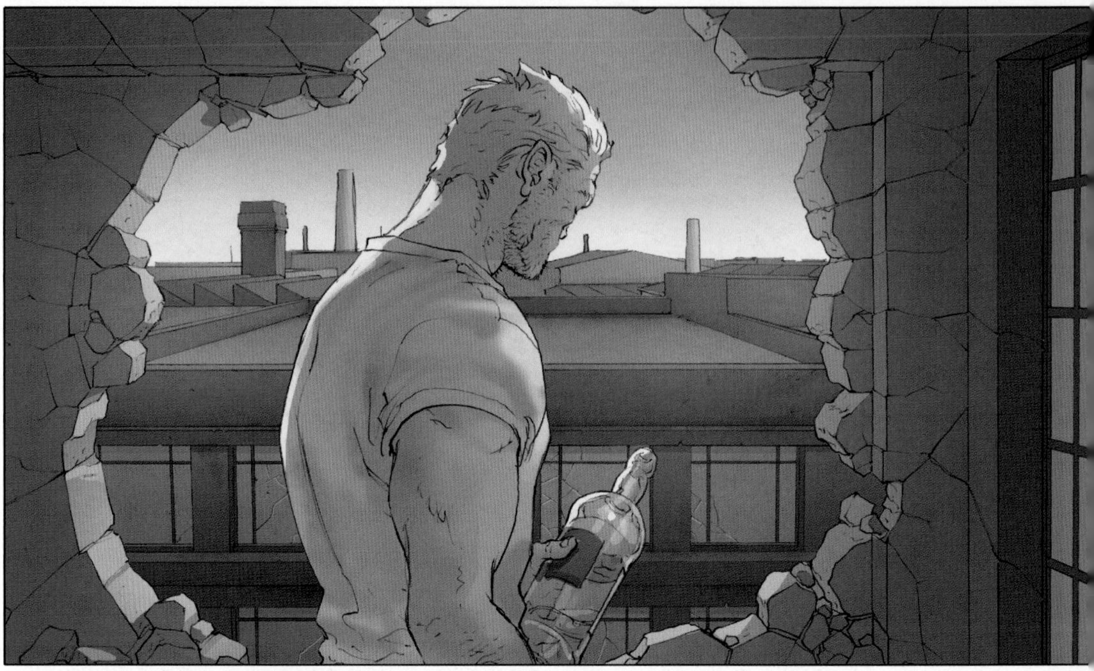

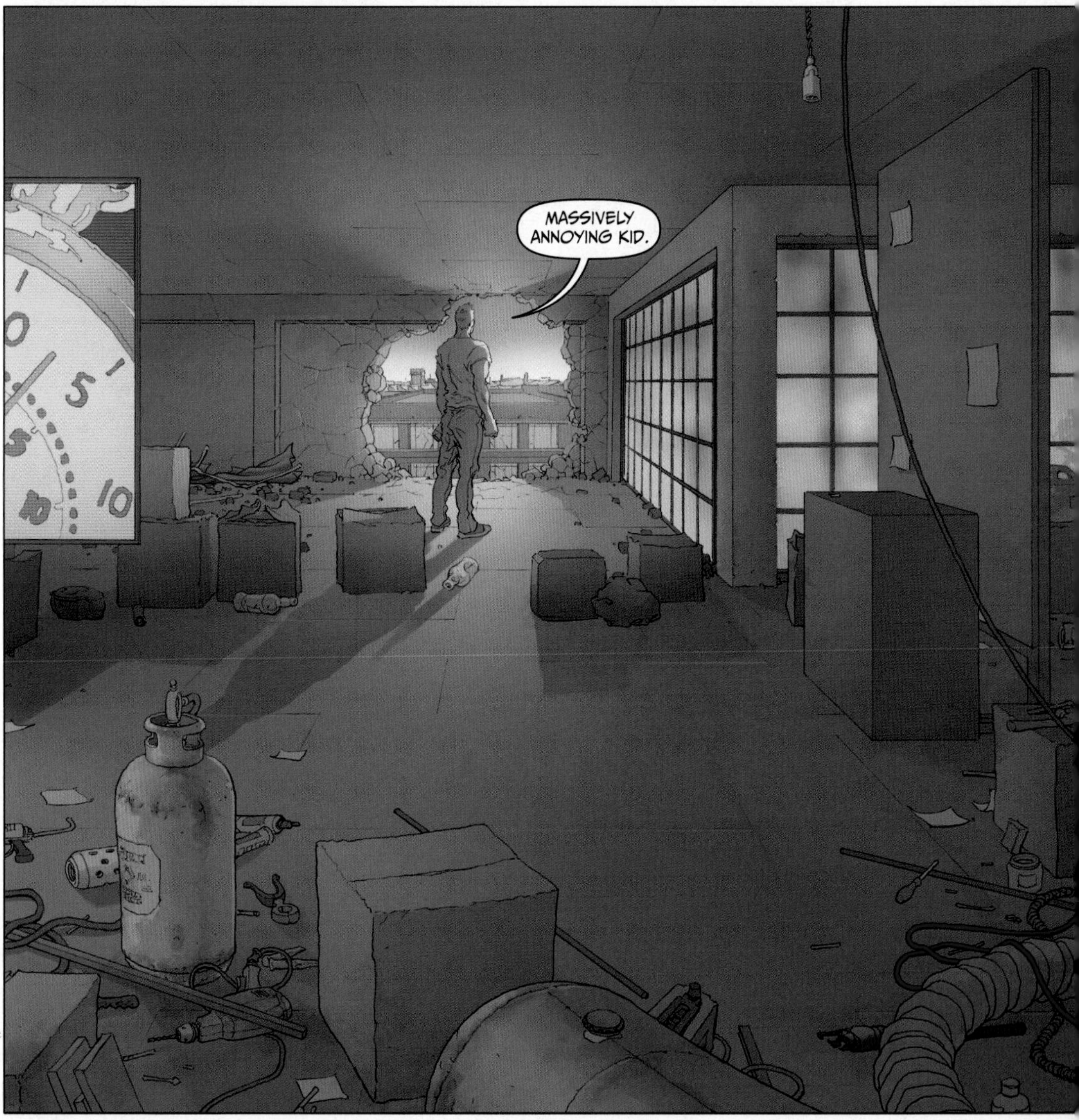
MASSIVELY ANNOYING KID.

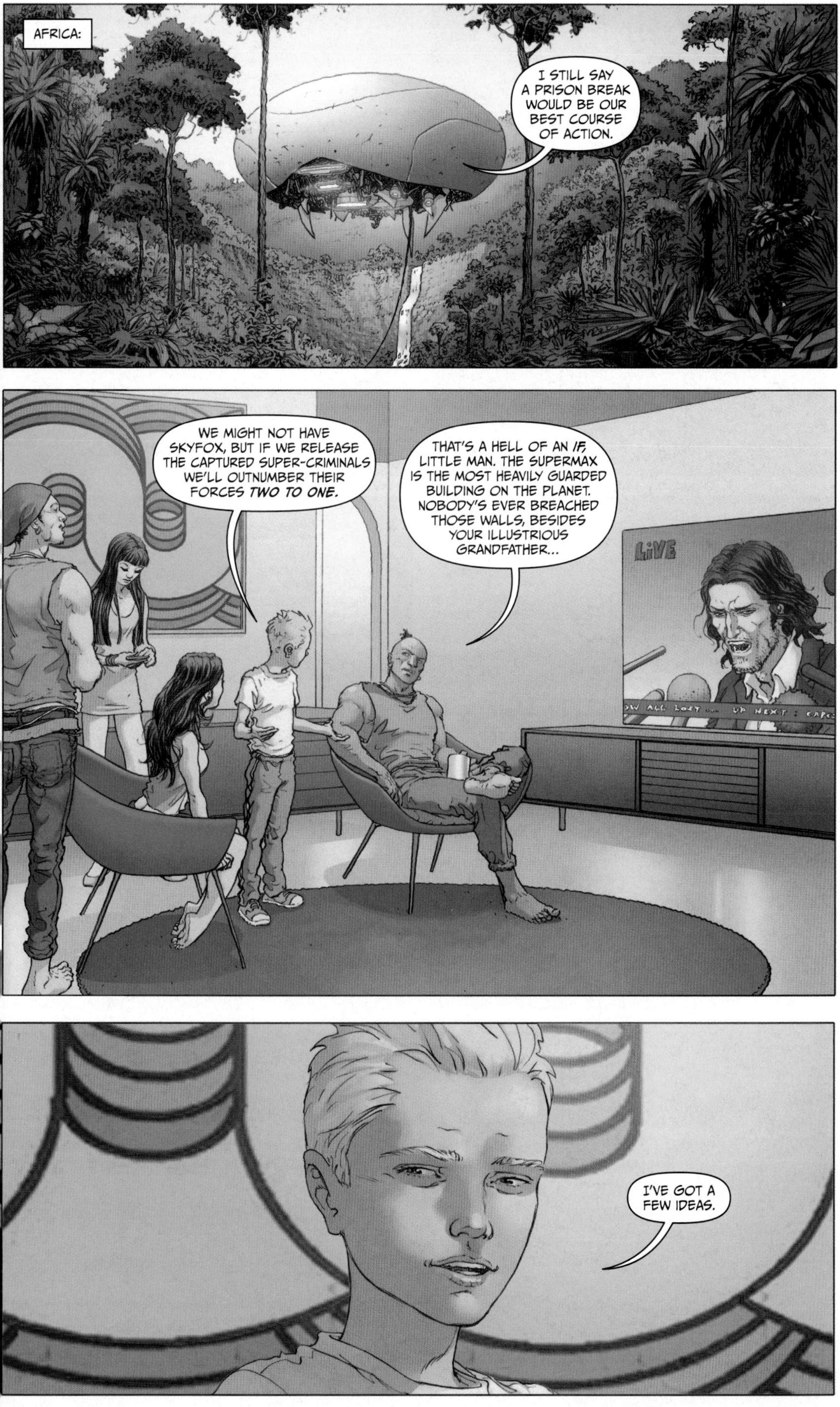
AFRICA:
I STILL SAY A PRISON BREAK WOULD BE OUR BEST COURSE OF ACTION.
WE MIGHT NOT HAVE SKYFOX, BUT IF WE RELEASE THE CAPTURED SUPER-CRIMINALS WE'LL OUTNUMBER THEIR FORCES *TWO TO ONE.*
THAT'S A HELL OF AN *IF*, LITTLE MAN. THE SUPERMAX IS THE MOST HEAVILY GUARDED BUILDING ON THE PLANET. NOBODY'S EVER BREACHED THOSE WALLS, BESIDES YOUR ILLUSTRIOUS GRANDFATHER...
LIVE
I'VE GOT A FEW IDEAS.

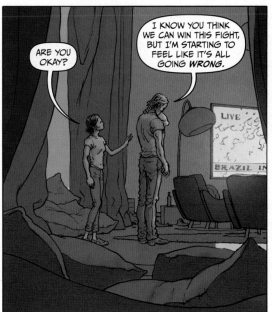

ARE YOU OKAY?

I KNOW YOU THINK WE CAN WIN THIS FIGHT, BUT I'M STARTING TO FEEL LIKE IT'S ALL GOING *WRONG*.

THEY'RE GAINING GROUND AND INTENSIFYING THE *SEARCH*. IS THERE REALLY GOING TO BE ENOUGH OF US WHEN IT COMES TO THE *FACE-OFF?*

WELL, IF THINGS ARE REALLY THAT BAD, I GUESS I SHOULD *GET ON* WITH THIS.

WHAT?

A LITTLE TRICK MY DAD SHOWED ME. SOMETHING HE MADE FOR MOM AFTER RESCUING SOME MINERS.

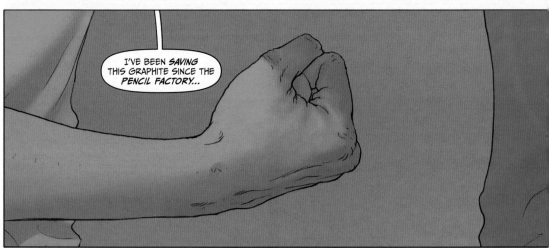

I'VE BEEN *SAVING* THIS GRAPHITE SINCE THE *PENCIL FACTORY*...

...NOW YOU KNOW WHY.

IF WE SURVIVE THIS, WILL YOU MARRY ME, MR. HUTCHENCE?

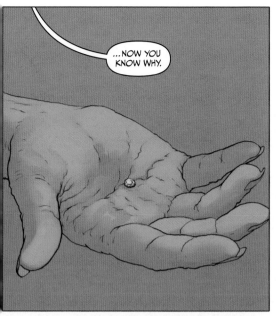

I'LL THINK ABOUT IT.

WHAT'S THE MATTER?

NOTHING. JUST *DISTRACTED* FOR A SECOND.

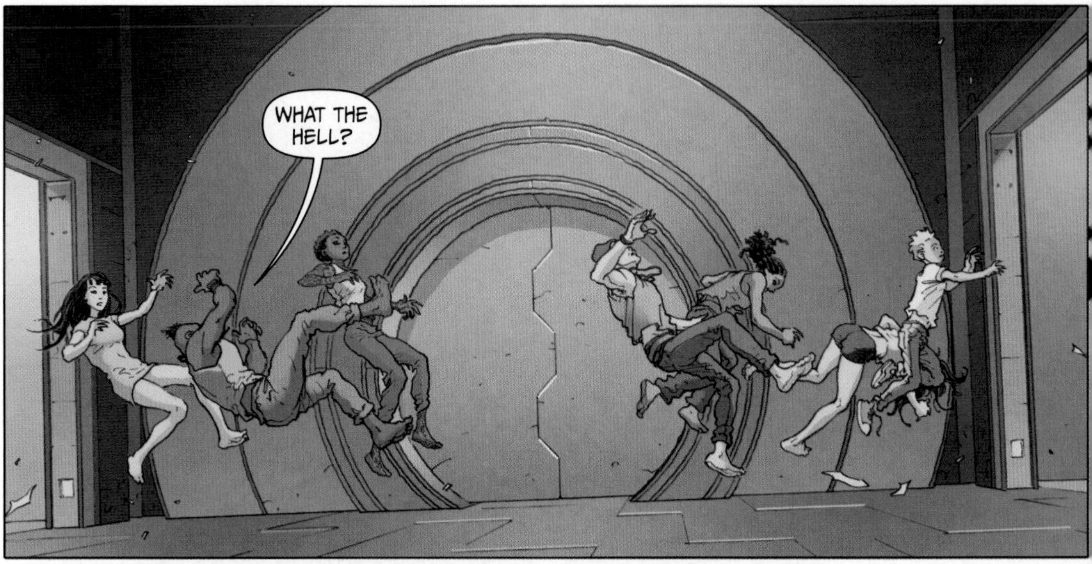
WHAT THE HELL?

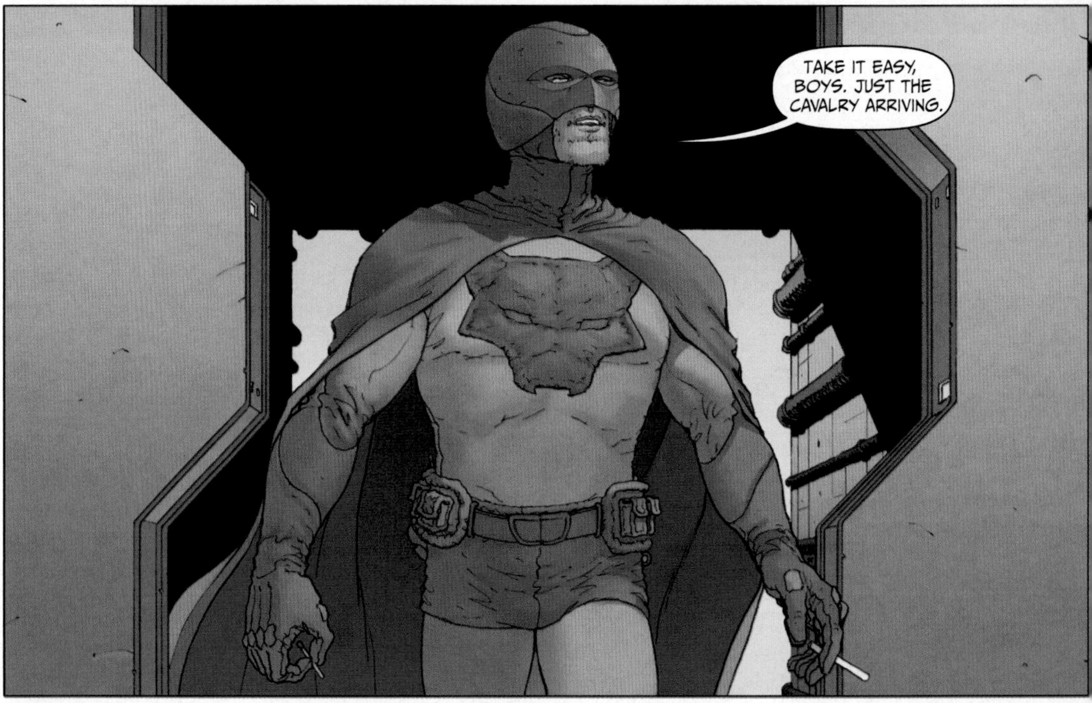
TAKE IT EASY, BOYS. JUST THE CAVALRY ARRIVING.

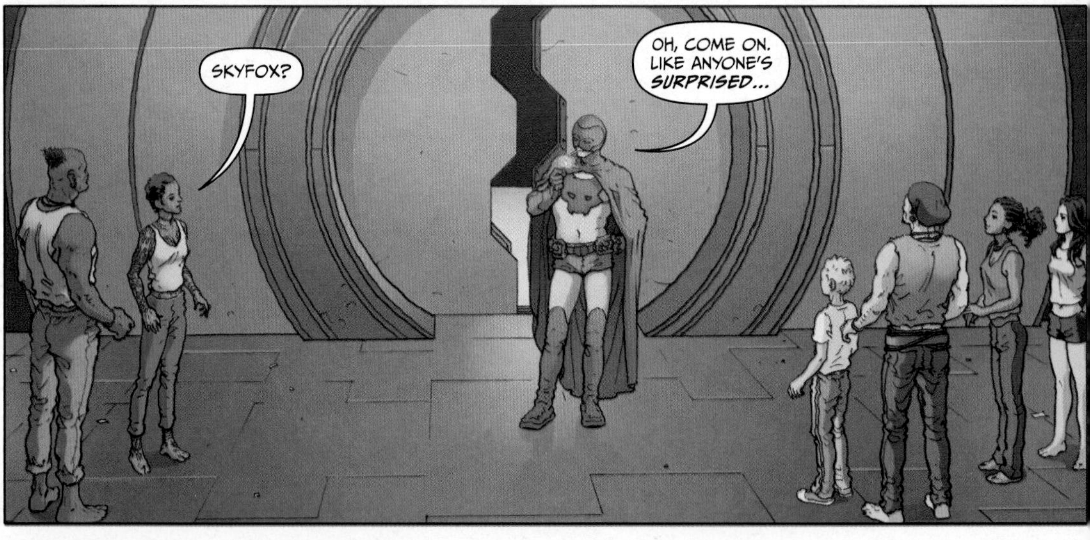
SKYFOX?
OH, COME ON. LIKE ANYONE'S *SURPRISED*...

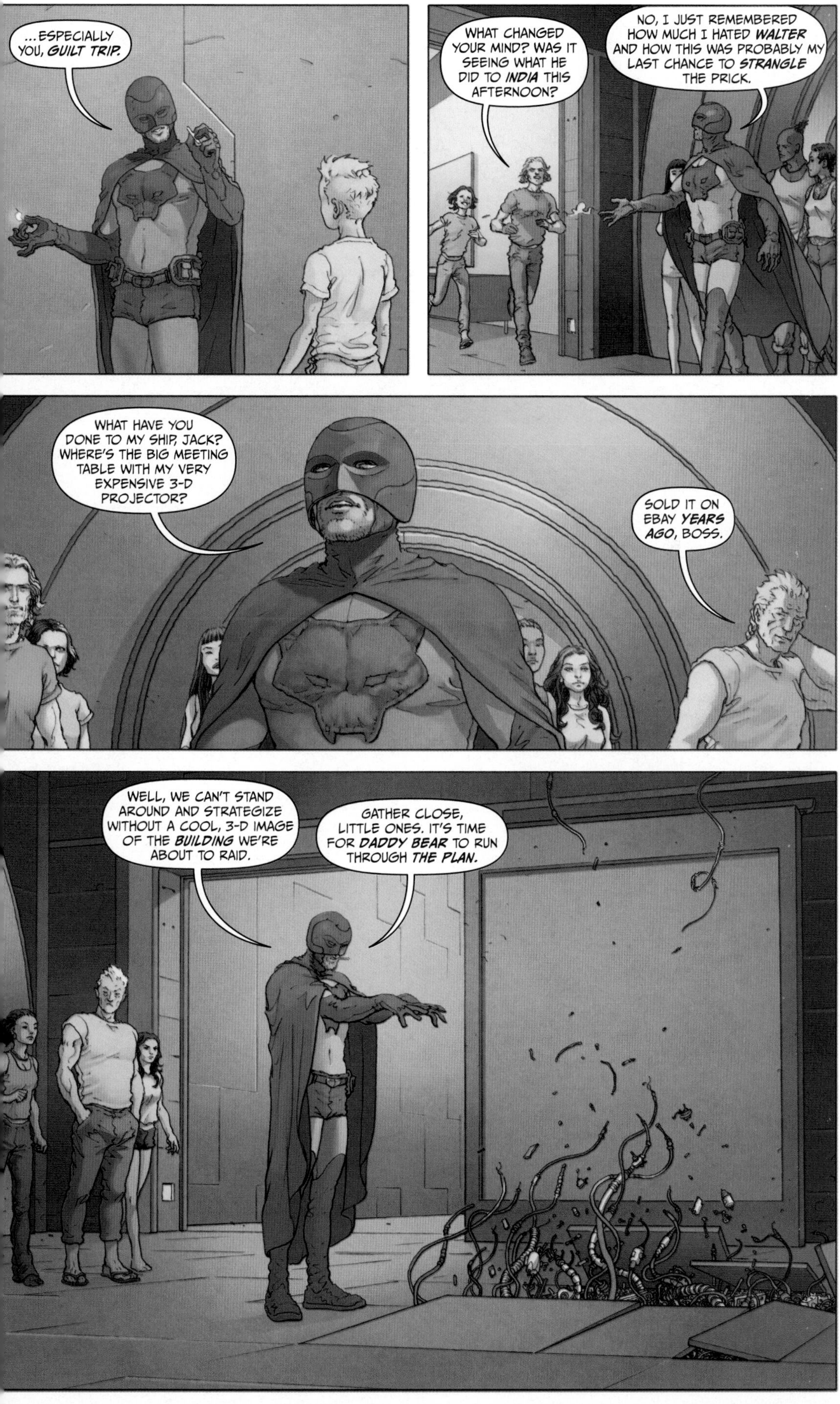
...ESPECIALLY YOU, GUILT TRIP.
WHAT CHANGED YOUR MIND? WAS IT SEEING WHAT HE DID TO INDIA THIS AFTERNOON?
NO, I JUST REMEMBERED HOW MUCH I HATED WALTER AND HOW THIS WAS PROBABLY MY LAST CHANCE TO STRANGLE THE PRICK.
WHAT HAVE YOU DONE TO MY SHIP, JACK? WHERE'S THE BIG MEETING TABLE WITH MY VERY EXPENSIVE 3-D PROJECTOR?
SOLD IT ON EBAY YEARS AGO, BOSS.
WELL, WE CAN'T STAND AROUND AND STRATEGIZE WITHOUT A COOL, 3-D IMAGE OF THE BUILDING WE'RE ABOUT TO RAID.
GATHER CLOSE, LITTLE ONES. IT'S TIME FOR DADDY BEAR TO RUN THROUGH THE PLAN.

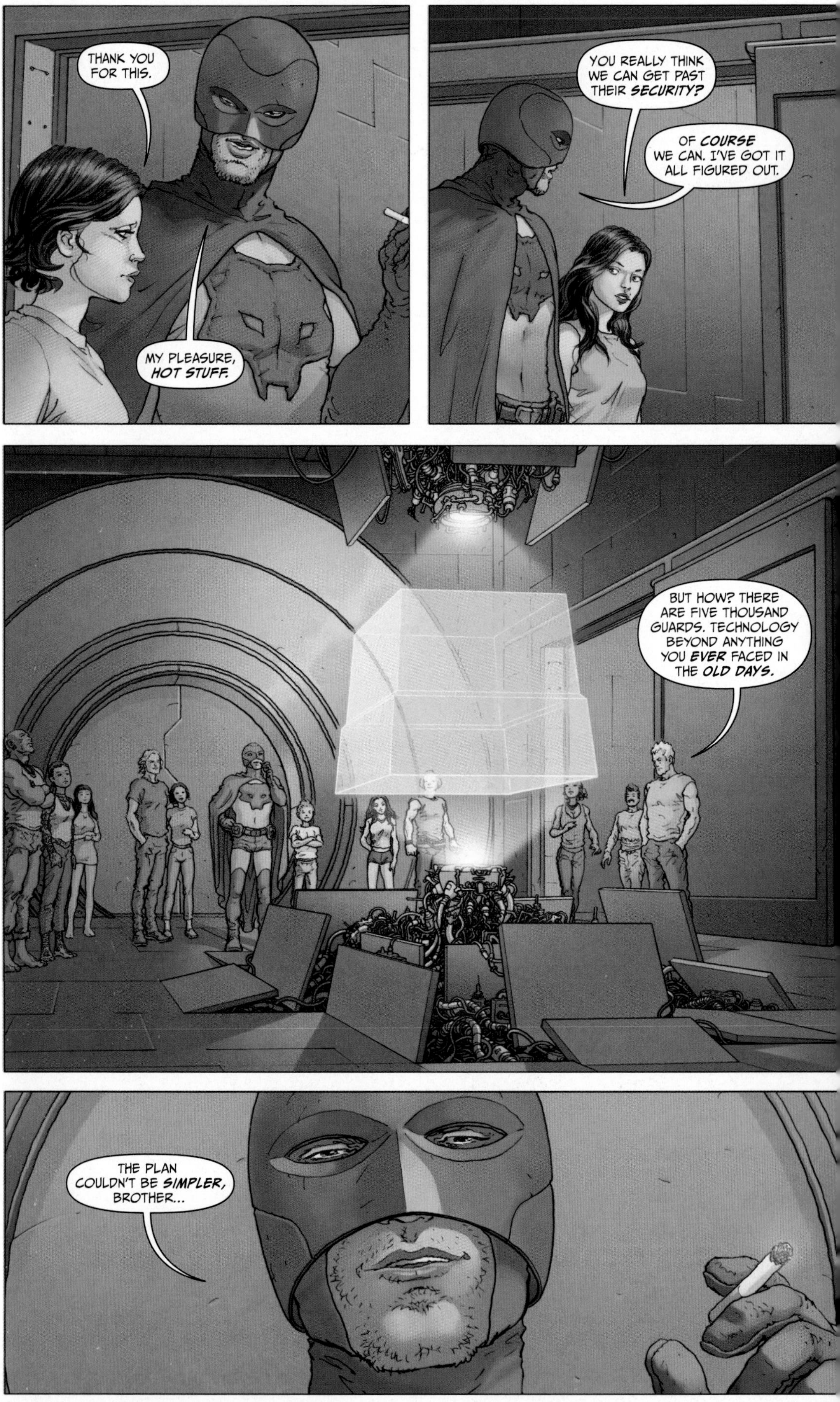
THANK YOU FOR THIS.
MY PLEASURE, HOT STUFF.
YOU REALLY THINK WE CAN GET PAST THEIR SECURITY?
OF COURSE WE CAN. I'VE GOT IT ALL FIGURED OUT.
BUT HOW? THERE ARE FIVE THOUSAND GUARDS. TECHNOLOGY BEYOND ANYTHING YOU EVER FACED IN THE OLD DAYS.
THE PLAN COULDN'T BE SIMPLER, BROTHER...

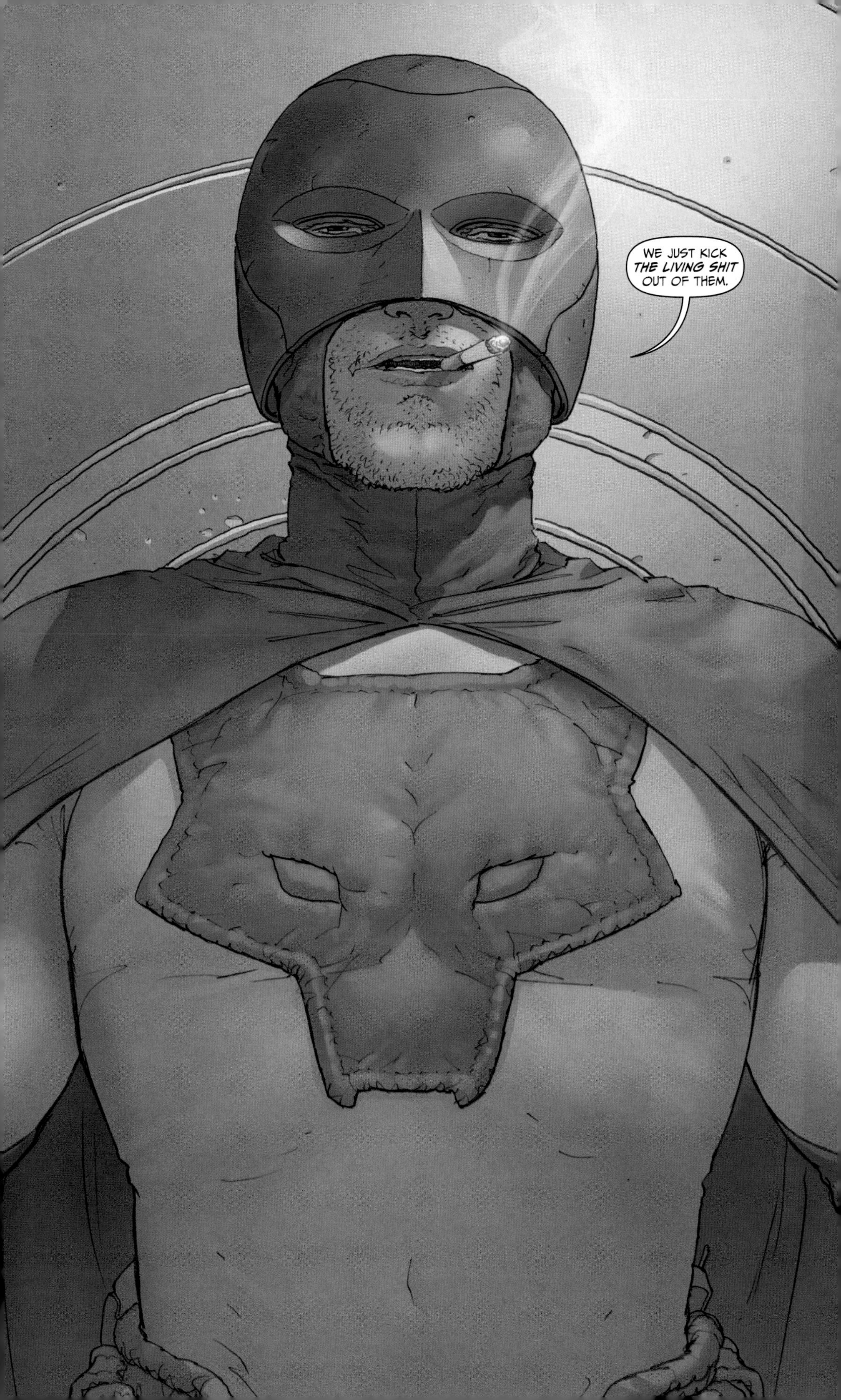
WE JUST KICK *THE LIVING SHIT* OUT OF THEM.

CHAPTER 4

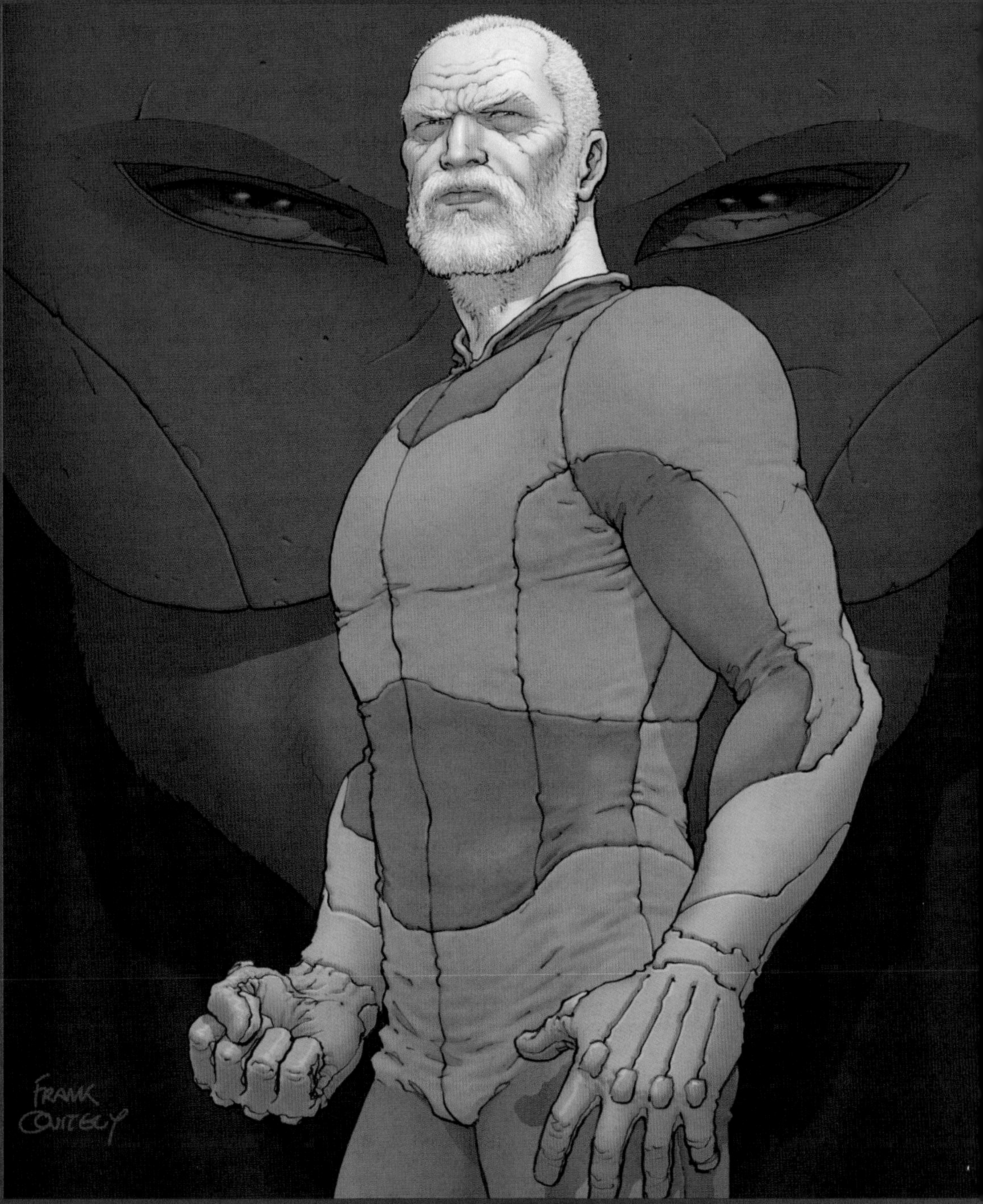
FRANK QUITELY

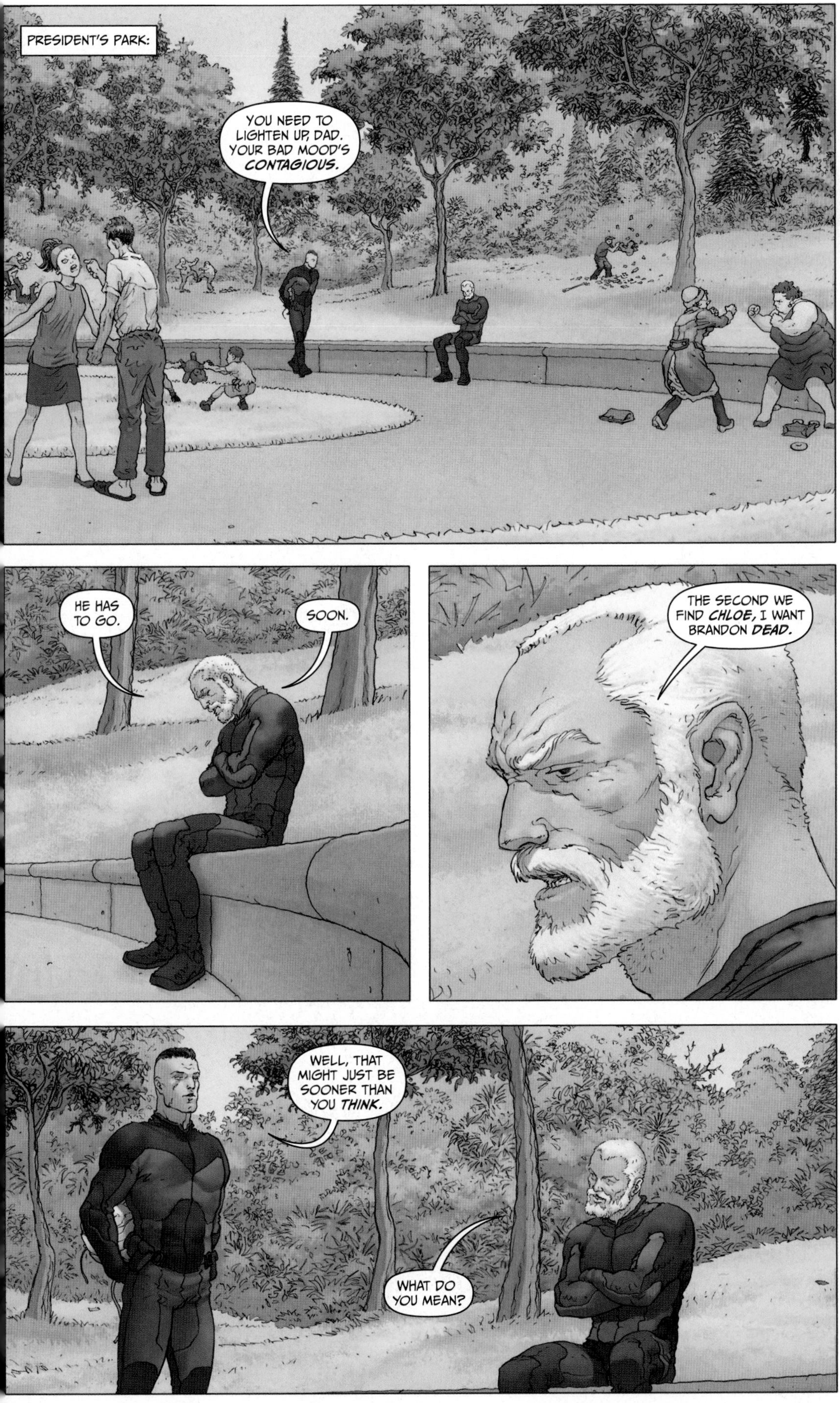
PRESIDENT'S PARK:
YOU NEED TO LIGHTEN UP, DAD. YOUR BAD MOOD'S CONTAGIOUS.
HE HAS TO GO.
SOON.
THE SECOND WE FIND CHLOE, I WANT BRANDON DEAD.
WELL, THAT MIGHT JUST BE SOONER THAN YOU THINK.
WHAT DO YOU MEAN?

I FOUND THIS MACHINE WHEN WE SCANNED THE MOON. IT'S A RADAR FOR PICKING UP *META-HUMAN GENES,* AND MY GUESS IS IT WAS BUILT BY CHLOE'S BOY.

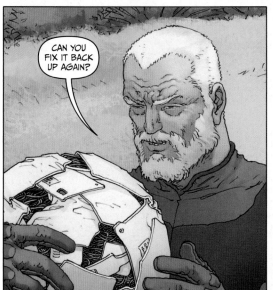

CAN YOU FIX IT BACK UP AGAIN?

DAD, I CAN FIX *ANYTHING.*

GOOD BOY, JULES. GOOD BOY.

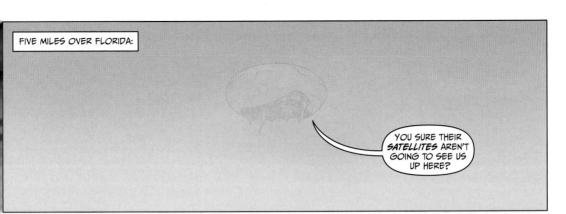

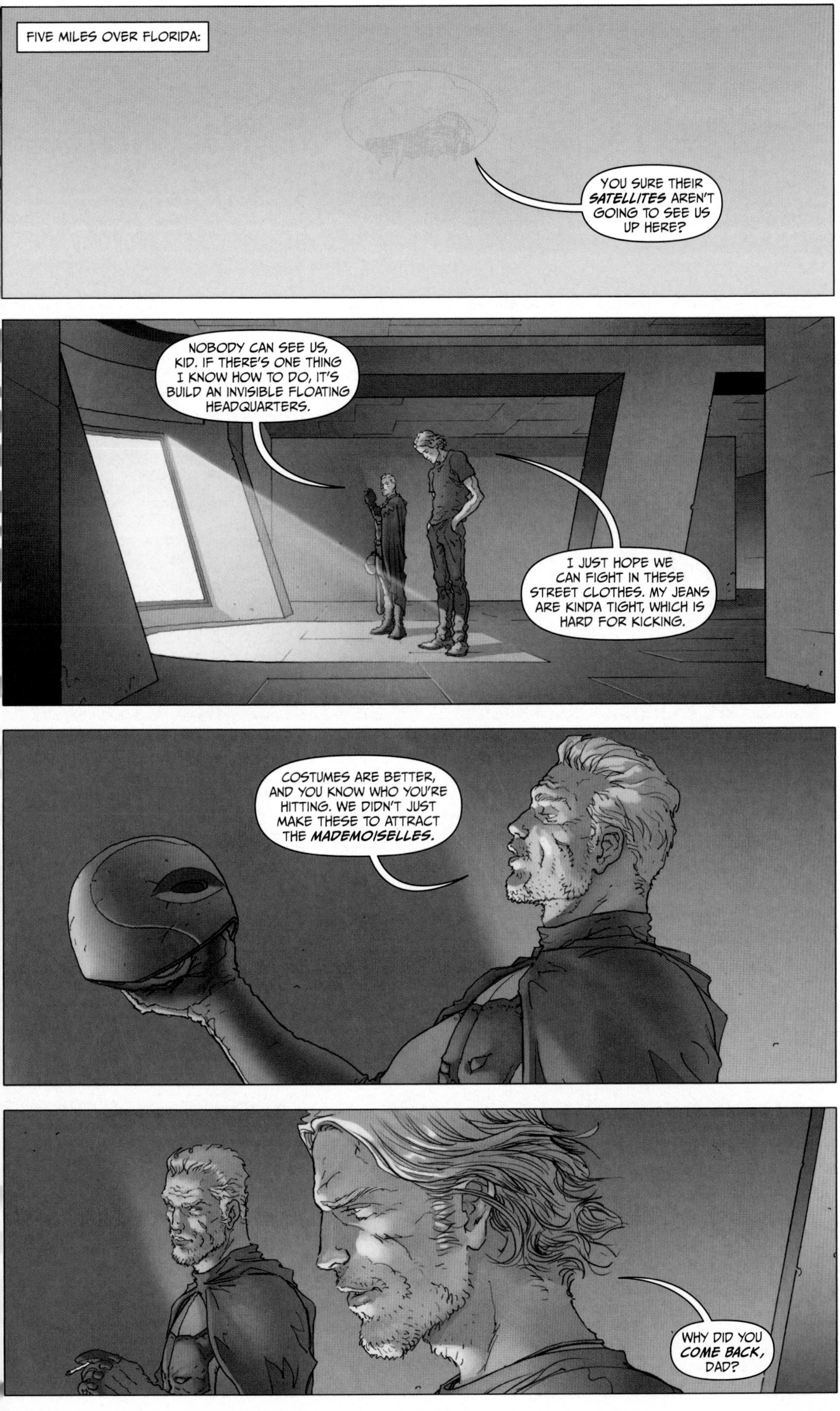
FIVE MILES OVER FLORIDA:
YOU SURE THEIR SATELLITES AREN'T GOING TO SEE US UP HERE?
NOBODY CAN SEE US, KID. IF THERE'S ONE THING I KNOW HOW TO DO, IT'S BUILD AN INVISIBLE FLOATING HEADQUARTERS.
I JUST HOPE WE CAN FIGHT IN THESE STREET CLOTHES. MY JEANS ARE KINDA TIGHT, WHICH IS HARD FOR KICKING.
COSTUMES ARE BETTER, AND YOU KNOW WHO YOU'RE HITTING. WE DIDN'T JUST MAKE THESE TO ATTRACT THE MADEMOISELLES.
WHY DID YOU COME BACK, DAD?

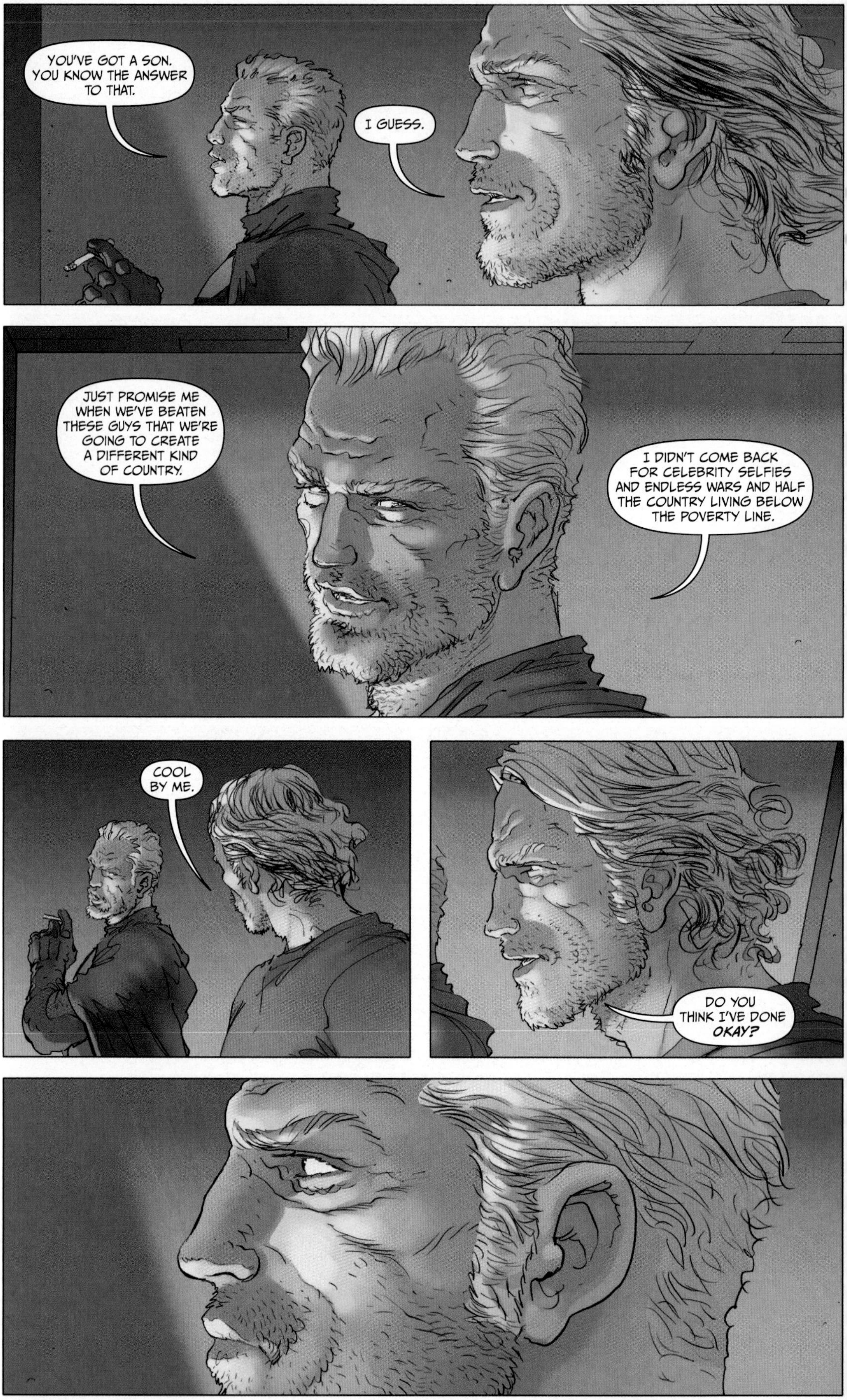
YOU'VE GOT A SON. YOU KNOW THE ANSWER TO THAT.
I GUESS.
JUST PROMISE ME WHEN WE'VE BEATEN THESE GUYS THAT WE'RE GOING TO CREATE A DIFFERENT KIND OF COUNTRY.
I DIDN'T COME BACK FOR CELEBRITY SELFIES AND ENDLESS WARS AND HALF THE COUNTRY LIVING BELOW THE POVERTY LINE.
COOL BY ME.
DO YOU THINK I'VE DONE *OKAY?*

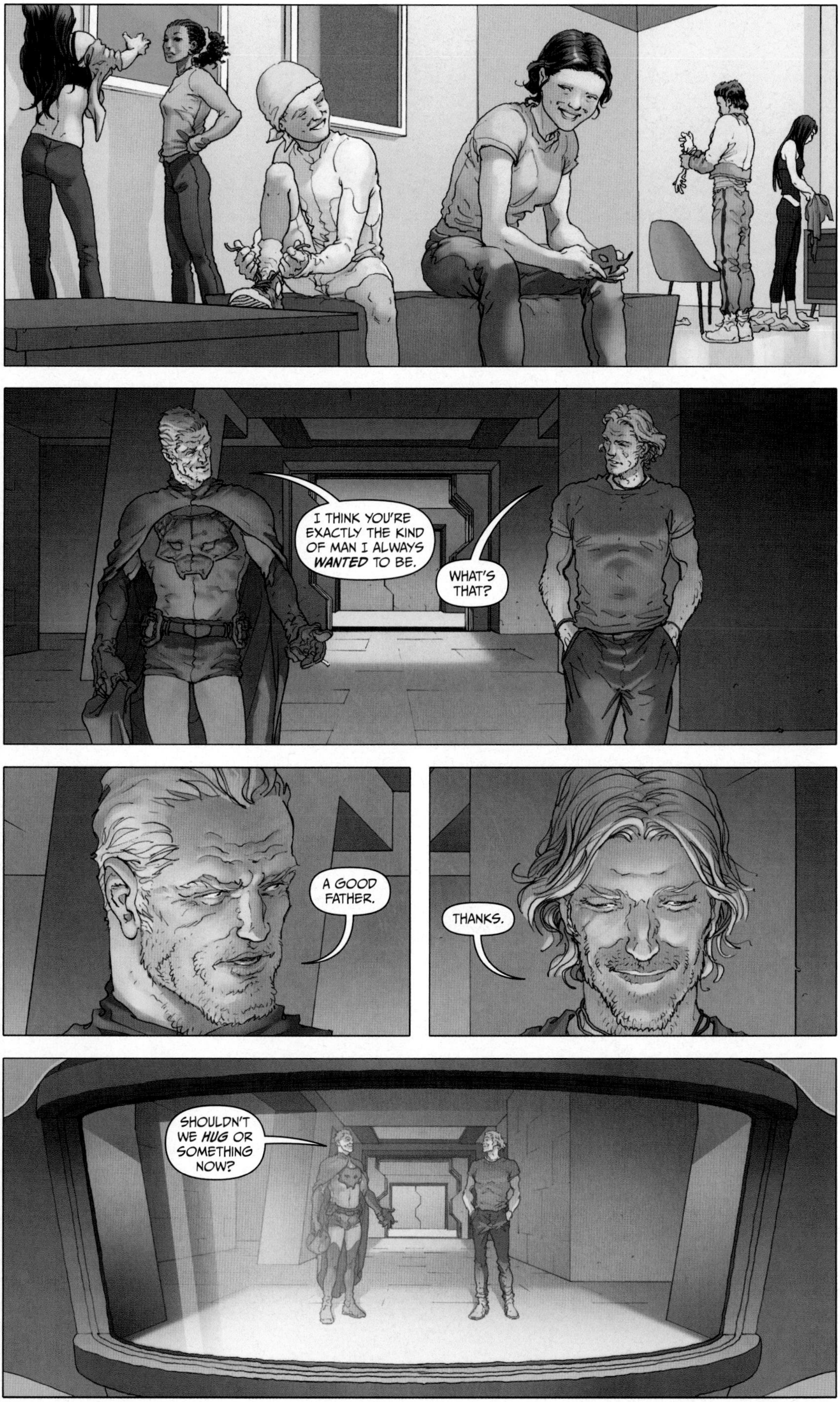
I THINK YOU'RE EXACTLY THE KIND OF MAN I ALWAYS *WANTED* TO BE.
WHAT'S THAT?
A GOOD FATHER.
THANKS.
SHOULDN'T WE *HUG* OR SOMETHING NOW?

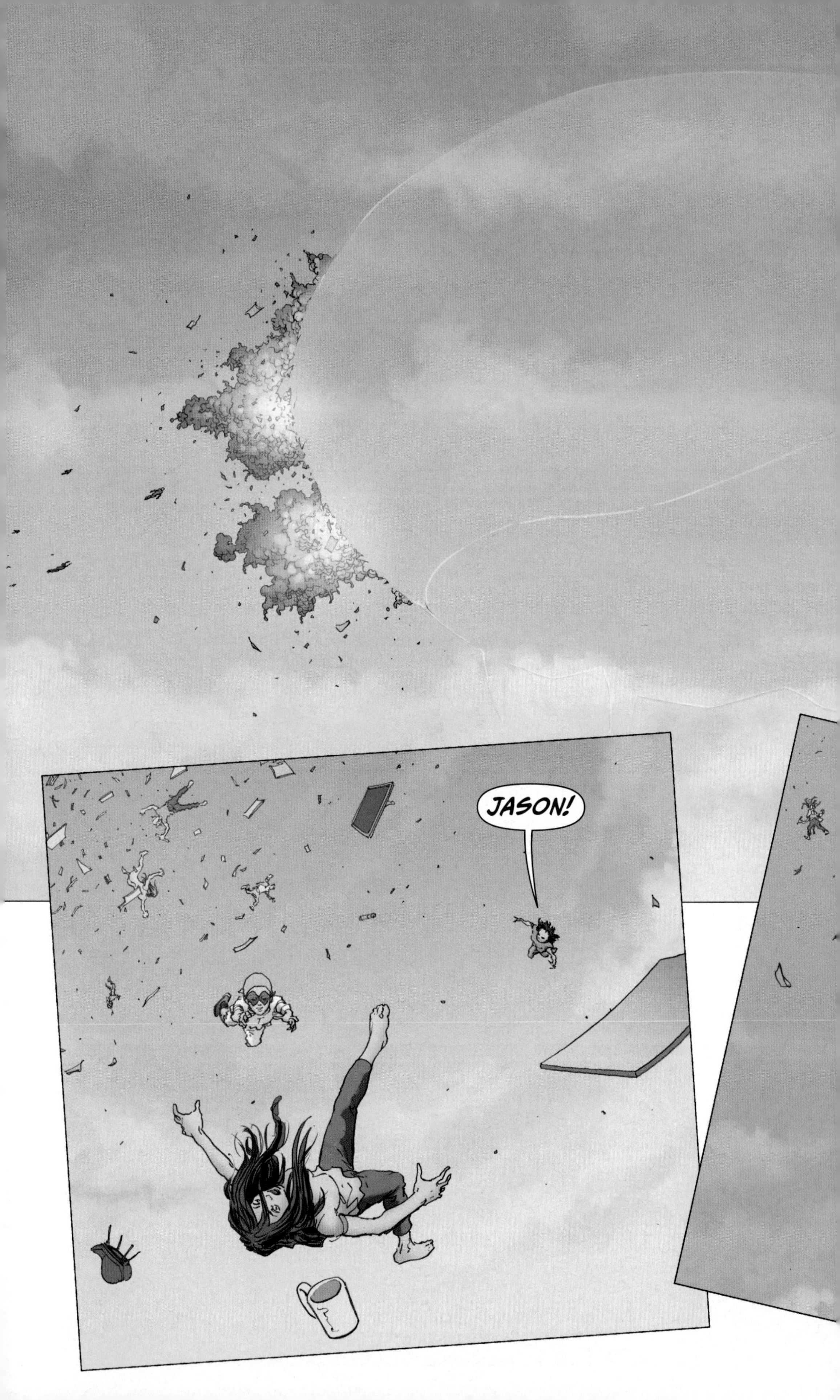
JASON!

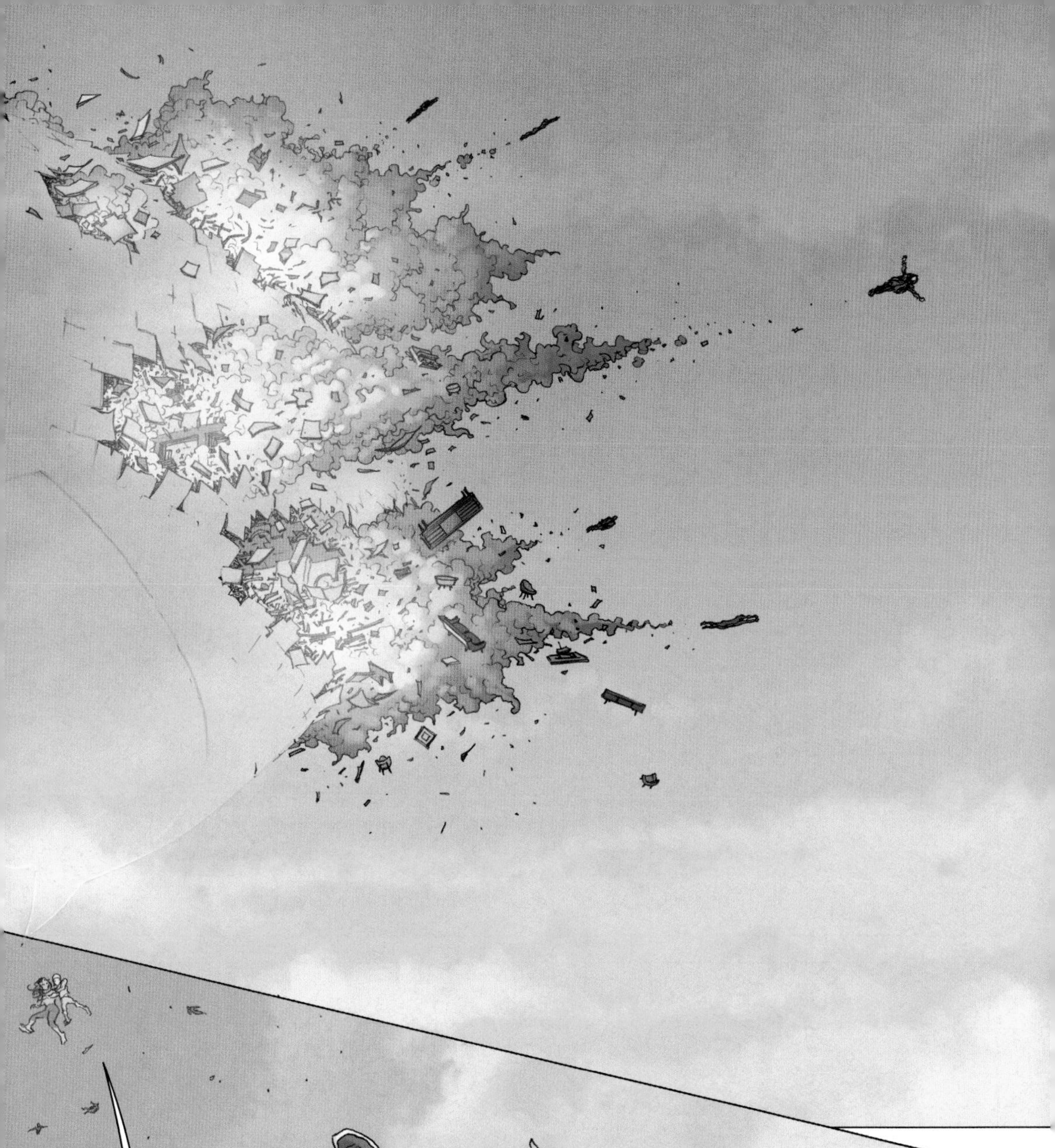
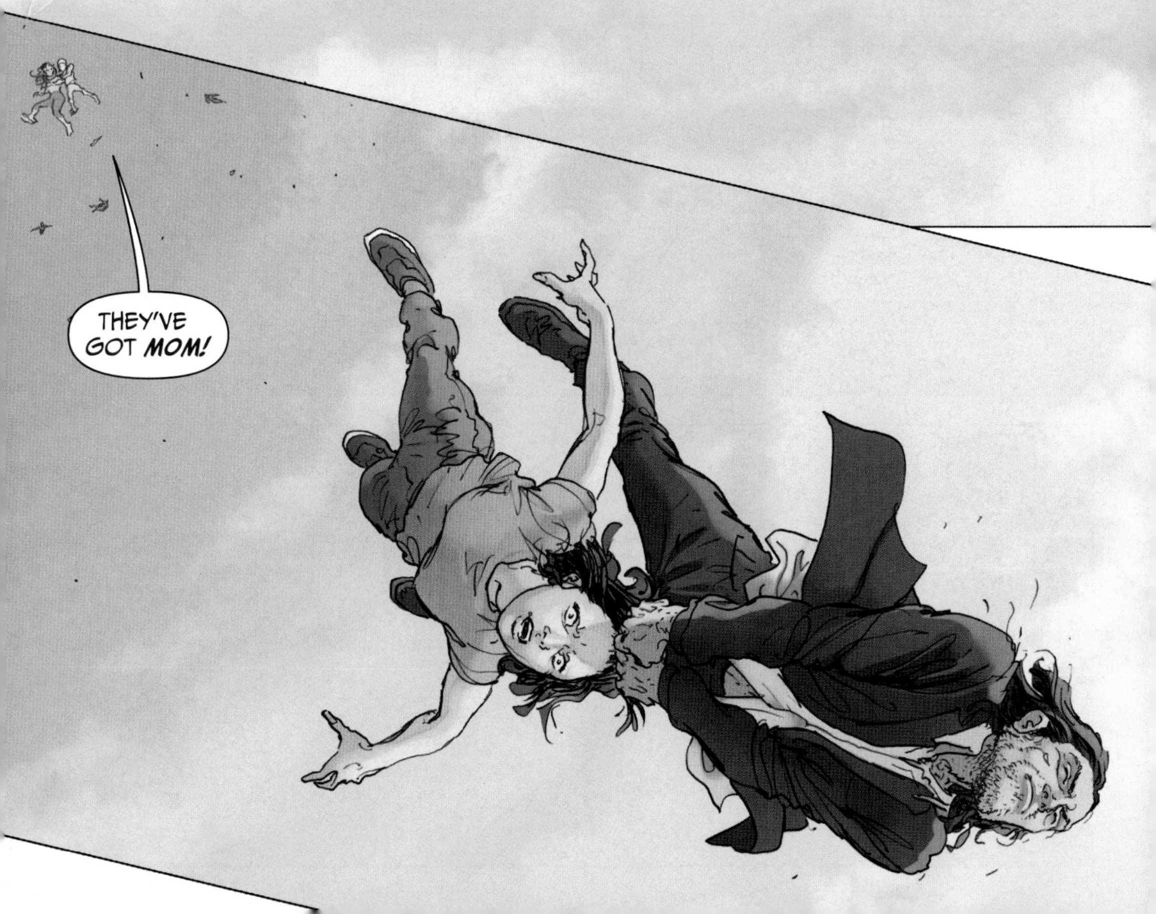
THEY'VE GOT MOM!

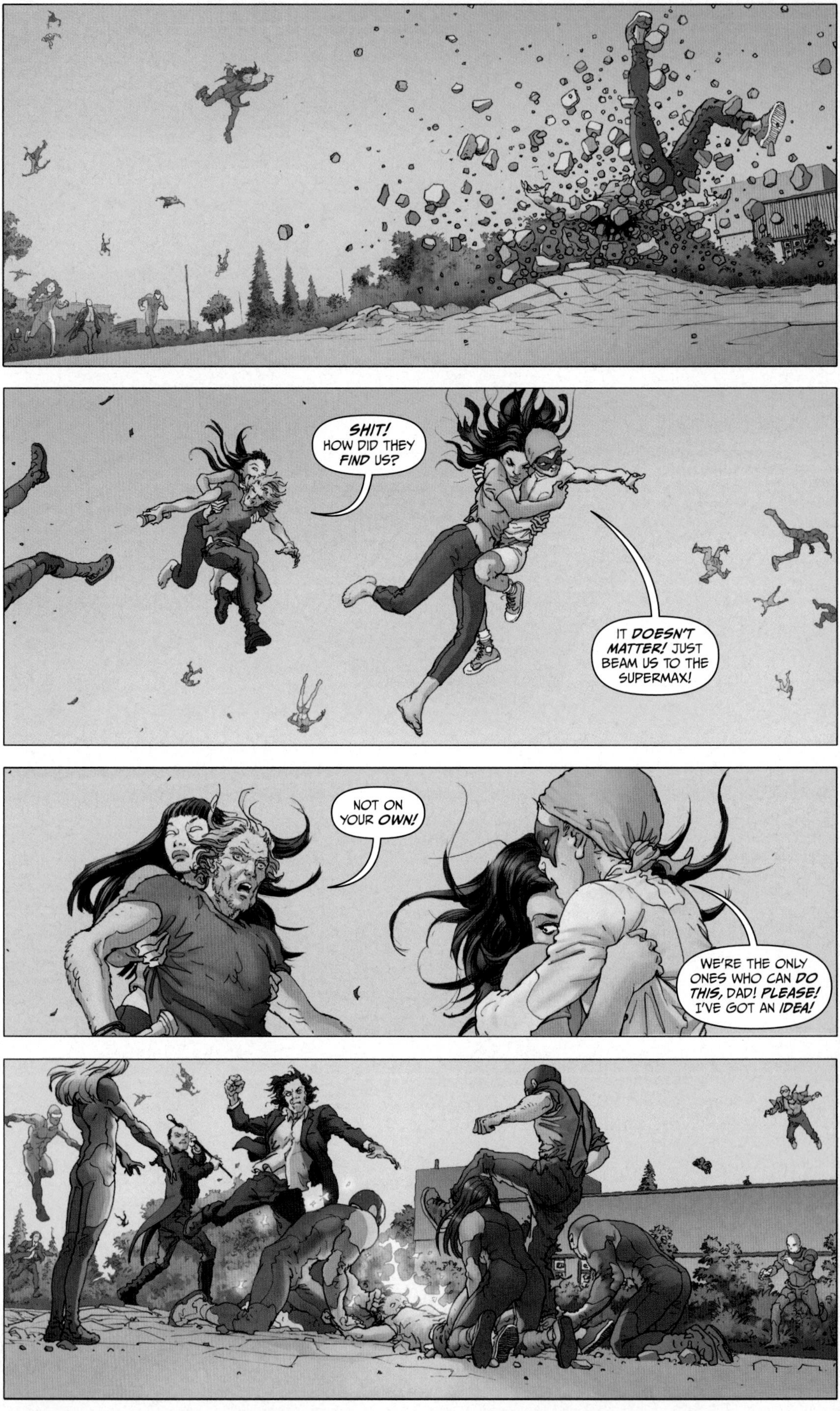
SHIT! HOW DID THEY FIND US?
IT DOESN'T MATTER! JUST BEAM US TO THE SUPERMAX!
NOT ON YOUR OWN!
WE'RE THE ONLY ONES WHO CAN DO THIS, DAD! PLEASE! I'VE GOT AN IDEA!

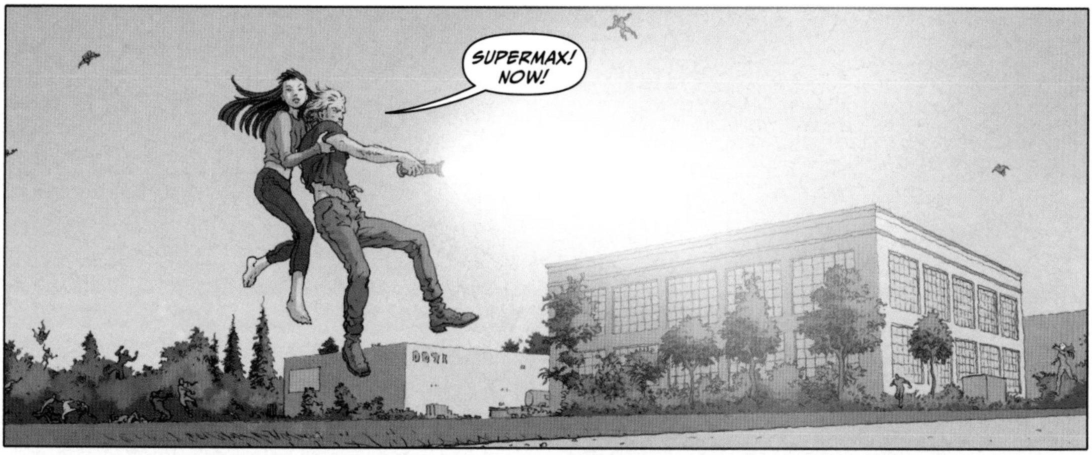
SUPERMAX! NOW!
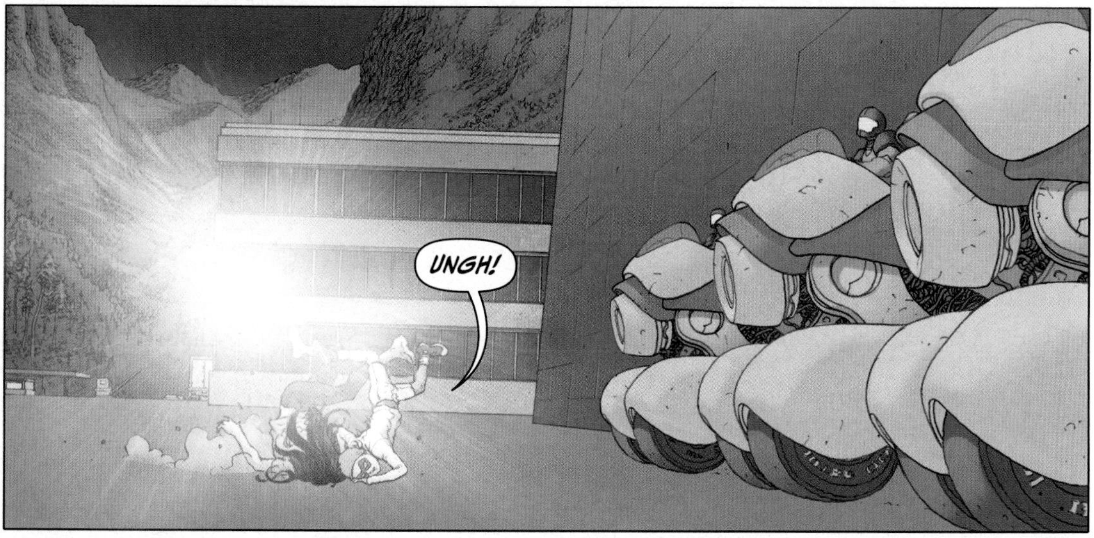
UNGH!
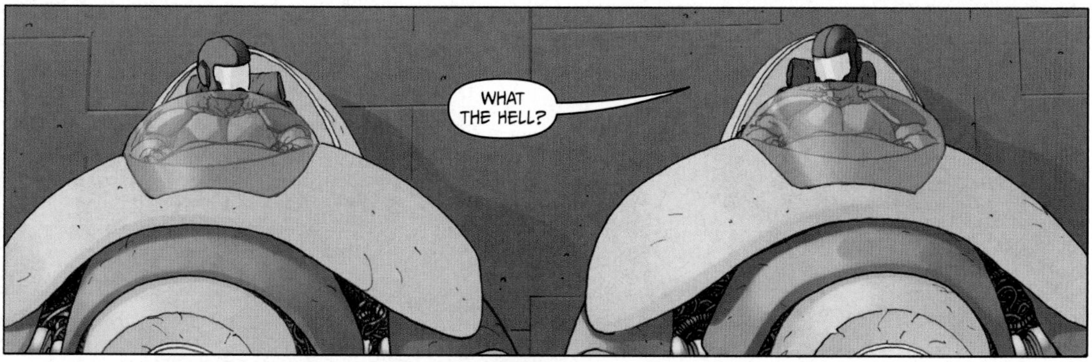
WHAT THE HELL?
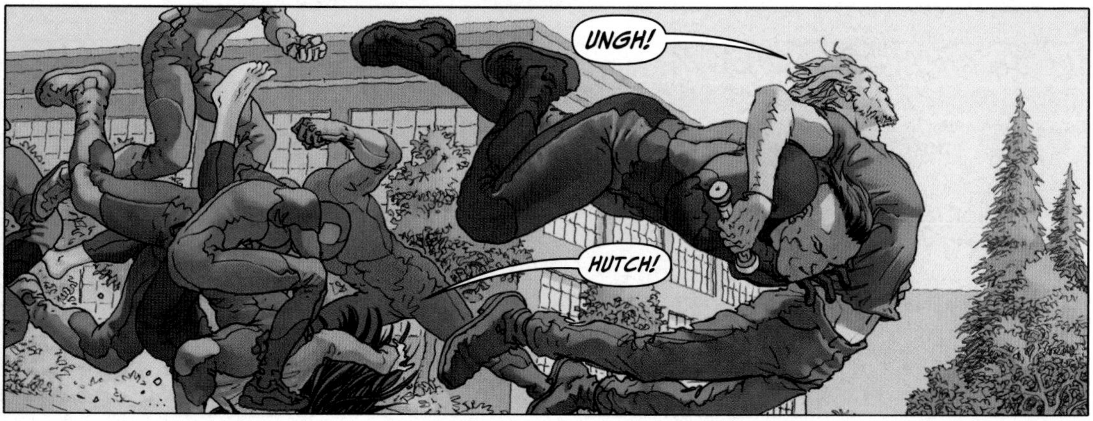
UNGH!
HUTCH!

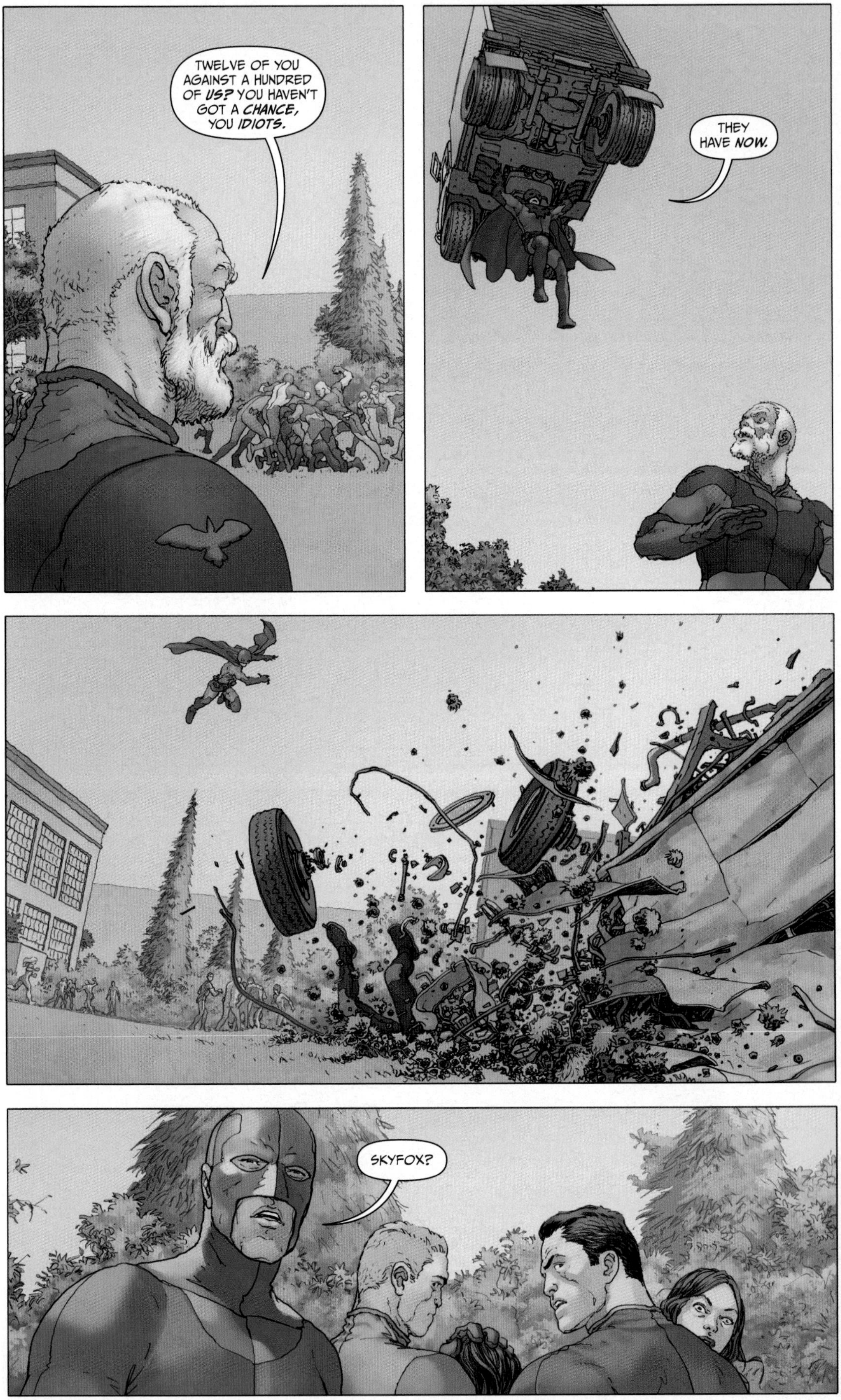
TWELVE OF YOU AGAINST A HUNDRED OF *US?* YOU HAVEN'T GOT A *CHANCE,* YOU *IDIOTS.*
THEY HAVE *NOW.*
SKYFOX?

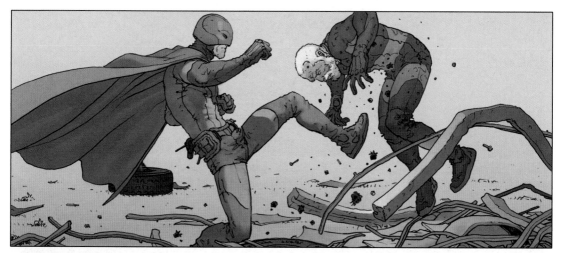

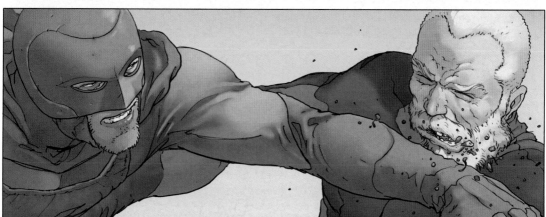

GET HIM!

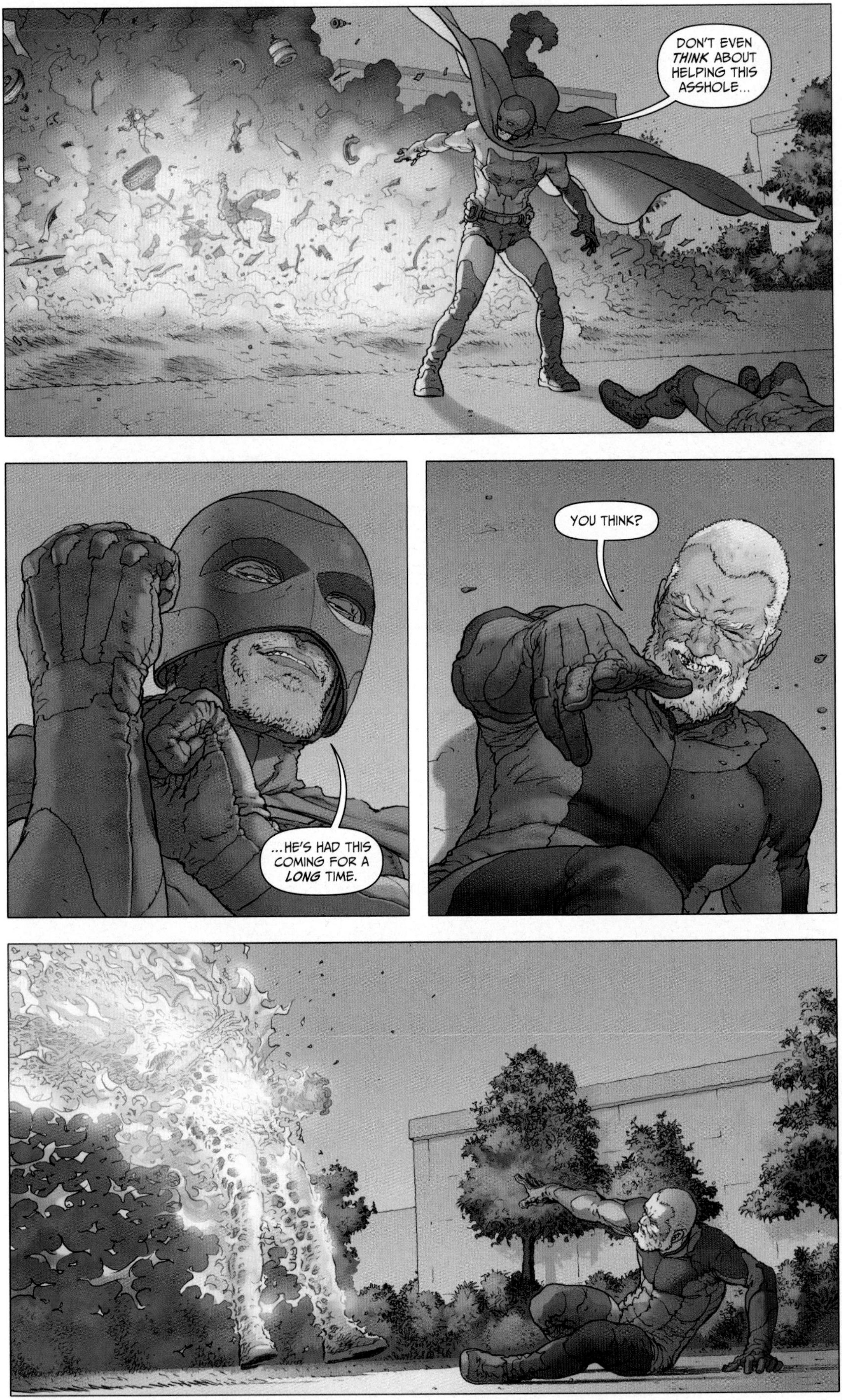
DON'T EVEN THINK ABOUT HELPING THIS ASSHOLE...
...HE'S HAD THIS COMING FOR A LONG TIME.
YOU THINK?

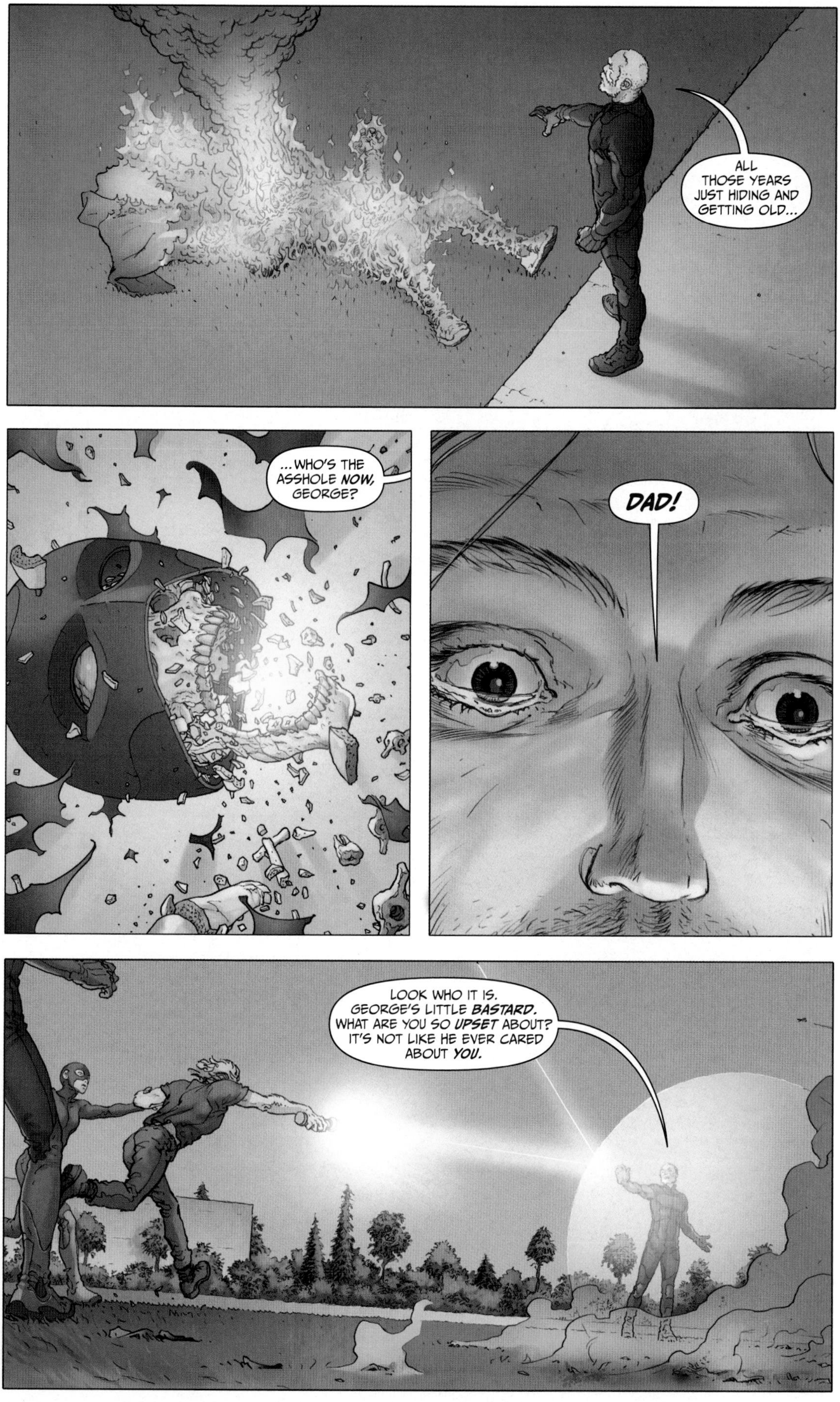
ALL THOSE YEARS JUST HIDING AND GETTING OLD...
...WHO'S THE ASSHOLE NOW, GEORGE?
DAD!
LOOK WHO IT IS. GEORGE'S LITTLE BASTARD. WHAT ARE YOU SO UPSET ABOUT? IT'S NOT LIKE HE EVER CARED ABOUT YOU.

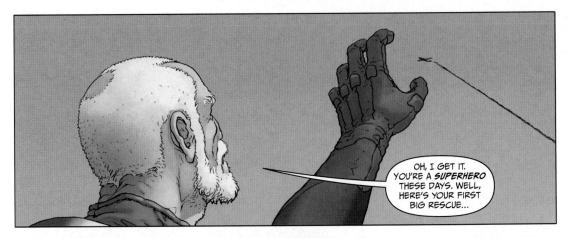

OH, I GET IT. YOU'RE A *SUPERHERO* THESE DAYS. WELL, HERE'S YOUR FIRST BIG RESCUE...

PLANE INTERIOR.

SAFETY.

SAFETY.

SAFETY.

SAFETY...

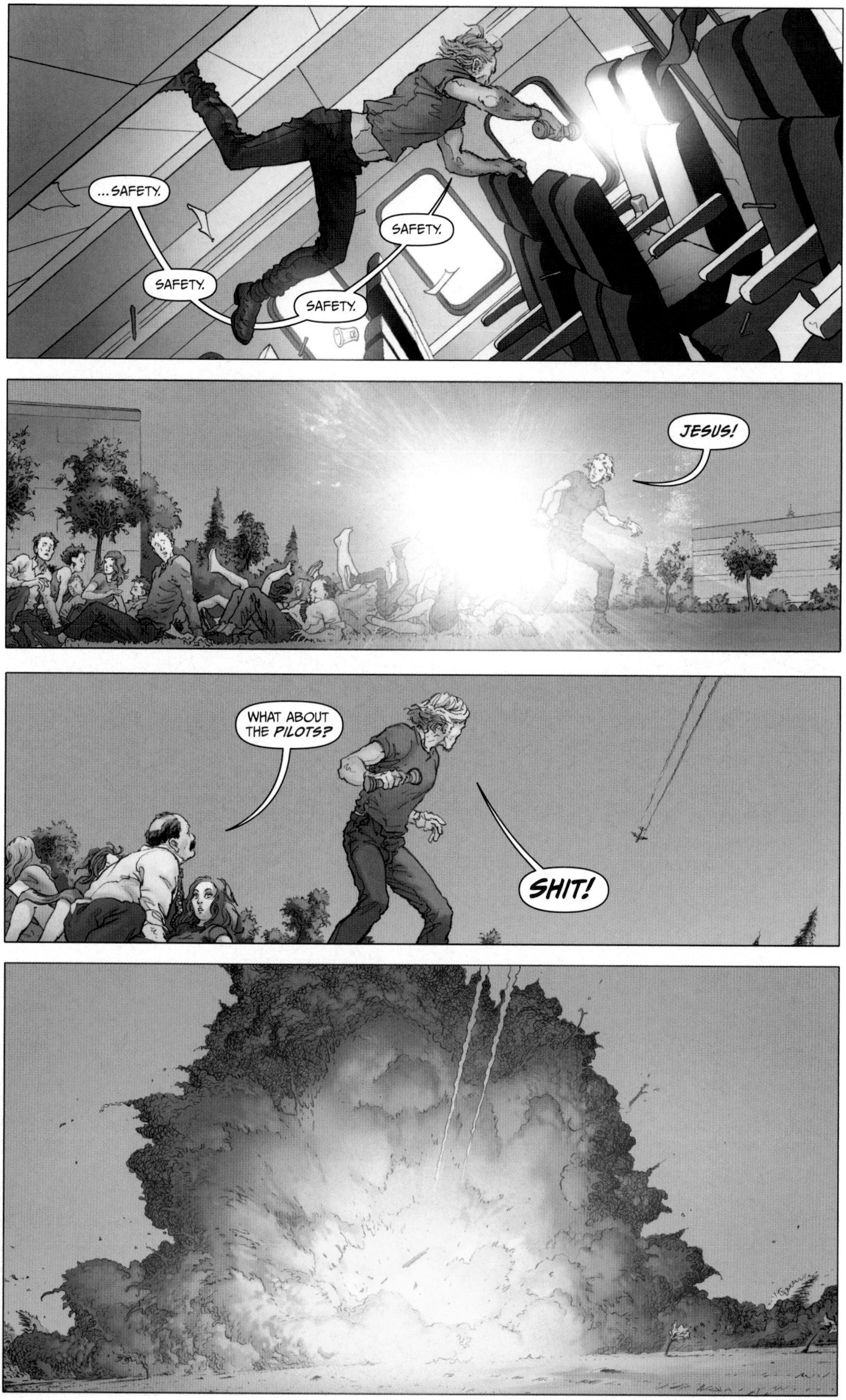
...SAFETY.
SAFETY.
SAFETY.
SAFETY.
JESUS!
WHAT ABOUT THE *PILOTS?*
SHIT!

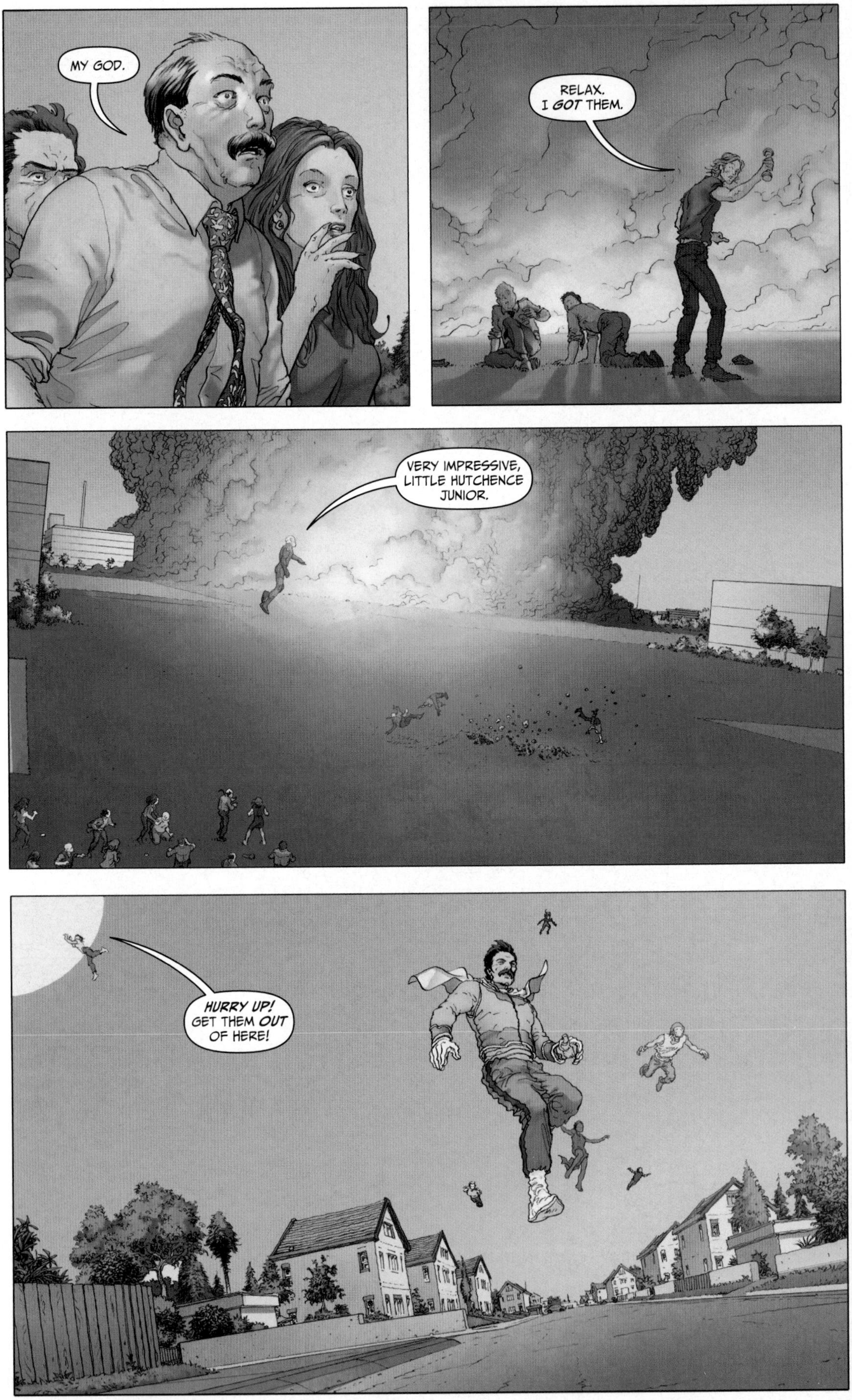
MY GOD.
RELAX. I GOT THEM.
VERY IMPRESSIVE, LITTLE HUTCHENCE JUNIOR.
HURRY UP! GET THEM OUT OF HERE!

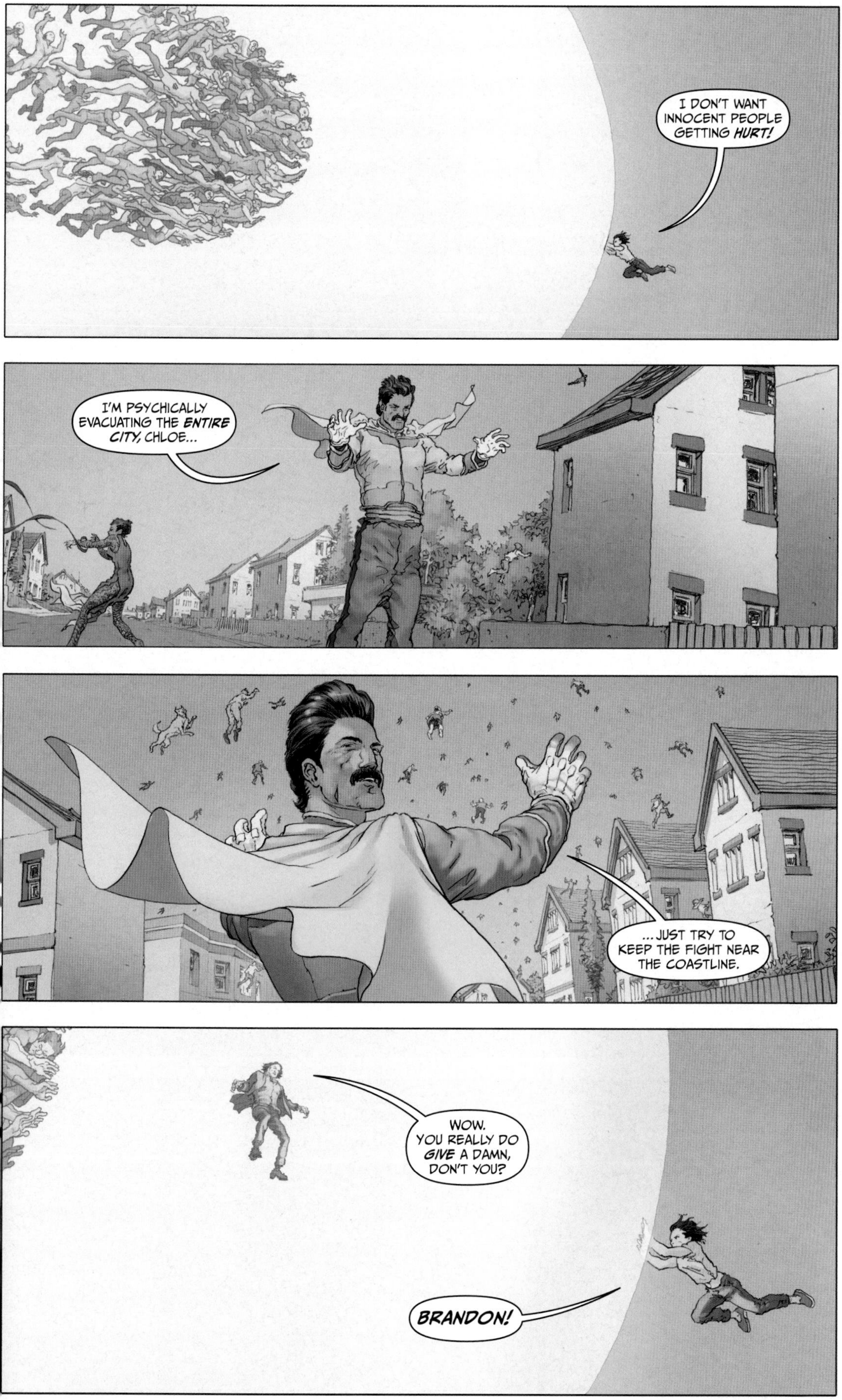

I DON'T WANT INNOCENT PEOPLE GETTING HURT!
I'M PSYCHICALLY EVACUATING THE ENTIRE CITY, CHLOE...
...JUST TRY TO KEEP THE FIGHT NEAR THE COASTLINE.
WOW. YOU REALLY DO GIVE A DAMN, DON'T YOU?
BRANDON!

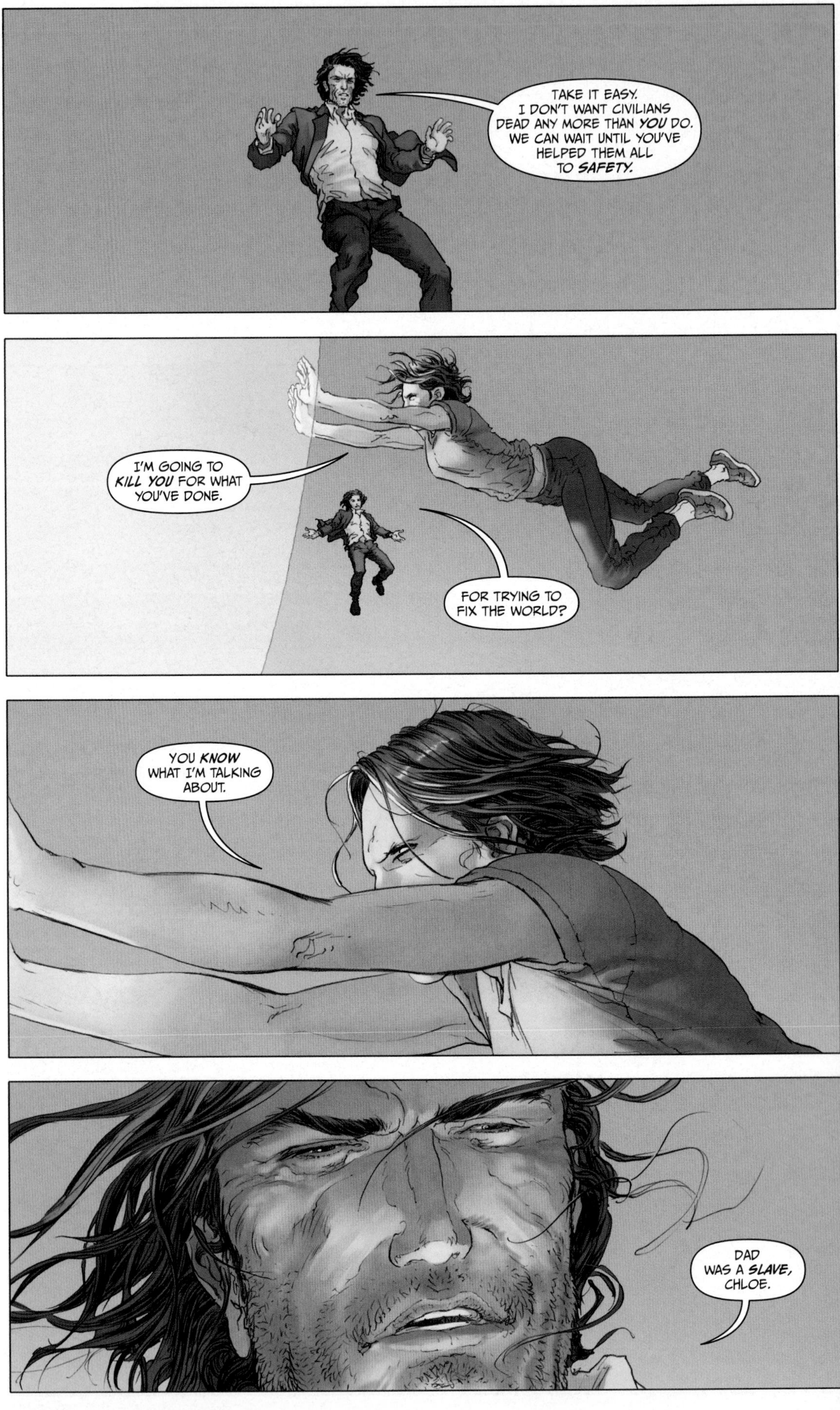
TAKE IT EASY. I DON'T WANT CIVILIANS DEAD ANY MORE THAN YOU DO. WE CAN WAIT UNTIL YOU'VE HELPED THEM ALL TO SAFETY.
I'M GOING TO KILL YOU FOR WHAT YOU'VE DONE.
FOR TRYING TO FIX THE WORLD?
YOU KNOW WHAT I'M TALKING ABOUT.
DAD WAS A SLAVE, CHLOE.

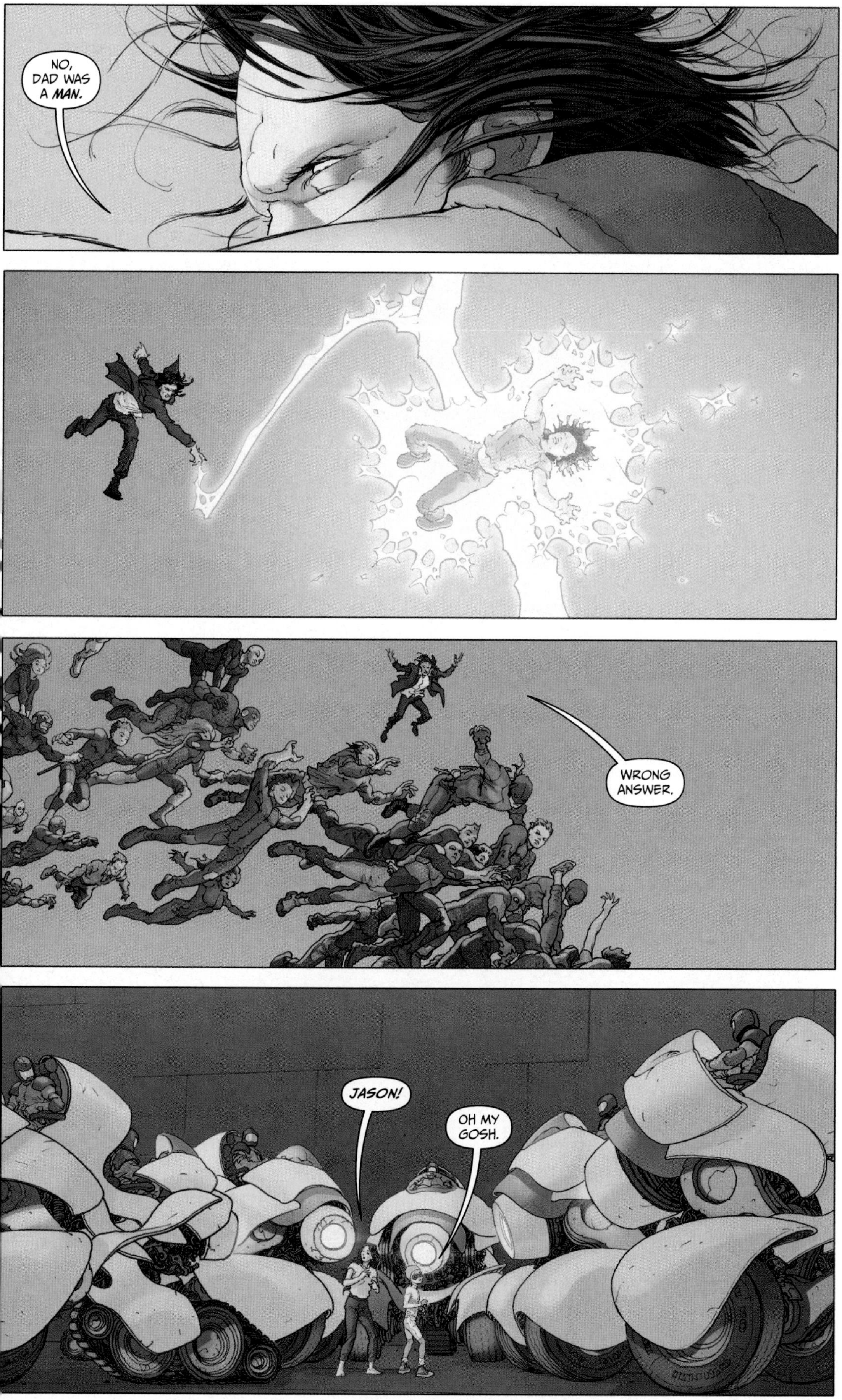
NO, DAD WAS A *MAN.*
WRONG ANSWER.
JASON!
OH MY GOSH.

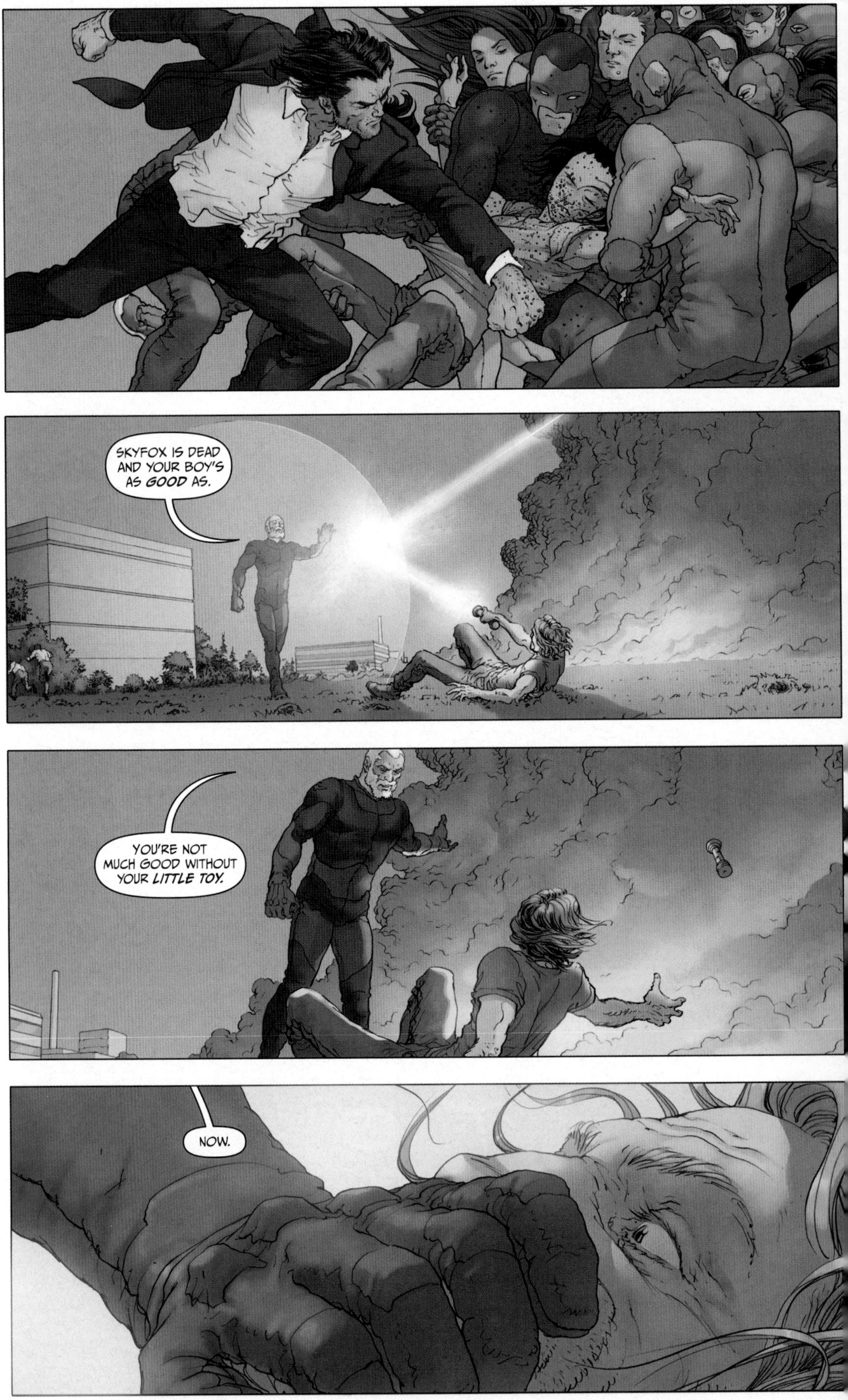
SKYFOX IS DEAD AND YOUR BOY'S AS *GOOD* AS.
YOU'RE NOT MUCH GOOD WITHOUT YOUR *LITTLE TOY.*
NOW.

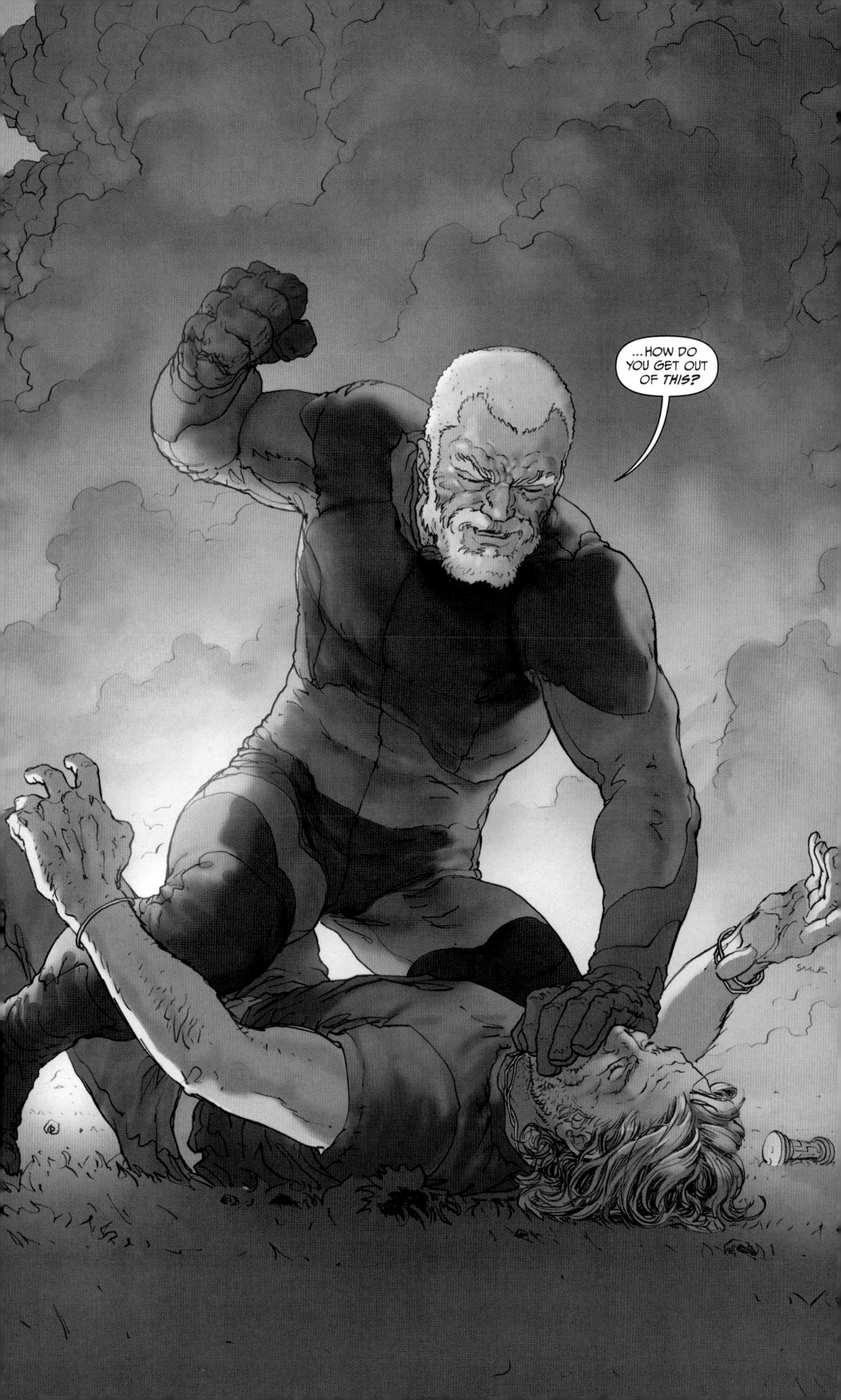
...HOW DO YOU GET OUT OF *THIS?*

CHAPTER 5

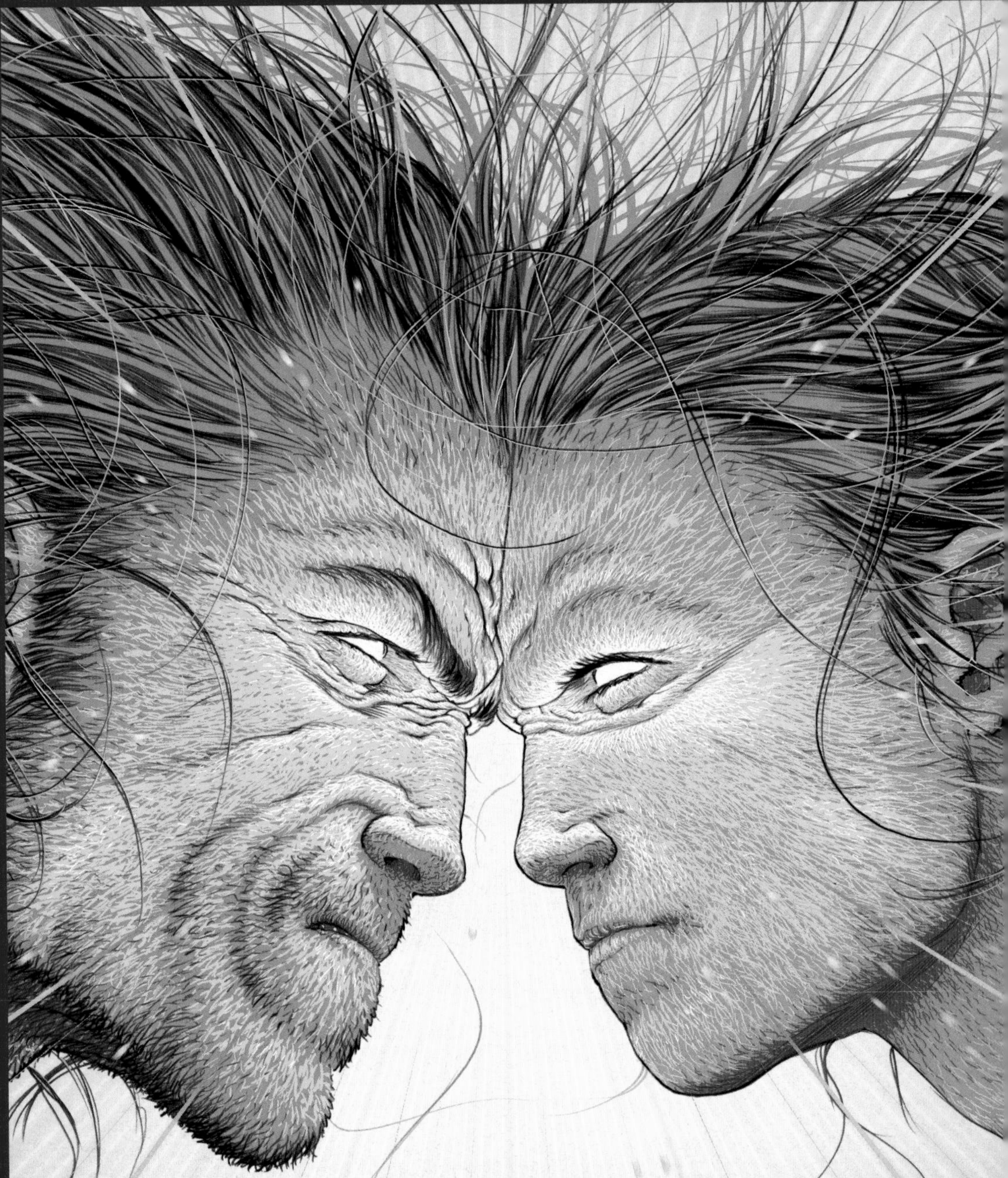

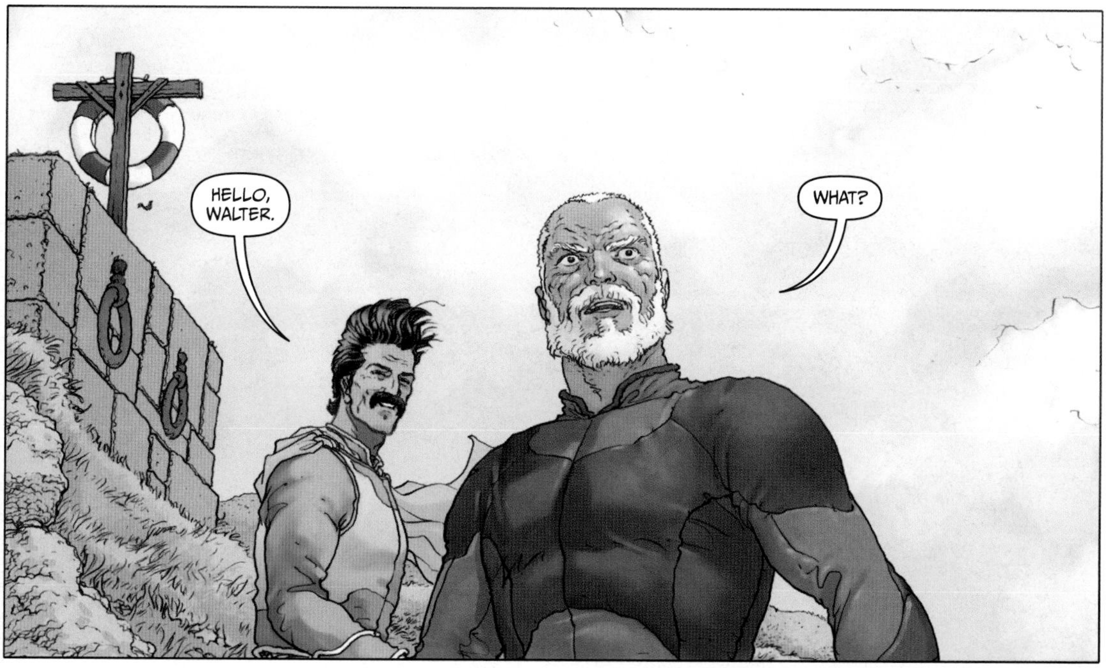
HELLO, WALTER.
WHAT?

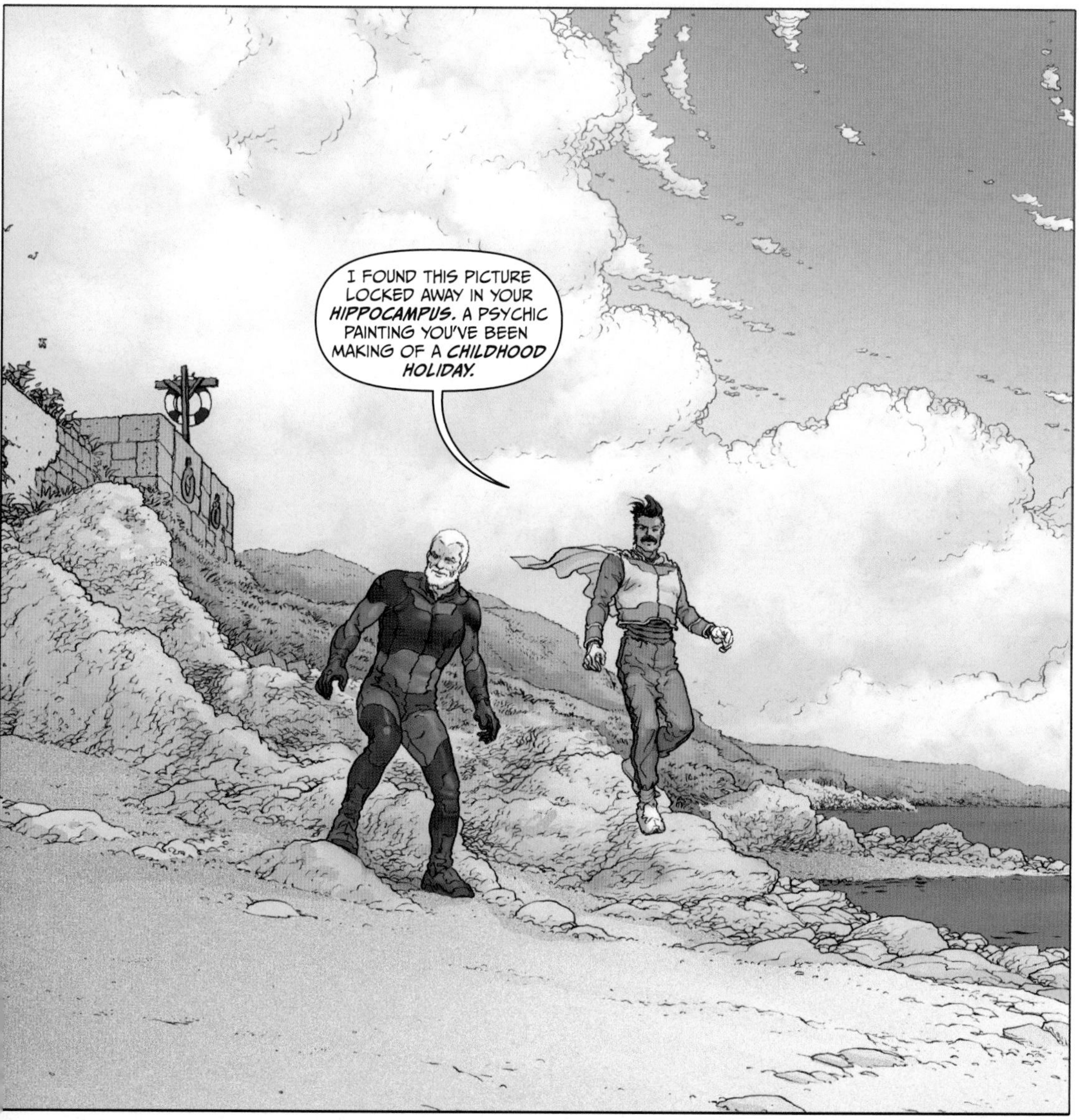
I FOUND THIS PICTURE LOCKED AWAY IN YOUR *HIPPOCAMPUS.* A PSYCHIC PAINTING YOU'VE BEEN MAKING OF A *CHILDHOOD HOLIDAY.*

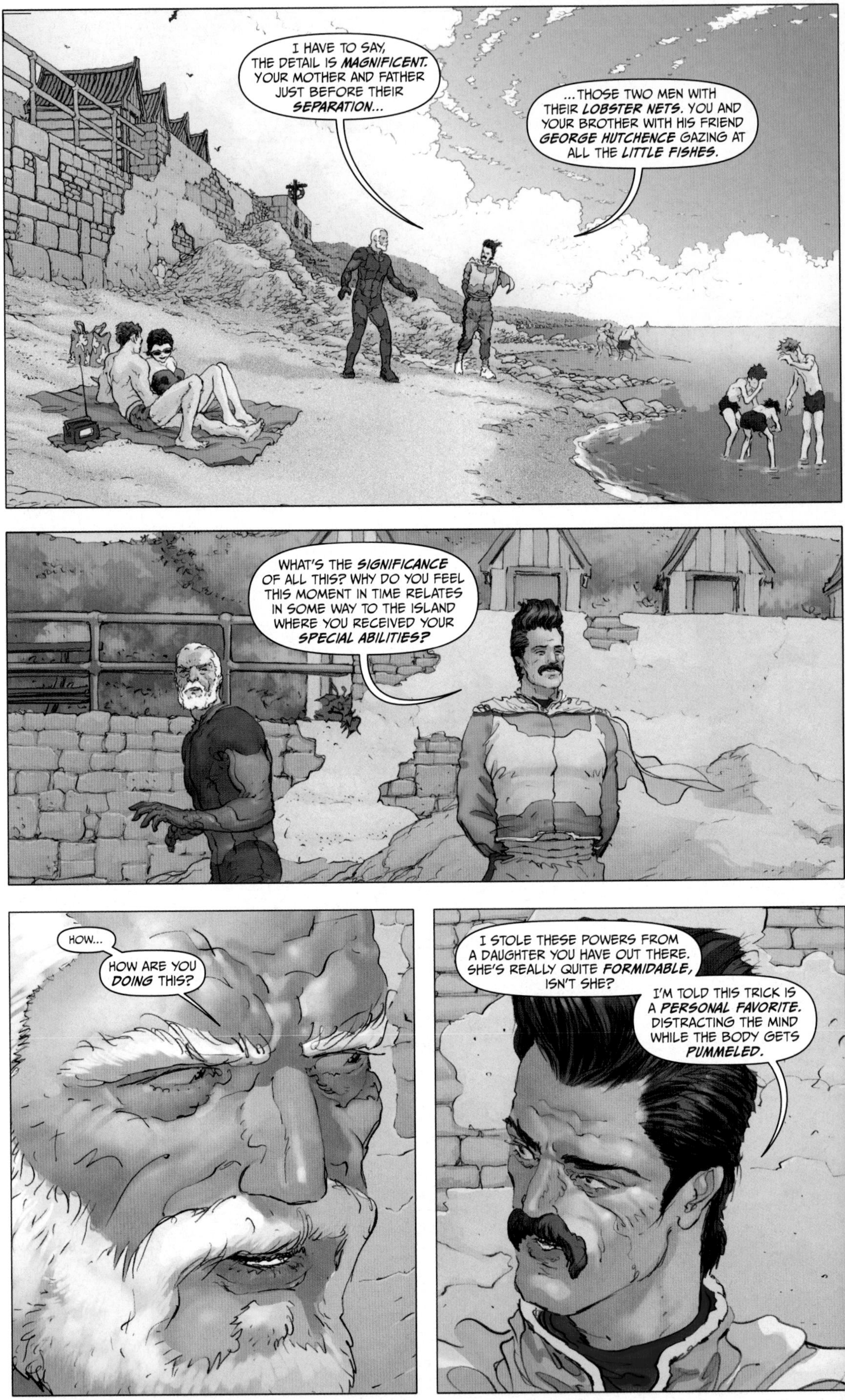
I HAVE TO SAY, THE DETAIL IS MAGNIFICENT. YOUR MOTHER AND FATHER JUST BEFORE THEIR SEPARATION...
...THOSE TWO MEN WITH THEIR LOBSTER NETS. YOU AND YOUR BROTHER WITH HIS FRIEND GEORGE HUTCHENCE GAZING AT ALL THE LITTLE FISHES.
WHAT'S THE SIGNIFICANCE OF ALL THIS? WHY DO YOU FEEL THIS MOMENT IN TIME RELATES IN SOME WAY TO THE ISLAND WHERE YOU RECEIVED YOUR SPECIAL ABILITIES?
HOW...
HOW ARE YOU DOING THIS?
I STOLE THESE POWERS FROM A DAUGHTER YOU HAVE OUT THERE. SHE'S REALLY QUITE FORMIDABLE, ISN'T SHE?
I'M TOLD THIS TRICK IS A PERSONAL FAVORITE. DISTRACTING THE MIND WHILE THE BODY GETS PUMMELED.

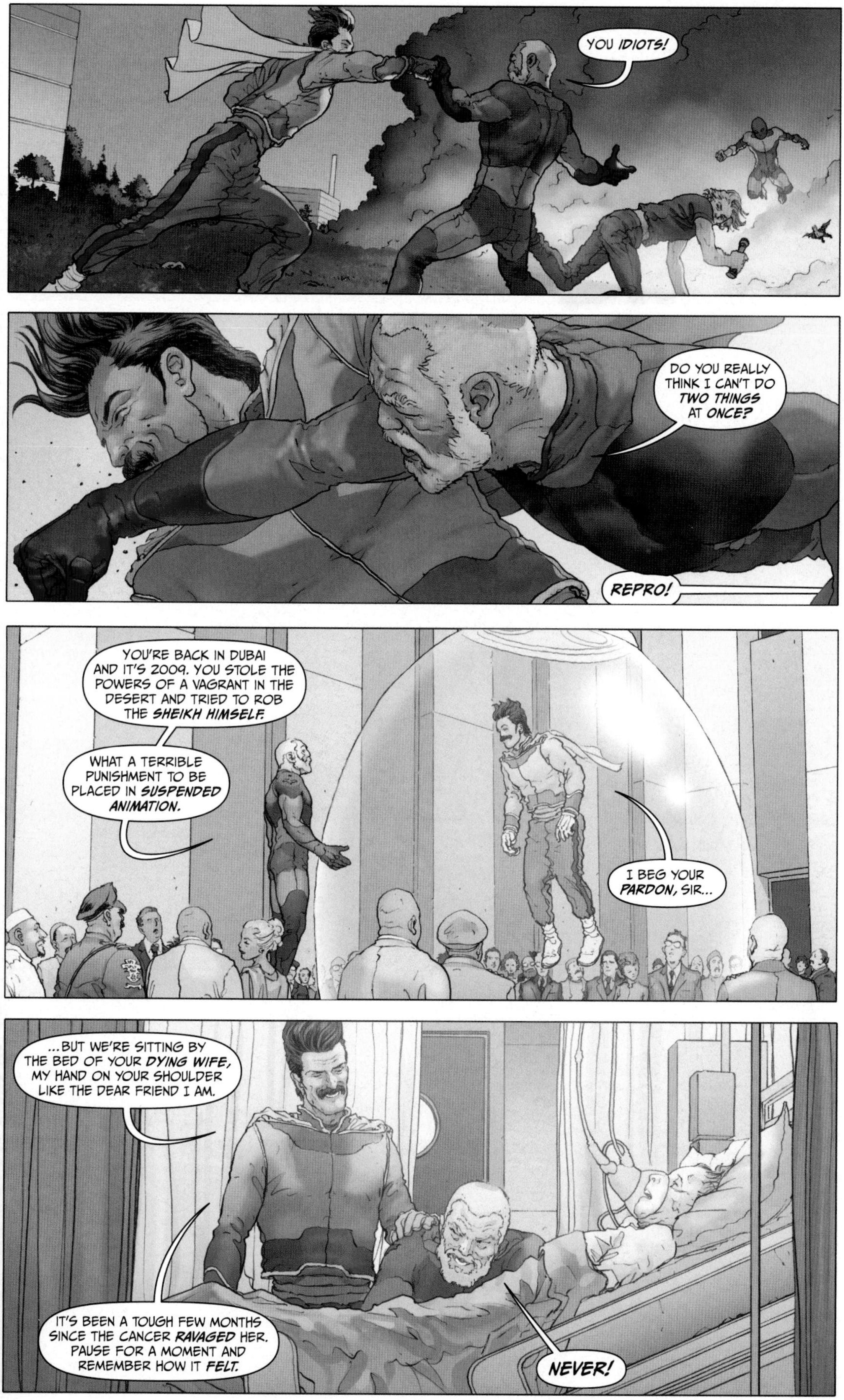

YOU *IDIOTS!*
DO YOU REALLY THINK I CAN'T DO *TWO THINGS* AT *ONCE?*
REPRO!
YOU'RE BACK IN DUBAI AND IT'S 2009. YOU STOLE THE POWERS OF A VAGRANT IN THE DESERT AND TRIED TO ROB THE *SHEIKH HIMSELF.*
WHAT A TERRIBLE PUNISHMENT TO BE PLACED IN *SUSPENDED ANIMATION.*
I BEG YOUR *PARDON,* SIR...
...BUT WE'RE SITTING BY THE BED OF YOUR *DYING WIFE,* MY HAND ON YOUR SHOULDER LIKE THE DEAR FRIEND I AM.
IT'S BEEN A TOUGH FEW MONTHS SINCE THE CANCER *RAVAGED* HER. PAUSE FOR A MOMENT AND REMEMBER HOW IT *FELT.*
NEVER!

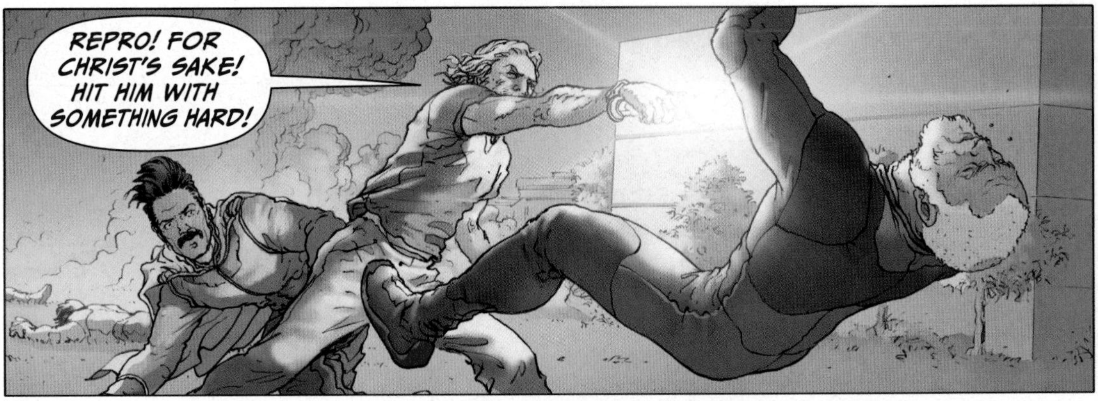
REPRO! FOR CHRIST'S SAKE! HIT HIM WITH SOMETHING HARD!

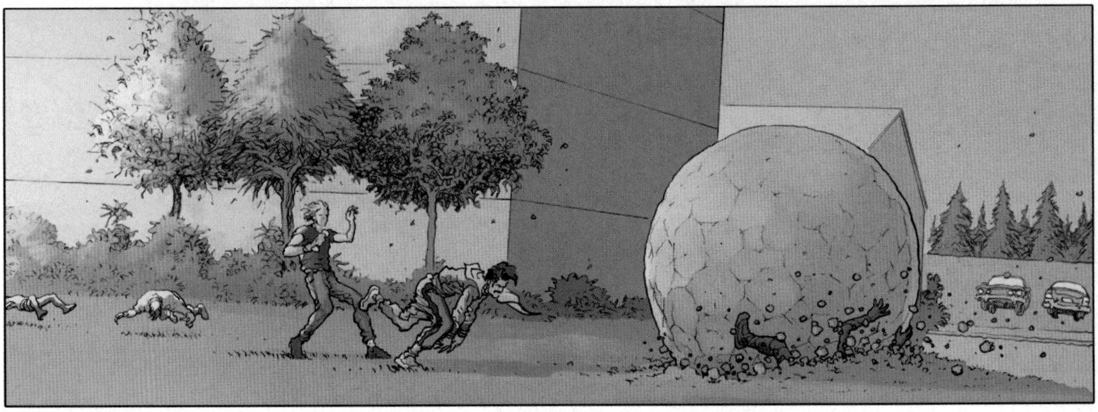

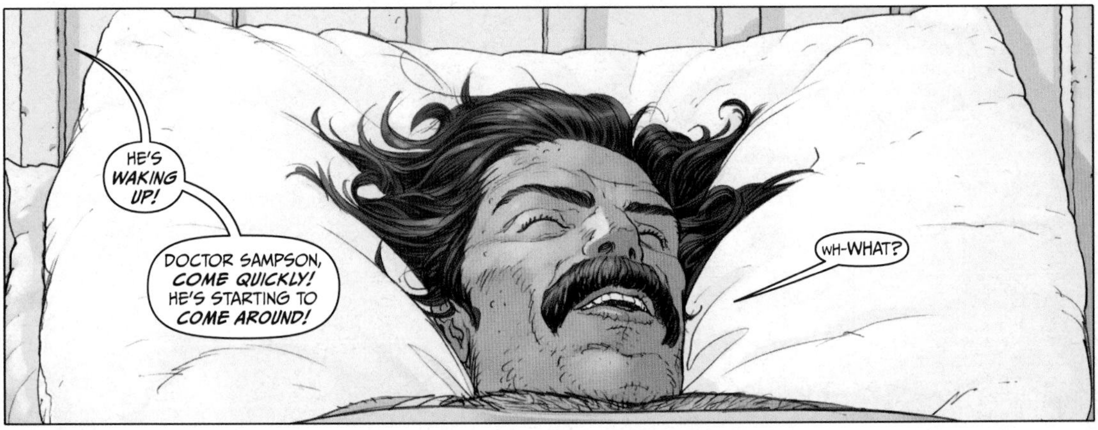
HE'S WAKING UP!
DOCTOR SAMPSON, COME QUICKLY! HE'S STARTING TO COME AROUND!
WH-WHAT?

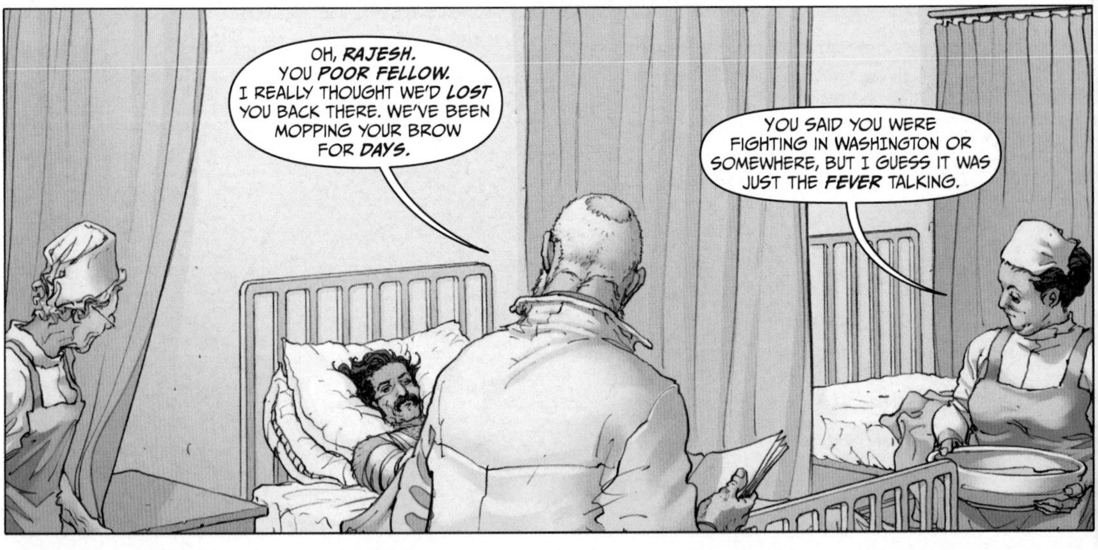
OH, RAJESH. YOU POOR FELLOW. I REALLY THOUGHT WE'D LOST YOU BACK THERE. WE'VE BEEN MOPPING YOUR BROW FOR DAYS.
YOU SAID YOU WERE FIGHTING IN WASHINGTON OR SOMEWHERE, BUT I GUESS IT WAS JUST THE FEVER TALKING.

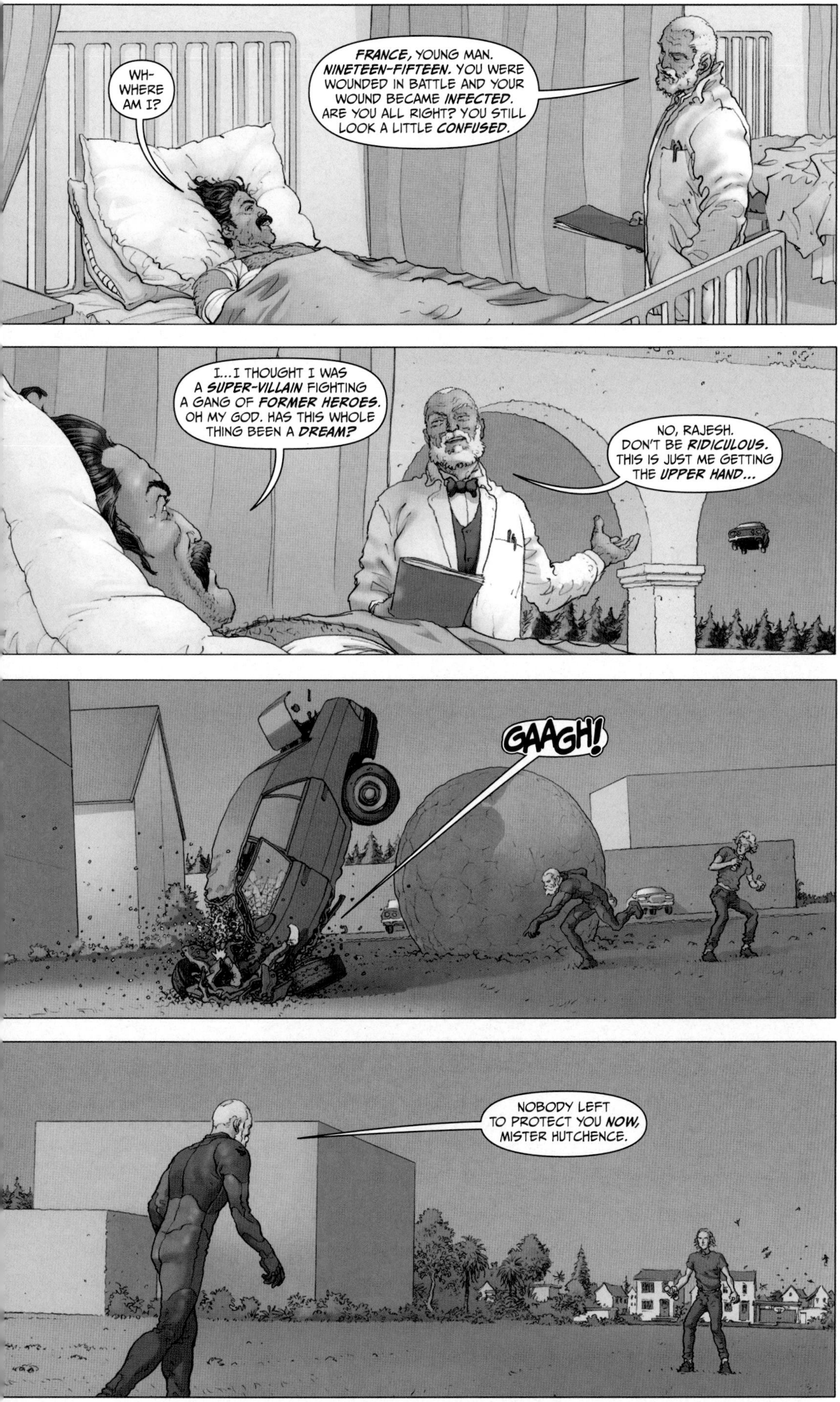
WH-WHERE AM I?
FRANCE, YOUNG MAN. NINETEEN-FIFTEEN. YOU WERE WOUNDED IN BATTLE AND YOUR WOUND BECAME INFECTED. ARE YOU ALL RIGHT? YOU STILL LOOK A LITTLE CONFUSED.
I...I THOUGHT I WAS A SUPER-VILLAIN FIGHTING A GANG OF FORMER HEROES. OH MY GOD. HAS THIS WHOLE THING BEEN A DREAM?
NO, RAJESH. DON'T BE RIDICULOUS. THIS IS JUST ME GETTING THE UPPER HAND...
GAAGH!
NOBODY LEFT TO PROTECT YOU NOW, MISTER HUTCHENCE.

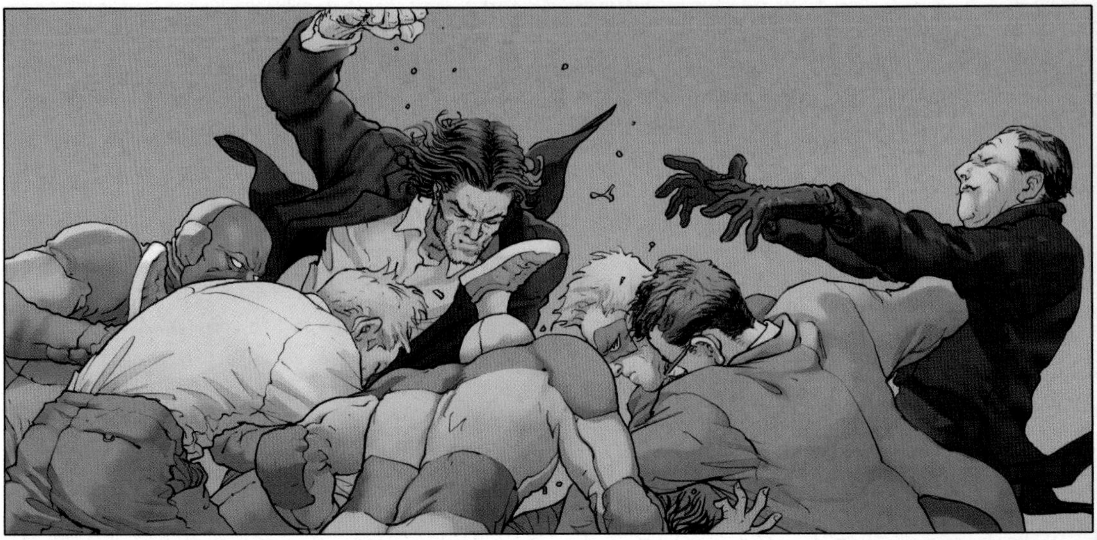
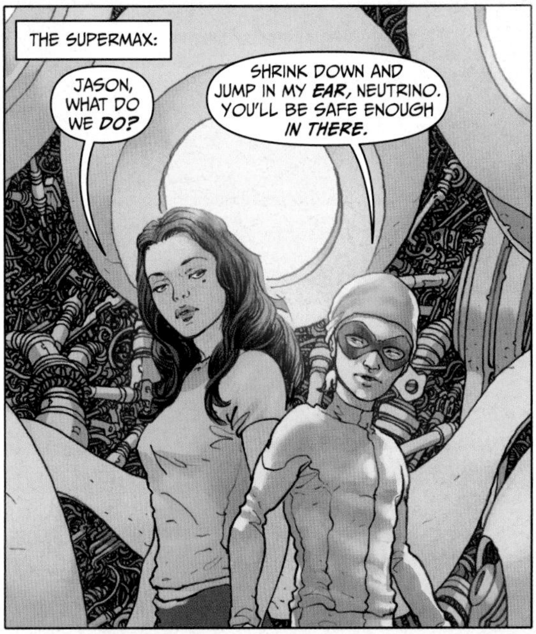
THE SUPERMAX:
JASON, WHAT DO WE DO?
SHRINK DOWN AND JUMP IN MY EAR, NEUTRINO. YOU'LL BE SAFE ENOUGH IN THERE.
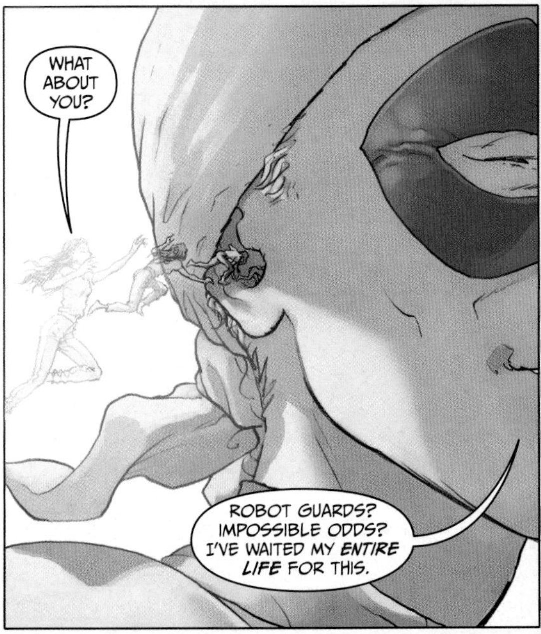
WHAT ABOUT YOU?
ROBOT GUARDS? IMPOSSIBLE ODDS? I'VE WAITED MY ENTIRE LIFE FOR THIS.
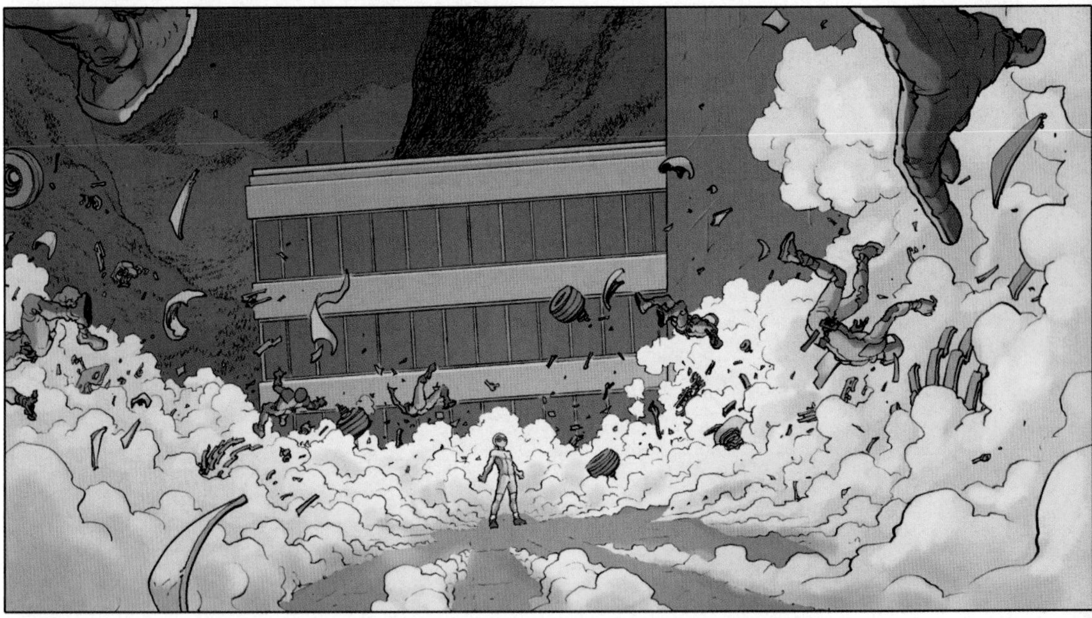

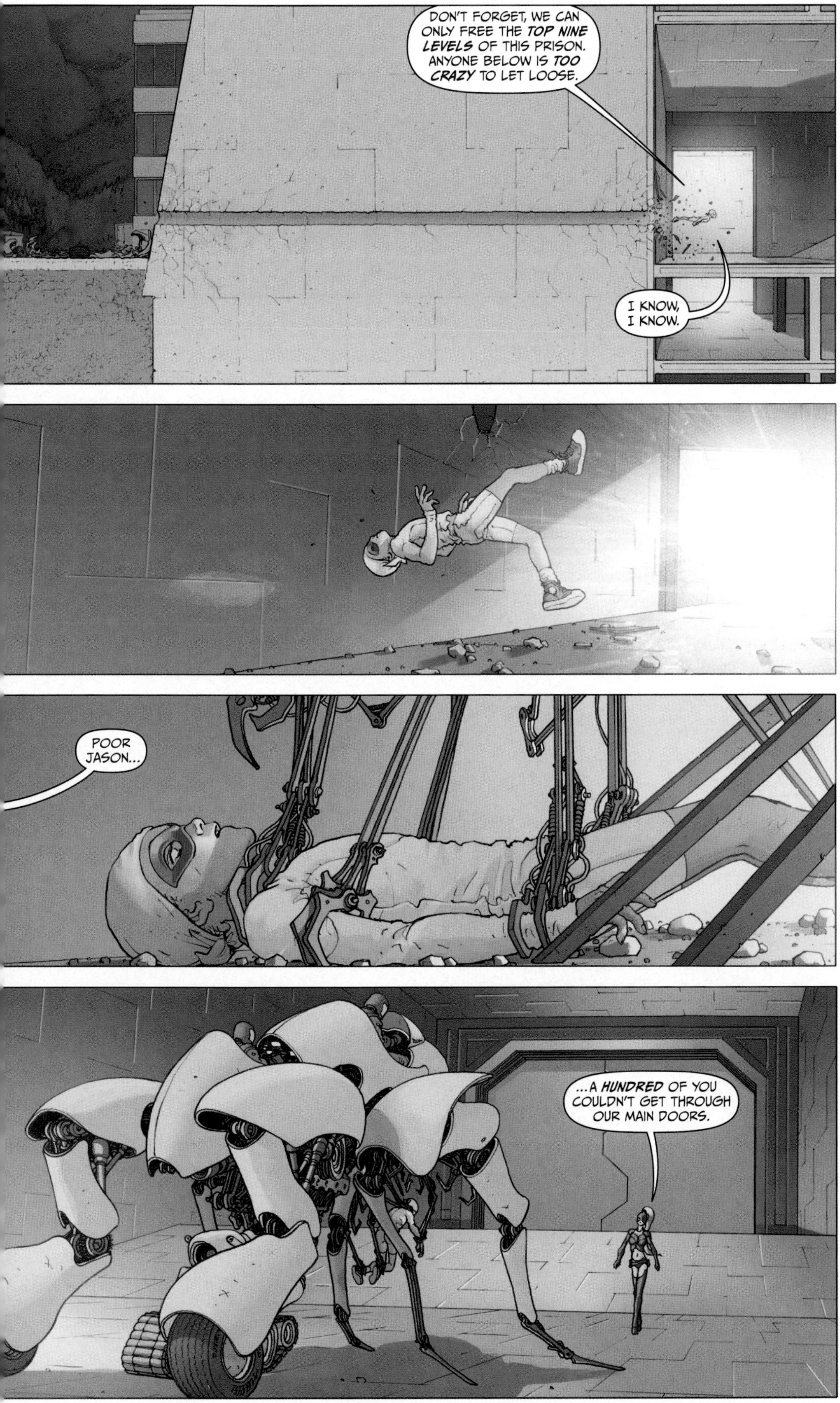
DON'T FORGET, WE CAN ONLY FREE THE TOP NINE LEVELS OF THIS PRISON. ANYONE BELOW IS TOO CRAZY TO LET LOOSE.
I KNOW, I KNOW.
POOR JASON...
...A HUNDRED OF YOU COULDN'T GET THROUGH OUR MAIN DOORS.

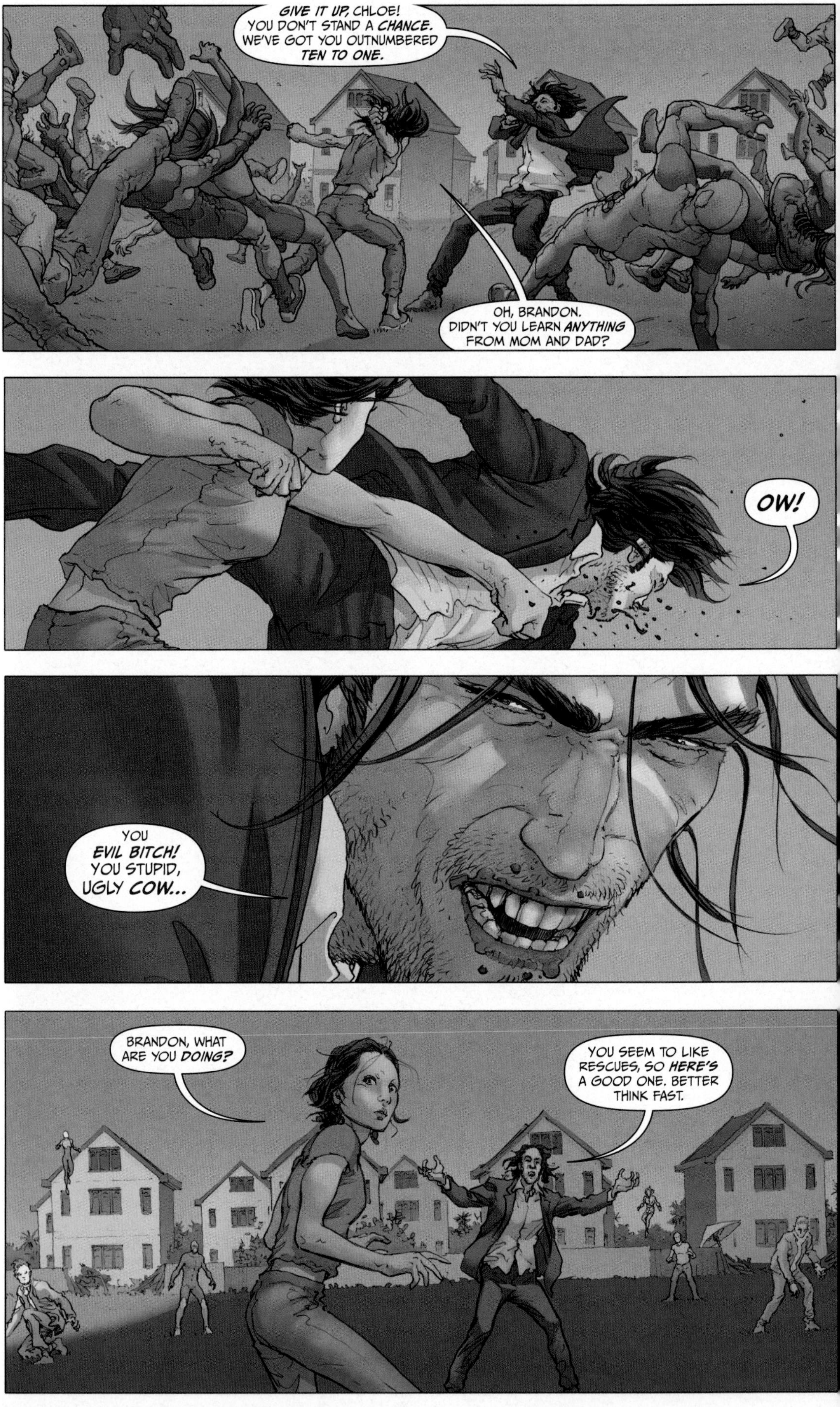
GIVE IT UP, CHLOE! YOU DON'T STAND A CHANCE. WE'VE GOT YOU OUTNUMBERED TEN TO ONE.
OH, BRANDON. DIDN'T YOU LEARN ANYTHING FROM MOM AND DAD?
OW!
YOU EVIL BITCH! YOU STUPID, UGLY COW...
BRANDON, WHAT ARE YOU DOING?
YOU SEEM TO LIKE RESCUES, SO HERE'S A GOOD ONE. BETTER THINK FAST.

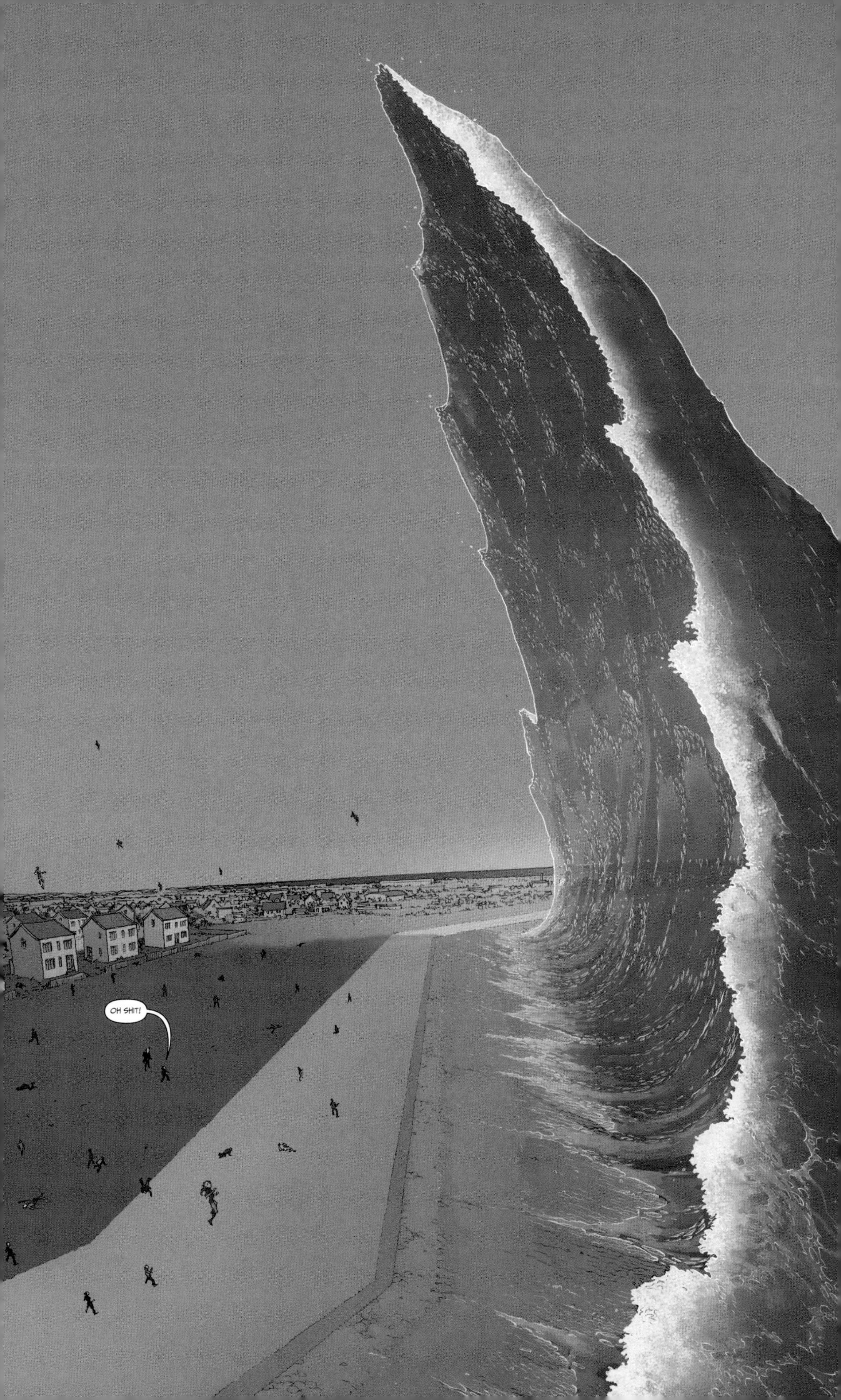
OH SHIT!

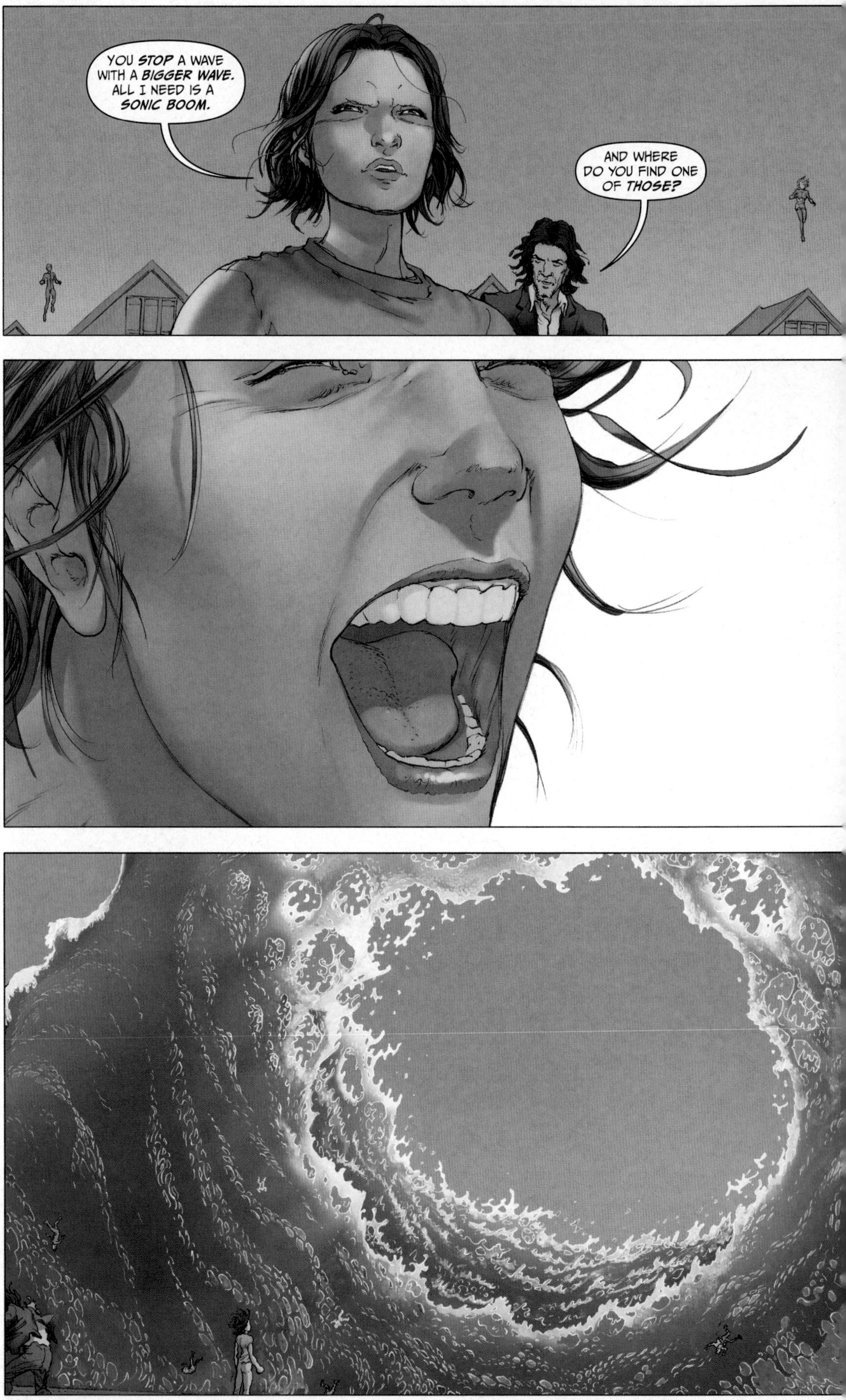
YOU STOP A WAVE WITH A BIGGER WAVE. ALL I NEED IS A SONIC BOOM.
AND WHERE DO YOU FIND ONE OF THOSE?

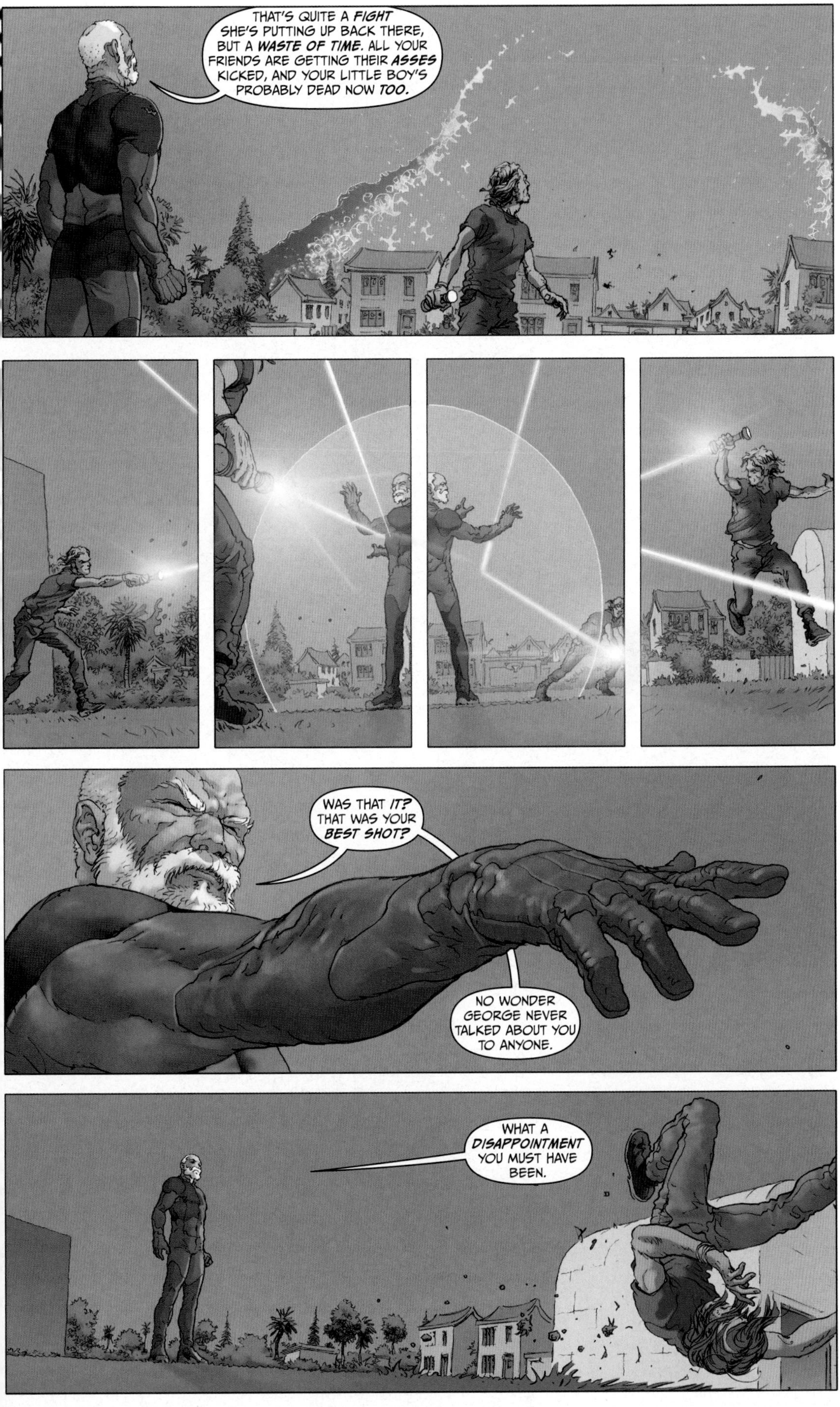
THAT'S QUITE A FIGHT SHE'S PUTTING UP BACK THERE, BUT A WASTE OF TIME. ALL YOUR FRIENDS ARE GETTING THEIR ASSES KICKED, AND YOUR LITTLE BOY'S PROBABLY DEAD NOW TOO.
WAS THAT IT? THAT WAS YOUR BEST SHOT?
NO WONDER GEORGE NEVER TALKED ABOUT YOU TO ANYONE.
WHAT A DISAPPOINTMENT YOU MUST HAVE BEEN.

YOU LOOK SO LIKE HIM IN HIS PRIME. THIS IS LIKE KILLING HIM TWICE.
I WISH HE COULD HAVE SEEN WHAT'S COMING NEXT. PRESIDENT WALTER SAMPSON.
COME ON, LITTLE BASTARD
I'LL EVEN GIVE YOU A FREE TRY.
WHICH ONE'S THE REAL ME?
GIVE IT YOUR BEST SHOT!
REAL WALTER'S HEAD.

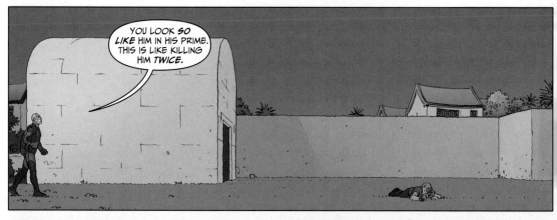

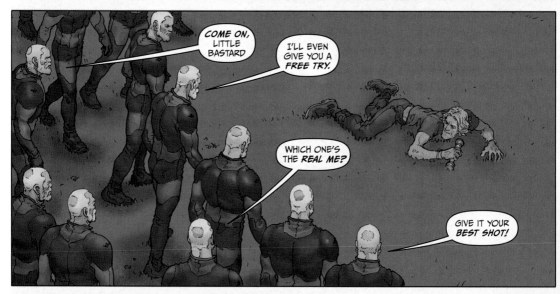

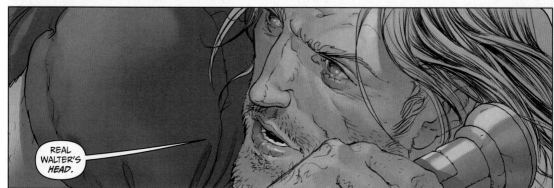

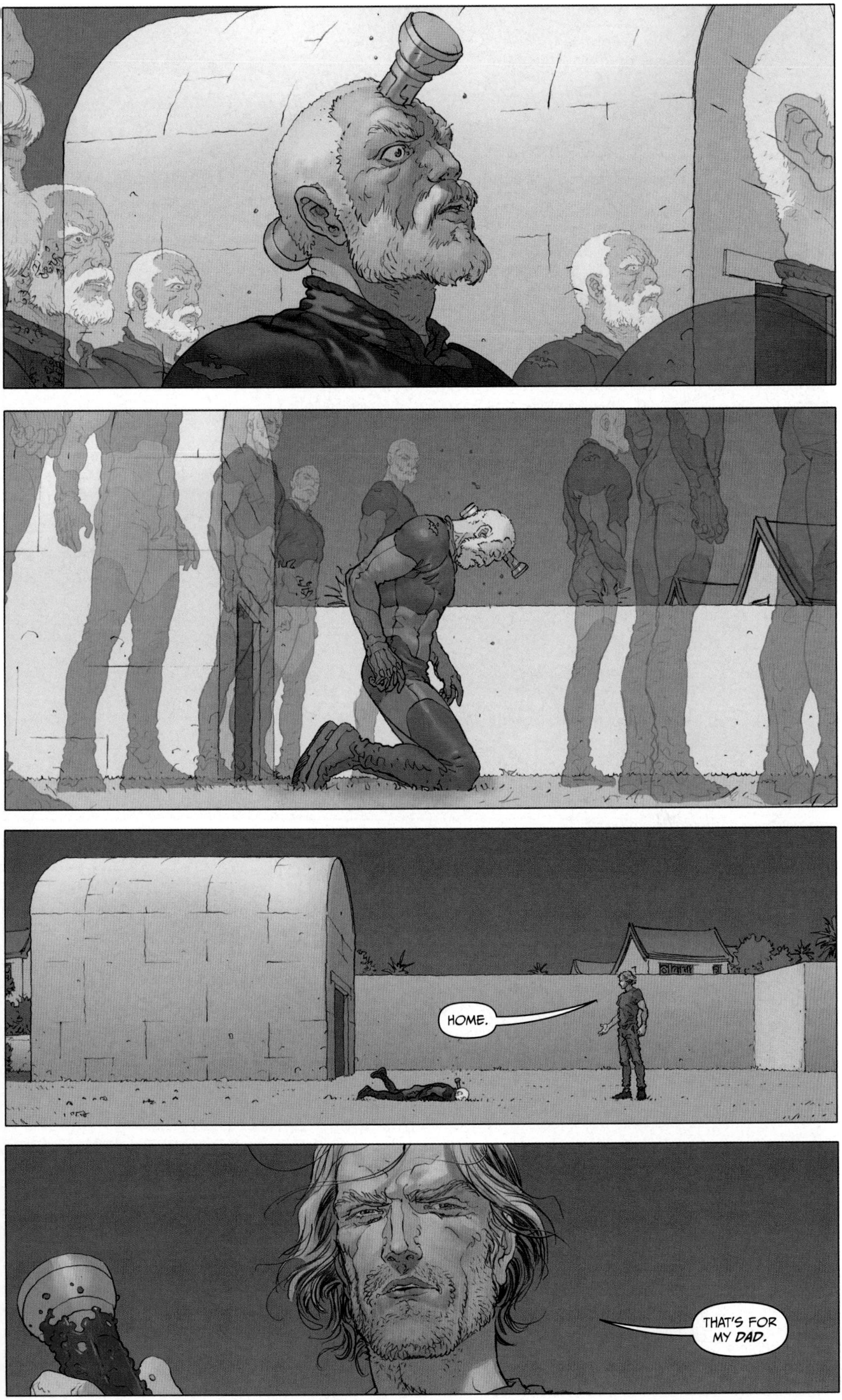
HOME.
THAT'S FOR MY DAD.

YOU'RE TOO LATE, MA'AM. NEUTRINO'S ALREADY IN THERE, FREEING ALL THE PRISONERS WE'RE GOING TO NEED.
BULLSHIT!
IF SHE HIT THE SENSORS, SHE'D HAVE TRIPPED THE ALARMS. IF SHE WENT MICROSCOPIC, SHE'D TAKE A MILLION YEARS TO GET THERE!
GIVE THEM A CALL IF YOU DON'T BELIEVE ME.
ALPHA-TEAM, THIS IS RUBY RED. WHAT'S THE SITUATION IN MAXIMUM SECURITY?

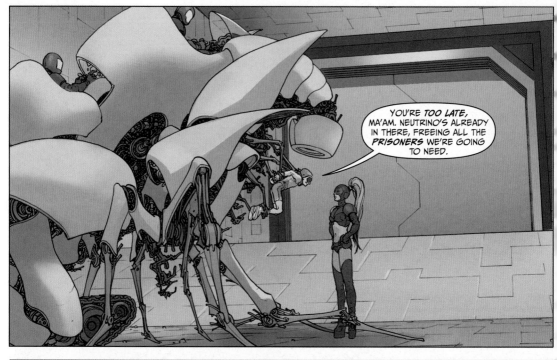

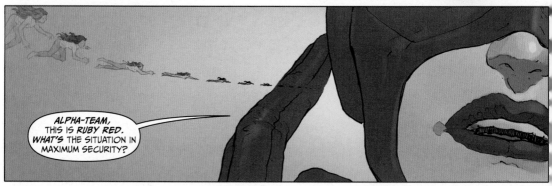

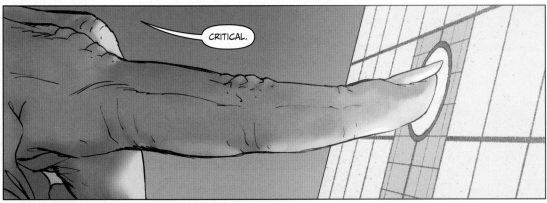

CRITICAL.

THANKS FOR THE RIDE ON THAT *SIGNAL*, BY THE WAY.

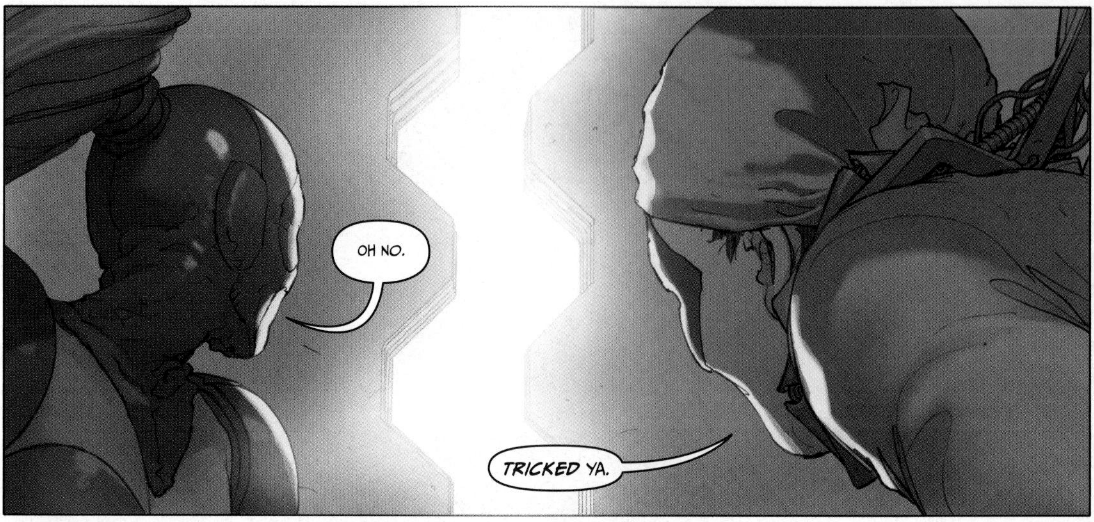
OH NO.
TRICKED YA.

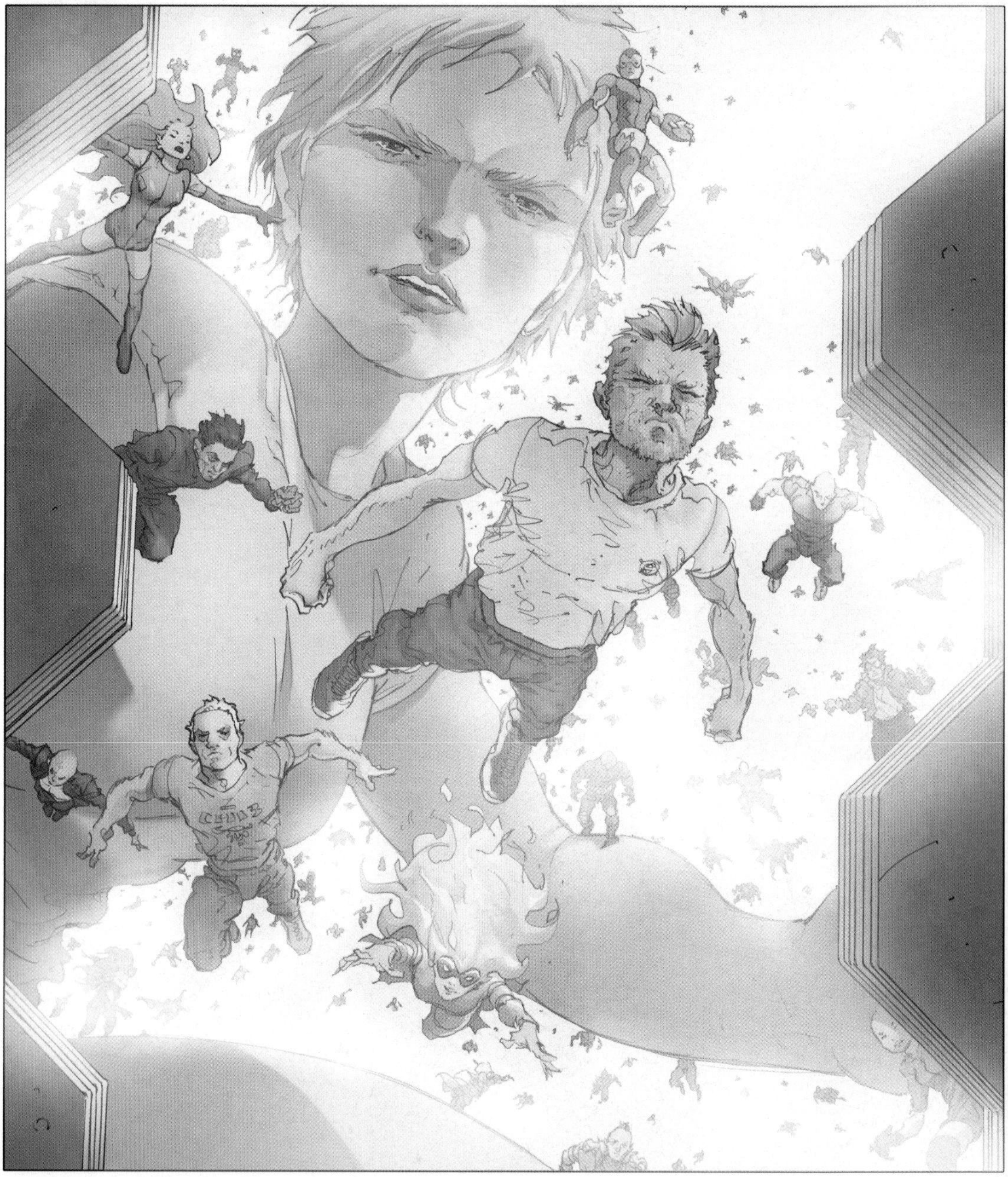

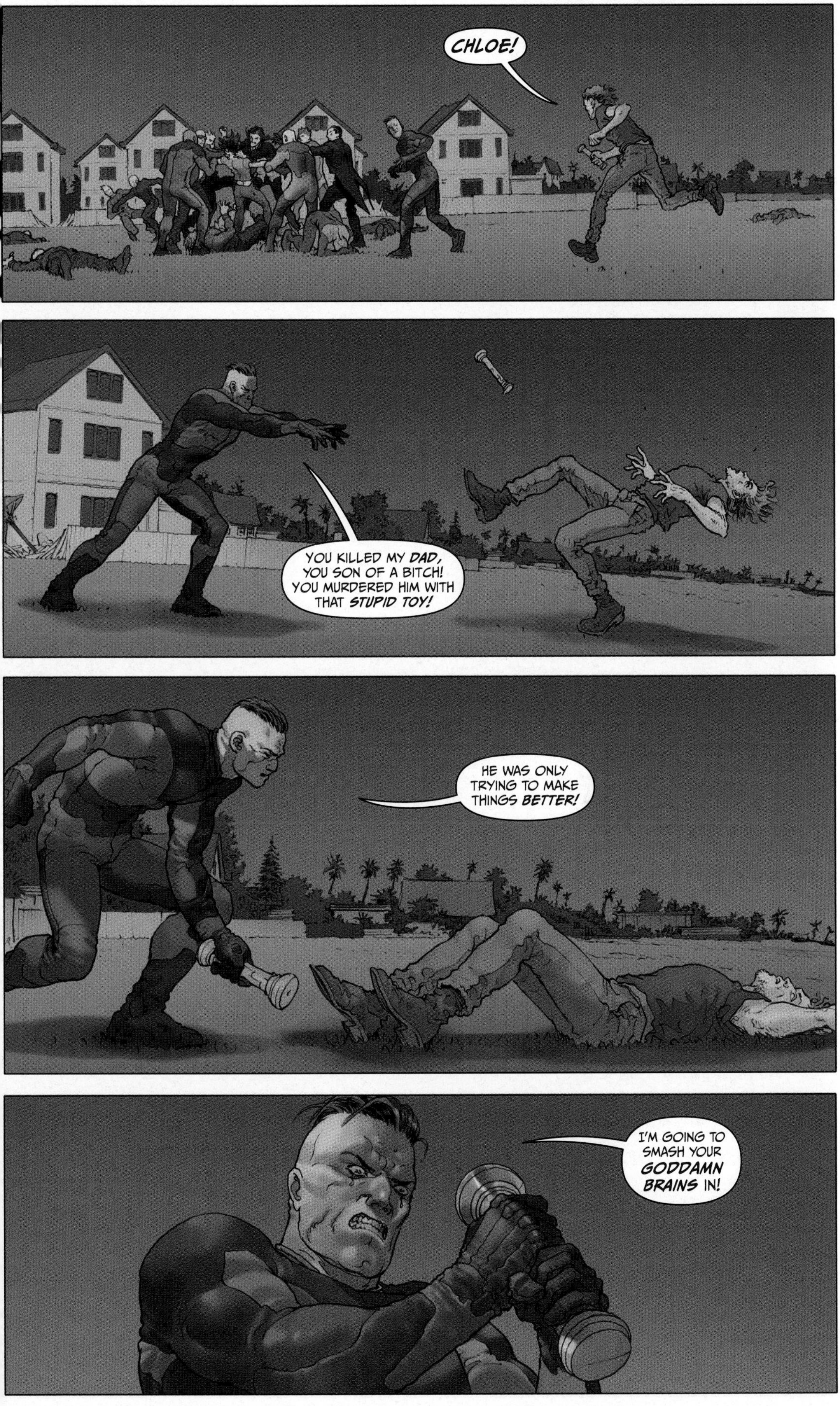
CHLOE!
YOU KILLED MY DAD, YOU SON OF A BITCH! YOU MURDERED HIM WITH THAT STUPID TOY!
HE WAS ONLY TRYING TO MAKE THINGS BETTER!
I'M GOING TO SMASH YOUR GODDAMN BRAINS IN!

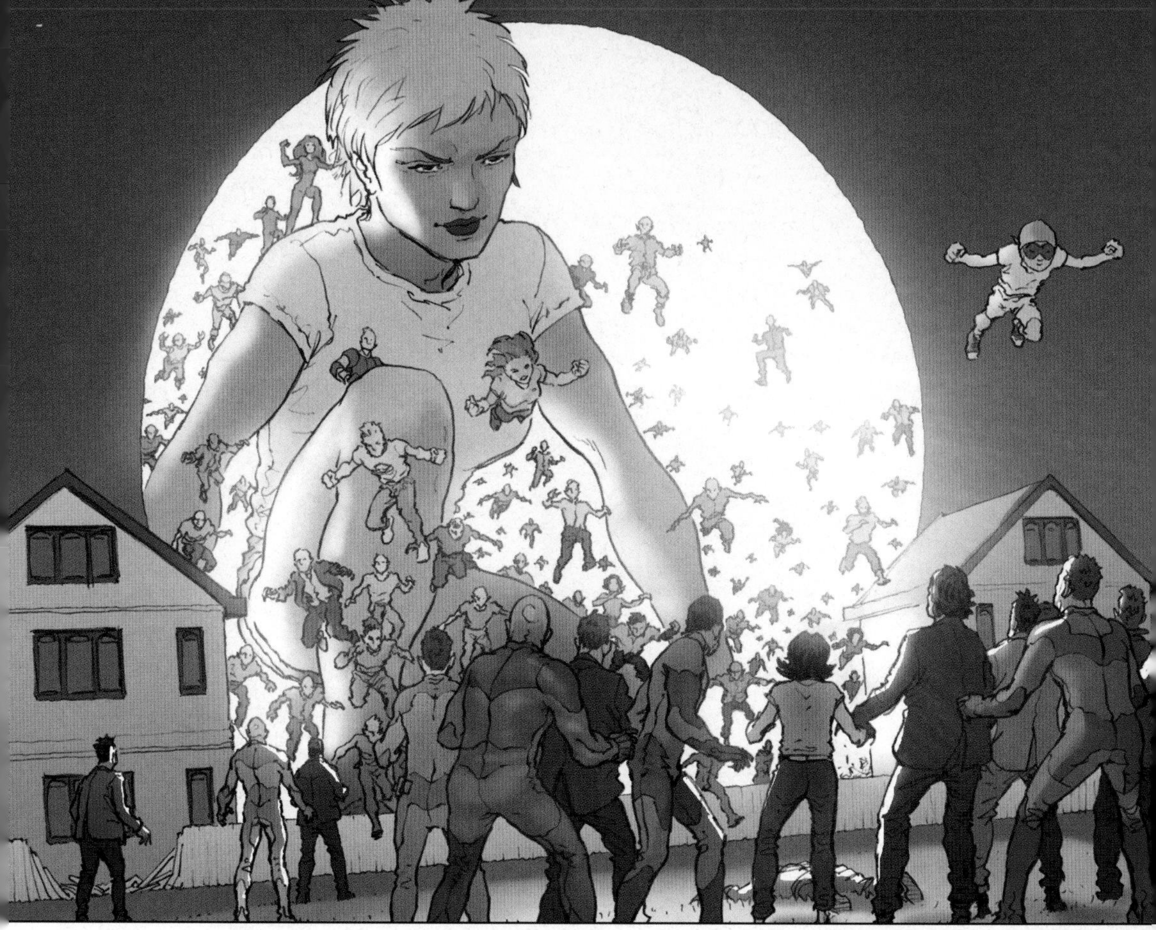
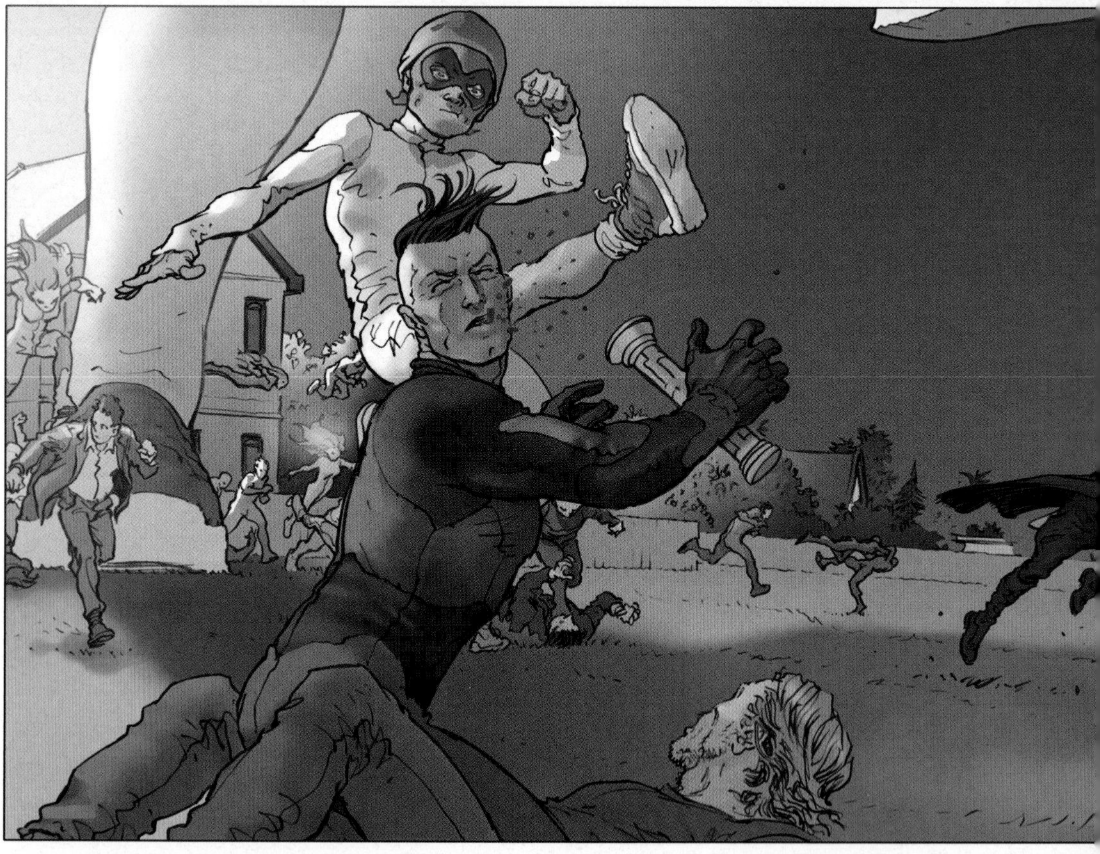

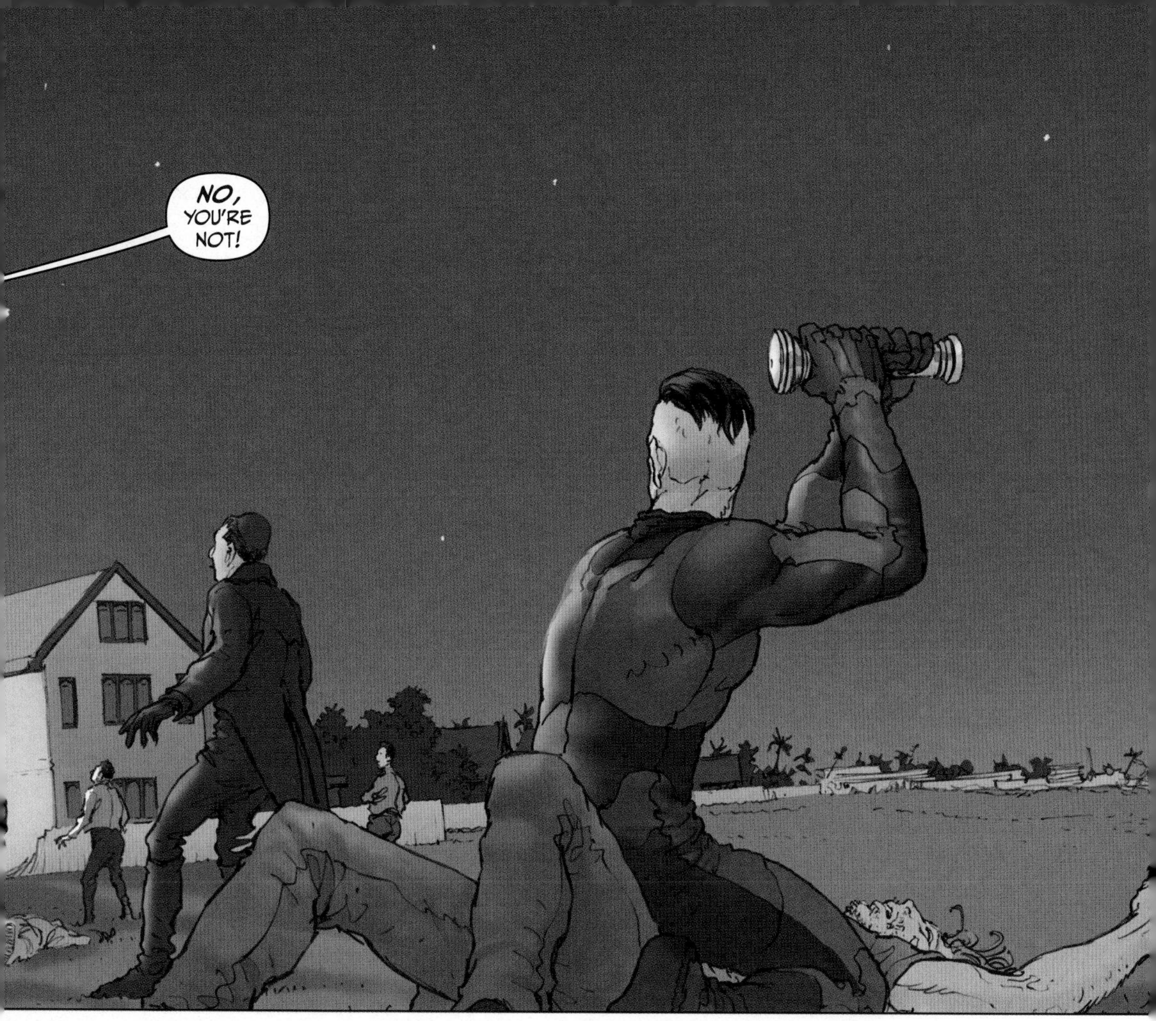
NO, YOU'RE NOT!

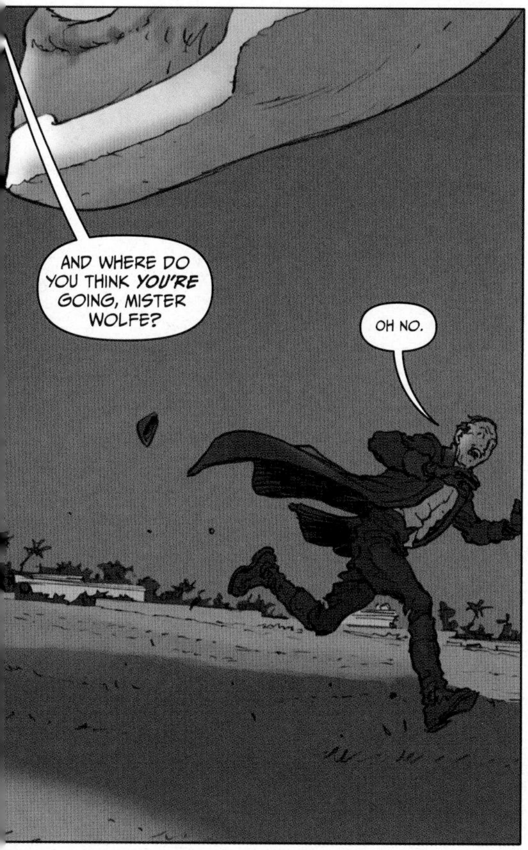
AND WHERE DO YOU THINK YOU'RE GOING, MISTER WOLFE?
OH NO.

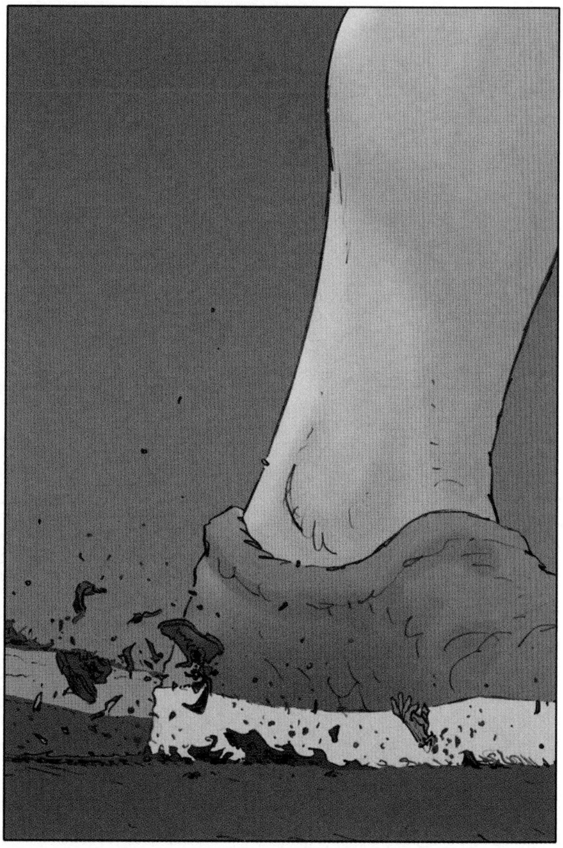

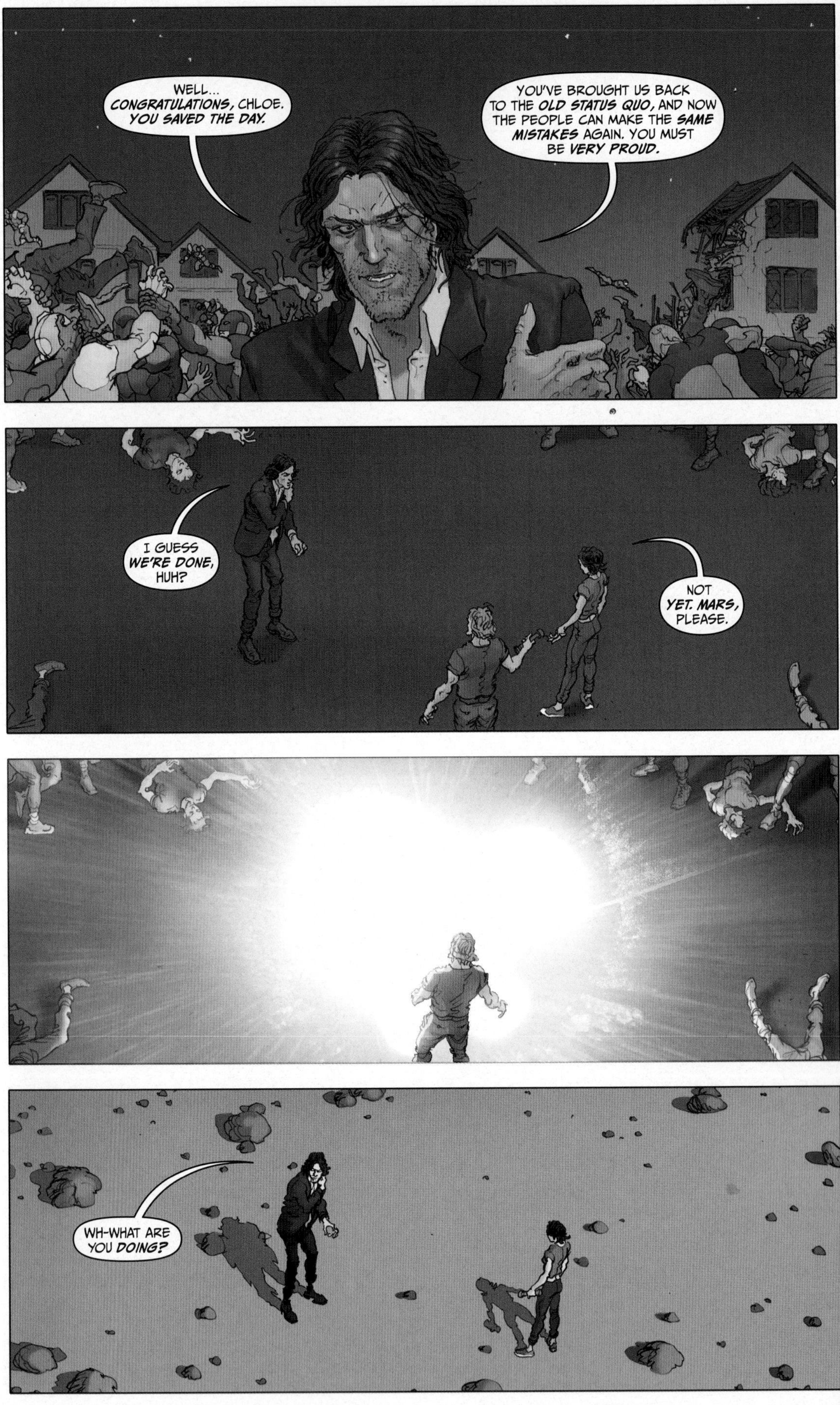
WELL... CONGRATULATIONS, CHLOE. YOU SAVED THE DAY.
YOU'VE BROUGHT US BACK TO THE OLD STATUS QUO, AND NOW THE PEOPLE CAN MAKE THE SAME MISTAKES AGAIN. YOU MUST BE VERY PROUD.
I GUESS WE'RE DONE, HUH?
NOT YET. MARS, PLEASE.
WH-WHAT ARE YOU DOING?

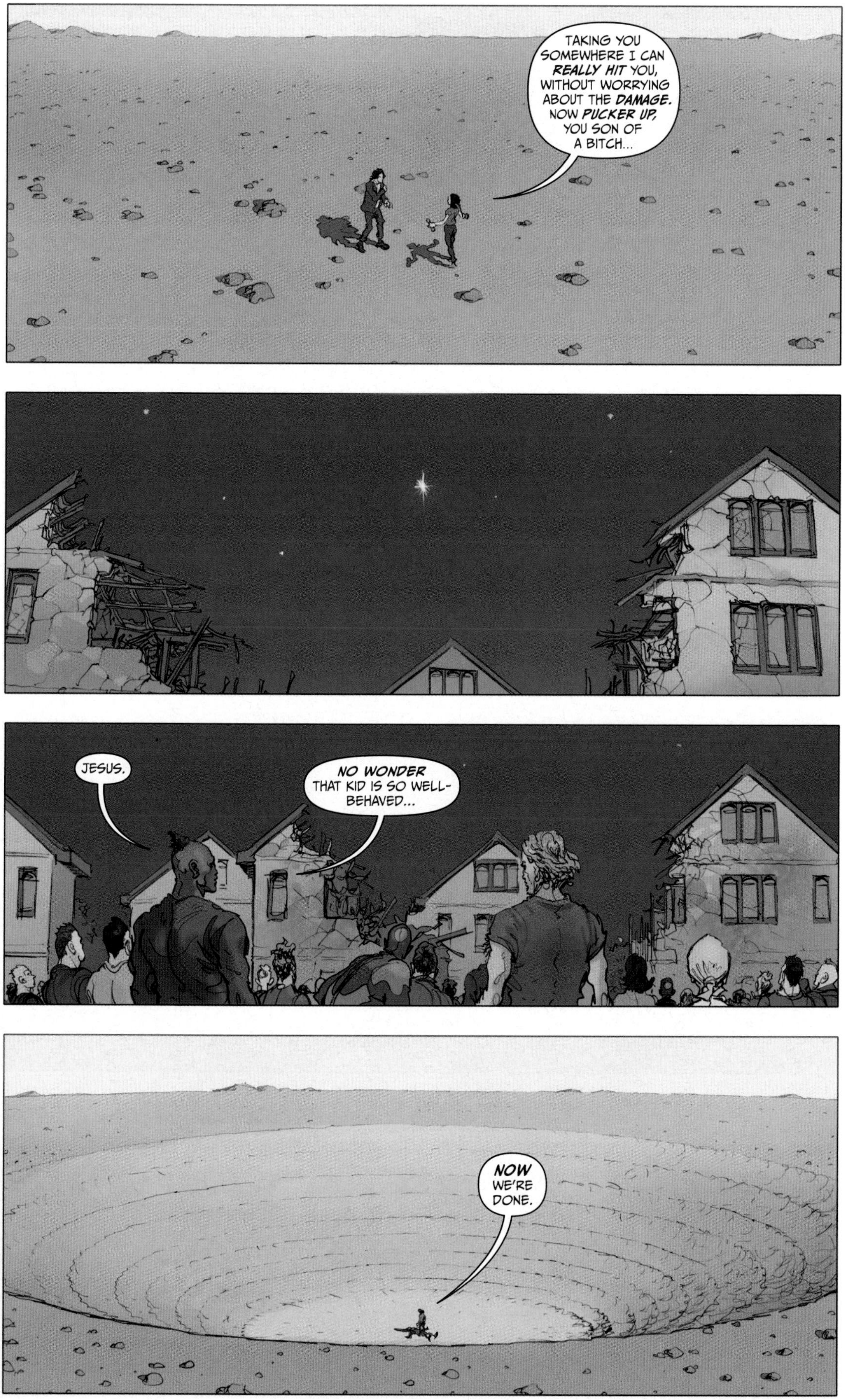
TAKING YOU SOMEWHERE I CAN REALLY HIT YOU, WITHOUT WORRYING ABOUT THE DAMAGE. NOW PUCKER UP, YOU SON OF A BITCH...
JESUS.
NO WONDER THAT KID IS SO WELL-BEHAVED...
NOW WE'RE DONE.

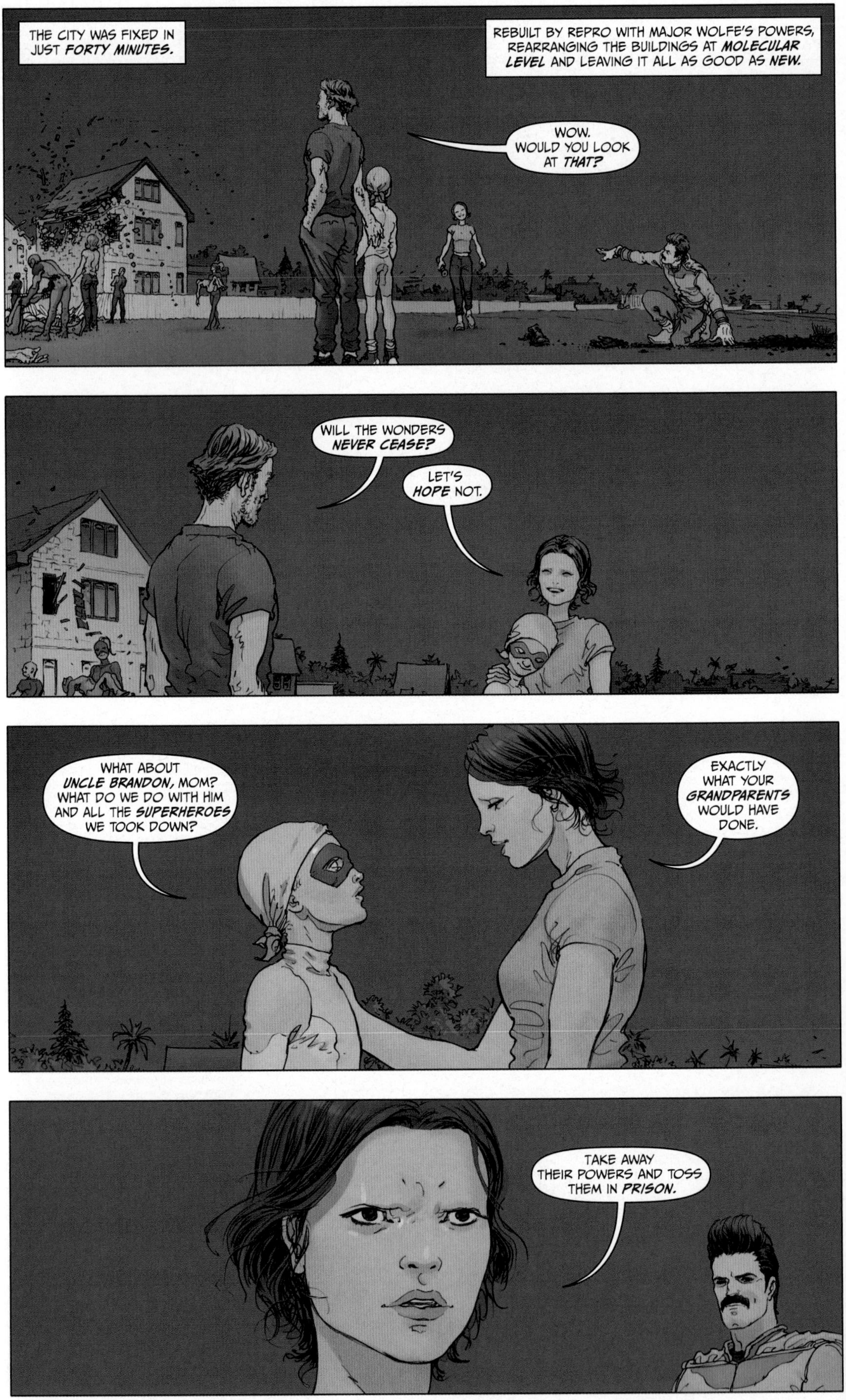
THE CITY WAS FIXED IN JUST FORTY MINUTES.
REBUILT BY REPRO WITH MAJOR WOLFE'S POWERS, REARRANGING THE BUILDINGS AT MOLECULAR LEVEL AND LEAVING IT ALL AS GOOD AS NEW.
WOW. WOULD YOU LOOK AT THAT?
WILL THE WONDERS NEVER CEASE?
LET'S HOPE NOT.
WHAT ABOUT UNCLE BRANDON, MOM? WHAT DO WE DO WITH HIM AND ALL THE SUPERHEROES WE TOOK DOWN?
EXACTLY WHAT YOUR GRANDPARENTS WOULD HAVE DONE.
TAKE AWAY THEIR POWERS AND TOSS THEM IN PRISON.

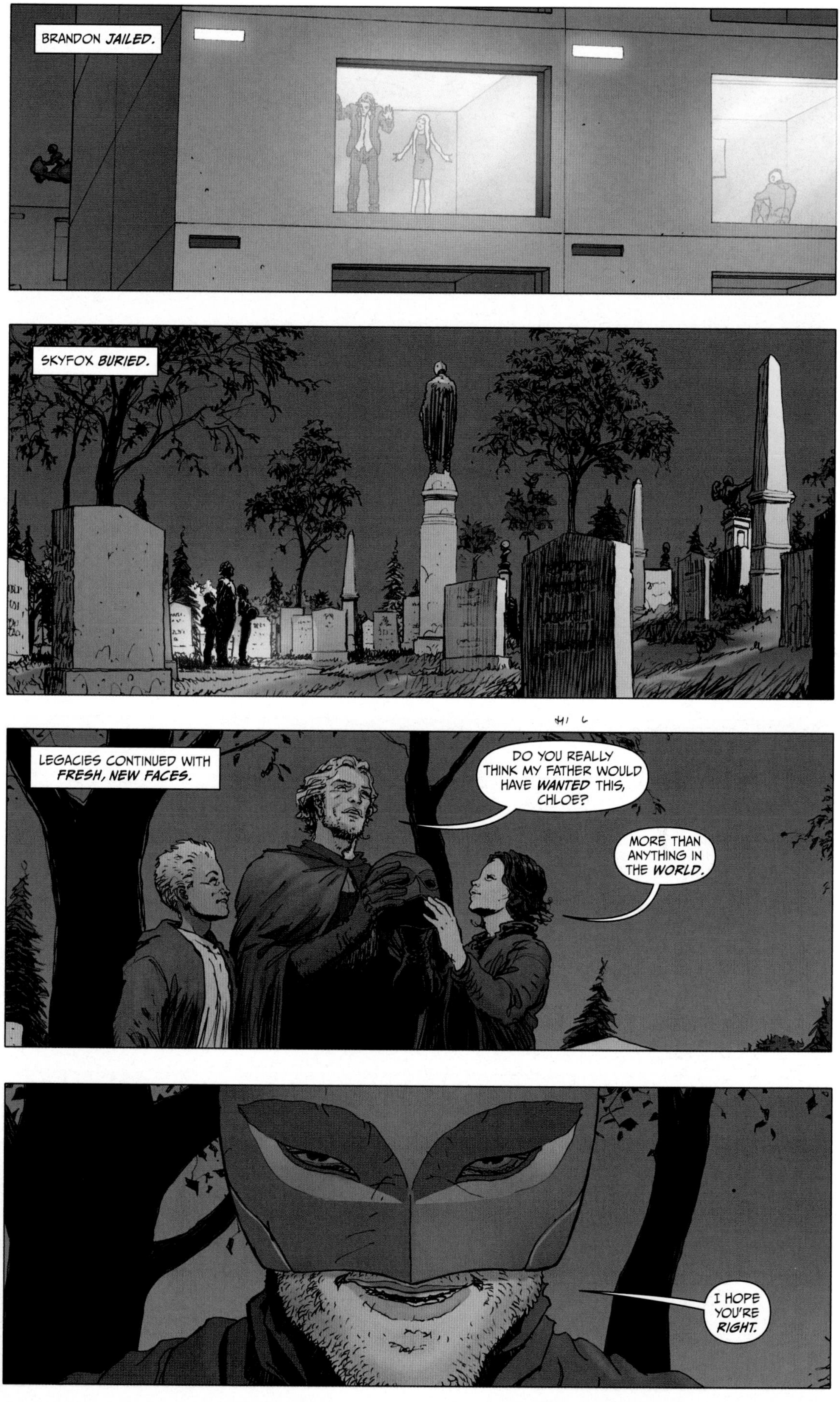
BRANDON JAILED.
SKYFOX BURIED.
LEGACIES CONTINUED WITH FRESH, NEW FACES.
DO YOU REALLY THINK MY FATHER WOULD HAVE WANTED THIS, CHLOE?
MORE THAN ANYTHING IN THE WORLD.
I HOPE YOU'RE RIGHT.

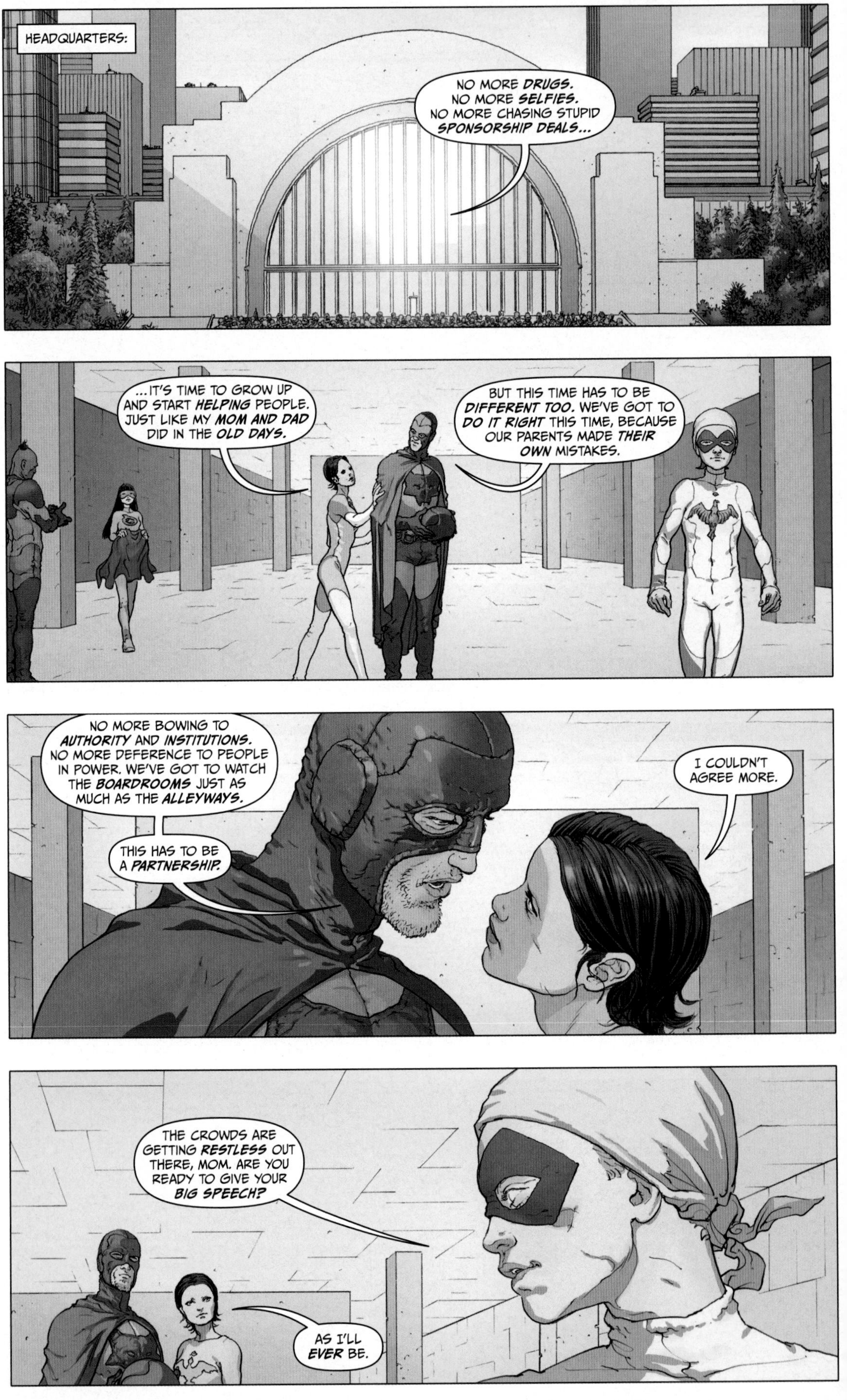
HEADQUARTERS:
NO MORE DRUGS. NO MORE SELFIES. NO MORE CHASING STUPID SPONSORSHIP DEALS...
...IT'S TIME TO GROW UP AND START HELPING PEOPLE. JUST LIKE MY MOM AND DAD DID IN THE OLD DAYS.
BUT THIS TIME HAS TO BE DIFFERENT TOO. WE'VE GOT TO DO IT RIGHT THIS TIME, BECAUSE OUR PARENTS MADE THEIR OWN MISTAKES.
NO MORE BOWING TO AUTHORITY AND INSTITUTIONS. NO MORE DEFERENCE TO PEOPLE IN POWER. WE'VE GOT TO WATCH THE BOARDROOMS JUST AS MUCH AS THE ALLEYWAYS.
THIS HAS TO BE A PARTNERSHIP.
I COULDN'T AGREE MORE.
THE CROWDS ARE GETTING RESTLESS OUT THERE, MOM. ARE YOU READY TO GIVE YOUR BIG SPEECH?
AS I'LL EVER BE.

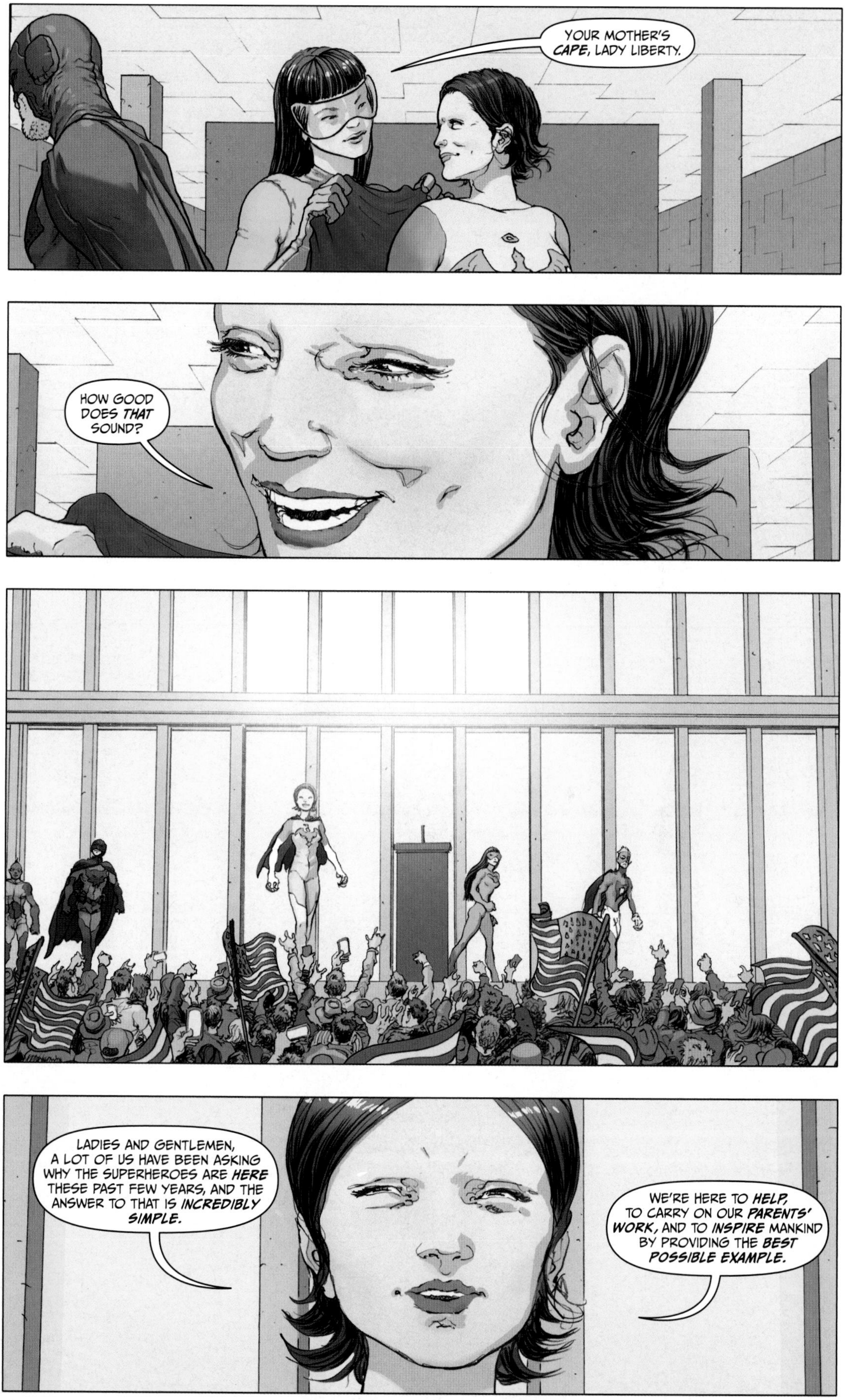

YOUR MOTHER'S CAPE, LADY LIBERTY.
HOW GOOD DOES THAT SOUND?
LADIES AND GENTLEMEN, A LOT OF US HAVE BEEN ASKING WHY THE SUPERHEROES ARE HERE THESE PAST FEW YEARS, AND THE ANSWER TO THAT IS INCREDIBLY SIMPLE.
WE'RE HERE TO HELP, TO CARRY ON OUR PARENTS' WORK, AND TO INSPIRE MANKIND BY PROVIDING THE BEST POSSIBLE EXAMPLE.

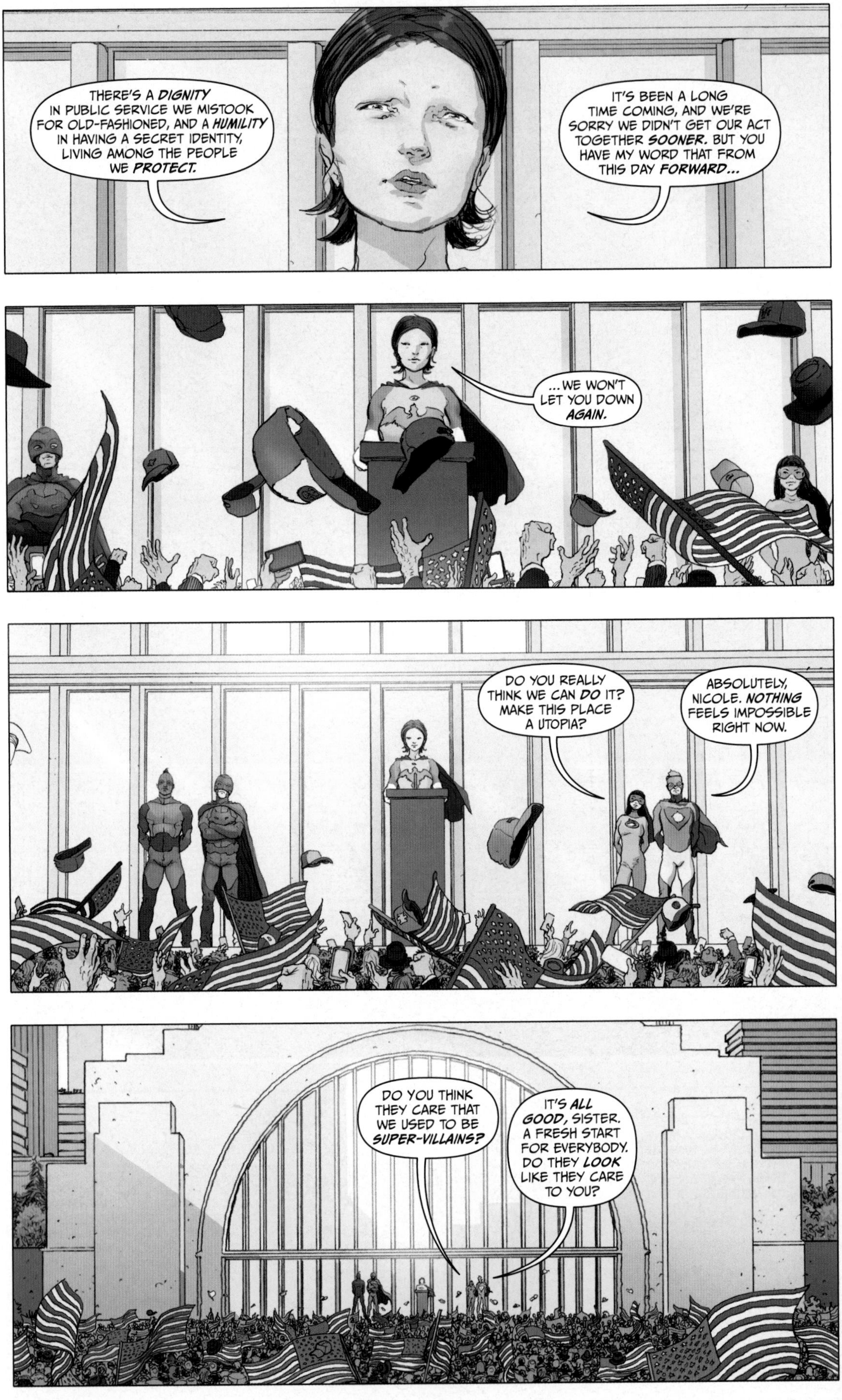

THERE'S A DIGNITY IN PUBLIC SERVICE WE MISTOOK FOR OLD-FASHIONED, AND A HUMILITY IN HAVING A SECRET IDENTITY, LIVING AMONG THE PEOPLE WE PROTECT.
IT'S BEEN A LONG TIME COMING, AND WE'RE SORRY WE DIDN'T GET OUR ACT TOGETHER SOONER. BUT YOU HAVE MY WORD THAT FROM THIS DAY FORWARD...
...WE WON'T LET YOU DOWN AGAIN.
DO YOU REALLY THINK WE CAN DO IT? MAKE THIS PLACE A UTOPIA?
ABSOLUTELY, NICOLE. NOTHING FEELS IMPOSSIBLE RIGHT NOW.
DO YOU THINK THEY CARE THAT WE USED TO BE SUPER-VILLAINS?
IT'S ALL GOOD, SISTER. A FRESH START FOR EVERYBODY. DO THEY LOOK LIKE THEY CARE TO YOU?

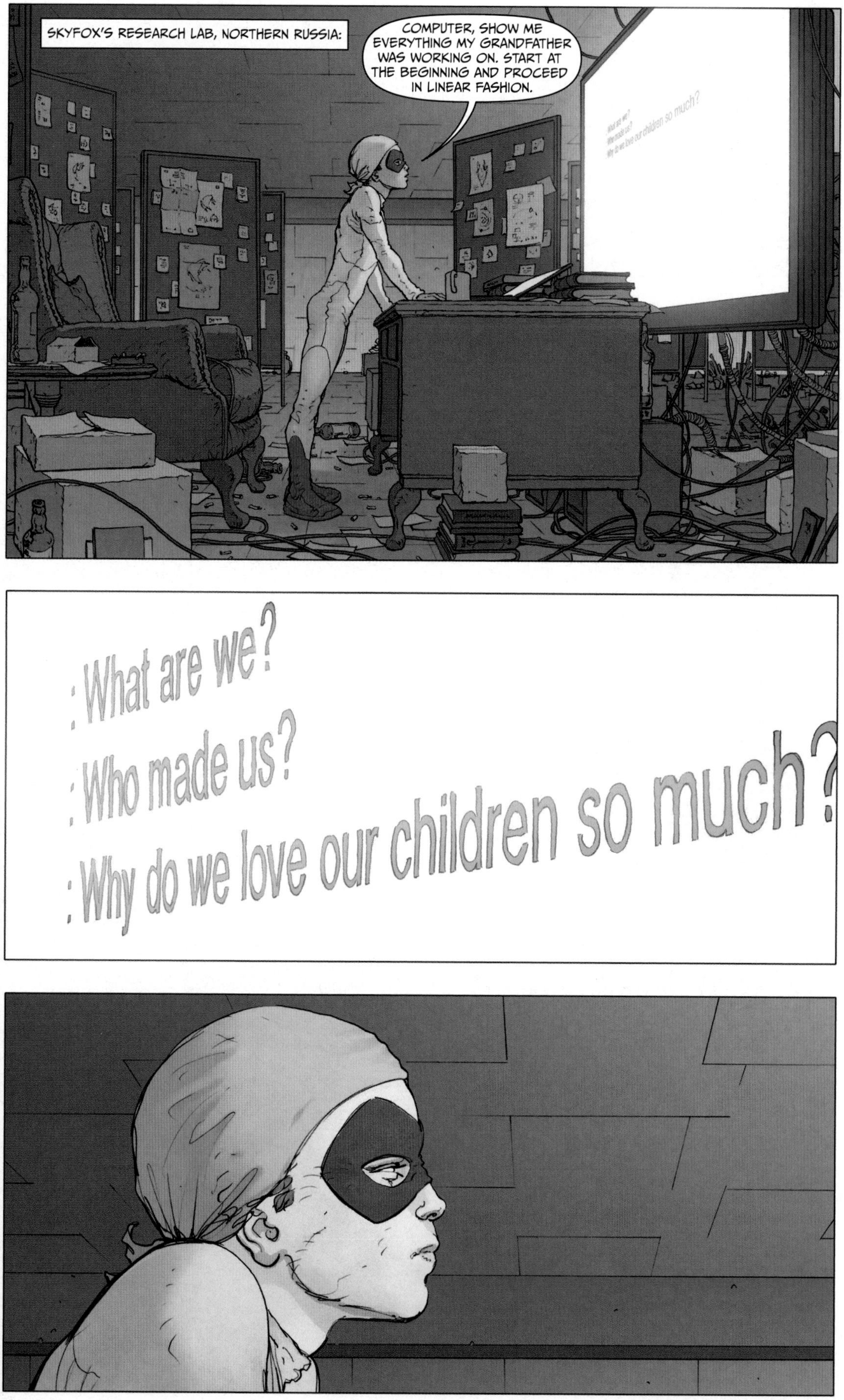
SKYFOX'S RESEARCH LAB, NORTHERN RUSSIA:
COMPUTER, SHOW ME EVERYTHING MY GRANDFATHER WAS WORKING ON. START AT THE BEGINNING AND PROCEED IN LINEAR FASHION.
: What are we?
: Who made us?
: Why do we love our children so much?

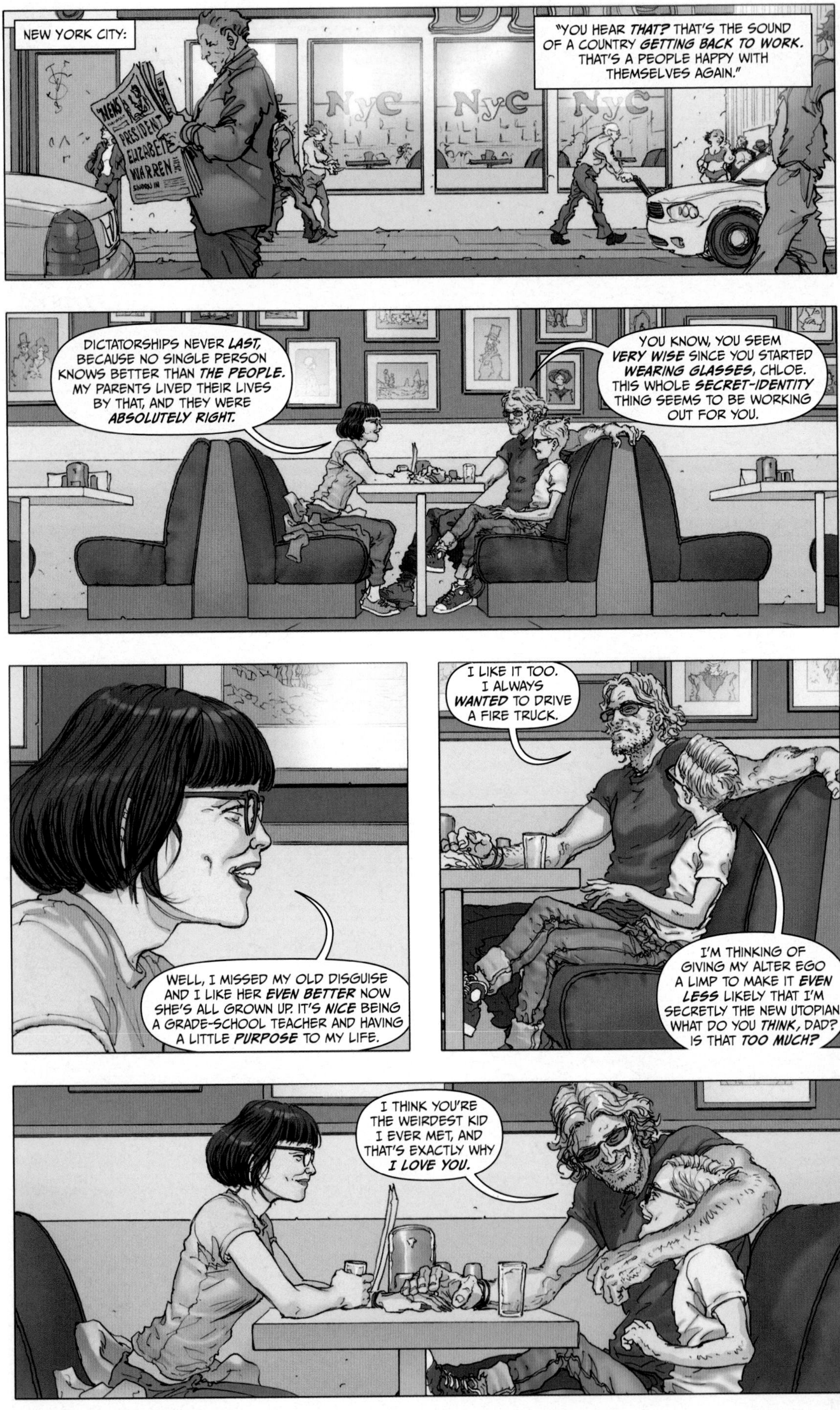
NEW YORK CITY:
NEWS
PRESIDENT ELIZABETH WARREN SWORN IN
"YOU HEAR THAT? THAT'S THE SOUND OF A COUNTRY GETTING BACK TO WORK. THAT'S A PEOPLE HAPPY WITH THEMSELVES AGAIN."
NyC
DICTATORSHIPS NEVER LAST, BECAUSE NO SINGLE PERSON KNOWS BETTER THAN THE PEOPLE. MY PARENTS LIVED THEIR LIVES BY THAT, AND THEY WERE ABSOLUTELY RIGHT.
YOU KNOW, YOU SEEM VERY WISE SINCE YOU STARTED WEARING GLASSES, CHLOE. THIS WHOLE SECRET-IDENTITY THING SEEMS TO BE WORKING OUT FOR YOU.
WELL, I MISSED MY OLD DISGUISE AND I LIKE HER EVEN BETTER NOW SHE'S ALL GROWN UP. IT'S NICE BEING A GRADE-SCHOOL TEACHER AND HAVING A LITTLE PURPOSE TO MY LIFE.
I LIKE IT TOO. I ALWAYS WANTED TO DRIVE A FIRE TRUCK.
I'M THINKING OF GIVING MY ALTER EGO A LIMP TO MAKE IT EVEN LESS LIKELY THAT I'M SECRETLY THE NEW UTOPIAN. WHAT DO YOU THINK, DAD? IS THAT TOO MUCH?
I THINK YOU'RE THE WEIRDEST KID I EVER MET, AND THAT'S EXACTLY WHY I LOVE YOU.

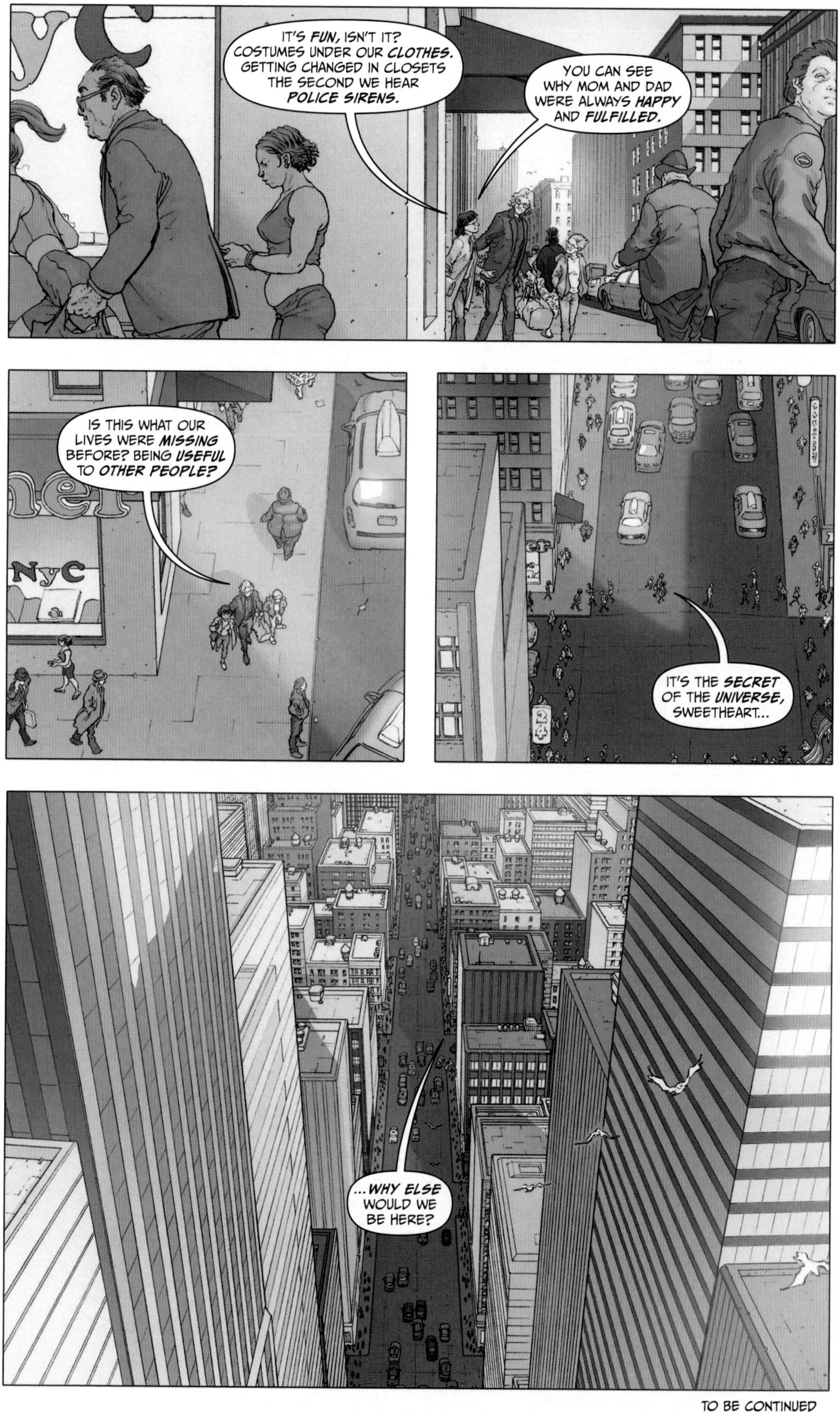
IT'S FUN, ISN'T IT? COSTUMES UNDER OUR CLOTHES. GETTING CHANGED IN CLOSETS THE SECOND WE HEAR POLICE SIRENS.
YOU CAN SEE WHY MOM AND DAD WERE ALWAYS HAPPY AND FULFILLED.
IS THIS WHAT OUR LIVES WERE MISSING BEFORE? BEING USEFUL TO OTHER PEOPLE?
NyC
IT'S THE SECRET OF THE UNIVERSE, SWEETHEART...
...WHY ELSE WOULD WE BE HERE?

TO BE CONTINUED

FIND OUT WHAT HAPPENS NEXT

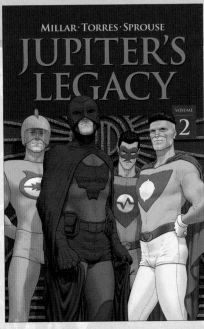

NETFLIX

THE STORY CONTINUES

JUPITER'S LEGACY

VOLUME 5

Why do we love our children so much?

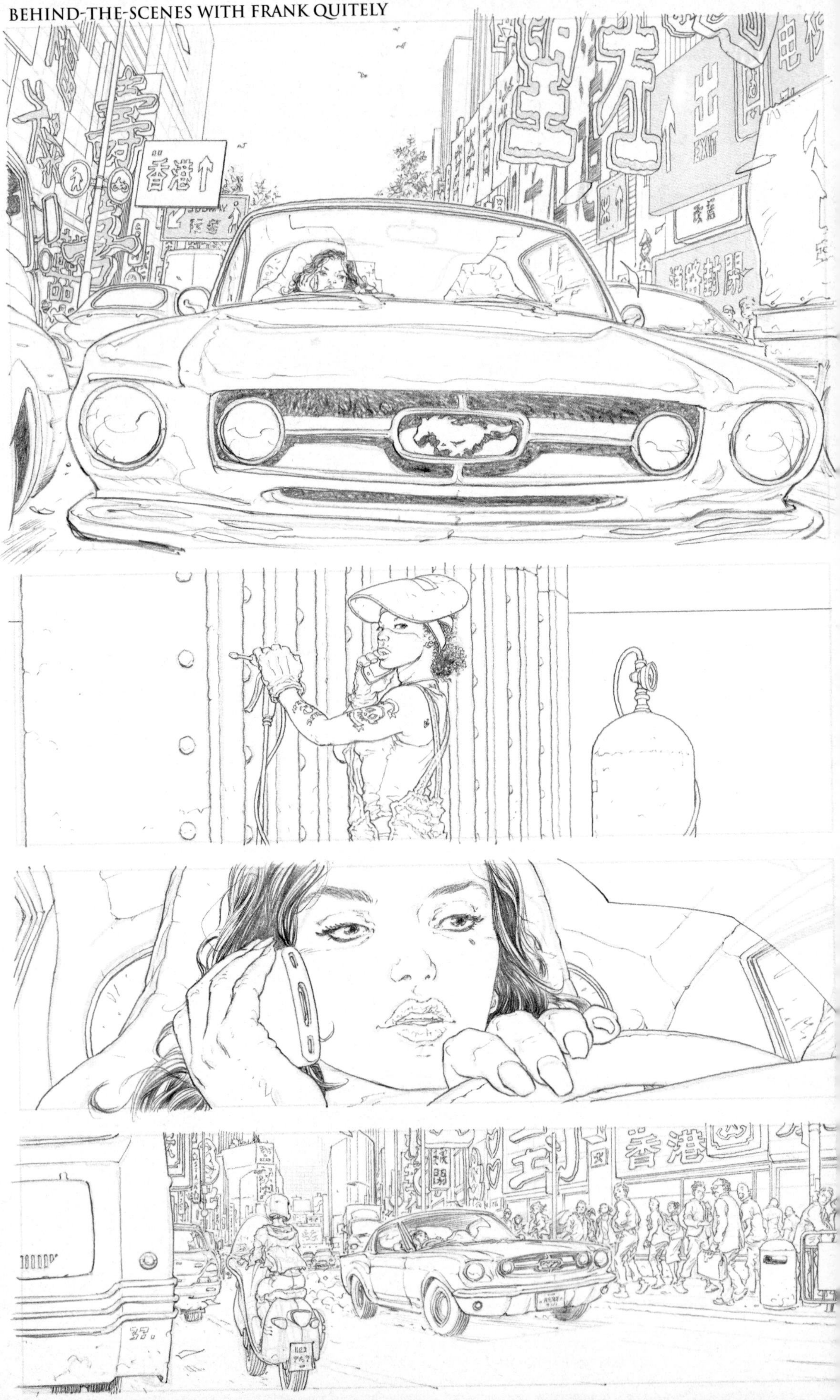
香港
SUBWAY
出
EXIT
香港

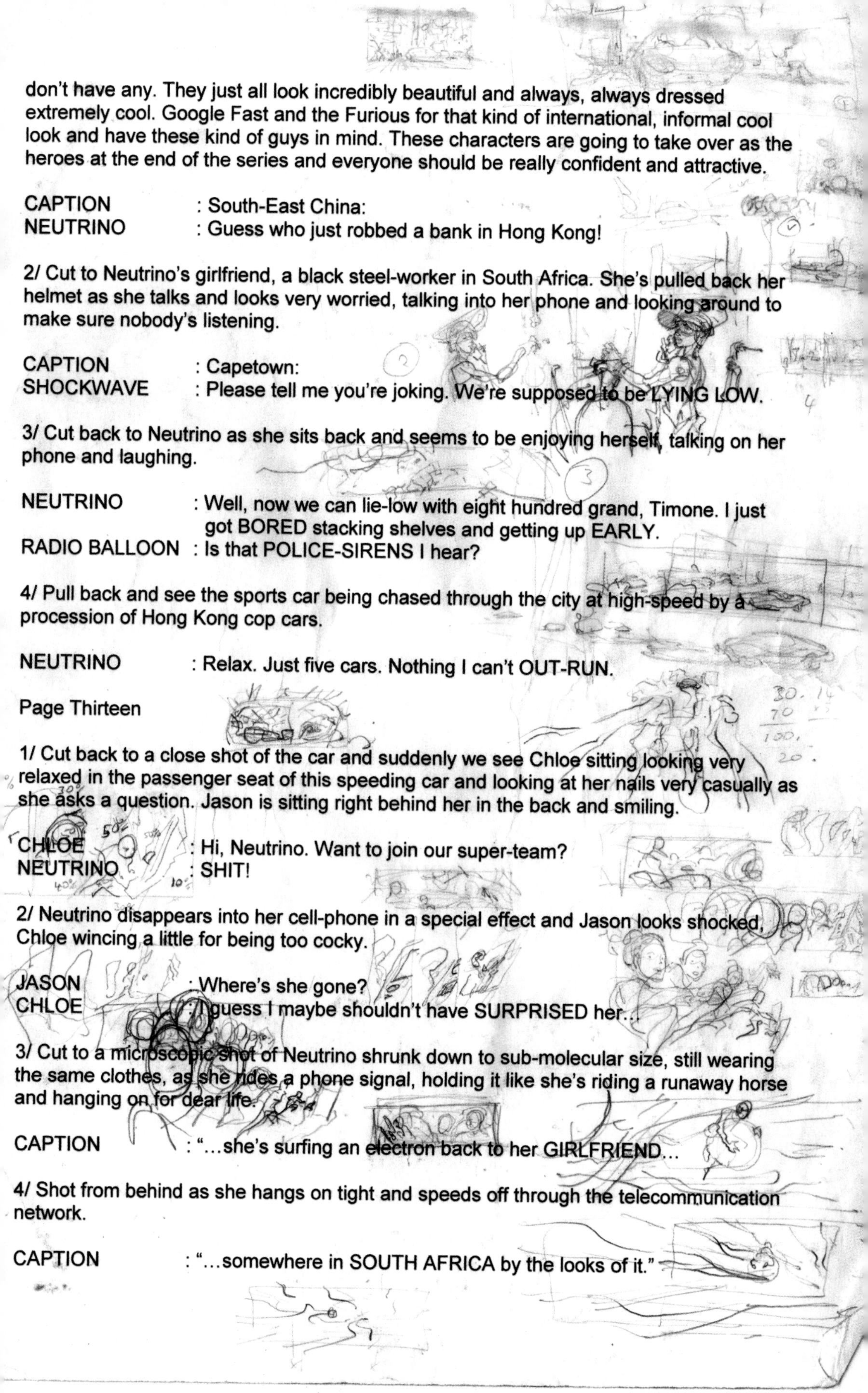

don't have any. They just all look incredibly beautiful and always, always dressed extremely cool. Google Fast and the Furious for that kind of international, informal cool look and have these kind of guys in mind. These characters are going to take over as the heroes at the end of the series and everyone should be really confident and attractive.

CAPTION : South-East China:
NEUTRINO : Guess who just robbed a bank in Hong Kong!

2/ Cut to Neutrino's girlfriend, a black steel-worker in South Africa. She's pulled back her helmet as she talks and looks very worried, talking into her phone and looking around to make sure nobody's listening.

CAPTION : Capetown:
SHOCKWAVE : Please tell me you're joking. We're supposed to be LYING LOW.

3/ Cut back to Neutrino as she sits back and seems to be enjoying herself, talking on her phone and laughing.

NEUTRINO : Well, now we can lie-low with eight hundred grand, Timone. I just got BORED stacking shelves and getting up EARLY.
RADIO BALLOON : Is that POLICE-SIRENS I hear?

4/ Pull back and see the sports car being chased through the city at high-speed by a procession of Hong Kong cop cars.

NEUTRINO : Relax. Just five cars. Nothing I can't OUT-RUN.

Page Thirteen

1/ Cut back to a close shot of the car and suddenly we see Chloe sitting looking very relaxed in the passenger seat of this speeding car and looking at her nails very casually as she asks a question. Jason is sitting right behind her in the back and smiling.

CHLOE : Hi, Neutrino. Want to join our super-team?
NEUTRINO : SHIT!

2/ Neutrino disappears into her cell-phone in a special effect and Jason looks shocked, Chloe wincing a little for being too cocky.

JASON : Where's she gone?
CHLOE : I guess I maybe shouldn't have SURPRISED her...

3/ Cut to a microscopic shot of Neutrino shrunk down to sub-molecular size, still wearing the same clothes, as she rides a phone signal, holding it like she's riding a runaway horse and hanging on for dear life.

CAPTION : "...she's surfing an electron back to her GIRLFRIEND...

4/ Shot from behind as she hangs on tight and speeds off through the telecommunication network.

CAPTION : "...somewhere in SOUTH AFRICA by the looks of it."

UNSEEN FRANK QUITELY THUMBNAIL ROUGHS AND PENCILS FOR PAGE 22, ISSUE 2

JASON : Well, now might be your BIG CHANCE, Dad.
HUTCH : What?

2/ The scanner is picking something up.

JASON : The META-GENE scanner. It's picking up another SUPER-HUMAN. Somewhere in Northern Russia.

3/ The others begin to gather around and look at the machine.

JASON : Caucasian. Male. Incredibly old... but carrying an enormous ENERGY SIGNATURE. Like nothing we've ever SEEN.
HUTCH : What are you trying to SAY, kid?

4/ Jason looks wide-eyed.

JASON : I think I've found your FATHER.

Page Twenty-Two

1/ End with a full-page splash and a big, powerful image of the Skyfox costume up on a wall, completely surrounded by mad graphs and post-its notes from two decades work. Standing before it and looking up at it we see George Hutchence AKA Hutch Senior. He'll have been through the most amazing character arc in Jupiter's Circle by this point and people will really lose their minds to see him back here. He's holding a cane behind his back and looking up here, an ancient, enigmatic vibe coming off him and the readers not even given a glimpse of his face. Light the panel for effect. We don't know where this is. We just know it's INTERESTING.

NO DIALOGUE

TO BE CONTINUED

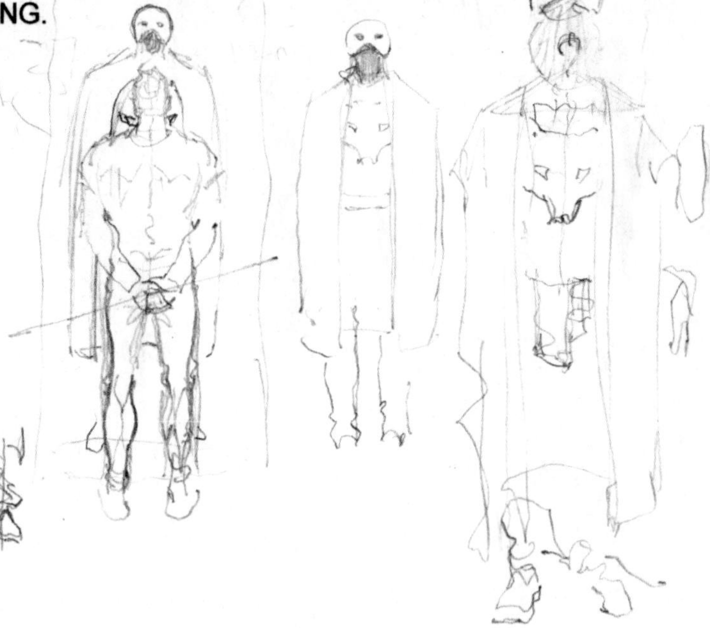
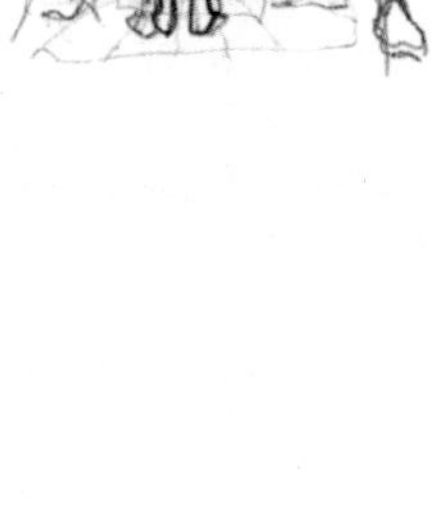

UNSEEN FRANK QUITELY THUMBNAIL ROUGHS AND PENCILS FOR PAGE 22, ISSUE 2

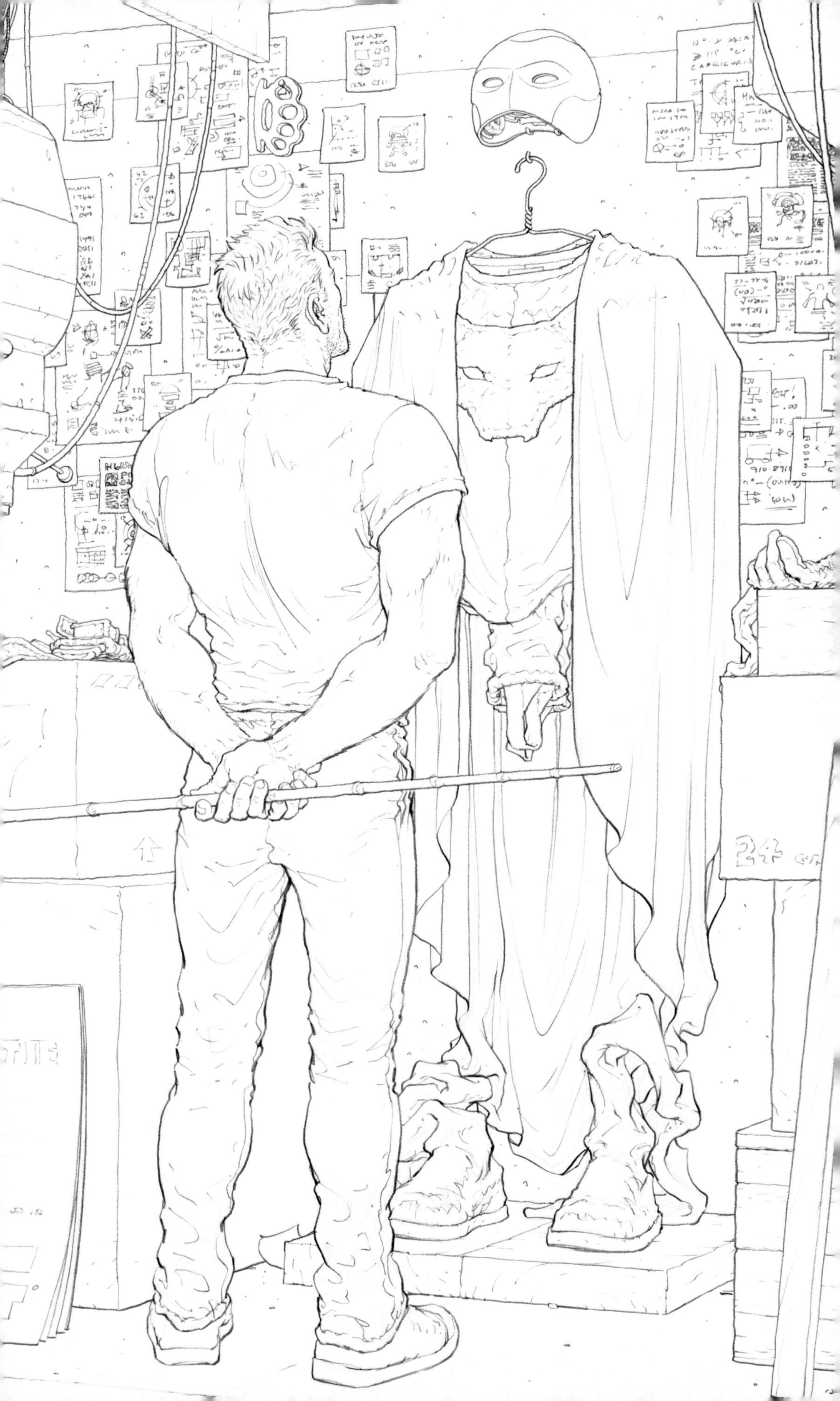

FRANK QUITELY'S FINISHED PENCILS FOR PAGE 15, ISSUE 2

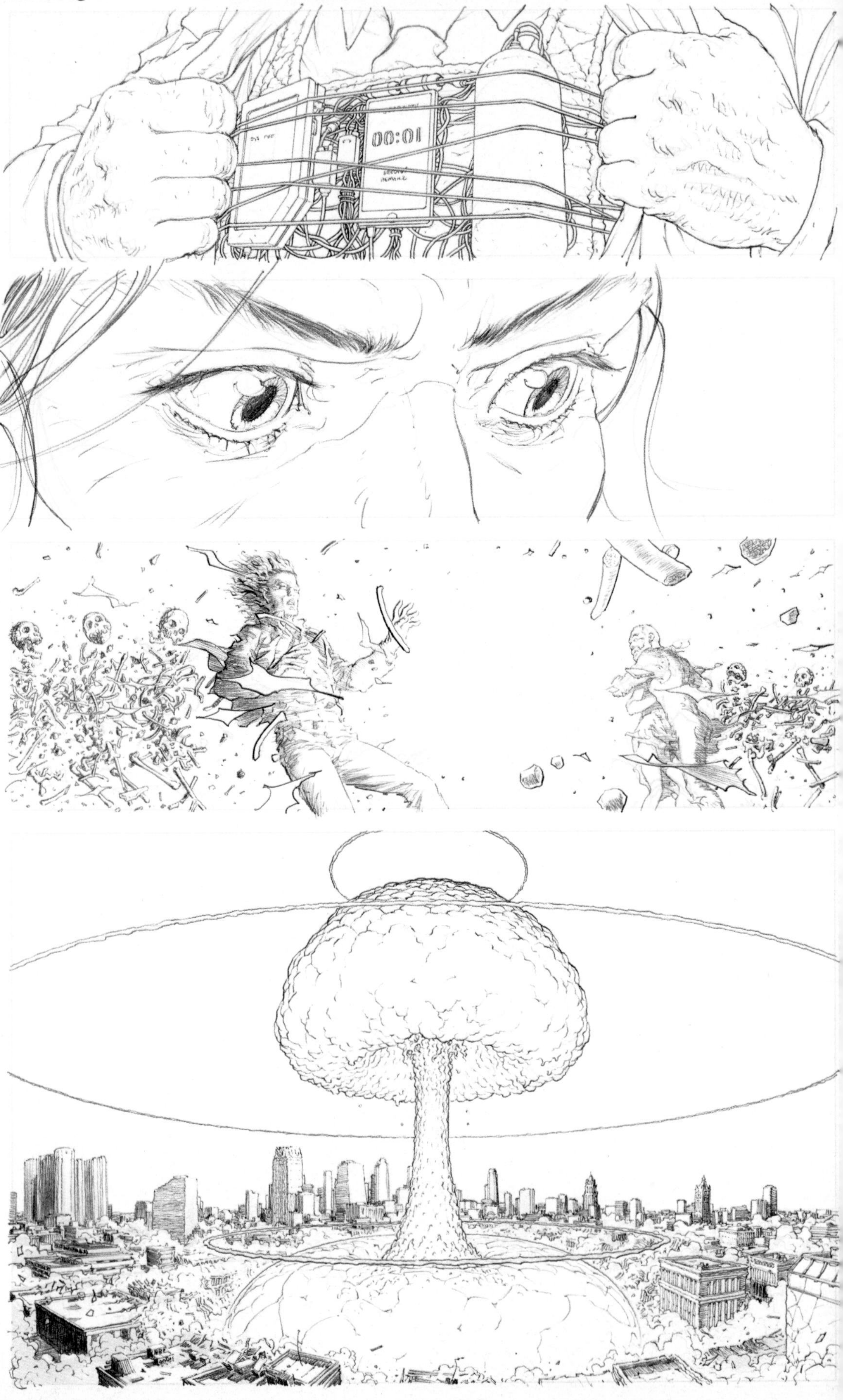
00:01

ROB MILLER'S FINISHED 'INKS' — DIGITALLLY PROCESSING THE PENCILS, PAGE 15, ISSUE 2

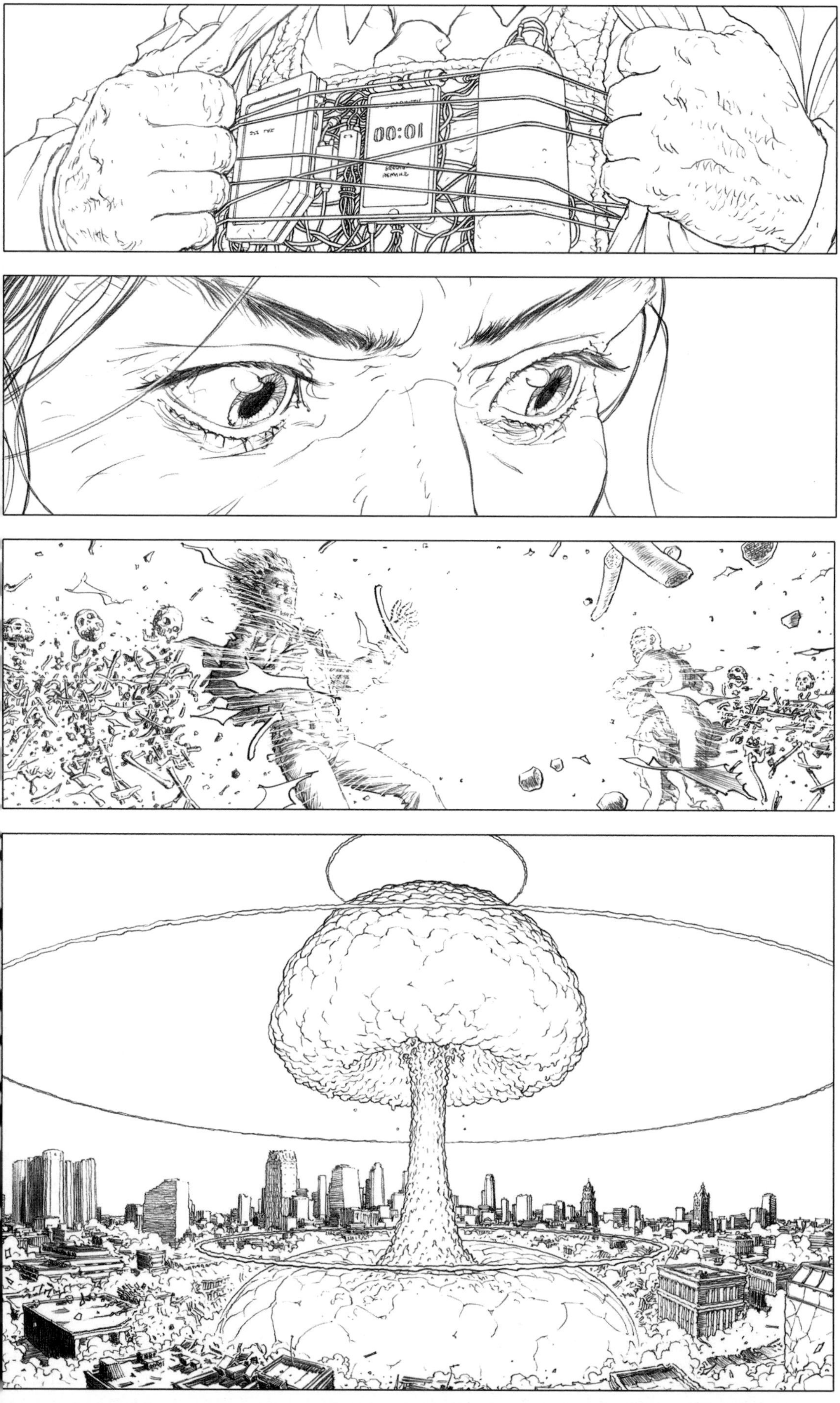

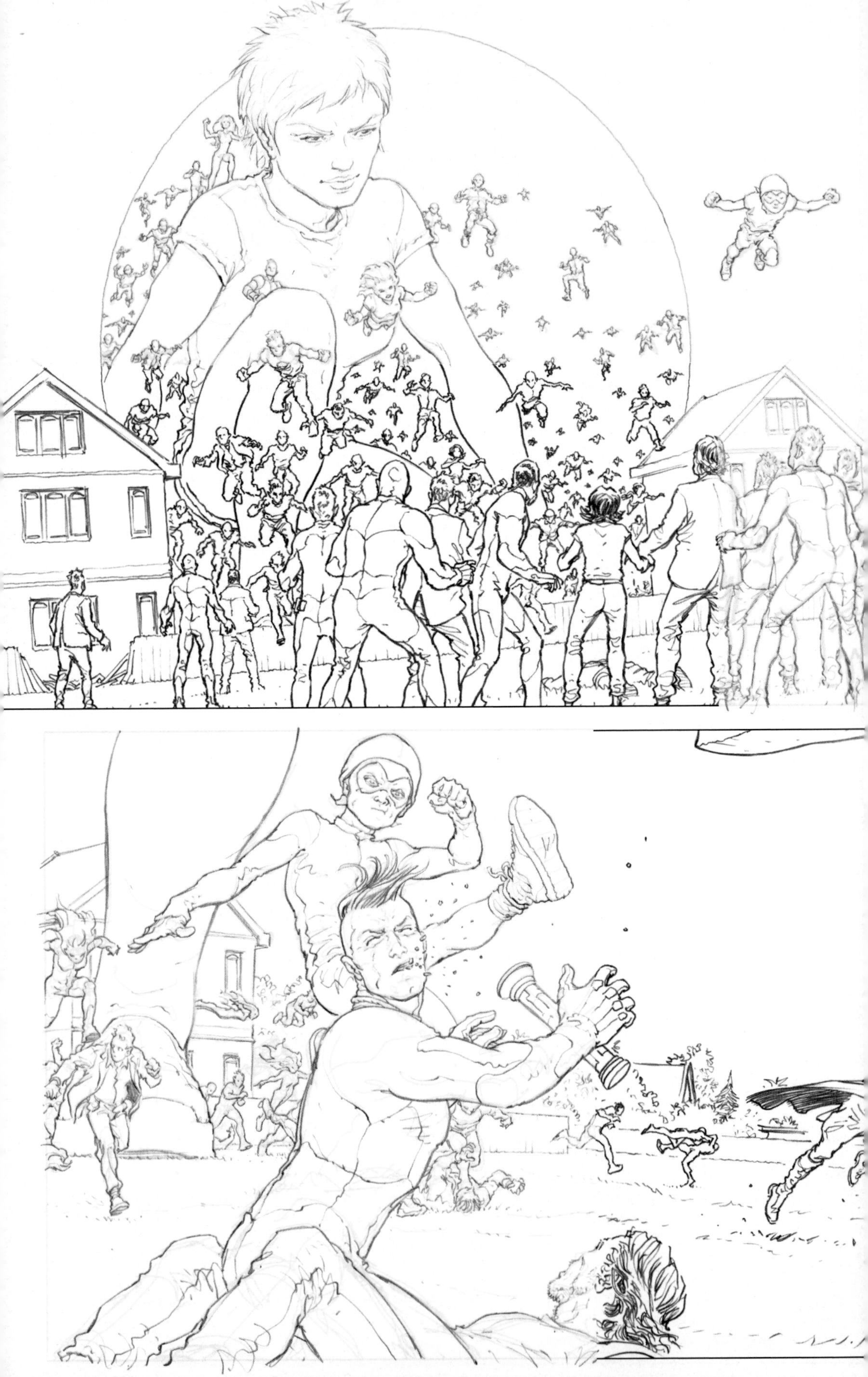

FRANK QUITELY AND ROB MILLER, PENCILS AND DIGITAL 'INKS', PAGES 18/19, ISSUE 5.

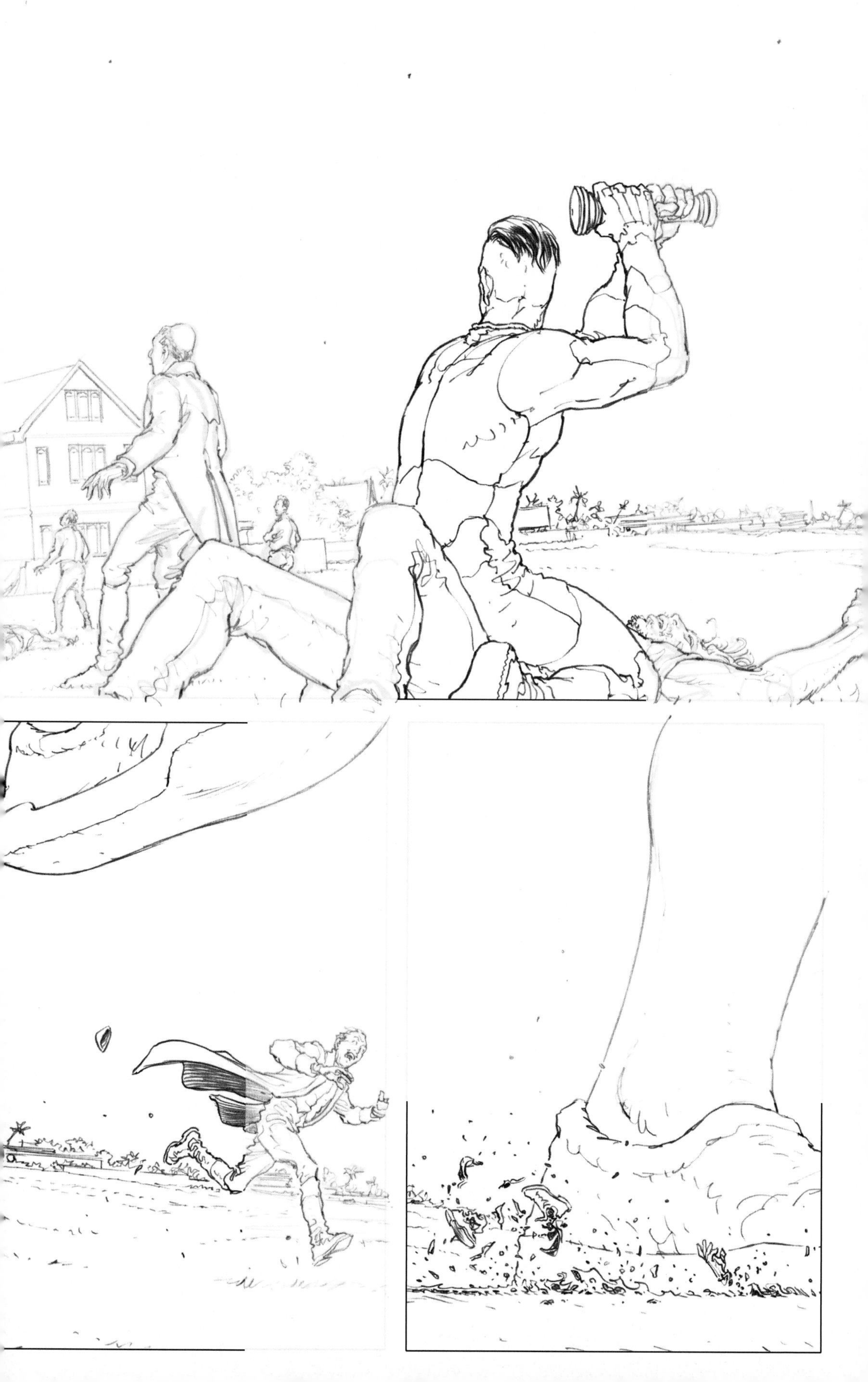

MARK MILLAR

Mark Millar is the *New York Times* bestselling author of *Kick-Ass*, *Wanted*, and *Kingsman: The Secret Service*, all of which have been adapted into Hollywood franchises.

His DC Comics work includes the seminal *Superman: Red Son*. At Marvel Comics he created *The Ultimates*, which was selected by *Time* magazine as the comic book of the decade, and was described by screenwriter Zak Penn as his major inspiration for *The Avengers* movie. Millar also created *Wolverine: Old Man Logan* and *Civil War*, Marvel's two biggest-selling graphic novels ever. *Civil War* was the basis of the *Captain America: Civil War* movie, and *Old Man Logan* was the inspiration for Fox's *Logan* movie in 2017.

Mark has been an executive producer on all his movies, and for four years worked as a creative consultant to Fox Studios on their Marvel slate of movies. In 2017, Netflix bought Millarworld in the company's first ever acquisition, and employed Mark as President of a new division to create comics, TV shows, and movies. His much-anticipated autobiography, *The Brian Grove Mysteries*, will be published next year.

FRANK QUITELY

Frank Quitely spent the first three years of his comic-book career in the independently published, Scottish adult-humour anthology *Electric Soup*. There he learned the basics of writing, drawing and lettering through his own black and white strip, *The Greens*.

Leaving writing behind, he spent a further two years painting the futuristic western *Missionary Man* and the Japanese sci-fi strip *Shimura*, both for the popular UK anthology *Judge Dredd Megazine*.

The next five years were mostly spent at DC Comics, producing ten black and white strips for Paradox Press' *The Big Books*, and six shorts and two mini-series for Vertigo, including *Flex Mentallo*. He also produced a selection of one-shots, original graphic novels and ongoing series at DCU and Wildstorm, including *Batman*, *JLA* and *The Authority*.

After two years on *New X-Men* at Marvel, he headed back to Vertigo for a fully painted *Sandman* short, and the creator-owned mini-series *We3*, followed by *All-Star Superman*, *Batman and Robin*, *New Gods*, and *Pax Americana*, all for DC Comics.

In 2017, Glasgow's Kelvingrove Art Gallery and Museum launched Frank Quitely : The Art of Comics, the largest collection of Frank's artwork ever displayed. The exhibition features his work on *All-Star Superman*, *Batman*, and – of course – *Jupiter's Legacy*.

SUNNY GHO

Sunny Gho studied graphic design at Trisakti University, Indonesia, before going on to work for companies such as Top Cow, Imaginary Friends Studios and now GLITCH. He founded Jakarta-based content business Stellar Labs, which specialises in content development across games, interactive content and animation.

He has colored an impressive array of comic-book titles, including Marvel's *Civil War II, The Indestructible Hulk* and *The Avengers*. For Millarworld, he has colored *Supercrooks* and *Superior*, and later took the helm on *Jupiter's Legacy 2* in early 2016.

In 2017, he will color the return of Millarworld's *Hit-Girl* –bringing the character's new, explosive adventures to life.

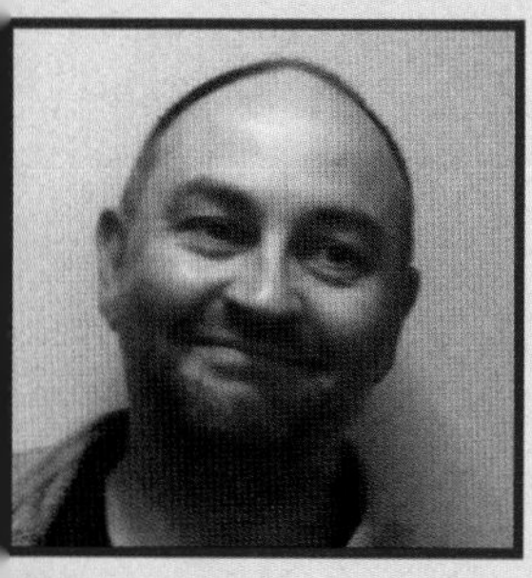

Peter Doherty

Peter Doherty's first work in comics was during 1990, providing painted artwork for the John Wagner-written *Young Death: Boyhood of a Superfiend*, published in the first year of the *Judge Dredd Megazine*. For the next few years he painted art for a number of Judge Dredd stories. He's worked for most of the major comics publishers, and has also branched out into illustration, TV, and movie work.

Over the last decade he's worked on projects both as the sole artist, and as a coloring/lettering/design collaborator with other artists, including Geof Darrow on his *Shaolin Cowboy* project, and more recently Frank Quitely and Duncan Fegredo, on the Millarworld projects *Jupiter's Legacy* and *MPH* respectively.

2017 found him working on *Kingsman*: *The Red Diamond*, *The Millarworld Annual* and quite a few life drawings.

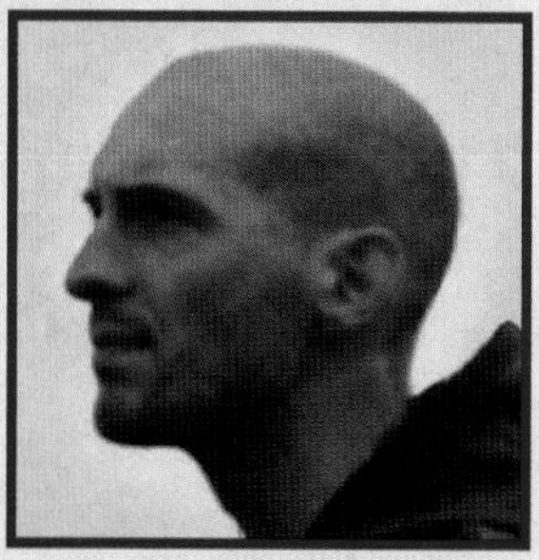

Rob Miller

Since stumbling onto the Glasgow comic scene in 2005 (via architecture, and Adam Smith's underground title *Khaki Shorts*) Rob Miller has been fortunate enough to assist Frank Quitely on his recent genre-defining works with Mark Millar and Grant Morrison.

Whilst working from Jamie Grant's highly regarded Hope Street Studios, he collaborated with many other Scottish comic professionals, including Alan Grant and Alex Ronald, and took the opportunity to publish prized collections of some of his favorite local underground artists : Dave Alexander, Hugh "Shug 90" McKenna and John Miller – under his own Braw Books imprint.

In his spare (!?) time Rob draws comics and makes music as *The Mind Robbers.*

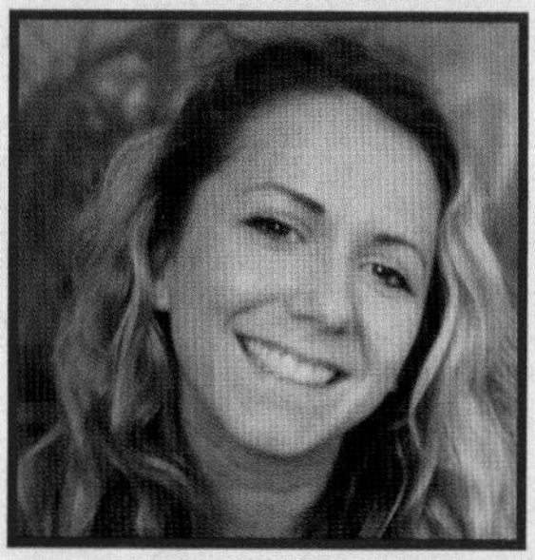

Rachael Fulton

Rachael landed at Millarworld in early 2016, taking the reins as series editor on *Empress* and *Jupiter's Legacy,* and working as associate editor on *Huck*. She is responsible for editing all Millarworld titles and currently manages teams on *Reborn, Hit-Girl, Kick-Ass, Jupiter's Legacy, Kingsman* and *The Millarworld Annual.*

She is a freelance journalist, and in a previous life was a TV reporter, producer, and features writer. Midweek she can often be found trying to hunt down artists and colorists, or on the phone to Peter Doherty.

She spends the rest of her time writing and volunteering in London.

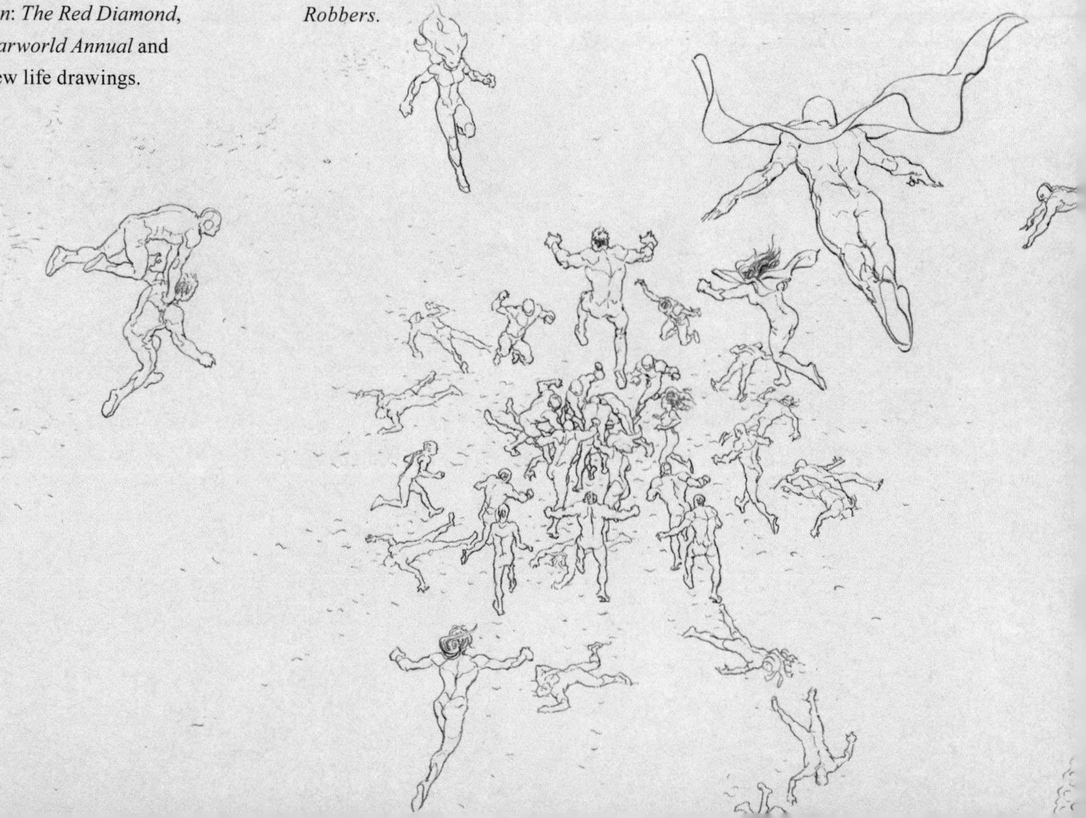

ALSO BY MARK MILLAR

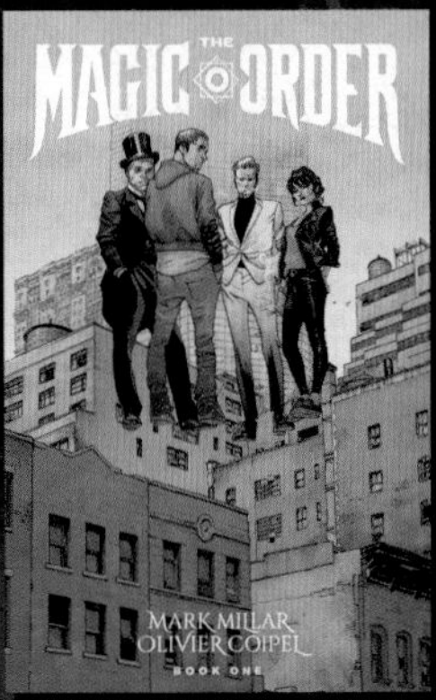
THE MAGIC ORDER
MARK MILLAR
OLIVIER COIPEL
BOOK ONE

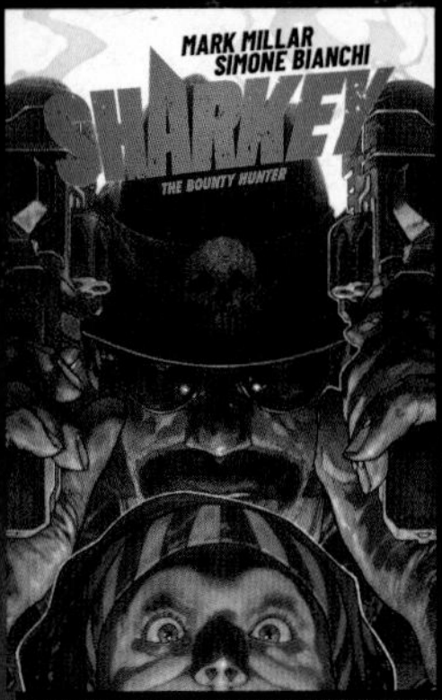
MARK MILLAR
SIMONE BIANCHI
SHARKEY
THE BOUNTY HUNTER

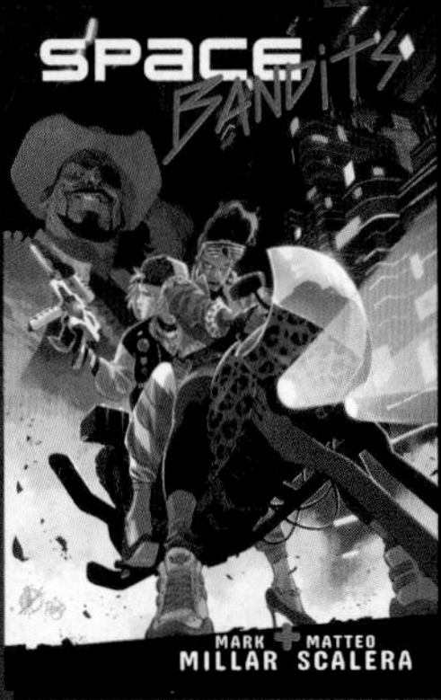
SPACE BANDITS
MARK MILLAR
MATTEO SCALERA

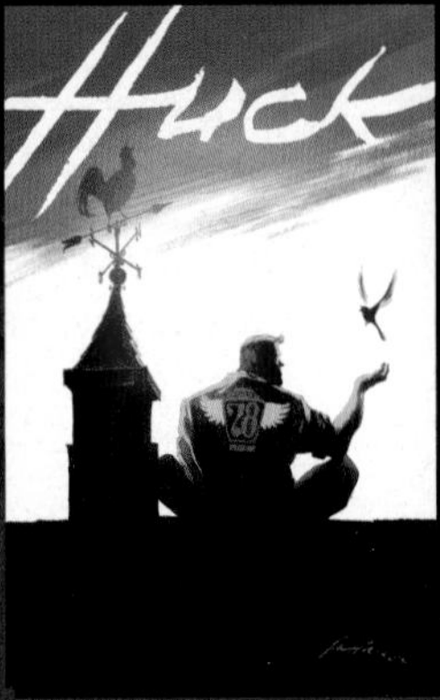
Huck

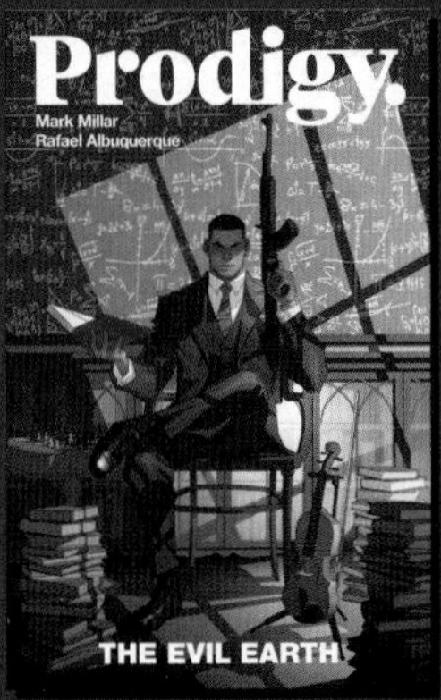
Prodigy.
Mark Millar
Rafael Albuquerque
THE EVIL EARTH

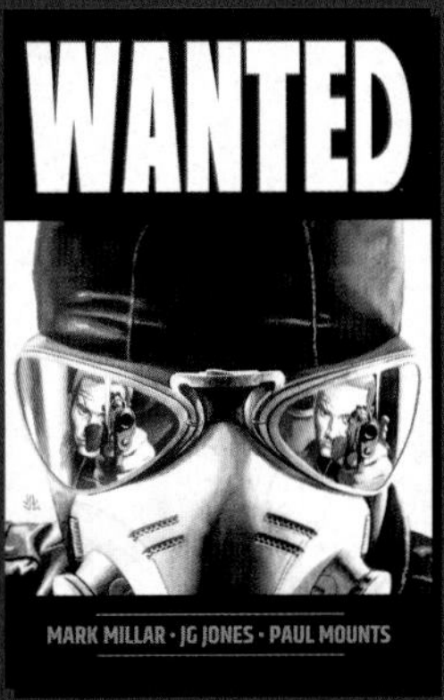
WANTED
MARK MILLAR · JG JONES · PAUL MOUNTS

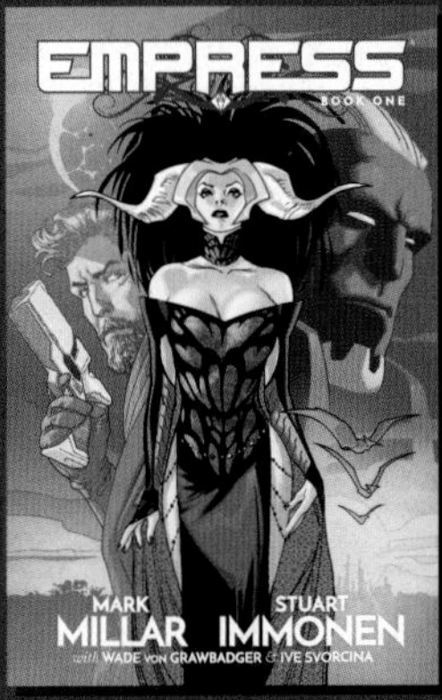
EMPRESS
BOOK ONE
MARK MILLAR
STUART IMMONEN
with WADE von GRAWBADGER & IVE SVORCINA

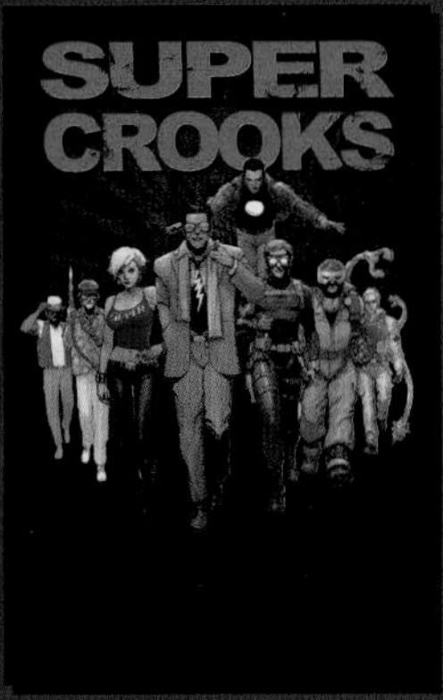
SUPER CROOKS

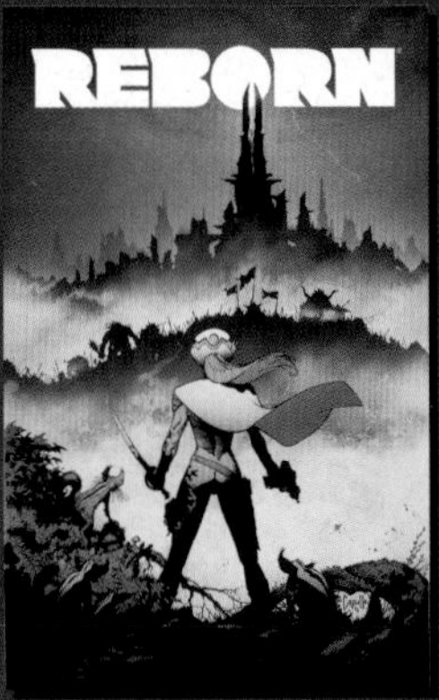
REBORN

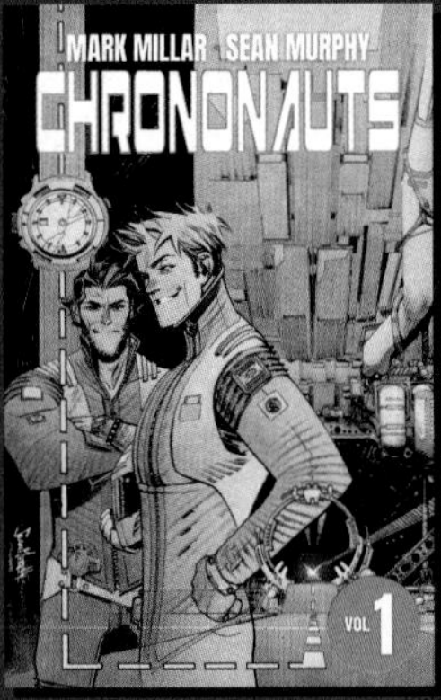
MARK MILLAR
SEAN MURPHY
CHRONONAUTS
VOL 1

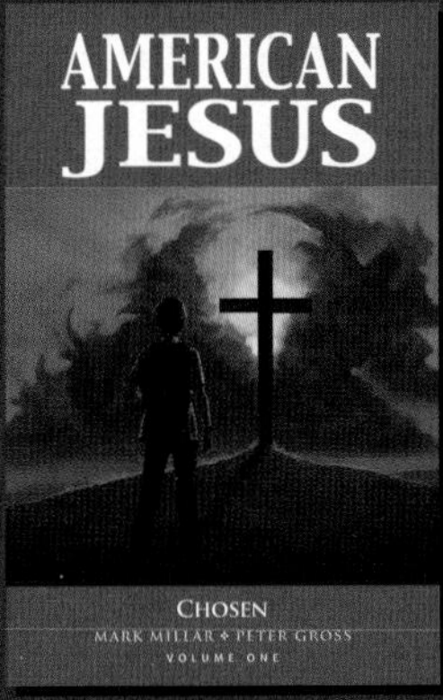
AMERICAN JESUS
CHOSEN
MARK MILLAR + PETER GROSS
VOLUME ONE

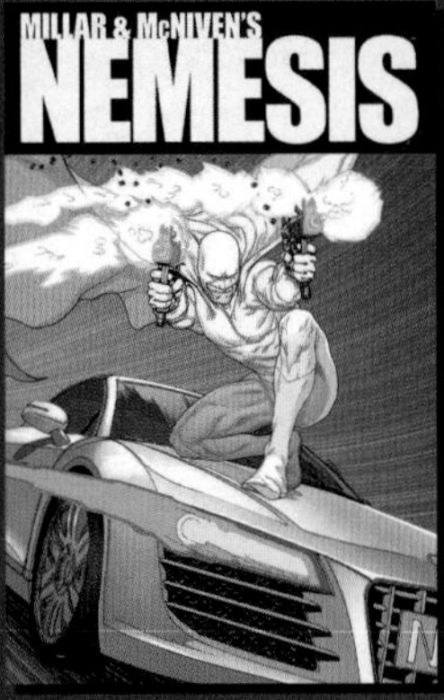
MILLAR & McNIVEN'S
NEMESIS

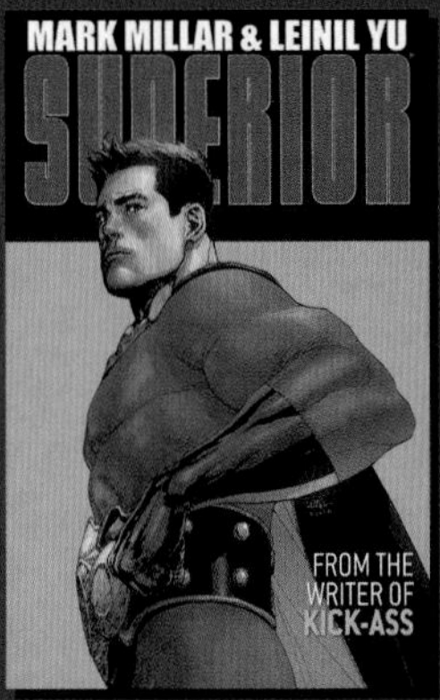
MARK MILLAR & LEINIL YU
SUPERIOR
FROM THE WRITER OF KICK-ASS

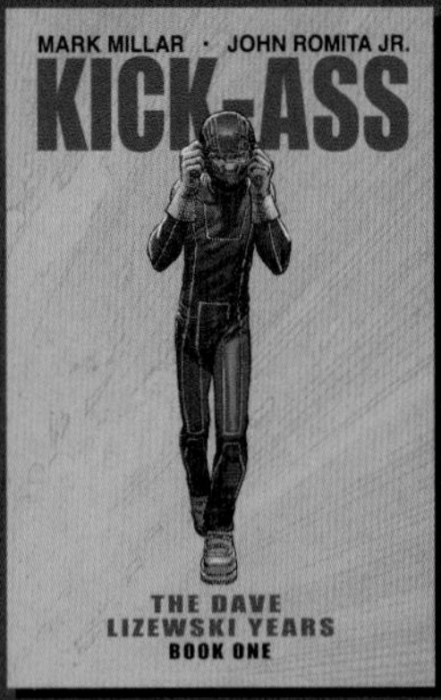
MARK MILLAR · JOHN ROMITA JR.
KICK-ASS
THE DAVE LIZEWSKI YEARS
BOOK ONE

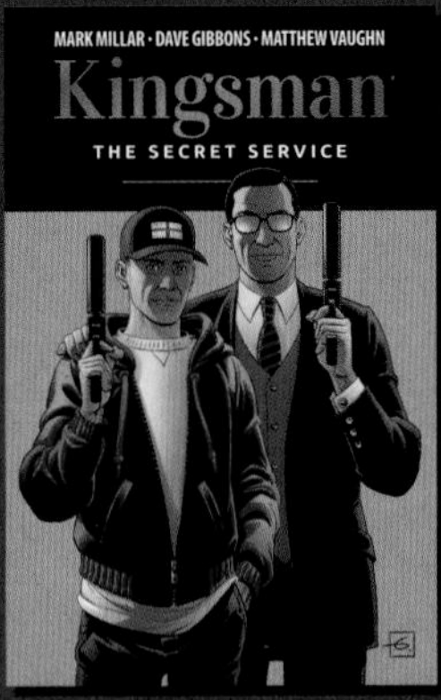
MARK MILLAR · DAVE GIBBONS · MATTHEW VAUGHN
Kingsman
THE SECRET SERVICE

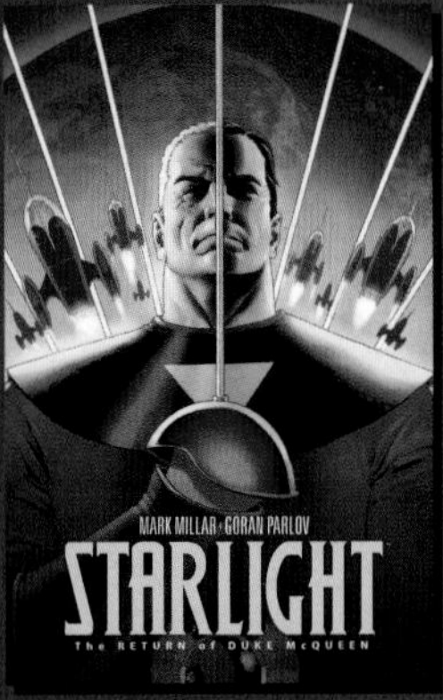
MARK MILLAR · GORAN PARLOV
STARLIGHT
The Return of Duke McQueen